RUN TO ME

DIANE HESTER

BANTAM

SYDNEY AUCKLAND TORONTO NEW YORK LONDON

A Bantam book
Published by Random House Australia Pty Ltd
Level 3, 100 Pacific Highway, North Sydney NSW 2060
www.randomhouse.com.au

First published by Bantam in 2013

Addresses for companies within the Random House Group can be found at
www.randomhouse.com.au/offices

National Library of Australia
Cataloguing-in-Publication entry

Hester, Diane.
Run to Me/Diane Hester.

ISBN 978 1 74275 642 4 (pbk.)

A823.4

Cover design by Christabella Designs
Cover photographs: woman © Knape/Getty Images, young boy © Christophe
Dessaigne/Trevillion Images
Internal typesetting and design by Midland Typesetters, Australia
Printed in Australia by Griffin Press, an accredited ISO AS/NZS 14001:2004
Environmental Management System printer

Random House Australia uses papers that are natural, renewable and
recyclable products and made from wood grown in sustainable forests.
The logging and manufacturing processes are expected to conform to
the environmental regulations of the country of origin.

For Michael

Prologue

'Jesse, come down from there, you might fall.'

'I'm throwing sticks in the water, Mommy. See how fast they float away.'

Shyler came up behind her son where he stood on the railing's lowest bar. Sliding her arm around his waist, her cheek pressed to his, she peered over the side of the bridge.

'The water's moving really fast, isn't it? Must be all that rain we had. Now come on, sweetheart, we better get going. Your baseball training went late today; it's starting to get dark.'

'All the sticks went under the bridge.' He held up the last one. 'I want to see where this one comes out.'

'All right, one more, then we have to leave. Daddy'll be home soon.'

With a five-year-old's flair he threw the stick, watched it hit the water, then jumped down to race to the other side.

'Look both ways before you cross.' Though he quickly obeyed, though they'd not seen a car since the edge of town, she couldn't help double-checking to be sure.

That's when she saw the three men step out.

1

They emerged from the bushes at the end of the bridge as though they'd come up from the banks below. But with no poles or reels they couldn't have been fishing.

She moved to where Jesse was scanning the water.

'There it is, Mom!'

'I see it, honey.' But in truth she was looking the other way, keeping watch from the corner of her eye.

The men had spread out across the road. Even before she could see their faces she knew the one in the middle was the leader, just from the way the others watched him, held back behind him as they started towards her.

Their sudden appearance could be totally innocent, random chance.

Still, why had they spread out across the road?

Jesse climbed down and took her hand. 'Timmy brought a rabbit to school today. A live one.'

'Did he? I bet that was nice.' She turned him to head back the way they'd come. Maybe they'd walk home the other way today, just to be –

Two more men had stepped out behind them.

'It had real soft fur, and big floppy ears. Can I get a rabbit, Mom?'

'We'll see.' Pulling him close, she looked from one group to the other. Clearly together, clearly an ambush. A mugging? Here? In their quiet little corner of New Hampshire?

'What is it, Mommy?'

She scanned the road in both directions. No cars, no people. The fields sweeping back to the woods either side held nothing but drying rows of corn. She knew there was a house just past the first turn. But trees lining the banks of the creek would screen them from view, muffle any cries for help. The bridge they had crossed nearly every day since Jesse started school had never felt so lonely and remote.

The men closed in, encircling them. Younger than she'd thought. Late teens perhaps. Taut and wiry, ragged as strays.

The one with his hands jammed in his pockets twitched like a puppet on invisible strings. Another had a snake tattoo on his neck, his eyes red-rimmed. The plaid flannel shirt on the gangly one made him a scarecrow, a jaunty beret an incongruous touch for the one incessantly scratching himself.

Stay calm. Don't provoke them.

She faced the fifth, the gang's leader. 'What do you want?'

A scar tugged the side of his mouth like a fish hook. 'Wallet,' he said.

She fumbled in her bag, handed it over. The others pressed closer as Fish Hook looked through it.

'You gotta be kidding. Five lousy bucks, that's all you got?'

'That's all I brought with me.'

An unseen hand jerked Puppet's strings. 'Oh man, no way.'

'That's bullshit, she's lying. She's gotta have more.'

'Here, take my bag if you don't believe me.' She held it out. The instant he snatched it, Puppet yanked Jesse away from her legs.

'No, please, let him go.'

Scarecrow and Beret cut between them as Puppet lifted the boy to the railing. 'Soon as you give us what we came for.'

She strained to see past them; Jesse's eyes were now huge and frightened. 'It's okay, baby, they'll be gone in a minute.'

Scarecrow leered. 'Yeah, baby, it's okay. Mama won't let her little boy fall.'

She couldn't pry her gaze from Puppet. Those twitching hands, that nervous dance . . . 'Please, let him down. There's rocks . . . the water . . . He can't swim.'

They shoved her back.

Fish Hook was throwing things from her bag. 'There's nothing in here.'

Bargain. Say anything. 'There's an ATM in town. I've got lots of money in my account. You can have it all.'

'Think we're stupid?' Puppet swung Jesse's legs over the edge.

'There's an iPod in my bag. A mobile, credit cards.'

'Not enough.'

'I have nothing else!'

A jab from behind. 'Empty your pockets.'

'Car!' Snake said, before she could move.

'Don't see nothin'.'

'I hear it, man.'

'Let's get outta here.'

Fish Hook threw the bag down, jerked his head. The others ran after him.

All but Puppet.

'Hey, what am I supposed to . . .?' His look grew frantic – the car was getting closer.

Raising her hands, a calming gesture, inching forward. 'Please, be careful. Don't –'

He let go and ran.

She sprang to the rail, the moment imprinting itself like a scar. Silken hair sliding between her fingers.

The terrified scream she would never stop hearing.

Chapter 1

Two years later.

Zack felt their stares on his back as he moved about the kitchen. The two of them, just sitting there, expecting him to make it all right. What the hell did they think he could do? He was just a kid himself.

He jerked up the bread box lid and peered in – two mouldy crusts and a donut that had probably been there since the year he was born, the little brown things scattered around it either chocolate sprinkles or petrified mouse turds. He slammed the lid and moved to the fridge. A six-pack of Bud, a jar of olives, a can of Cheese Wiz. Something black and fuzzy that might once have been a carrot lay in a puddle of slime at the bottom. Zack grabbed the Wiz and shut the door.

From the cupboard he'd pawed through earlier, he took down the half-eaten box of Ritz. He fished the cleanest plate from the sink, tipped the remaining crackers onto it, squirted each with a dollop of Wiz and plunked the plate on the kitchen table.

Reece and Corey sat dead quiet staring down at it.

'I thought you guys said you were hungry.'

'We are.' Reece shifted. 'It's just . . .'

'Just what?'

Reece shoved a knuckle into his mouth. Zack pulled it out again. He couldn't stand it when the kid chewed himself. Corey rested his chin on the table, hiding his face beneath a mop of blond curls.

Be cheerful, reason with them, Zack told himself – that's what you did with little kids. 'Well, that's all there is so you better eat it.'

Reece shook his head, inching his hand towards his mouth again.

'You sure? They're pretty good.' Zack picked one up and popped it in his mouth. 'Mmm, yum.'

Corey looked up. 'But the crackers. They're Frank's.'

'Yeah, so what? Frank's not here, so you get first dibs. Now go on and eat.'

Neither boy moved.

'I said eat!' He thumped the table.

They jumped in unison, then hid their faces. Corey's shoulders began to quake.

Zack clenched his jaw. The only thing worse than when they nagged him was when they cried. It twisted everything up inside him, made him feel sad, scared and angry all at the same time.

Slowly, as always, his resistance ebbed. He sidled up to Corey and gave him a nudge. 'Scooch over, Runt.'

The boy slid aside and Zack perched half his butt on the chair.

'Now listen, you guys, I'm in charge and I say it's all right for you to eat this, so that means it is.'

'But what about Frank?' Corey's voice carried the threat of more tears. He often played at being the baby, but this time Zack knew his fear was real.

'You let me worry about Frank.'

They stared at the plate. Reece chewed the skin on the back of his hand. Corey bit down on his quivering lip.

Zack heaved a sigh. 'Okay, what if . . .' He couldn't believe he was going to do this. 'When Frank gets home you can tell him *I* ate all the crackers, all right?'

The pair looked up as though he'd just offered to walk barefoot over broken glass for them. In a way, he supposed he had.

They each grabbed a cracker and started to eat, for the moment happy. Probably a good time to mention the other thing. 'There's something else I needed to tell you.'

They waited, expectant.

'You gotta stop following me around everywhere.'

'How come?' Reece said.

'Well, I got things to do, that's why.' Not to mention how uncool it was to be seen with a five- and a seven-year-old.

'Why can't we do them with you?'

'Because the places I go aren't safe for little kids. Like yesterday, that old building. It's okay for me to go in, I'm big, but you could get hurt in dumps like that. Plus you can't run as fast as me. I mean, what if one of those guys had spotted us?'

'What guys?' Reece said.

'There, ya see, you didn't even notice.'

'I saw him,' Corey piped up. 'The one with the suitcase.'

'Sports bag. And I didn't mean him. One guy on his own wouldn't matter; I'm talking about the others that showed up after him. You gotta pay attention to stuff like that. You get caught doing what I do and they put you in jail.'

They sat absorbing the weight of his words.

'So why do you go in places like that?' Reece said.

7

Zack stuck his chest out. 'To lift stuff. Buildings that aren't used any more have all sorts of junk lying around, stuff you can hock or get a deposit for.'

From the front of the house came a knock at the door. Zack got up.

'You mean you steal stuff?' Corey said, his eyes like saucers.

'Where do you think your candy bars come from? Think Frank buys 'em for you?' Zack left them with their mouths hanging open and walked to the living room.

He unlocked the front door, and opened it just enough to peer out. On the other side of the tattered screen stood a man and a woman, each with a briefcase.

The man stepped forward. 'May we speak to Frank or Julie Leary, please?'

'Not home,' Zack said.

'When will they be back?'

'How should I know?'

'Do you know where we might find them?'

Zack gave a laugh. 'The nearest bar?'

'Son, it's very important we speak to your parents.'

He jerked the door back. 'They're not my parents.'

A second's pause. 'Yes, of course. Any idea when they'll be home?'

'You got shit in your ears? I said, I don't know.'

'Well, would you mind if we waited for them?'

Zack took a closer look at the man. Gelled brown hair slicked back off a male-model, clean-shaven face. Younger than Frank and a lot more polite. The woman's dark hair just skimmed her shoulders. Pants, smart jacket, big round eyes. They seemed safe enough. But the briefcases, the man's suit and tie . . .

'You're not Mormons, are you?'

The man smiled. 'No.'

'Jehovah's Witness?'

'We're not from any church.'

Zack shrugged. 'Guess you can wait as long as you want then.' He started to close the door but the man spoke up again.

'What I meant was, could we wait inside for them?'

'Nup, can't let any strangers in.'

The man nodded, then tilted his head. 'I'm guessing you're Zackary Ballinger, is that right?' He opened his briefcase and pulled out some papers.

'How'd you know that?'

'You look the right age. Nine, isn't it?'

'Ten,' Zack corrected, standing taller.

'That's right. And the others? Let's see . . . Reece Dennings, seven; Corey Ingles, five. They inside too?'

'Maybe.' Zack frowned. 'Hey, who the hell are you?'

'I'm Mr Westgate and this is Ms Knowles. We're with the New Hampshire Department of Child Welfare.'

Zack went still. Social workers. Just like the ones who'd brought him to this dump, and the ones who'd brought him to the dump before that. He didn't know these particular workers but he knew what a visit from one could mean. 'What do you want with Frank and Julie?'

'It'd be better if we discussed that with them.'

They stared at each other.

'So.' The man slipped the papers back in his case. 'Now that you know who we are, may we come in?'

Zack squinted up at them. Would anyone say they were a social worker if they weren't? Robbers maybe. But there wasn't anything worth stealing here.

'Lemme see something.'

'You mean an ID?' Another smile. Then the pair pressed laminated cards to the screen, complete with their pictures. Their names were Westgate and Knowles all right.

Still Zack hesitated, imagining what Frank's reaction would be if he came home and found these strangers in his house. Then again, knowing what they were probably here for, it might just be worth it to see Frank squirm.

He unlocked the screen door and held it open.

Chapter 2

Westgate stepped into the tiny living room and stopped as though he'd been slapped in the face. 'Christ, what's that —?' He cut himself off.

'What's what?' Zack said, pretending innocence. He'd never grown immune to the smell but at least he was used to it.

The man's gaze swept over the dirty dishes heaped on an end table, the mouldering remains of food that clung to them, the grease-stained furniture, the take-away wrappings, the overflowing ashtrays. 'Never mind.'

The woman pulled a handkerchief from her bag and held it to her face. She was thin and tough-looking like she worked out a lot, like maybe the padding in her jacket's shoulders wasn't all padding. 'Is the place normally this . . . untidy?'

'Hell, no. Usually it's worse.'

She pursed her lips at him.

'Go ahead and sit down if you want,' Zack said, warming to the game of baiting them.

'We'll stand, thank you.'

'You sure? They could be a while. It's pay week and they usually stay till closing. Unless Frank gets in a fight, of course, and gets kicked out before that.'

The man had moved to one of the doors that opened off the living room. Zack watched him survey the rickety bunk bed and single mattress on the floor of his bedroom. With his fancy clothes and slicked back hair he looked like some kind of trendy businessman. Up this close he even smelled clean. What would he think of the dirty clothes that littered the floor, the bedding that hadn't been changed in months?

The woman stood eyeing him. 'How did you get that bruise on your cheek?'

'Baseball. A pitch came back at me.'

'So you're a pitcher, eh?' Westgate swung away from the door. 'Bit late in the season for baseball, isn't it? Would've thought you'd be playing football in September.'

'Like I'm really big enough to play football.'

The man stepped closer and lowered his voice. 'That's not how you got the bruise, is it, son?'

Zack said nothing. It wasn't that he wanted to cover for Frank, it was that he didn't know whether he could trust these strangers any better.

The man waited a moment longer then, realising he wasn't going to get an answer, moved to the next door. 'Hello, boys, I'm Mr Westgate. It's okay, you go right on eating; we're just having a look around.'

Zack hurried over to stand beside him. He was starting to regret having let the pair in. Social workers or not, dump or not, he felt suddenly resentful of these smartly dressed strangers poking through the house.

Westgate scanned the kitchen from the safety of the doorway – the dish-choked sink, the grimy stove, the cascading rubbish bin – ending with the plate of crackers on the table.

'Ritz and Cheese Wiz,' he said to the boys. 'That your dinner?'

Reece and Corey, frozen with crackers poised at their lips, looked to Zack.

'Yeah, that's dinner,' he answered for them. 'We're fresh out of lobster.' He took the man's arm and pulled him back into the living room. 'I think you better go and come back tomorrow.'

'We'd like to ask you a few more questions, if that's okay,' the woman said.

'I don't want to talk to you anymore.'

'Come on, Zack, help us out here.' Westgate flashed him a kid's-best-friend smile. 'If you do the right thing we might be able to get you and the others out of here.'

Zack felt his cheeks get hot. Where were these people when there wasn't even crackers and Cheese Wiz to eat? When Julie spent days drunk on the couch? When Frank went apeshit and knocked them around?

'What if we don't want to leave?'

The man gaped at him. 'You can't . . . I mean . . .' His smile returned. 'You don't understand. I'm saying we can get you out of here for good.'

'And take us where? Some other dump? Some other *family* that doesn't give a rat's ass about us?'

Zack turned away. Bad Boy Ballinger strikes again. If he could only learn to control that side of him – the part that was like a whole other person inside his head, the agro punk who never took shit, no matter who from – maybe he wouldn't keep getting sent to places like this.

Westgate leaned down, his expression softened to one of sympathy. 'I know the system's failed you in the past, son, but I give you my word –'

The promise was cut off by shouts from the kitchen. 'Little shits! What are you doing with those?'

13

Zack heard Corey yell his name then Reece give a shriek. The next instant both boys burst into the living room, ran towards him and hid behind his back.

Franklin J. Leary waddled out after them, stumbled to a halt and stared dumbly at the strangers in front of him. Before he could speak, Julie swayed through the door behind him. 'What's going on?'

'Frank and Julie Leary?'

'Who the hell are you?'

The pair introduced themselves and showed their IDs.

A series of expressions crossed Frank's face – confusion, surprise, fear, hostility – then he turned and shot Zack a look so savage it made him step back.

Corey reached up and tugged at his arm. 'Zack, what's happening?'

'Dunno, just listen.'

Westgate cleared his throat. 'Mr and Mrs Leary, I'll come straight to the point. Our department has received a number of calls from concerned individuals regarding the treatment and condition of the boys in your care.'

Frank and Julie spluttered in outrage. 'What goddamn individuals?' Frank demanded.

'That's confidential. All you need to know is that, upon our initial inspection of these premises, we've found those reports largely substantiated.'

'Aw, now come on.' The ingratiating smile looked like a grimace on Frank's round face. 'You don't want to go believing everything these fellas tell you. They're just kids.'

'The boys told us very little, Mr Leary. They didn't have to.' The woman glanced around in disgust.

'Well, sure, the place is a mess at the moment.' Frank waved a hand. 'My wife's been sick. It isn't like this all the time.'

'It's more than just the state of the house,' Westgate said.

'The food, is that it? You're wondering why there's nothing to eat? Well, hell, I only got the cheque today. We just haven't done the shopping yet, that's all.' Frank took in the man's doubting expression. 'All right, I'll admit we may have let a few things slide. But we'll take care of everything the minute you leave. I give you my word.'

When Westgate said nothing, Frank exhaled. 'There, see? All sorted out. So what happens now? Some kind of slap on the wrist, I suppose.'

Westgate glowered. 'It's going to be more than that, I'm afraid. For starters your support payments are hereby terminated.'

'What? You can't do that!'

'In fact we can. What's more, once our report has been processed these boys will be removed from your care and you'll be banned from ever fostering children again.'

Zack heard Corey gasp behind him. 'What did he say?'

Reece grabbed his other arm. 'Are we getting out of here?'

'Shut up, I'm tryin' to listen.' The excitement in their voices made Zack think twice. He hadn't believed Westgate the first time he'd said it, but maybe there was a chance he was telling the truth.

Frank sneered. 'Aw, you mean I don't get to wipe no more snotty noses and listen to all their pissing and moaning?'

'I said those measures were for starters, Mr Leary. Once we conduct a full investigation there's a good chance criminal charges will be laid.'

So much colour drained from Frank's face, Zack thought he was having a stroke. Though the house was cold, sweat broke out on his fleshy features. He swept a plump hand over his cue-ball head.

Stepping towards Westgate, he lowered his voice. 'All right, look, you know that cheque we got today? We ain't spent more than a hundred of it. The rest is yours.' He whispered an amount. 'If you just . . . well . . . tweak that report a bit.'

Zack slumped. No way Westgate would turn that down.

Silence engulfed them. Westgate looked at Zack and the boys. Some kind of change came over his face. Here it was then. In a minute he'd walk out, leaving the three of them to face Frank's fury.

Westgate drew a steadying breath. 'Mr Leary, nothing would give me greater pleasure than to see you do a spell in prison. However, if we proceed through the proper channels, these boys might have to remain in your care for as much as another week. I don't know if I could live with myself if I let that happen.'

Frank frowned. 'What are you saying?'

The man pulled some papers out of his briefcase. 'If you and Mrs Leary would sign this form, agreeing to let us take the boys now, tonight . . .' he hesitated, as though his next words were distasteful to him, 'I won't report either your attempted bribe or the more serious offences I've witnessed here.'

Frank's eyes widened. 'Shit, yeah, I'll sign that right now!'

'You understand the other conditions still apply.' The woman produced a pen from her bag. 'Your payments are terminated and you'll never foster children again.'

'Yeah, yeah, I get it, we're off your Christmas list.' Frank passed the form and pen to his wife. With a final burst of swearing he turned and stormed back into the kitchen. A moment later Julie followed him.

'He signed it,' Reece whispered. 'What does that mean?'

Westgate slipped the form back into his case. 'It means you don't have to stay with these people any more. It means you can leave here with us right now and we'll find you another place to live.'

Corey and Reece slowly emerged from behind Zack's back. Their grips on his arms had grown positively painful.

Reece looked around him. 'Will it be better than this?'

'Absolutely. There'll be nice beds, decent clothes and plenty to eat.'

'Will we get to stay together?' Corey murmured.

The man considered this. 'You boys have been through a lot together, huh?'

The younger two nodded.

'Well then, we can't let anyone separate you, can we? Don't worry, I'll make sure you stay together.'

At their glowing smiles, Westgate straightened. 'Now go and get your things so we can get out of here.'

'Don't worry about clothes,' the woman added. 'Just grab anything special that's yours.'

Corey and Reece raced into the bedroom. Zack stood his ground, gazing at Westgate.

'Nothing you want to take with you, son?'

He shook his head.

At his unflinching scrutiny, Westgate winked. 'Didn't I tell you I'd get you out of here?'

Zack stared back. Why didn't he feel the excitement the others did? Was it something he could see in these people they couldn't? Or was it all the broken promises that had gone before?

The younger boys charged back into the room, Reece in his treasured Red Sox sweatshirt, its pockets bulging with baseball cards – the only things his mom hadn't hocked before she'd OD'ed. Corey clutched Ali, the Kermit-green alligator his dad had given him before he'd walked out that final time.

Taking Zack's hands, they followed their rescuers out into the night.

Chapter 3

They drove for an hour, ending up in a quiet neighbourhood where street lights illuminated tidy yards and people walked poodles and golden retrievers.

'It's too late to drive to the shelter tonight,' Westgate said as he and Ms Knowles led them up the path to a two-storey house. 'We'll sleep here and head off first thing in the morning.'

'Don't worry, there are plenty of beds upstairs so you can all share a room,' the woman added.

Through the front door was an open area – dining table on the left, darkened living room off to the right, between them stairs to the second floor.

'Here you are, boys. Make yourselves comfortable,' the woman said. When the younger two simply clung to Zack's arms, the woman bent down and fluffed Corey's hair. 'Aren't you just the cutest thing? Look at these curls!'

He squirmed with delight. 'What's your name?'

'You mean my first name? It's Vanessa. You can call me that instead if you like.'

'Me too?' Reece added.

'Well sure.' She pointed at Westgate. 'And his name is Phil.'

'What about him?' Zack nodded to a figure he could just make out in the shadows of the living room. He sensed more than saw that the man was watching them.

'That's Mr Tragg,' Westgate answered. 'He isn't part of our child-caring team so best not to bother him.'

'If he's not one of you then why's he here?'

'He helps out in other ways.'

Vanessa clapped her palms together. 'So who wants a sandwich? We have peanut butter, bologna, cheese, ham . . .'

Her voice sounded phoney-cheerful to Zack but it worked well enough on Reece and Corey. They let go of his hands for the first time since leaving the Learys' and stood staring up at her all goo-goo eyed. As they told her what they wanted, Zack looked around.

Another strange house. How he hated this feeling. He'd been in so many these last three years. Smells were the worst. Even when they weren't bad they were creepy and somehow they always brought on his dreams.

The nightmare was always the same – a remnant from the one time he'd visited a pound. Only in his dream it wasn't dogs in the cages, it was boys. And when the attendant came and hauled him out, dragged him outside to the idling truck – the one with the hose that ran from the tail pipe up into the little box at the back – that's when he woke, gasping and choking and drenched in sweat.

He'd had his own home once upon a time. And if not a full family at least a mom. But unlike Reece and Corey – and most other foster kids he had met – his mother hadn't been forced to give him up. His mother hadn't been an addict or a drunk. She simply hadn't wanted him any more.

Oh, she'd said she did, but that was a lie. If it was true, she'd never have agreed to marry Paul. She'd have told him to go fuck himself when he said he didn't want her bastard, that he wanted to start a family of his own. But no, she caved in, put her own son in foster care – swearing up and down she'd come back and get him some day – then went off and got herself killed in a car crash. The only good thing about it all was that Paul died, too.

'Now before you eat I want you all to have a nice hot bath and put on the pyjamas I laid out for you.' Vanessa was herding them towards the staircase. 'Throw your clothes in the big plastic bag. We've got new ones for you and you'll get them tomorrow. The bathroom's upstairs on the right. Go on up and I'll call you when your sandwiches are ready.'

Reece and Corey took off at once.

Zack stood his ground. 'How'd you guys know to have all this stuff here? How'd you know to have pyjamas and clothes and beds all ready for us?'

The woman's smile didn't light up her eyes. 'This is what's called a safe house. We use it as a temporary shelter for lots of children so we always have clothes and other things on hand. Now why don't you go up and look after your brothers?'

'Isn't that your job?'

The smile vanished.

'Now, listen here, buddy.' Westgate stepped forward.

'Yeah, I'm going; don't blow a gasket.'

The tub was half-filled when Zack reached the bathroom. Corey and Reece, their clothes strewn from one end of the room to the other, were seated inside it, madly frothing the water with their hands to create more bubbles.

What were they so damn happy about? Didn't they realise there was every chance they'd end up in a place just as bad as, if not worse than, the Learys'? No, probably not, since the Learys' was the only foster home they had known.

Zack began picking up their clothes and shoving them into the rubbish bag. 'Knock it off, will ya? You're getting water all over the place!' He'd worked his way across the floor before noticing the others now seemed *too* quiet. He straightened and turned.

A stranger stood in the doorway. Bigger than Westgate with pock-marked skin and dark flat eyes. This had to be Tragg, the guy from the living room.

Zack side-stepped in front of the tub.

The man moved past him without a word, lifted the toilet seat, unzipped his pants and started to pee. Looking over, he smiled at the three of them frozen and staring. Their silence only amused him further and he let out a laugh.

'Zack?' Corey's voice quavered a little.

'Just stay there.'

Tragg shook himself, zipped up his pants and turned to face them. From the breast pocket of his shirt he pulled out a box of Junior Mints and opened the lid.

Again amusement tugged at his lips. 'Want some candy, little boys?' Then he shook out a mint, tossed it in his mouth and left the room laughing.

Zack exhaled the breath he'd been holding.

'He's creepy,' Corey whispered.

'Yeah, and ugly.' Reece made a face in imitation and Corey gave a nervous giggle.

'Hey, don't make fun of Hatchet Face; you might hurt his feelings.' Zack pulled an even uglier face and the next thing the boys were laughing again.

Reece and Corey seemed to have forgotten their run-in with Tragg by the time they all sat down to dinner. It helped, Zack was sure, that the man had once again retreated to the living room and was nowhere in sight. But the incident had left him vaguely unsettled, and more than ever he wanted to learn all he could about these people.

'What time are we leaving in the morning?' he said.

Vanessa stood, pouring them each some milk. 'Well, we're not exactly sure we'll be leaving tomorrow. It depends.'

'On what?'

'On whether the shelter has room for you. At the moment they're full.'

'There's more than one place that could take us though, isn't there? They can't all be full.'

Before she could answer, a hand shot over Zack's shoulder and snatched half the sandwich off his plate. The sharp scent of mint was suddenly in the air.

He looked up to find Tragg standing over him.

'Kid's right. There ought to be room at each place for one of them. Easiest thing is to just split 'em up.'

As protests erupted from Corey and Reece, the man pushed the sandwich wedge in his mouth, chewed and swallowed it, holding Zack's gaze the entire time.

Vanessa had finished settling the others by the time Tragg walked back into the living room. 'Don't worry, Zack. If we have to stay here an extra day you'll have plenty to eat and lots to do.'

Zack nodded, grabbed his milk and took a big gulp.

Chapter 4

Westgate's voice murmured up the stairwell. 'Come on, admit it. I wasn't bad. Even I believed the lines I was feeding them. Honestly, I missed my calling, I could've been an actor.'

'You're as conceited as one, I'll give you that,' Vanessa replied.

Zack inched closer to the top of the stairs. Reece and Corey were asleep in one of the bedrooms behind him. He hadn't yet told them of his fears, of his growing conviction that something was wrong and these people weren't who they said they were. Before he did, he had to be sure.

Using the banister for cover, he knelt and peered down into the living room. Vanessa was perched on Westgate's lap, one arm draped around his neck, a wine glass in her other hand.

'You weren't bad yourself,' the man said. 'Reading them stories, getting them water, fussing over that stupid stuffed animal. I've never seen your nurturing side. Getting in touch with the mommy within, are you?'

'Fuck off, Nolan.'

Vanessa pushed off from Westgate's lap and crossed to the window. Nolan? Why had she called him that? Hadn't she said his first name was Phil?

The man said something Zack didn't catch and Vanessa responded.

'Neighbourhood snitch told us the kids were in foster care so it seemed the best way to get our hands on them.'

'But how did Tragg organise things so fast?'

'Lazaro's got a man inside the department. The IDs, forms, the kids' records, even the complaints about their careers . . . Everything he gave us was legit.' She turned to him grinning. 'And the best thing is, the Learys will never follow it up 'cause they're guilty as sin and never gave a shit to begin with.'

'What about the kids' real parents?'

'What parents? Ballinger's dad split before he was born and his mother's dead. The other two are in a similar boat. There's nothing to worry about, Nolan. I'm telling you.'

'In theory at least.'

Zack was feeling sicker by the minute. Again the woman had used the name Nolan. He didn't understand all they were saying, but one thing was clear – these people didn't sound like social workers.

Vanessa threw a hand up and stepped to the table to refill her glass. 'If you're that concerned, I suggest you tell Lazaro you changed your mind.'

'Tell your uncle I want to pull out?' The man laughed. 'Like he'd really let me walk away now. Besides, I don't want to. I'd just like to know what happens from here.'

'As soon as it's safe, we'll take the three of them back to the warehouse. Tragg's got someone casing the place and they'll let him know.'

'As soon as it's safe?'

'Some snoopy neighbour heard the commotion and called the cops. They've been crawling all over the place ever since.'

'Well, how do you know *they* haven't found the bag?'

''Cause they weren't looking for it. A few specks of blood is all they'll find. Tragg got rid of the body when he left.'

Body? Zack clutched the slats with a white-knuckled grip. These definitely weren't social workers.

Breathing hard, he pushed to his feet, then stood frozen. He'd heard enough – more than he wanted to! – but he just couldn't tear himself away.

'Boy, your pal Tragg sure fucked up.' Nolan had lowered his voice a notch. 'How does he end up killing Giles *before* finding out where he stashed the money?'

'It wasn't intentional. He was working at getting the info out of him and things got out of hand.'

'And the kids were there. They saw all this?'

'We don't know if they witnessed the killing but they were definitely there when Giles went in. They were spotted running out the back of the building.'

Zack fought to comprehend what he was hearing. A building? Someplace they had all been together?

'One of Tragg's men followed them home,' the woman went on, 'but there were too many people around to grab them.'

'So Tragg thinks the money's still there in the warehouse.'

'He's had his eye on Giles for a while, thinks he's been skimming from Lazaro for ages.' The woman raised her glass in a toast. 'And right now those three snotty-nosed brats could be our only hope of getting it back.'

A punch of realisation left Zack gasping. The abandoned warehouse! Where he'd gone two days ago scavenging for scrap. Where Corey and Reece had suddenly appeared, having followed him in. Yes, they'd been there. Yes, they'd all seen a man come in carrying a sports bag. Yet none of them had seen where he'd hidden it. And when these people found out they didn't know . . .

Slowly he backed away from the stairs. He had to wake the others. They had to get out of here! They'd put on the clothes Vanessa had left for them and after the grown-ups were all asleep –

Fingers clamped around his throat, shoving him back. He hit the wall and clutched at the hand now sliding him upwards by his neck. Tragg's minty breath enveloped his face as his feet left the floor.

'Well, well, who's the Nosy Parker, eh?'

The fingers tightened. Zack gasped for breath. He pressed his bare soles against the wall, trying to take the weight off his throat. The hand held him firm.

'Hearing some interesting tidbits, are we?' Tragg leaned closer. 'Should've heard them earlier, reading your file. Eight foster homes in less than three years – that's gotta be some kinda record. Why is it nobody wants you, eh? Not even Mommy.'

Even through his panic, Zack felt the stabbing pain of each word. He dug his fingernails into Tragg's flesh but the man only smiled.

'So what's the story, Zacky-boy? She leave you in a dumpster somewhere or sell you for the price of a fix?'

Zack kicked out. The effort was blind but he knew from Tragg's grunt and instant release that he'd managed to connect with someplace vital. He slid to the floor, grabbed for the banister and half-fell, half-scrambled down the stairs.

'What the hell!' Nolan said, when he landed in a heap at the bottom.

Still gagging from the remnant pressure on his throat, Zack back-pedalled away from the steps as Tragg descended. He managed to scurry around the table in time to avoid the man's kick.

'What's going on?' Vanessa demanded.

'He was listening to you. Little shit heard everything you said.'

26

With the table between them, Zack got to his feet.

Nolan stepped towards him. 'What is it you think you heard, son?'

'Nothing. I didn't hear anything. I just got up to go to the bathroom.'

'I know what he heard, 'cause I heard it too.' Tragg turned his rage on the pair. 'Two fuckwits using a name they shouldn't have!'

The woman came slowly around the table from the other side. 'Well, that's nothing to worry about, Zack. Lazaro's just the man who runs the shelter we're taking you to.'

He backed away from her. 'That's bullshit! *You're* bullshit! We're getting outta here!' In the second it took him to draw breath to shout, Nolan was on him, clamping a rough hand over his mouth.

Zack bit down. The man yelped and swore. Zack twisted free, dodged a chair. And ran straight into Tragg's back-handed blow.

His tongue was a ball of cotton in his mouth. He tried to swallow but something was holding his jaws apart, stretching his lips back so far he thought they would tear. He was on the floor but felt it sliding away beneath him – hands under his arms, dragging him backwards. He opened his eyes.

An unfamiliar kitchen – ceiling beams, copper-bottom pots on butcher hooks, some kind of weird-looking antique stove . . .

And Nolan's inverted face staring down at him.

Zack gasped and tried to strike out but found his hands bound with electrical tape. The dish towel they had used to gag him muffled his shouts.

'Put him in there.' Vanessa's voice came from out of sight behind him.

Nolan stopped and swung him around to face a low hearth. A half-sized door stood open before him revealing a small dark space laced in cobwebs. No way in hell were they putting him in there!

Zack shot his legs out, jamming his feet against the doorframe.

Now on his knees, Nolan grunted with the effort of pushing him towards the opening. 'For Christ's sake give me a hand here, would you?'

Zack heard approaching steps. Then a large push-broom swung into view and rammed his feet off the frame. With a final grunt, Nolan shoved him inside.

'Shit, what's that?' The man sat back and swiped at his face. 'Spiders. Jesus, don't –' He sprang to his feet. 'Where is it? Get it off me!'

As the man danced around, Zack saw Vanessa brushing him down. For a tantalising moment they were both distracted. They mightn't even notice if . . .

Another pair of legs appeared in the doorway.

Tragg squatted down to fill the opening. Pulling the Junior Mint box from his pocket, he inspected the cramped dark space.

'Nice place you got here, Zacky-boy.' He rolled a mint out onto his tongue and lapped it back, a toad catching flies. 'Plenty of creepy-crawlies to keep you company. Hope there's none of those recluse spiders, they can be nasty. Great big fangs, dripping venom . . .'

Fighting his panic, Zack forced a two-word reply past the gag.

'Oh now, Zack, that's not very nice.' Tragg's smile vanished. He popped another mint, then rattled the box. 'One left. You better have it. Wouldn't want you to get hungry in the night.'

He tossed the box. It hit Zack's forehead and dropped to his lap.

'Oops, can't eat with your hands tied, can you? Too bad.'

Laughing softly, Tragg got to his feet – 'Sweet dreams, Zacky' – and locked the door.

Chapter 5

The piece was ruined. With a single careless stroke of the chisel she'd destroyed a solid two days' work. Shyler set the carving on the workbench and eyed it in hopes of repairing the damage.

From the outset the owl had been slightly lopsided but that never bothered her. More like a living specimen than the soulless symmetry of something manufactured. Now, however, due to her distracted efforts, an entire inch of the tail had sheered off. There was no way to salvage it. She hurled it onto the kindling pile, then sat back and rubbed her eyes.

It was late; she should quit. She had more than enough pieces for this month's delivery. Poor old Bill probably hadn't sold half of the last lot. But at the prospect of going back in the cabin, sitting by the fire, alone with her thoughts . . .

She reached for another chunk of wood, took up the gouge and began again.

She needed the diversion of work right now, something to keep her mind occupied. Already the nightmares had started again, and while she'd not yet had a panic attack she'd felt the familiar warning signs that one was threatening. With the second anniversary less than one week away, she was heading into her roughest time. She would need every crutch, every trick to get through it.

Two years. It didn't seem right. Had she made no progress in all that time? Despite it being her only option, the cabin was her haven, Deadwater the safest place she knew. Deep in the northern woods of Maine – the last remaining wilderness in the east, home to more moose and bears than people – the vacation home she'd built with her father had offered the perfect retreat from the endless questions, the doubting looks, the oh-so-carefully-worded suggestions.

The relief she'd experienced in escaping that torment had given her a sense she was moving forward. Now, after ten months on her own, her equanimity once again slipping, she had to wonder if that 'progress' had only been an illusion.

Some things you just can't do alone.

She gouged a meaty chunk from the wood. 'And sometimes you don't have a choice in the matter.'

As bad as the first year had been, people had still believed her story, rallied around her, offered support. But slowly that had come to change.

Considering the detailed description you gave of the men who attacked you, we find it odd no one else remembers seeing them.

First the police, then family, then friends. In the end who had there been left to trust? Who trusted her? When even your therapist hints it might not have happened the way you remembered . . .

You said they came up from under the bridge, yet we found no footprints down by the creek.

She gripped the chisel and closed her eyes as the question she'd asked a thousand times whirred yet again inside her head. Had she suppressed what really happened?

Had there really been men on the bridge that day? Had one of them actually let Jesse fall? Had she truly risked her life to save him, jumping in after him, nearly drowning? Or had she, as the police came to think but couldn't prove, invented the story, her heroic acts, just to ease her own guilt? The guilt of a mother too distracted, too self-absorbed to notice her son was leaning dangerously over the edge?

We found a muddy shoeprint on the north side railing. Size four – that was your son's size, wasn't it?

Just the thought it might have happened the way they implied brought the darkness bearing down on her. She could see why a parent would desperately seek to block such a truth.

But, God help her, it wasn't the truth! Did they honestly believe anything she thought or said or did could make the reality any easier to bear?

She took a savage jab at the wood. The blade glanced off and found the soft flesh at the base of her thumb.

With a cry she dropped both wood and chisel and clutched her hand. Beneath the light she surveyed the damage. Not good. Not life-threatening by any stretch, but bad enough it might require a trip to Doc Muir. A trip she was in no condition to make, either financially or emotionally. Stupid, stupid . . .

Unless she could patch it up herself.

She shut off the light and left the workshop. Wind whipped her hair as she ran the short stretch to the cabin, the dark hissing forest showering her passage in twigs and swirling autumn leaves.

Inside, however, her hoped-for reprieve was not to be had. Closer inspection revealed a bit of flesh protruding from the wound. Touching it felt like stroking a nerve. Even if she could bring herself to push it back in, it would never stay. And the wound would never heal as it was.

In the pantry she got down the first aid kit and, with trembling fingers, wrapped her hand in a strip of gauze. Doctor Muir's office. A public place. Filled with patients. Talking, staring, asking questions.

She shoved the kit back and rested her forehead against the shelf. Trip to the doctor? She'd done it before, back before her medicine had run out. Now? In her current state? Well *that* would be progress – nowhere to hide, no deluding herself.

Clenching her undamaged hand in a fist, she strode from the pantry. She could do it. It wouldn't be easy, but taking the next step never was.

And anyway, she had no choice.

Chapter 6

Three holes, each as round as his finger, formed a triangle in the top of the door. When Zack saw thin rays of light stabbing through them he knew it was morning.

The fact both heartened and terrified him. Surely they'd be letting him out soon, if only to use the toilet. But the thought of this last stretch of time in the box, when he could actually see what was around him . . . After all the hours he'd managed to hold himself together, why did that prospect seem so terrible?

The cubicle had been so dark through the night, so utterly can't-see-your-hand-in-front-of-your-face lightless, it had actually been a blessing. What he couldn't see didn't scare him so much. The problem had been his other senses.

Twice he'd felt something crawling over him, the hair-fine touch of multiple legs. Once he'd heard something scuttling about – a mouse or rat – perhaps in the walls, perhaps right there in the wood cupboard with him.

Those moments had tested him to the limit, challenged his resolve not to break down into the whimpering baby he knew was hiding beneath the surface. He couldn't give Tragg the satisfaction.

Unable to stretch out, he hadn't slept. But using a sharp edge of rock jutting from the wall he'd finally managed to scrape off his bindings. For all the good it did him. No matter how hard he kicked at the door it didn't budge. And he could tell from the dead flat sound of his shouts that they never reached beyond the kitchen.

And so he'd waited, using the time to try and come up with some kind of plan for getting them out of here. First he'd have to convince Reece and Corey there actually was a danger. They were both so smitten with Vanessa that could be difficult.

Then he had to work out how three small boys could outsmart or overpower three adults. Especially when they'd be expecting them to try. In all the hours he'd been stuck in the cupboard he hadn't come up with a single idea.

From beyond the door came the sound of voices. Scrambling closer, Zack peered out through one of the holes.

Past the edge of the kitchen table he could just glimpse the dining room. No one in sight. He strained to listen. He could hear voices but nothing distinct. The sounds grew closer. Shadows flickered. At last he caught Vanessa's words.

'I've got a surprise for you boys this morning. If you can be ready and out in the van in five minutes we'll stop and get donuts on the way to the shelter.'

Out in the van? Zack's hopes dissolved. Tragg must have got the all-clear from his man. They were leaving and he still hadn't thought of a way to escape.

Movement at the corner of his eye drew his gaze. In the feeble light feeding in through the holes, a spider worked at repairing its web. Zack watched the pea-sized creature thoughtfully, feeling his initial revulsion give way to speculation. Last night they had driven an hour to get here, which meant they'd be driving an hour back . . .

All at once he was groping around for the mint box Tragg had thrown at him. When his fingers closed on it he opened the lid and, using a stick from the floor, gently scooped the spider into it.

Voices from the dining room.

'What about Zack?' Corey sounded anxious.

'Don't worry, he's coming. He's just in the bathroom,' Vanessa assured. 'So what do you say? Can you guys be ready?'

'We're ready now!' Reece shouted.

'Well, what are we waiting for? Let's go!'

Noises receding.

Zack braced himself. This was when they would come and get him. He wondered if it would be Tragg or Nolan and if they would tie him up again, replace his gag. How would they explain that to Reece and Corey?

Silent moments. Clutching the mint box, Zack peered out. No more shadows moved in the dining room. The house was still.

Panic washed over him in deepening waves. Had they left without him? Maybe they'd decided they didn't need him, that the others could tell them what they wanted to know. Once they got Corey and Reece in the car all they had to do was drive away.

The dam that had served him well through the night began to crack. Left in this hole with no food or water, what would become of him? He flashed on the image of his shrivelled remains, sucked dry by dozens of feasting spiders.

The dam finally burst.

'Hey! Lemme out! Hey! I'm in here! Hey! Hey!'

He pummelled the door till his hands went numb, then leaned back and had a go with his feet.

Suddenly a blinding light stabbed his eyes. A hand reached in, took hold of his ankle. He had just enough time to grab the mint box before being hauled out into the room.

He lay squinting up at the kitchen ceiling. When Tragg's face appeared above him, he tried to scuttle back. The man thumped a foot in the middle of his chest, pinning him in place.

'Now you listen to me, kid. You're going to go out and get in that van and not say a word to your little buddies, you got that? Because if you so much as open your mouth someone's going to get hurt. And it might not be you. You get what I'm saying?'

With no breath to speak, Zack quickly nodded.

Tragg removed his foot, reached down and lifted him by the front of his pyjama shirt. He thrust him towards a chair where some clothes were lying. 'Put those on and make it quick.'

Zack obeyed, anxious about changing in front of him but too afraid not to. To his surprise he still clutched the box with the spider. He managed to keep it out of sight long enough to slip it into his pocket.

He straightened from tying his sneakers to find Tragg eyeing him.

'Hey, Zacky, what say you save us all a lot of trouble and tell me now where the guy hid the case?'

'What guy? What case?'

Tragg smirked. 'You really don't want to be playing games with me.'

'What'll you do with us after we tell you?'

'Then you *did* see Giles.'

'Sure. We all did.'

'Well, no problem then. The minute you tell me we'll let you go, I give you my word.'

Zack knew the man was lying, but stalling would at least buy them some time. 'It's . . . well . . . I can't explain it. I'll have to show you.'

Tragg thought for a moment then reached out and pulled him to within an inch of his face. 'You better not be fucking with me.'

Zack felt the funny stirring in his chest. Bad Boy didn't like being pushed around. And he didn't much care how big or nasty the person was doing it.

He made a show of surveying the man's ravaged skin. 'Geez, you musta had the world's worst case of zits as a kid. Probably all them Junior Mints, huh?'

Zack held his breath. No matter how scared he got himself, Bad Boy always said what he wanted. But he'd never mouthed off to someone like Tragg before!

'Little Zacky likes to live dangerous.' Tragg shoved him towards the kitchen door.

Zack walked ahead of him into the dining room. 'You know they got cures for hatchet-face these days. You should check into it. Don't want to go around scaring little kids.'

'I like scaring little kids.'

'Bet they're not the only ones, though.' He braced himself for a blow from behind. *Please, don't do this!* But BB Ballinger was on a roll. 'Must be hard getting laid with a face like that.'

Two steps from the front door Tragg slammed him into it and pinned him while he hissed in his ear. 'You're going to be checking out a set of false teeth if you don't put a sock in it.'

He yanked Zack back by the collar of his sweatshirt and opened the door. 'Right, let's go. And remember what I said.'

Hand on his shoulder the entire way, Tragg escorted him out to the van. The door stood open and Corey and Reece were already buckled into the middle row of seats. Nolan was at the wheel and Vanessa stood talking to Corey through a window.

'But aren't you coming with us?' the boy was pleading.

'No, I have to stay here and wait for the next lot of children to come through.' When she saw his expression she quickly added, 'Don't worry, I'll see you at the shelter in a day or so.'

Corey brightened. The boy's hair, which normally stuck out in all directions, had been neatly combed, and Ali the alligator had a new button eye to replace his missing one. Vanessa's work? Had to be. No way Nolan or Tragg would have done it.

Zack glared at her. The fact she would pretend to care about Corey was almost as bad as what Tragg planned to do to them. For an instant nothing mattered more than that he expose these people for what they were. But Tragg still had a grip on his shoulder and the adoration in Corey's eyes was something he didn't have the heart to destroy.

With a feeling of helplessness he climbed up into the seat beside them. Tragg waited, watching him closely as he buckled his seatbelt.

'Zack! Where were you last night?' Corey said the instant he saw him.

Reece clutched his arm. 'Yeah, we woke up this morning and your bed was empty.'

Zack caught the warning look from Tragg. 'You dipsticks, I was there all night. I just got up early to get ready, that's all.'

With a satisfied smirk, Tragg rolled the door shut. He rounded the van and got in the front to ride shot gun. Nolan started the engine, saluted Vanessa and drove from the driveway.

Chapter 7

Doctor Chase Hadley strode from the treatment room into the office and returned his last patient's file to the receptionist's desk. Through the archway across the hall he could see five people in the waiting room – including a pair of school-age boys who seemed bent on breaking every item in the toy box.

The round middle-aged woman seated at the desk glanced up from her computer. 'And you thought Deadwater was such a small town you'd get to spend all your afternoons fishing.'

He couldn't help smiling. In the three weeks they'd been working together he'd found Elaine Kirkland to be direct and unflinching in her observations. As well as possessing an uncanny knack for reading his thoughts. 'Looks like I'll just have to make do with weekends.'

'Being the only practice for a hundred miles and with all the logging camps in the area we do get busy occasionally. Just be glad we haven't had one of those awful log spills. Crush injuries are the worst. At least that's what Doctor Muir always said.'

Chase nodded. He couldn't argue. 'Right, who's next?' At the sound of something breaking across the hall he bent to her ear.

'Please tell me it's the juvenile demolition crew while there's still something left of the waiting room.'

'Well, that depends.'

'On what?'

'Whether you're prepared to barter for your services.'

'Barter? You're kidding.'

She shook her head.

He frowned a moment then narrowed his eyes. 'Yes, you are. Come on, admit it. Dumb city boy out in the sticks, you think I'll fall for it. Next, you'll be telling me this is how all . . .'

Elaine continued to shake her head. When his words trailed off she pointed up the hall.

Chase stepped into it and peered towards the back of the building. In the light streaking in through the door to the parking lot a young woman paced the width of the corridor. Long jean-clad legs, brown corduroy jacket, shoulder-length blonde hair. He couldn't see her face for the glare, but from the speed of her strides and the tension held in those slender shoulders, he guessed she wasn't elated at being there.

'Who is she?' he said.

'Shyler O'Neil. Doctor Muir treated her only twice but she bartered both times; the last was six months ago. I don't think she realised he'd retired.'

'So she came in expecting the same arrangement.'

'I told her you might not be willing to continue it but that I would ask you.'

Chase stepped back. On seeing his receptionist's smile he realised he'd lingered over studying the stranger a bit longer than necessary. 'What kind of barter are we talking about?'

'I don't know; she makes things.' Elaine began shuffling papers on her desk.

'She's not going to pay me in pot holders, is she?'

'You'll have to work out the fine points between you. All I'm asking is, will you see her?'

He accepted the file she held out to him and skimmed the notes of his predecessor. First visit dated November last year, the second in March, both for recurring bouts of cystitis. 'There's a few things missing here – address, phone number, emergency contact.'

'If you can get any of that information out of her I'll be happy to record it. But don't hold your breath – she doesn't say much.'

'You saying she refused to give her details?'

'It's possible she just keeps forgetting, I guess.'

'So what do we know about her?'

She shrugged. 'Nothing.'

'Elaine,' he admonished, 'you mean to tell me in a town this size, a dedicated gossip such as yourself –'

'Caring professional, if you don't mind.'

'. . . doesn't have the lowdown about a patient?'

'Sorry, Doctor, but if anyone knows her I haven't talked to them.'

Chase tapped the folder against his palm. This was a great way to start a new practice. If word got out, he'd be running a welfare clinic for sure.

He sighed. 'All right, send her in.'

Eyes straight ahead. Don't look into the waiting room. Acknowledge the receptionist.

Shyler talked herself towards the treatment room door. Her feet grew heavier with every step. She'd been anxious enough about coming to the clinic. When she'd arrived and learned she'd be seeing a new doctor, a total stranger, she'd nearly turned around and driven home again.

Unspoken though it had been, she'd had an understanding with Doctor Muir. From her very first visit he'd seemed to know not to pressure her. Their distance from 'civilised' medical circles had perhaps made it easier for him to bend the rules where she was concerned. Would this new doctor be as accommodating?

The door stood ajar. She stopped before it and looked at her hand. The cut wasn't all that bad really. It didn't even hurt so much any more. Surely if she just kept it tightly bandaged –

'Go ahead in.' The receptionist was waving her on. 'The doctor's waiting.'

She took a deep breath and stepped through the door.

Her heart dropped. The man seated behind the oak desk was half the age of Doctor Muir, not much older than herself. Thick brown hair, solid shoulders, athletic build. When once she'd had an eye for such things she'd have thought him attractive. Now her main concern was his age – a younger practitioner, not long out of medical school, would surely be a stickler for rules.

He looked up and smiled. 'Shyler? Come in. Have a seat.'

Ignoring the chair beside his desk, the one he'd indicated, she crossed the room and perched on the edge of the treatment table. 'Thank you for seeing me without an appointment, Doctor.'

He paused a moment then pushed to his feet, tall and straight, and came round the desk. 'That's all right. What can I do for you?'

She held out her hand.

'Done some damage to yourself, have you? Let's take a look.' His voice was soft, his manner calm. He pulled up a stool and sat before her, then reached for the mag-light above their heads.

Say something, anything, she goaded herself. *Explain how it happened. Act normal. The last thing you want –*

He took her hand, his touch strong and sure, gentle and warm. She couldn't block thoughts of how long it had been. A lock of his hair dropped over his brow as he bent his head. A waft of soap and spicy aftershave.

'Okay, this isn't so bad,' he said. 'A couple of stitches is all it needs. You'll be fine.'

Without getting up, Chase rolled the stool to a neighbouring cabinet and opened a drawer. As he got out what he needed he cast a surreptitious glance at his patient.

The glimpse he'd caught of her out in the hall had not done her justice. Olive-green eyes, porcelain skin, hair the lustre and shade of raw silk. Delicate features marred slightly by apprehension, but no surprise there. Not many patients enjoyed getting stitches.

He rolled the stool back and laid his things on the tray beside her. 'Shyler, I'm going to have to numb the site. It'll probably sting more than when you cut yourself so just take a deep breath and try not to move.'

She clamped her jaw as the needle went in. Her feet did a little dance on the step stool; she clenched her other hand in a fist.

'Hang in there. Almost done.'

Shyler ground her teeth and hung on. Sting, he'd said. She couldn't imagine getting the stitches without the injection would hurt any more.

'There.' He straightened. 'You can relax, the worst is over.'

Relax? She'd laugh but knew what it would come out sounding like.

Chase disposed of the syringe and sat back to let the drug take effect. 'I guess Elaine told you about Doctor Muir. He retired only recently, which is probably why you weren't aware. I just took over the practice three weeks ago.'

He waited but she didn't respond. Usually patients asked questions at this point. Some to be friendly, others simply to know what sort of man they'd be dealing with. Shyler apparently wasn't curious.

She didn't seem to have relaxed much, either. Her feet were still tapping, her fingers writhing in her lap, her top teeth scraping her bottom lip. Didn't she believe him that the worst was passed?

He took up her hand. Tension hummed along her arm like energy through a high voltage wire. Her pulse was fast.

Gently he prodded the skin near the wound. 'How are we going? You still feeling that?'

A wordless nod. A shuddering breath. No eye contact. Nothing terribly out of the ordinary. Yet somehow he sensed this was more than simple fear of the procedure.

'While I think of it, we don't seem to have any contact details for you in our file. Perhaps you could give them to Elaine on your way out.'

Another quick nod. But this time a shift, her hand tugging slightly as though to pull free. He gently restrained it. 'So you don't have a problem with giving your details?'

Shyler looked up, ignored the warmth she read in his gaze. 'Of course not. Why should I?'

'Your file says you've been here twice. Normally –'

'I was in the process of moving then so I didn't know which address to give.'

'Well that explains it.'

Despite his smile she sensed his suspicion had not been allayed. Best to get him off the topic entirely. 'Where were you practising before you came here?'

'Boston. That's where I got my degree. Elaine thinks that makes me a city boy, but actually I grew up in Maine. Just north of Camden. Ever been there? Not a bad spot.'

It wasn't his habit to babble to strangers. In fact many considered him on the reticent side. But Chase hoped his talking would put her at ease. Whatever the reason, she still looked tense.

'When I left Maine to study I always planned to come back some day, open a practice in my home state. Though I have to admit, I never dreamed I'd be living this far north.'

Judging the site to be fully anaesthetised he began the procedure. 'I came here for my father mainly. He had an accident about five months ago and is in a wheelchair. He'll make a full recovery eventually but I thought it might help him if he got back to work. He's a painter – wildlife and wilderness landscapes. The area here is perfect for that.'

He glanced up occasionally as he worked. Overall she seemed in good health. Her clothes, though casual, were well presented and she smelled of fresh air and, oddly, of cedar.

With the first stitch completed, he repositioned her hand for the second, casually noting the feel of her arm. Good muscle tone, not underweight. But he'd noted that fact out in the hall. Even half concealed by her jacket her physique was pretty much . . . well . . . perfect.

'My father taught art at Camden University and was about to retire when he had the accident. By the time he got out of the hospital the house he'd planned to buy had been sold and the lease had run out on his campus apartment. So when this practice came up it seemed a good place for both of us. At least for a while.'

He tied the last suture, cut the silk, and got to work on the sterile dressing. 'Don't get me wrong, the area's beautiful. As an avid hiker and cross-country skier how could I not love these forests?'

Her arm moved more freely as he wrapped it in gauze. Though she'd not responded directly to his words she did appear to have relaxed a bit.

'Elaine's convinced I'll never last. "Once a city boy, always a city boy." And I'll admit the pace here is different from Boston. It'll certainly take some getting used to. I guess I'll just have to wait and see.'

With the dressing complete, he laid her hand gently back in her lap. He glanced up briefly into her eyes and for an instant felt helpless to look away. 'Who knows? Maybe I'll find a reason to stay.'

At hearing his own words his fixation broke. He pushed back the stool and got to his feet. 'That's it. All done.'

He turned away, bent over his desk and recorded the visit in her file. 'If that cut were any bigger I'd suggest a course of antibiotics. But seeing as you've kept it clean I think we can get by without them. You'll need to come back so I can remove the stitches, though. Let's make it next Wednesday. Any time is fine, I'll just fit you in. No need to –'

Chase slowly set down his pen and blinked at the object that had appeared on his desk.

The miniature carving was so lifelike he half-expected it to get up and move. Perfectly symmetrical palmate antlers rose from the creature's elongated head. Together with the distinctive muzzle and stout equine build the animal was instantly recognisable.

With a sense of wonder he picked it up and turned it in his hands. The moose was no more than six inches high. Hundreds of needle-fine gouges effectively rendered the fur on its body and the dewlap that hung from beneath its throat was thinner than a toothpick. How did anyone carve something so fine?

Shyler cleared her throat. 'Your receptionist told you about my bartering arrangement with Doctor Muir.'

'Your arrangement?' Her meaning registered and he looked at her stunned. 'You made this?'

Despite herself she arched a brow. 'That surprises you?'

47

'Please, that wasn't a sexist remark. I'm in awe of anyone who works with wood. I'm not renowned for my carpentry skills.' He studied the figure again. 'Not that what you do is even remotely in the same league. This is exquisite.'

Of all the things she'd expected she might feel in confronting this stranger, shy embarrassment wasn't one of them. She'd never received any praise for her work. Though her pieces sold well enough from Bill Ramsey's store she never lingered to hear buyer feedback. 'Then . . .'

'Will I accept this as payment for the consultation?' Chase straightened and held out his hand. 'Yes. Thank you.'

Shyler stepped out into the reception area and paused to take a few deep breaths. She'd held it together. Despite the man's questions, the stressful procedure, she'd behaved almost like a normal human being. A few seconds more and she'd be out of here, the whole affair safely behind her. Just one remaining danger to side-step.

She opened her eyes. Elaine the receptionist wasn't at her desk. Glancing back to make sure the doctor wasn't watching, she hurried through the office, turned to head for the door – and froze.

A miniature fire truck glided towards her out of the waiting room across the hall. It rolled to a stop in front of her feet, followed closely by a freckled, chubby-cheeked little boy.

The boy bent down and picked up the truck. Had she simply smiled and walked away he'd no doubt have run straight off again. But her rigid pose and frozen expression caught his eye. He stood, head cocked, staring up at her.

Steel jaws clamped around her chest. Only one last danger and here it was. She hadn't been fast enough. She hadn't gotten out in time.

The boy kept staring, a bit uncertain now. She tried to smile but her lips wouldn't move. He took a step back. *Oh no, please, don't be afraid.*

A woman came towards them out of the waiting room. She murmured an apology and drew the boy away, casting a wary look over her shoulder.

Shyler turned and raced up the hall.

She tasted blood as she neared the back door and raised her bandaged hand to her mouth. When she drew it away she saw a bright red stain on the gauze. Somehow, at some point, she'd bitten her lip.

Chapter 8

Twenty minutes after leaving the 'safe house' Nolan turned the van into a one-pump gas station on a lonely country road. He steered around an idling transport truck and parked in the shade at the edge of the lot.

'Take those two.' Tragg jerked his head at Reece and Corey, then shifted his gaze to Zack. 'I'll stay with him.'

'But I need to –'

Tragg silenced the man with a look. Zack half-smiled. Even grown-ups were afraid of Hatchet-face.

The two men got out. Nolan slid the back door open and waved impatiently at the younger boys. 'Well, come on. We don't have all day.'

As the three walked away, Tragg stood watching Zack through the door. 'Having fun, kid?' He popped a Junior Mint into his mouth.

Zack stared sullenly out the window. He hated the sound of the man's laugh. It threatened to shatter the façade he'd worked so hard to maintain since leaving the house.

Projecting an air of cowed acceptance, he'd kept his gaze on the road the whole time, watching for a place to enact his plan.

What that plan was exactly hadn't come to him until the moment they'd pulled in here. Now, as the details took shape in his mind, he fought to contain his growing excitement.

The spot seemed perfect. Not a single car had gone by since they stopped. The stretch up ahead was fairly straight and had a field on either side. Huge oak trees lined the shoulders but were far enough apart that, with luck, they wouldn't run into one. At any rate it was worth the risk.

Zack reached into his sweatshirt pocket and closed his fingers around the mint box, praying its occupant was still alive.

'You gotta go?'

Tragg's voice jolted him so much he jumped. He shook his head, then held his breath as the man's suspicious gaze crawled over him. A moment later Reece and Corey climbed back in the van, each with an apple cider donut.

Tragg turned to Nolan. 'Don't leave them alone.'

'But I haven't –'

Nolan swore as Tragg walked away. He set his coffee in the dashboard holder and handed the last donut to Zack. 'You guys stay put. I'm just going to duck behind the van for a second.'

The instant he was out of earshot, Zack leaned towards Reece and Corey. 'We gotta get out of here.'

They stared at him blankly. 'What? Why?'

'These guys aren't who they say they are. And they're not taking us to any shelter.'

'But Vanessa promised we'd get a new home.' Reece wiped cinnamon sugar from his lips.

'She was just saying that so we wouldn't play up.'

Corey looked stricken. 'But Vanessa said –'

'She lied, all right?' Zack lowered his voice. 'There isn't time to explain it all, you just gotta trust me.'

He shot a quick glance around at Nolan whose head was just visible through the van's rear window. 'Don't let on I told you anything. Pretend to go along with whatever they say and just be ready when I give you the signal.'

'Ready for what?'

'To do what I tell you!'

Zack saw that Nolan had finished peeing and was heading back for the driver's door. He straightened in his seat and turned to the others. 'Buckle your seatbelts.'

'That's right, boys,' Tragg said, climbing into the front. 'Do what your big brother tells you.'

Zack's heart stopped. He'd been so busy watching Nolan he'd failed to check the other way. Had Tragg heard what he'd said to the others? From the steady glare the man now had fixed on him it was clear he was wondering.

'Zack's not our real brother,' Reece spoke up. 'He's our foster brother.'

His innocent tone drew Tragg's attention and seemed to dispel any suspicions he might have had. When Nolan got in, Tragg turned his menacing glare on him. 'I told you not to leave them alone.'

The man's whispered words were more frightening than a shout.

'I didn't. I was right here the whole the time, I swear.' Nolan fumbled the key in the ignition. He started the van, stalled it, and finally managed to get it going. They pulled from the station and started up the road.

With a deep breath, Zack slipped his hand in his sweatshirt. He would have only one chance. And it had to be in the next few moments, before the van got going too fast.

He kept his eye on the speedometer as he eased the mint box from his pocket. Twenty-five miles an hour now. Just a bit faster.

The two men hadn't yet buckled their seatbelts. Bonus! Please, just a little longer. Approaching thirty. He moved his fingers to the lid of the box.

Then he saw it. Something he couldn't have seen from the gas station. A ditch along their side of the road. What would it do? Improve the odds or work against them? He'd have to chance it. He leaned forward slightly, opened the box and shook its contents onto Nolan's shoulder.

Tragg caught the movement from the corner of his eye and spun around. Like a striking snake his hand shot out and snatched Zack's wrist in a crushing grip. 'You wouldn't be dumb enough to try something, would you?'

Zack bit down to keep from crying out.

The van lurched sharply.

'Shit! Oh, shit!' Nolan jerked the wheel as he slapped at his face.

Tragg let go. 'For Christ's sake watch –' was all he got out before being slammed against his door.

The van lurched again. Flashing images, squealing tyres.

Through the last blurred seconds Zack saw the oak tree rushing towards them.

Chapter 9

Zack sat gasping. By some miracle they'd missed the tree but their final impact had been a lot harder than he'd anticipated. The van's nosedive into the ditch had thrown him against his shoulder belt with enough force to wind him. Otherwise he felt okay.

Beside him, Reece and Corey sat speechless, eyes filled with shock. No blood, no mangled body parts. At least they hadn't been injured either.

The men in the front had not fared as well. Tragg lay crumpled against the dashboard, Nolan slumped over the steering wheel.

A groan from Nolan spurred Zack into action. 'Come on, let's go.' He threw off his belt.

The others sat frozen, their incredulous expressions making it clear he hadn't convinced them they were in danger.

'I said, come on!' He undid their belts, turned for the door and let out a gasp.

Face streaked in blood, Tragg glared back at him from between the front seats. With a quavering hand he pulled something small and dark from his pocket. And aimed it at Zack.

Though the sight threatened to loosen his bladder he could

not look away. The hole seemed enormous, opening wider as Tragg moved the pistol towards his face.

When the man's arm jerked Zack thought it was over – he hadn't heard the shot because he was dead.

But as the arm lowered further he saw Tragg's face and realised what had happened. The vicious sneer of moments ago had changed to a dull, questioning stare. The pistol slipped from the gunman's hand as he slumped unconscious against the seat.

Zack sat gaping for precious seconds. Again it was the sound of Nolan moaning that snapped him out of it. 'Let's go. Move!'

This time the others needed no convincing. As he slid the door open and scrambled out they were right behind him.

'Hey, get back here!' Panic at the sound of Nolan's voice helped them clamber out of the ditch.

Up on the road there were no cars in sight.

Reece grabbed his hand. 'What do we do?'

Zack looked around. No houses, no people. Only the gas station a hundred yards back. With the transport truck still idling out front!

'This way!' They ran.

Halfway there he slowed to look back. Nolan was staggering out of the ditch. He walked in circles on the shoulder of the road, then spotted the three boys running. 'Damn it, get back here!' He started after them.

Zack quickly made up the ground he'd lost. He reached Corey first, who was lagging behind, grabbed his hand and dragged him along. The three of them reached the station together.

'Over here!' Zack hurried them to the back of the truck. Then stood staring up at the towering beast.

With the rumbling engine, noxious fumes and massive wheels, it felt like some kind of sleeping dragon. Corey could just about walk beneath it without bending down. It was almost as ugly and scary as Tragg.

Zack stepped closer. The two back doors had lever handles but there was no way he could reach them from the ground. He would have to climb up. And that would take time they might not have.

He checked Nolan. The man was still weaving but getting closer. If a car came along, or he recovered enough to start running . . .

Zack turned back. A round bit of steel, like the end of a trumpet, stuck out from the bottom of the truck. He climbed up onto it and grabbed a handle, heaved with all his weight and pulled.

The door creaked open, nearly pushing him off his perch. He let it swing past him, then reached his hand down to the others.

'Corey first. Reece, push him up to me.'

As he heaved Corey up, Zack threw an anxious glance at the shop. The truck stood just to the left of the entrance, clearly visible to anyone inside. If they happened to be looking that way. He prayed the truck was far enough to the side that no one would notice them.

With Corey safely inside the truck, Zack climbed in after him. But even as he reached down to give Reece a hand, the shop doors opened and a man came out.

Zack held his breath. The man's interest in his wallet was all that was keeping him from spotting the boys as he strode towards the truck. The instant he disappeared around the front of it, Zack yanked Reece up into the hold.

His relief was short-lived. Nolan had spotted the driver as well and had broken into a shambling jog. 'Hey! Wait! Don't go! Hey!'

For a moment, Zack felt a crushing defeat. Then the engine roared and he realised the sound of its idling had been enough to drown out Nolan's shouts. But would the driver see him when he checked in his mirror?

Again Zack braced. The truck started forward. The back door swung towards him and he quickly grabbed it.

Nolan was still shambling along the shoulder, waving his arms, shouting after them. But those massive oak trees that had posed such a threat now cloaked the man in heavy shade. He was no more than a ripple in a sea of shadow.

The truck commenced its slow acceleration. Closing the door, Zack smiled and flipped Nolan the bird.

Chapter 10

Whistling a verse of 'Downeaster Alexa', Dr Chase Hadley set his last patient's file on the desk and picked up his jacket from the chair beside it.

'Someone's in a good mood,' Elaine commented, her fingers flying over her keyboard.

'Had a good day. What about you?'

She shot him a look over the top of her glasses.

'Sorry, you're still converting those files. I guess that's no picnic.'

'It's not your fault. If Doctor Muir hadn't been such a fossil we'd have kept our records on computer to begin with.'

'Well, don't stick with it too long, will you? You're bankrupting me with all this overtime.' He shoved his arm through the sleeve of his jacket and spied the carving he'd set on the cabinet.

Smiling, he picked it up. 'Elaine, did Shyler . . . Did Ms O'Neil give you her contact details?'

'No. Why?'

He turned to blink at her. 'She said she was going to.'

'Sorry, haven't seen them. I was getting a coffee when she came out of your room, but she didn't leave them on my desk.'

He frowned at the carving then pushed back a sense of disquiet. 'Guess she forgot again.'

'She ran past me as I came out of the kitchen. Flew out the back door like the devil was chasing her.'

'Must have been in a hurry. I'm sure she'll give them to you next time she comes.' He turned, about to wish her goodnight, but something in her silence made him step back. 'You don't think she will.'

'Give us her details? Doesn't seem likely. If she wouldn't give them to Doctor Muir –'

'Wouldn't? She told me she'd been moving back then and didn't know which address to give.'

Elaine arched a brow. 'Her last two visits were four months apart. A bit long to have no address, don't you think?'

Ten minutes later, as he pushed through the door of old Bill Ramsey's general store, Chase was still pondering Elaine's remarks. Her words had rekindled his earlier concerns – ones he'd dismissed as products of his own over-sensitive radar – and now the questions were surfacing again.

Shyler had been tense and withdrawn at her visit, a fact he could conceivably attribute to the stress of the procedure. But what if, as he had briefly sensed, it was due to something more than that? She'd had no money to pay for her visit, presumably because she didn't work. Was that because she couldn't find a job or didn't want the exposure of one?

If Shyler had lied about why she hadn't given her details, it cast these facts in a totally different light. Each on its own was hardly suspicious, but taken all together –

'Just about ready to close up, Doc, if you're wantin' something.'

'Thanks, Bill,' he said to the Grizzly Adams clone behind the counter. 'I'll just be a minute.'

The store was a relic from a different era. Bare wood floor, glass-topped counters and a cash register that belonged in a museum. Barrels and crates displayed many items. Iron rakes stood beside fishing rods and brooms, kerosene lamps hung with coils of garden hose. If the store had been in Quincy Market it would have been labelled environmentally trendy. Here it was simply that things had never changed.

Chase walked the aisles collecting the items on his father's list. He was just heading back to the counter when a familiar object caught his eye.

He picked it up. A white-tailed deer, carved with distinctive needle-fine gouges to depict its fur. Around him he saw others now, their style too similar to be anyone else's.

'Bill, do you know the woman who does these carvings?'

The man looked up from sweeping the floor. 'Shyler? Sure do. Comes in regular every other month. Makes all them feeders and mailboxes, too.'

Chase turned to where he had nodded. Displayed on a table in front of the window was an assortment of handmade wooden items. Picture frames of rough-cut pine. Mailboxes that looked like colonial mansions. Platform feeders with the silhouettes of birds carved into the rims.

'You wouldn't happen to know where she lives, would you?' Chase called over.

'Sorry, Doc, couldn't tell ya.'

He picked up a log cabin made of birch twigs. Its cedar roof shingles appeared to have been cut and attached individually. 'Do you know her well? Know much about her?'

'I know her stuff's real popular with tourists.'

'Does she live with anyone that you know of?'

'Never said. Lady keeps pretty much to herself.'

'Well, has she ever come in the store with anyone?'

'Not that I've seen.' Bill stopped sweeping and leaned on the broom. 'Now you mention it, I've never seen her anywhere else.'

'So she just comes in here every other month, you pay for her delivery and she leaves.'

'Oh, no, we barter. I keep a tally of how much she's sold and she picks out groceries for that amount.'

Chase put the cabin back on the table. Bartering again. No cheque – no bank account or ID required.

''Course, this time o' year she falls behind some.' Bill stood before him, having swept his way closer.

'Falls behind?'

'Not as many vacationers coming through town to buy her stuff.' The old man shrugged. 'Pretty lady. I let her run up a bit of a tab.'

The old man's gaze lingered this time – the scrutiny of the local for the town newcomer.

'Guess it seems odd, me asking all these questions about her.'

'Don't seem funny at all, Doc. Figure a respectable fella like you must have their reasons.'

Chase sighed as the man walked away. All right, so maybe he was worrying over nothing. Elaine could be wrong about Shyler deliberately withholding her details and the other issues surrounding the woman could be perfectly innocent.

He picked up a crow from the table of carvings and smiled at a sudden realisation – he'd probably have asked the same questions anyway. The simple truth was he was interested. And not in an entirely professional sense. Chase Raymond Hadley, who'd never done an irrational thing in his life, who never took chances or acted impulsively or followed hunches, *that* Chase Hadley was smitten by a woman he'd met only once and about whom he knew absolutely nothing at all.

Shaking his head he put the crow down. 'This'll be all, Bill.' He carried his basket of goods to the counter.

As he opened his wallet he noted the barred owl next to the register, its feathers rendered with the same exacting detail as the moose's fur. These pieces would have taken hours to make. And their prices didn't come close to doing them justice.

'Hang on a second.' He ran back, grabbed up an armful of items from the display table and returned to the register. Bill watched, impassive, as he set them one by one on the counter.

Chase shrugged. 'I like to support struggling artists.'

Bill began ringing up his purchase. 'Like I said – pretty lady.'

Chase carried the boxes up the ramp, noting with pleasure the solid feel of the plywood construction beneath his feet. He'd built the ramp the week they'd moved in and still felt pride in his bit of handiwork. Bracing the boxes against the back door, he twisted the knob and entered the kitchen.

The house, a classic colonial design, had needed only minor modifications to accommodate his father's wheelchair. The dining room was now his father's office and the original den had become his bedroom. Chase had the entire second floor but only made use of two of its four rooms – one for a study, the other his bedroom.

But the best feature of the house, the reason Chase had chosen to rent it, was the glass conservatory off the living room. With its natural light and commanding view of the lawn and woods it was the perfect place for his father to paint.

As he set the boxes on the kitchen table he heard the buzz of his father's wheelchair approaching from the living room. A moment later the robust figure of Allen Hadley swept into the room.

'Hey,' he said in his usual greeting.

'Hey, yourself.' Chase hung his jacket on the hook by the door and surveyed the kitchen. The breakfast dishes were right where they'd been when he'd left that morning. Rolling up his sleeves, he stepped to the sink. 'How was your day?'

'I finished the Lynxes.'

'Great. That puts you ahead of schedule, doesn't it?'

'If "ahead" means being two weeks behind.' The man's gaze grew distant. 'I was thinking I'd do the bobcats next. I had a terrific idea for the scene – a male in deep snow, leaping after a snowshoe hare. Lots of action. Winter shadows to offset the white. What do you think?'

Chase nodded. But the lengthy description had the ring of diversion. 'Can't wait to see it. Did you do your exercises?'

Allen shifted in his chair. 'Well, you'll be pleased to know I sat down this morning and actually worked out –'

'Did you do your exercises?'

He sighed. 'No.'

Chase aimed a soapy finger at him. 'After dinner. Or no TV.'

The man let out a good-natured huff. 'You'd think I was five the way I get treated around here.'

'And we both know the response to that one, don't we?'

'Probably wouldn't have finished the Lynxes if I'd stopped to bother with all that nonsense.' Allen buzzed his chair to the fridge and opened it.

'Exercises here instead of three months in a rehab centre. Wasn't that the deal, or am I mistaken?'

'Did I ever tell you you've got a lot of your mother in you?' Allen's muffled words issued from the fridge.

'In fact I seem to remember the word "religiously" used a few times,' Chase added, unfazed by his comment.

Clutching an armful of salad ingredients, Allen reversed and closed the fridge. 'All right, let's not argue. Especially when you're winning. I'll do them right after dinner, okay? You can even count.'

'Don't think I won't.'

'Yeah, I know how you doctors like to watch folks suffer. Bunch of sadists.' Allen plunked the groceries on the counter and pulled a cutting board out from beneath it. 'You shouldn't have done it.'

The man's voice had gone suddenly serious. Chase turned back to the sink. 'Done what?'

'Taken the practice. You had no business moving way up here in the middle of nowhere. You were happy in Boston.'

'I was, was I?'

'You had friends, contacts, a social life. That's where you should be. Not holed up in some wilderness babysitting a crippled old fart.'

Chase cocked his head. 'You know, now that I think about it, *you've* got quite a bit of Mom in you too.'

'Well, I know what she would've thought of all this.'

'It's not a life sentence for either of us, Dad. Once you're out of that chair for good I can find a different practice if I want.'

'I know. And don't think I don't appreciate it. It's just . . . Well, it kills me to think I've become such a burden.'

Chase regarded him over his shoulder. 'Nice try, Dad, but you still have to do your exercises.'

'Smart alec kid.'

With the salad completed, Allen buzzed his chair to the kitchen table and began unpacking the first of the boxes. 'Any chance we can get to Presque Isle this weekend? I'm nearly out of Sienna acrylic and I could use some more canvases.'

'I suppose my hike around the lake can wait.'

Allen had finished emptying the first box and now sat staring into the second. 'What's all this?'

Wiping his hands, Chase came over. 'Those are bird houses and that's a feeder. Thought we might put them up in the yard.'

Allen reached in and held up the moose. 'And this?'

Chase took a moment, gazing down at it with the same sense of wonder he'd felt at first seeing it. 'A patient gave me that today as payment for a consultation.'

His father turned the carving this way and that, scrutinising it with an artist's eye. 'He's good.'

'She.'

'Oh?' His bushy brows rose. 'Unusual hobby for a woman. We should hire her to fix that ramp you built.'

Chase frowned. 'What's wrong with my ramp?'

'So, this woman carver . . . Anyone I know?'

'No one you or anyone else knows, apparently.'

'A lady of mystery, eh? Good looking?'

A red flag suddenly appeared on the field. 'Didn't really notice.'

'Eligible age?'

Chase turned away. 'Start the spaghetti, Dad, I'm hungry.'

Allen went back to studying the moose. 'A mysterious stranger giving my son gifts. And here I was worried you wouldn't meet anyone.'

Chapter 11

'It's me.' Nolan stepped away from the hospital room door and moved to the opposite side of the hall. He could still see Tragg but had eliminated the chance of the man's waking up and overhearing his conversation.

'Where are you?' Vanessa's voice issued from his mobile phone.

'A hospital in Conway. We had a slight accident.'

'What! How bad?'

'Bad enough. I'm fine and the van's okay but Tragg's laid up. At least for a day or two. Concussion or something.'

'What about the boys?'

'That's why I'm calling. They . . . got away.'

A heartbeat of silence. 'I don't believe it. How could –'

Nolan quickly gave her the details.

'How's Tragg taking it?' she asked when he'd finished.

Nolan glanced back into the room and felt his throat tighten. Even bruised and unconscious the man had a look that could turn his blood cold. 'He doesn't know yet. Hasn't woken up since the kids took off.'

Vanessa blew out a breath through her teeth. 'Wouldn't want to be in your shoes right now.'

'It'll be okay. I got the licence plate number and company name off the truck they got on.'

'So?'

'It's been less than an hour. If your uncle's people can find out where it's headed there's a good chance I can catch up to it.'

This time she laughed. 'You're kidding, right?'

Nolan clamped down to keep from swearing. 'Will you just call Lazaro and see what you can find out? And do it fast. I'd like to get them back before Tragg wakes up.'

She sighed. 'All right, give me the details.'

The truck's gentle rocking soothed Zack's initial adrenaline shakes. That, plus the knowledge he'd outsmarted Nolan, boosted his mood from what it had been that morning.

But he could tell the others were far from happy. They huddled together in the small space near the door as cold air and dust swirled around them.

'You're bleeding,' Reece said, pointing to his leg.

Zack looked down, saw that one leg of his jeans was torn and rolled it up. There on his calf, half concealed by a layer of dirt, was a dark red blotch. He spat on the cuff of his sweatshirt sleeve and used it to wipe away some of the grime.

The cut was only an inch or so long but it was almost as deep. If he pushed the skin a certain way the edges gaped like the mouth of a fish. He stared in wonder at how little it hurt and that he hadn't even felt it when it happened.

'Must've cut myself climbing out of that ditch. Or into the truck.' He rolled the pants leg down and dismissed it.

'My stomach hurts.'

Zack sighed. Corey always had to be the centre of attention. Any time someone else got hurt, somehow he always felt sick as well. 'You're just hungry, that's all.' As Zack was himself, he suddenly realised.

He inspected the boxes stacked around them. They were all sealed with tight plastic bands, impossible to break. If he only had a knife or something sharp . . .

On the floor beside him he spotted a two-inch metal staple. He snatched it up, jabbed it into the nearest carton and ripped a small hole in its side.

Toilet paper.

He tried the next box. Laundry detergent. And the ones after that. Dish liquid, toothpaste, motor oil.

He dropped the staple and sat back down. 'I'll find us something to eat when we get there.'

'When we get where?' Reece said softly. 'Where are we going?'

'How the hell should I know?'

'How long will it be?'

'If I don't know where we're going how can I –'

'Who'll take care of us?'

Corey's frightened little-boy voice just made things worse. Why were they always asking him questions he couldn't answer? 'Who took care of us up till now? You think Frank and Julie ever gave a crap about us?'

Corey bowed his head. A minute later there were tears on his face.

Zack paused to get a grip on himself. One thing he had always sworn – he would never let the Bad Boy out around them. That part of him that felt like a whole other person, the side he sometimes couldn't control, the one that mouthed off to men like Tragg no matter the risk. Sometimes that part of him scared even him.

'What's wrong now?' he said at last.

'I left Ali on the van.'

Crying. Over a skanky stuffed animal. Corey was just too dumb to realise his dad had only given it to him because he felt guilty for walking out on him. But just at that moment Zack didn't have the heart to explain.

He pushed off the box, dropped to the floor and slung his arm around Corey's shoulder. 'Don't worry, we'll find another one.'

Reece scooted closer to the boy's other side. 'I know how you feel – I lost all my baseball cards, too.' He held up a single dog-eared specimen. 'All I got left is this dumb Eric Gagne.'

The man clipped the chain to his collar and dragged him down the darkened corridor. At the end, a garage with only one vehicle – the idling truck.

He fought and kicked but the man was stronger, lifting him towards the open compartment, pushing him in, slamming the door.

The air inside burned his lungs like fire. Absolute blackness swallowed his pleas. But a terror far deeper evoked his screams – *this is what happens to unwanted boys . . .*

Zack jerked awake, somehow managing to stifle his cry. He sat up, blinking around in confusion.

He was in a truck all right, but not the one of his recurring nightmare. This one was bigger and loaded with boxes, and Corey and Reece were in it with him.

Yes, he remembered now – the men, the accident, their lucky escape. But something had changed.

They were no longer moving.

He scrambled to his feet and rushed to the door, his sudden movements waking the others. Before they could speak he held up his hand, then bent to listen. No engine noises. No sound of voices. They'd definitely stopped. But where and for how long?

One thing for sure, they couldn't just go marching out in the open. Three young boys, alone, climbing off the back of a truck . . . If anyone saw them they'd turn them over to the police. And grown-ups never believed what kids said, they only listened to other grown-ups. Which meant the cops would just hand them back to Nolan and Tragg.

Zack shuddered, recalling the gun, the yawning black hole just inches from his face.

Something touched his hand and he jumped. Reece and Corey had come up behind him, their expressions anxious. He placed a finger to his lips then pressed his ear to the door again. Nothing.

Slowly he raised his hand to the lever. The light seeping through the seams of the hold didn't seem as strong as it had been earlier. He sensed it was dusk, perhaps even later. With any luck the shadows would cloak them. He pushed on the handle and eased it down.

With the door open only a finger's width, Zack peered out. Some kind of depot. Lots of trucks, some with huge logs chained to their beds. No one in sight. He pushed the door wider and the scent of pine flooded the hold. Reece and Corey squeezed up beside him.

The twilight was deepened by surrounding trees – forest so thick and dense with shadow he couldn't see more than a few yards into it. A strange kind of forest. Bare straight trunks in staggered rows, their greenery forming an impenetrable canopy high above.

Perhaps it wasn't so late after all, Zack thought, climbing down from the truck. The forest just blocked out most of the sun, its damp, cold, pine-scented breath raising goosebumps along his flesh. He reached up and helped the other boys down.

'Where are we?' Reece said, clutching his arm.

'Don't start that again,' Zack hissed. 'Just shut up and follow me.'

The trucks were parked in two long rows that stretched either side of a gravel track. Zack led them towards the road at the end, using each vehicle in turn for cover.

He needn't have bothered. There was no one around. Even the little office building they came to stood dark and deserted. In the end they ran the final stretch.

Once on the road, Zack breathed a sigh of relief. If anyone came by and saw them now they'd just think they were some local kids out for a walk.

But with one problem solved, the next arose. It was getting dark. They'd soon be unable to see where they were going, and there wasn't a house or shop in sight. Just an endless corridor of massive trees.

They'd been walking about fifteen minutes when pinpoints of light appeared up ahead. A car approaching. Zack heard the gurgle of water nearby – a stream flowing beneath the road.

'This way!' The two boys followed him down the embankment.

When the car finally passed, its headlights lit up the culvert enough to show three large concrete pipes passing beneath the road's surface. Water flowed through only two of them.

The third, blocked at one end by a tangle of branches, would be their shelter for the night.

Chapter 12

Nolan pulled the rental car into the depot and began slowly driving up and down the rows of parked trucks. He rounded a corner and let out a curse. Too late – the boys were already here.

He rolled to a stop with his headlights fixed on the truck's rear door. If he hadn't had to wait over an hour for Vanessa to get back to him with its destination he might've made it here in time. Shaking his head, he climbed from the car.

On the bright side, he could be sure of one thing – once the truck had left the gas station there were few other places it could have stopped before getting here. Maine boasted only a handful of roads in its northern quarter and most were privately owned by logging companies. Odds were the boys had come this far. Hell, if he was really lucky the little shits were still on the truck.

But as he walked towards it he saw the back door was slightly ajar. Hopes dashed, he yanked it open and peered inside. Nothing but boxes, packed so closely there was no way the boys could be hiding among them.

Cursing again, he pulled his ringing mobile from his pocket. And froze at the sound of the voice that spoke to him.

'Tragg? Hey, buddy, how are you feeling?'

'Well, let's see. I wake up in a hospital with the mother of all headaches after some fuckwit drives me into a ditch. Then some battle-axe nurse tells me I'm all alone here, that the fuckwit and my passengers have split. How would you guess I'm feeling, *buddy*?'

Nolan launched into a hasty explanation. He revamped the accident and the boys' escape, playing up how hard he had tried to stop them getting on the truck.

When he'd finished, the silence from the other end was even more ominous than Tragg's first words.

'I haven't just been sitting around,' he added quickly. 'I tracked where they were headed and I'm in the town now. I actually found the truck they were on and the engine's still warm so –'

'Screw the truck. What about them?'

Nolan tried to swallow but his mouth had gone dry. 'They're not here. But, hey, the good news is they can't have gone far in the dark and there's no one anywhere around to help them.'

'Find them.'

'Sure. Don't worry, I'm on it.'

'Don't worry? I'm not sure you get the importance of this. Not only are those kids the only ones who saw where Giles hid his stash but the oldest also knows things that could hurt Lazaro. Things he *wouldn't* know if you and the bitch had kept your mouths shut.'

Nolan felt it wise not to argue.

'I'll be laid up here a couple more days; you've got that long to get them back. Otherwise the first thing I'll do when I get out is head up there to give you a hand. That plain enough for you, *buddyboy*?'

'Yeah, got it.'

'Call me tomorrow.'

Nolan closed the phone and slumped against the back of the truck. He could always run for it – this one-horse hamlet couldn't be more than a hundred miles from the Canadian border. But it would never work. If the boys got away and eventually talked, Tragg would stop at nothing to find him.

He hung his head. It didn't seem right . . . Damn it, it wasn't right that he should cop the rap for this alone. He opened his phone again and punched in a number.

When Vanessa answered he gave her the bad news.

'Well, they can't have gotten far on foot,' she said.

'Unless they hitched a ride with someone.'

'Oh, come on. Lazaro's man told me the place was remote. Population less than a thousand.'

Nolan stared up at the towering trees. 'Remote's not the word. It's a frigging wilderness. Not a house in sight and I didn't pass another car in the last eighty miles.'

'Then there's not many places they could be hiding.'

Nolan laughed. 'Only a thousand square acres of forest, that's all. I could use some help with this.'

'Forget it. I'm busy.'

'I'm sure it can wait.'

'Maybe I don't want to wait. Hell, it isn't my fault you lost them.'

'But it's your fault they know about Lazaro.' Her silence told him he'd gotten her attention. 'That's what Tragg thinks. I mean if you hadn't said the name at the house it wouldn't be so urgent we find them, would it?'

'Shit.'

He smiled.

'All right, I'll be there first thing in the morning.'

Chapter 13

Firelight winked in the pot-bellied stove that warmed the workshop. A lone gypsy moth, a rare sight this late in the season, fluttered around the hurricane lamp that hung from the rafters, casting shadows, crazed and ghostly, across the walls.

Shyler took a sip of brandy, set the glass on the workbench beside her and resumed sanding the roof of the martin house. She didn't normally drink while she worked but, still recovering from her trip into town, felt the need for something to settle her.

Brushing a strand of hair from her face, she caught the scent from her bandaged hand. Gauze, antiseptic and the barest hint of something else. Soap? Aftershave? Something . . . *him*. Suddenly the doctor's face was before her.

If anything had made her ordeal less distressing it had been Doctor Hadley. There was something about him, something more than looks and a competent manner. Soft-spoken, gentle, yet radiating an aura of quiet strength, he'd made her feel calmer and more relaxed – and a few other things she preferred not to dwell on – than any man she'd met in a long time.

Despite her fears, her determination to tell him nothing about herself, he'd somehow managed to draw her out. Not goaded her into it, as many had tried, but simply let her feel it was all right, that he would listen. And, wonder of wonders, she had believed it, however briefly. She'd spoken more to him in their twenty minutes than at both her visits to Muir combined.

She felt the slightest prick of conscience recalling she hadn't left him her contact details as she had promised. What she had told him wasn't a lie – the first time she'd visited Doctor Muir, last November, she'd only just returned to the cabin and hadn't expected to stay very long. Just a few weeks, months at the most, she'd told herself. To get over the divorce, losing her job, her friends, the apartment, and . . . everything else. Just a bit of time to pull herself together and then she'd move on. Find a new job. Start a new life.

Only it hadn't worked out that way. Nor was it likely to in the future. When the mere sight of children was enough to bring on your panic attacks, how did you ever go back to teaching? And without a job to get money for treatment, how did you ever get over your problem? Not without asking for help, you didn't, and that was patently out of the question.

And so here she was, ten months later, still at the cabin.

She gazed towards the workshop's darkened window, seeing in her mind's eye the forests beyond. The misty hillsides, shrouded peaks and flowered meadows she'd hiked nearly every summer of her childhood. Sometimes she wondered if part of the reason she'd come running back here was in the hope of finding that girl still out there. Trusting and safe, wholly at peace. So far she hadn't.

The winter past had been grim at the start, the long hours of cold and darkness closing in on her, the isolation she'd initially craved driving her slowly beyond despair. Until the day she'd unlocked the door and entered this room, her father's old workshop, and stepped back in time.

As she'd cleared the benches and sorted the tools the memories had come flooding back – those wonderful summers she'd spent helping him build the cabin. The hours he'd devoted to teaching her the skills had instilled in her his love of the craft, a love reawakened the minute she'd returned to where it all started.

Once revived, that love had gotten her through the winter. With the tools and wood he'd left behind, his presence alive in the dusty rafters as though he was watching over her, she'd renewed her practice of woodwork and carving. By spring she'd had enough decent pieces to consider selling them, and with the last of her food running out, she'd approached Bill at the general store. Their arrangement had kept her going ever since.

By her second visit to Muir in March she'd known she wouldn't be leaving the cabin, but by then the anger had taken hold of her and she'd refused to give him her details on principle. Not in a loud defiant way but by simply 'forgetting', as she had today.

She accepted that her logic on the issue was probably flawed, as it had become on so many things since 'the accident'. But she couldn't help clinging to her imagined safeguard, her protective barrier, one of the few things she still had any control over. The world that had forced her into seclusion was not going to turn around and follow her here!

And as calm and assuring as Doctor Hadley had seemed, she wasn't ready to trust him that far. Nor anybody else.

Chapter 14

At the first hint of light – probably an hour or more past dawn, owing to the forest's shade – Zack crawled out of the concrete pipe. His calf felt stiff as he took his first steps, but he doubted it had anything to do with how or where he'd spent the night.

In fact their makeshift bed hadn't been much worse than his filthy mattress back at the Learys'. Before it had grown completely dark he'd gathered armfuls of pine needles and dead leaves and spread them over the floor of the pipe. Not only had it proved a soft bed, it had also provided insulation and levelled the surface so the three of them could sleep side by side. Combined body heat and the absence of drafts had kept them warm.

No, the stiffness in his calf was something else – he felt a twinge of pain now as well. He limped to the stream, sat on a rock and rolled up the leg of his jeans. Cupping water up with his hands, he washed away the crusted grime. The wound beneath was no longer bleeding but was red and puffy around the edges. Funny that it hurt more now than yesterday. Still, it didn't hurt near as much as his stomach. God, he was starving!

He rolled the pants leg back into place, pushed off the rock and turned to see Reece coming out of the pipe.

'Corey won't get up. He says his stomach hurts.' He pulled a twig from his short brown hair. 'So does mine.'

'Yeah, mine too.'

'You said you'd find us something to eat.'

'I will. Gimme a chance, okay?'

Zack scanned the only sliver of sky visible above the road. Thick grey clouds skimmed the tree tops. If they stayed by the pipe they'd have shelter from rain.

He turned back to Reece. 'Right, here's the deal – you and Corey are going to stay here and I'm going to walk up the road a ways. If I find a shop or a house I'll get some food and bring it back to you.'

'What if you don't find anything?'

'Then I'll come back and walk the other way. There's gotta be people around. We just haven't found them yet.'

Eyes bright with tears, Reece nervously scanned the woods.

Zack stepped closer. 'Come on, don't worry; we'll be okay. You just stay and look after Corey. He's only little.'

'If someone comes by, couldn't we just tell them what happened to us and ask for help?'

'No! We can't. They'd never believe us.'

'But if we told the police –'

'They'd just send us back to Nolan and Tragg.' Zack bent down to look him in the eye. 'You gotta promise – you can't talk to anyone. You can't even let anyone see you.'

Reece nodded and dragged his sleeve across his nose. 'You're gonna come back, aren't ya?'

'Don't be a turkey. 'Course I will.' Zack straightened, gave the boy's shoulder a gentle shove, then turned and started up the embankment.

At the top he checked that no cars were coming before stepping into the open.

As he started up the road he gave Reece a parting thumbs-up. 'Won't be long. Just remember – stay out of sight.'

Shyler drove the final stretch into town with more than her usual sense of disquiet.

From careful observation she'd long since learned what days were safest to visit Bill's store. She could have gone in yesterday – the same day she'd come to see the doctor – and saved herself this extra trip. But yesterday had been delivery day, that one day of the month when the supply truck came and the general store did its heaviest trading. No way would she go near the place then!

Today, however, was a different story. The day after delivery day was usually Bill's slowest, especially in the morning, which was why she always came at this time. Well worth the bother of an extra trip. Or so she had thought. In reality the safeguard that usually reassured her didn't seem to be working this time.

Because of yesterday. Because of one minor change in her routine – a single unplanned trip to the doctor.

Shaking her head, she steered the pick-up into the parking lot at the back of Bill's store.

Walking helped work the stiffness from his leg. By the time Zack reached the first set of buildings – an office block for a logging company on one side of the road with a doctor's office diagonally opposite – his leg was feeling almost normal again. Strong enough that he could walk a bit further.

Beyond the next bend he came to what was possibly the centre of town, if there even was one: three houses and a general store flanking a T-junction. He ran up the shop steps straight at the door and nearly cracked his head when it didn't open.

Peering through the glass, he saw bins of apples, squash and potatoes arranged around a table heaped with bread. Aisles of canned and packaged goods receded into the shadowy depths. He tore his gaze from a shelf of cookies and stepped back to study the front of the shop.

No business hours were posted in the window but it was so light out now, he felt sure the place had to be open. Maybe there was another door. He went down the steps and started around the side of the building.

As he neared the back, he heard the crunch of footsteps on gravel and quickened his pace. On clearing the corner he saw an old pick-up backed up to the rear of the shop. A woman with blonde hair was unloading boxes and placing them beside the door.

Zack hesitated. He'd already accepted he'd have to show himself to get what he wanted. But in a town this size people would recognise a stranger. He'd need a convincing story to tell them.

'Hi,' he said, stepping out and starting towards her.

The woman, just pulling a box from the truck bed, spun around so fast it startled him to a halt.

'Sorry, didn't mean to scare you.' His apology had no effect. She still looked as though she was about to scream.

'Can I help you with that?' He took another cautious step. If she said yes he might even get a couple of bucks out of it. Then he could buy food instead of stealing it.

But the woman didn't answer. She simply turned away and went back to unloading the truck.

Zack stood frowning. How could she not have heard what he said? Was she afraid of him? Did she think he was going to mug her or something?

'My family's camping up there a ways.' He waved a hand vaguely. 'They sent me to pick up something for breakfast. What time do you open?'

The woman pulled another box off the tray and carried it to the door.

'We're going to be around here for a while and there's not a whole lot for kids to do. You wouldn't have a job I could do? Sweeping or stacking, something like that. Just for a few days.'

Having set the last box with the others, the woman walked around to the front of the truck, opened the driver's door and got in.

Suddenly the Bad Boy was in Zack's head. What was wrong with her? Even if she was deaf or didn't speak English she could at least look at him.

He stepped up and rapped on her window. 'Hey, lady, I just –'

The engine roared and the truck shot forward.

Zack jumped away from the spinning wheels. He stood staring after it, mouth agape, then picked up a handful of gravel and threw it.

Not deaf. Not stupid. The bitch was crazy!

A mile up the road, Shyler forced herself to slow down. The steering wheel was shaking so badly in her hands she feared she might veer off into a tree.

Encountering children was always bad. Like yesterday in the doctor's office. At least she'd been half prepared for it then. Unexpected encounters were worse. Especially with boys. And especially when they looked so much –

But could that be any excuse for her actions?

She sat up taller and raised her chin. On this occasion she'd done what she had to – avoided his gaze, refused to speak, gave no indication she'd even heard him. All necessary considering what would have happened otherwise. She was sure he would understand if he knew.

But he didn't know.

She slumped. Oh, God, what must he have thought? Kids lacked confidence at the best of times. To have an adult completely ignore him, treat him like he didn't exist, wasn't important . . .

She gripped the wheel.

And what if he'd been in some kind of trouble? Needed her help? What if he'd been lost or hurt or –

The jaws slammed shut. She stamped on the brakes.

Clutching the wheel so tightly it hurt, she began the count. Inhale – one . . . two . . three . . .

Her body fought her with every beat, prodding her to renew her flight. Sweat trickled between her breasts, turning her bra to a cold damp vice around her chest.

Seven . . . eight . . .

The muscles of her legs quaked so badly she could barely keep her foot on the pedal. The usual countermeasures weren't working. Her heart was slamming against her ribs. Just the thought she might one day again be responsible . . .

She squeezed her eyes shut and clenched her teeth. 'I am alone. There is no one else. No one needs me to keep them safe.'

With the words a sob escaped her lips, a spasm so sharp it broke the paralysis. She chanted the phrase in her head and out loud. With each repetition the band constricting her chest eased further. On the fifth, it fell away completely. She hauled in an unencumbered breath. Her arms, trembling and weak from exertion, dropped to her sides.

She rested her head back against the seat.

No one needs me. So painful a truth. For any sane person a cause for despair.

For her, the lifeline to which she must cling.

Chapter 15

'You coming home for lunch? Got a chicken I can roast.'
'Save it for dinner, Dad, I can't today. Have to talk to Doc Muir about something.' Turning from the counter with his plate and mug, Chase took a seat at the kitchen table across from his father.

'Muir the fella you took over from? Thought he'd left town.'

'According to Elaine he's still around. At least I hope so.'

Chase took a thoughtful bite of his toast. He'd been unable to shake his niggling concerns regarding the woman who'd come to his clinic the day before. He was hoping a quick conversation with Muir would shed some light on Shyler's situation. One way or another he had to put his mind at rest.

'Sounds important,' his father said.

'Sorry?'

'Whatever you need to see Muir about.'

'Well, I'm hoping it's nothing but, yes, it could be.'

'Anything you want to talk about? You're not sick, are you?'

'No, Dad, I'm fine.'

'Must be the office then. Problems with the building? I told you you should've had a builder check it out first.'

84

'It's not the building, it's regarding a patient.'

'Yeah? Which one?'

Chase simply shifted his gaze to the man.

'Oh, come on, that confidentiality nonsense doesn't apply to your own father.'

'You're right, it's all just an evil conspiracy to curtail a doctor's freedom to gossip.'

'Fine, don't tell me. Thought I might be able to help, is all.' Allen leaned towards him. 'Just could be I know a few things. Things Doc Muir never put in his files.'

'Dad, we've only been here three weeks and you haven't left the house. What could you possibly –'

'Like Marg Whetherston's gout, for example. Which has more to do with her fondness for port than the family predisposition she claims.'

'Thanks, but I figured that out on my own.'

'And Herbie Laracourt, who didn't break his leg felling that tree but climbing out Shellie McManus's window.'

Chase sipped his coffee to hide his surprise. Now *that* he hadn't known.

'And Geraldine Sprenkle who uses more than Valium to ease the boredom of her lonely nights. And –'

He thumped the mug down. 'Dad, how do you do it? How on earth do you know all this?'

Allen tapped his temple. 'Side effect from the accident. Ever read *Dead Zone*?'

'Dad.'

'Gina told me.'

'Gina, our cleaning lady?'

'Well, she told me the bit about Marg Whetherston. The rest I got from Abagail Watson.'

Chase's frown deepened. 'Who's Abagail Watson?'

'Runs the local mobile library. For people who can't get out much. I signed up last week.' Allen smiled. 'Been reading a lot of fine literature lately.'

Chase shook his head.

'What, I can't have a coffee with a lady now and then?'

'You mentioned two ladies.'

The man turned sheepish. 'Actually, it's six. They formed a book club and asked me to join. Said they needed a man's perspective.'

'Well, I'm glad you're getting to know the locals, but I hardly think hearsay is a reliable source of facts about my patients.'

Allen shrugged. 'Suit yourself.'

Chase took another sip of coffee. He fought back the urge as long as he could, then finally gave in. 'Did Gina or Abagail ever say anything about a local woman who sells her wood craft from Bill's store?'

'No, but I could ask. Seeing as you're more than professionally interested I'm sure they'd do their best to find out.'

Chase coughed up the crumb he'd inhaled. 'Dad, I am not –'

'And that's why we have four bird feeders and a dozen houses cluttering up the kitchen.'

'You know what? Forget it.' Chase mopped up the coffee he'd spilled – served him right for encouraging the man – and got to his feet. 'I'll see you tonight. Leave the dishes. I'll get them after dinner.'

'Nonsense, I'll do them. Don't I always?'

Chapter 16

Slumped in the rental car's front seat, Nolan jerked awake at a rap on the window. For a moment he didn't know where he was, nor did he recognise the face peering in at him through the windscreen. Until she spoke.

'You going to sit there all day or what?'

Nolan opened the door and got out, wincing at the brightness of the morning sun.

'Good to see you're on top of things as usual,' Vanessa quipped as he stood rubbing his neck.

'You try spending a night in a car with no blanket in the friggin North Pole. I didn't get to sleep till –'

'Is this the truck?' She pointed at the one he'd parked behind.

'Yeah, that's it.'

She scanned the ground beneath its rear door. After a moment she started wandering, still hunched, along the depot's dirt driveway.

'The ground's soft here. You can see their footprints,' she said as she slowly moved towards the road, 'in the spots where you didn't tramp all over them.'

Nolan watched her with grudging respect. Unlike him she had dressed for the setting – hiking boots, camouflage fatigues, fleece-lined jacket. Her take-charge attitude was a pain at times but she could usually be relied on to get things done. Though sometimes he wondered just what she was trying to prove and to whom.

Then again perhaps he knew. In the weeks since they'd met in that North End bar, he'd got the sense from odd things she'd said that everything in her life came back to one person. Lazaro. Her uncle. The man who'd raised her.

Nolan shook his head. He just didn't get it. The lifting weights, the survival training, the toughing things out when it wasn't required . . . Was she trying to prove she was as good as her cousins, Lazaro's sons? Why go to all that effort when the guy would give her whatever she wanted without her ever lifting a finger?

Things were different for someone like him – the reason he'd hooked up with her in the first place. To get where he wanted to go in life he needed connections like Lazaro, had to be prepared to start at the bottom, take the shit jobs. Jobs like this one. And if that included massaging Vanessa's ego, letting her walk all over him, ride him with spurs on every issue . . . Well, at least the sex was some compensation.

Out on the road she looked around briefly before walking back to him. 'The tracks fade out when they hit the gravel but they definitely headed up that way.' She waved a hand. 'Was it dark when you got here?'

'Just about.'

'And you said the truck's engine was still warm.' She added things up. 'I'm betting they didn't make it far. Which means they slept in the woods somewhere.'

She pulled her car keys out of her pocket, clicked the remote and locked her door. 'Right, let's go.'

Nolan looked from her to the trees. 'You mean in there?'

'Afraid of ruining those Gucci loafers? Too bad. Get moving.'

The berries were squashed and staining his fingers by the time Zack reached the culvert again. Together with the peanuts he'd taken from a bird feeder in someone's yard, they constituted the sum of his food-finding efforts.

In the end he hadn't been able to get anything from the general store. The man who'd eventually shown up to open it had watched him like a hawk as he'd walked around the aisles. As much as Zack had wanted to grab something, he couldn't take the chance of being caught for shoplifting and handed to the police.

No, the nuts and berries would have to hold them until he could enact his revised plan – he'd return to the store, this time with Reece, whom he'd get to create some kind of diversion while he stole what they needed.

It meant that now two of them would have to show themselves but Zack figured that was okay. As long as the three of them weren't spotted together – and provided he gave a convincing story – he doubted anyone would become suspicious.

Besides, there wasn't a whole lot of choice.

Reaching the embankment he checked to make sure no cars were coming before sliding down it. The minute he hit the bottom Reece rushed out of the culvert at him, red-faced and crying.

'There's something wrong with Corey! He fell asleep again and I can't wake him up! I think he's dead!'

The boy's panic was contagious. Zack dropped the berries and raced to the pipe.

'Not dead, he's unconscious,' he said after checking that Corey was breathing. The boy's round face was as pale as his hair.

'He kept crying that his stomach hurt,' Reece hiccupped. 'I thought it was just because he was hungry, like you said, but . . .'

'But what?'

'He said he hurt it when we had the accident. He landed on the arm rest when we crashed into the ditch. He didn't want to tell you 'cause he thought you'd be mad.'

Zack turned back. With a rush of dread he rolled up the hem of Corey's sweatshirt, and sucked in his breath. The bruise that spread across the boy's left side was shiny, swollen and dark red.

Instantly Reece started crying again. It was all Zack could do not to join him. He forced himself to climb from the pipe and drag Reece with him.

'Here,' he said, fishing the peanuts from his pocket. 'Eat these while I think what to do.'

Reece hesitated only an instant before accepting them. Between sniffles he shelled the nuts and wolfed them down. By the time he'd finished, Zack had decided.

'There's a doctor's office up the road. We'll take him there.'

Reece looked horrified. 'You said we shouldn't talk to anyone!'

'I know, but we have to. Corey's sick.'

'But what if the doctor calls the police? What if they send Corey back to –'

'It's better than letting him die!'

Zack swore at the force of his outburst. He knew it wasn't just fear that had goaded him. If he hadn't caused the accident . . . If Corey hadn't been too afraid to tell him he'd been hurt . . .

Reece had lapsed into crying again. Zack reached out and hugged the boy to him. 'It'll be all right. Corey'll be safe and so will we. We'll sneak him into the doctor's office and leave again before anyone sees us. Then . . . then we'll hide in the woods and watch the place and as soon as he's better we'll go back and get him.'

'But how will we know when he's better?'

'When it's dark I'll go over and look through the windows. I'll find out what room he's in and every day we'll check how he's doing. Now come on, you gotta help me with this.'

Zack dragged Reece towards the pipe again. 'I can carry him but I need you to push him up onto my back. Get in there behind him.'

Reece stepped carefully over the still, little form then stood crying softly. 'I don't want him to go. They'll take him away.'

'No, they won't. It's gonna be fine.' Zack sat down with his back to Corey and lifted the boy's legs in either hand. 'As soon as he's better we'll help him climb out the doctor's window and come away with us. Now push him up!'

At last feeling pressure against his back, Zack leaned their combined weight forward. With Corey's limp form draped across him, he pushed up onto his hands and knees and crawled from the pipe.

'What if the doctor calls the police?' Reece choked out, trailing him towards the embankment.

'Even if he does, they won't take Corey anywhere until he's better. We just have to make sure we get him back before they do.'

Chapter 17

'Shyler O'Neil?'

Chase waited as the man on the other end of the phone worked to connect the name with a face.

'Oh, yes – blonde woman, late twenties, quiet,' Muir said at last. 'I take it she recently paid you a visit.'

'Yesterday. Needed a couple of sutures in her hand.'

'I didn't know she was still around. She still bartering for her appointments?'

'Yes, she is.'

'Sorry to hear that. I would've thought she'd be over her money woes by now. Hope you didn't have a problem with it. Would have warned you if I'd remembered, but it's been a while since I've seen her.'

'No, I was fine. It didn't bother me.'

'So what can I do for you?'

'Well, I have some concerns regarding Shyler and I'm hoping you can shed some light on them.'

'Sure, if I can.'

'For one thing we didn't have her contact details so I asked her to leave them. She said she would, but in the end she didn't.'

'Same as last time as I recall. I assumed she forgot.'

'Which is just what I thought. But Elaine seems to think she's deliberately withholding the information.'

Muir gave a laugh. 'Elaine sees mysteries where there aren't any. A lot o' folks around here do, probably the only entertainment they get. There's no great mystery surrounding Shyler. She lives in a cabin out off one of the old logging tracks. Used to vacation there with her family.'

'Family?' Chase felt a stab of disappointment. 'You mean a husband and children?'

'Oh, no, this was years ago, when she was a girl. Came up here with her parents every summer. Don't know from where.'

'So you knew her back then?'

'Not really. Ran into them now and again at the store. Enough to know who they were but that's it.'

'Do you know where this cabin is exactly?'

'No, sorry. Never felt a need to.'

Chase thought a moment. 'Did she ever explain to you why she couldn't pay for her visits?'

'No, and I never pressed her about it. I figured she just fell on hard times and needed a spell to get back on her feet.'

'How did Shyler seem to you otherwise?'

'How do you mean?'

'She didn't seem overly anxious? I mean, if Elaine's right and she's deliberately withholding her contact details . . .'

'Look, the woman might have been mildly depressed. Quiet, as I said, and certainly rundown. But nothing you wouldn't see in a dozen other patients every day. Sorry, Hadley, but I'm not sure I understand your concerns.'

Chase exhaled. Where had he heard those words before?

*

The forest was intolerable. An endless procession of wooded slopes, sodden hollows, and rocky streams. His Guccis had been ruined in the first hundred yards, his pigskin jacket not long after. And, believing he'd have matters sorted out well before this, Nolan hadn't brought a change of clothes.

At the top of another lengthy rise he collapsed, gasping, against a tree. 'What do you say we rest a while?'

'Can't. Keep going.' Vanessa marched ahead of him barely breathing hard.

'What, are you on steroids or something?'

She stopped and laughed. 'I find it helps to keep in mind what'll happen to us if we don't catch those kids before they talk. You do remember your good friend Tragg?'

Nolan sent her a sour look. As if he'd forget. 'Us? What do you have to worry about? Lazaro's your uncle. Tragg wouldn't dare –'

'If you think for a minute that'll protect me if we fuck this up . . . !'

Vanessa stood trying to regain control. Nolan seemed to think her connection with Lazaro was some kind of warm-and-fuzzy relationship. He sat at her feet like a starving stray begging for scraps, second-hand crumbs dropped from the table.

Never mind that she was fighting for crumbs herself. Deprived of a life outside 'the family', expected to perform whatever hack work Lazaro asked, yet forever denied the respect and affection he bestowed on his sons. Bestowed on even henchmen like Tragg.

She had no delusions why Lazaro had assigned her to securing these boys from their foster home. It wasn't because of any trust in her competence. He'd simply have realised a woman social worker would be less threatening, more believable in the plan he'd devised. So – as always – he'd used her.

Yet on this occasion she didn't care. Intended or not, she planned to make use of this chance he'd given her. Planned to do the job so fucking well he'd finally be forced to acknowledge her worth.

If Nolan didn't screw things up totally first!

'We could rest a few minutes,' he tried again. 'It's after two; we've been slogging through this jungle for hours and I haven't had anything to eat yet today.'

She sighed and walked back to him. 'Not a real trooper, are you, Nolan?'

'Playing Daniel Boone wasn't on your list of job requirements.'

'Neither was your being a man. Guess you can't take anything for granted these days.'

She looked away from him in disgust, then scanned the slope they'd just ascended. 'All right, I'll go back and get the car. You take a short rest, then keep searching. Give me about an hour then head for the road. I'll pick you up. We'll grab something to eat and start again.'

Nolan saluted her as she walked away. Noting the sticky feel of his fingers, he looked down and swore. The tree he was leaning against – some kind of pine – had oozed sap all over his pants. He pushed off and slumped to the ground.

Long after Vanessa had disappeared from view he was still sitting with the pine needles pricking his legs. He'd be damned if he'd traipse around the wilderness alone. Bad enough he'd ruined his clothes and had to take abuse from Attila the Cunt, he'd not spend another minute wandering a place that could very well have –

A sound pricked his ears and he spun around. At the bottom of the slope, one of the boulders from a granite outcropping was somehow rocking itself against a tree. His eyes narrowed then widened again. Not a boulder. A frigging bear!

He launched himself up, scrambled over the nearest rise, tripped on a branch and tumbled head-first down the next slope.

At the bottom he climbed from the stream he'd landed in and ran for the road. The hell with this!

A stitch in his side and shortness of breath finally overrode his panic. He staggered to a halt a bare stone's throw from an embankment rising up to the road and turned to survey the forest behind him.

Nothing. No movement. No sign of the bear. He paused briefly to savour his relief then started for the embankment again.

Three large concrete pipes passed beneath the road at its base. The stream flowed through two of them but, there, near the third . . .

Nolan stopped. A scrap of paper anywhere else would never have attracted his attention. But here, in these wretched God-forsaken wilds, it was the first piece of litter he'd come across. He walked to the conduit and picked it up.

A baseball card. Creased and torn but not nearly as filthy as he would have expected of something left out in the rain and the elements. It hadn't been lying here very long.

Frowning, he stared at the face of Eric Gagne. He remembered escorting the boys from the Learys' house – the youngest had taken some ugly stuffed animal, Zack had brought nothing, and the third . . . Hadn't he collected baseball cards?

Nolan bent and peered into the conduit. The area just inside its opening was thickly blanketed with leaves and pine needles. They were spread too evenly and appeared too fresh to have been deposited by flood waters.

This time it was the sound of a car approaching that drew his attention. He rushed to the embankment and climbed to the road in time to flag Vanessa.

'I found where they spent the night,' he told her as she rolled down her window. 'There's a conduit just here beneath the road. I found this lying by one of the pipes.' He gave her the card.

Vanessa opened her door and got out. 'Okay, you take the car and keep going that way. See if you can spot them. I'll try to pick up their trail.'

They traded places and she bent to the window. 'Look for any place they might have gone in – a barn, a shed, anywhere they might have tried to get food. But don't ask anyone if they've seen them.'

'You really think I'm that stupid?'

She walked away without giving a reply.

Chapter 18

It was late afternoon by the time they reached the doctor's office. As they crouched in the bushes across the road, Zack gently lowered Corey's limp form to a bed of sugar maple leaves.

He guessed it had taken them three times longer to walk the same distance he had that morning. Because they couldn't risk being seen on the road, they'd travelled through the forest where unseen twigs and rocks had tripped him and mulch-covered slopes had sent him sliding.

But he'd also started to feel a bit weird and that had slowed him down even more. Though he'd coped with Corey's weight at first, by the time they'd come within sight of the office he was practically staggering. Now, as he flopped back against a tree trunk, his legs felt rubbery and his body quaked.

Reece sat beside him, peering through the undergrowth at the white shingled house across the road. 'How come we're just sitting here?'

'Too many cars over there now, too many people. We have to wait till some of them leave.' Zack closed his eyes and laid his head back.

'One of them's leaving!'

He jerked awake. How long had he been out? Two minutes? Five? Probably no more, but it had been the thick black void of the deepest sleep. Struggling to pull himself from its grasp he pushed forward to kneel beside Reece.

Three cars were left in the office parking lot. If one of them belonged to the doctor and maybe another belonged to a nurse, it meant there was only one patient there. And if that patient was in with the doctor, the waiting room should be empty. Maybe.

Zack shook his head. Too many maybes, too many ifs.

He reached out and picked up Corey's hand. The boy's lips were chapped, his fingers icy and, except for the circles under his eyes, his skin was so pale you could see his veins. Zack wanted desperately to wait and be sure, but maybe Corey didn't have that long.

He turned to Reece. 'Okay, help me lift him up again.'

He crossed the road a bit further back so no one would see him from the office's windows. Moving through the trees that edged the parking lot he swung around to the rear of the building. With no way of knowing who might be watching, he took a deep breath and ran for the door.

His run was more of a shambling trot and by the time he'd crossed the short distance his whole body was shaking again. For a moment the porch grew dim before his eyes, then the mist cleared and he struggled up the steps.

Bent nearly double to balance Corey's weight, he opened the door and peeked around it. A wide corridor stretched before him. At the end he could see the building's front door and the corner of a desk. The reception area? No doubt the waiting room was through the archway just across from it. He slipped inside and started up the hall.

Doors either side opened successively on a laundry/bathroom, kitchen/lounge and storage area. To his relief all were empty.

As he slid past the last one, more of the front desk came into view. He heard the clicking of a computer keyboard. Then the soft whoosh of wheels – a chair rolling back.

A few steps further and he saw the computer, but whoever had been typing had moved out of sight. The sound of a cabinet rattling open came from further back in the room. Heartened, he eased up and peered around the corner.

A woman with grey hair stood with her back to him at a bank of filing cabinets that lined the far wall. To his left, as he'd hoped, was the empty waiting room. He tip-toed across it, laid Corey down on one of the couches and retreated up the hallway.

Nolan pulled the car to a stop by the silhouette waiting at the side of the road. Vanessa climbed in, slammed the door and slumped in the seat.

'No luck?' he ventured.

'Plenty – all bad. Their tracks were all around the stream and the culvert. I followed them for about a mile then lost them over some rocky ground. You?'

'I didn't actually see them but I might have a lead.'

Her head snapped around.

'There's a general store just up the road. When I went in to grab a bite I overheard the owner telling someone about a boy who came in early this morning. The kid was alone and the guy felt sure he was looking to steal something but he watched him too close to give him a chance. In the end the kid left without buying anything.'

'Could be a local.'

Nolan shook his head. 'The owner said he didn't recognise him. And in a town this size he'd know most kids.' He waited while she chewed her lip. 'I think it was him – the oldest one, Ballinger. Which means the three of them are still in the area.'

'Maybe.'

'Come on, they've gotta be. By the number of cars that pass on this road what are the odds they caught a lift?'

She drew a deep breath and blew it out again. 'Well, we'll have to assume they didn't, won't we? If they did, we've lost them – they could be anywhere. And that's not going to make Tragg very happy.'

Nolan swallowed. 'So where does that leave us?'

'It's too dark to try and pick up their trail any more today. We might as well find a place for the night.'

Nolan watched as her frown slowly cleared. When she finally turned to him she was almost smiling. 'Then first thing tomorrow we stake out that store. If they went in there once, chances are they'll show up again.'

The carving had taken command of his desk. Nearly every patient who'd come through his doors since he'd opened that morning had commented on it. Even people he wouldn't have credited with the slightest artistic appreciation had remarked how perfect and lifelike it was – loggers with work-roughened hands, mothers with babies, the elderly right down to grade school children, all had been intrigued.

Yet not one of them had known the woman who'd carved it.

How could it be? Chase reflected, turning the object in his hands. Shyler had been to see Muir on two occasions, the last six months ago. How did a woman live in a town as small as this for all that time and make no friends and only two contacts? Not only would she have to want it that way but also she'd have to work damn hard to accomplish it.

But was that in itself any cause for concern? Dan Muir didn't seem to think so. Even if she was withholding her details, her desire for solitude could be perfectly innocent. She could be a writer, Muir had argued, holed up in her remote cabin for the purpose of finishing her latest book. Or a scientist doing some kind of research on the wilderness environment.

Chase shook his head. She wasn't a writer, or a scientist, she was a carver. And no occupation he could think of explained her reticence and heightened anxiety.

Yes, despite what Doctor Muir had assured him, he still had concerns regarding the woman.

'Who are you hiding from, Shyler O'Neil? Everyone, or someone in particular?'

Chase set the figure back on his desk, rose and went out into the office. 'Right, who's next?' he said to Elaine.

'That's it,' she answered, straightening over an open file drawer. She grabbed the folders she'd stacked on the cabinet, pushed the drawer closed and crossed to her desk. 'You're done for the day. These are tomorrow's files I'm doing.'

Chase looked across the hall to the waiting room. 'Maybe you better check again.'

Following his gaze, she gave a small 'Oh!' at the sight of the boy asleep on the couch. 'I'm sorry, I could've sworn . . .' She sat at the computer, drew up the schedule then shook her head. 'No, I was right. Ella Thomas was your last appointment.'

'Must be a walk-in. I'll take care of it.'

Chase crossed the hall and approached the couch, noting as he did the pronounced pallor of the child's face. His frown deepened as he scanned the otherwise empty room. Surely the boy wasn't here alone. Whoever had brought him must be up the back using the bathroom.

He eased a bit closer but stopped short of actually bending

down. The last thing he wanted was for the boy to wake and see a total stranger standing over him. And technically, without a parent present . . .

But the boy wasn't just pale, his breathing was shallow. In the end Chase couldn't stop himself reaching out to check his pulse.

'Elaine!' he shouted. She was at his side almost before his voice had faded. 'Run up the back and get his mother.'

As Elaine ran off he conducted a more thorough examination, his alarm growing by the second. He raced to the closet, pulled out a blanket and was just draping it over the unconscious boy when Elaine returned.

'I checked the restroom. No one's in there. And no one's out in the parking lot either.'

'There's got to be.'

'I'm telling you there isn't. The only cars in the lot are ours.' She stepped to the window. 'And no one's out front.'

'Well, then who . . .?' Chase shook his head – questions could wait. 'All right, get Presque Isle hospital on the phone. Tell them we need emergency evac for a John Doe child, approximately six, with hypothermia and internal injuries.'

Chapter 19

The store was closed by the time he reached it but a light
out the front illuminated a rubbish bin beside the door.
As hungry as he was, Zack stood staring at it for several long
minutes, unable to bring himself to open the lid. Finally
accepting that he had no choice, that Reece needed food even
more than he did, he reached inside and began pushing things
around.

He chose only scraps that were semi-protected or hadn't come
in contact with any of the nastier, more putrid rubbish – half a
ham sandwich in a plastic bag, an apple with only two bites out
of it, a bit of cherry pie still in its wrapper, a half-box of Cracker
Jack and a nearly full carton of chocolate milk.

Reece was still sitting in the bushes across from the doctor's
office when he returned with his booty.

'Did you find anything?' the boy asked eagerly as Zack sat
down.

'Yeah. Here.'

In the faint light cast from the office windows Reece stared at
the half-eaten sandwich. 'There's bites out of this.'

'I got a little hungry on the way back.'

Reece raised the sandwich to his face and winced. 'It smells gross!'

'Yeah, well, that's 'cause it came out of a garbage can. Sorry I couldn't get anything better but it's dark out in case you hadn't noticed.' Zack heaved a sigh when the boy didn't answer. 'Look, none of this stuff smells any better so just eat it, okay?'

Reece bowed his head. Any second he was going to start bawling.

'All right, here.' Zack shoved all the other things at him and took the sandwich. Hoping to put an end to the matter he nodded across the street. 'Anything happen while I was gone?'

'I didn't see anything. No one went inside or came out.'

They sat side by side, watching the office as they ate. With the surrounding forest so dark and dense the place seemed to glow in its small patch of moonlight.

'You think the doctor lives in there?' Reece said around a mouthful of pie.

'Nah, that's just where he sees sick people.'

'Then why's he still over there? How come that other person's still in there with him?'

'They're taking care of Corey, that's why. They want to make sure he's all right before they . . . go home.' Even as he said it, Zack realised his mistake. No grown-up would leave a small boy alone even if he wasn't sick.

'You mean they might not go away until Corey's all better? How can we go and check on him then?'

'When it's darker we'll look through the windows. If they have their lights on they won't be able to see us.'

Zack felt his patience beginning to strain. The only bad thing about giving Reece food was that it had revived him. Before he'd left to walk to the store the boy had been sitting hunched and silent. Now he was starting with the questions again!

'But what if they have their curtains closed? What if we can't see him? What if Corey wakes up and we're not there? He won't know where he is. He'll think we left him.'

Before he could answer, Zack heard the sound of a car approaching. 'Get down!'

The two boys peeped through a gap in the undergrowth as an ambulance pulled into the doctor's driveway and disappeared around the back of the building.

Zack jumped up and grabbed Reece's arm. 'Come on. We gotta see what's happening.'

They moved onto the road and dashed for the woods on the other side. Ten yards back the building's rear door came into view – the ambulance standing open before it. In the light from the hall, two men emerged wheeling a stretcher with a tiny figure strapped to its bed.

Reece jumped up. 'No! You ca –'

Zack grabbed him and covered his mouth, then peered anxiously through the bushes. The sound of the stretcher wheels hitting the gravel must have masked Reece's cry – the two men continued to push it forward. They loaded it into the back of the ambulance, slammed the doors and, a moment later, drove from the parking lot.

Zack stood, unable to move. It had happened so fast he hadn't had time to even think what to do.

Reece broke free of his grasp and faced him. 'That was Corey. They took him away!'

'I know.'

'But you said they wouldn't. You said we'd get him back again. Where'd they take him? Where did he go?'

Zack took his arm again. 'Shut up, will ya? You want them to hear?'

'I don't care if they hear! You said we would stay together. You said everything would be all right.'

'I thought it would be.'

'No, you didn't. You hated Corey! You wanted those men to take him away!'

'What? Don't be stupid. Corey was hurt. What was I –'

'He wouldn't have been hurt if it wasn't for you! It's your fault! You did it! You and your stupid spider accident! We'll never –'

'Shut up! Shut up!' It was Zack's voice that shouted the words, but the Bad Boy's hand that shot out towards Reece.

Reece fell back, sprawling amid the moss and dead leaves. He lay for a moment blinking in shock, then rolled on his side and started sobbing.

Zack stared down at him, equally stunned. Revulsion hit him with such sudden force he bent double and puked his dinner onto the mulch. The spasms were painful but somehow he felt he deserved every one – one day the Bad Boy would do something so awful, he wouldn't be able to pull him back again.

He straightened and wiped his mouth on his sleeve. It wasn't fair! Kids like Reece and Corey needed someone smart and strong and good to take care of them. Not a pathetic throw-away like him!

With a flash of hope he looked towards the house. The grey-haired lady and another man had just come out the back, said their goodbyes and were walking towards their cars. Maybe if he went to them . . . told them the truth . . . asked for help . . .

Angrily he blinked his tears away. What was he thinking? No one would believe a kid like him.

As the cars filed past him out of the lot, Zack looked down at Reece again. Rotten as it was, he was all the kid had at the moment.

He knelt beside him. 'Everything's going to be all right. Corey'll be safe because he's unconscious. As long as he doesn't tell them his name, they won't know who he is so they can't give him back.'

Reece didn't answer. He'd rolled into a ball and lay crying and shivering.

Zack began pushing up leaves all around him. When he'd made a big pile he crawled in beside him and pulled the boy close. 'Tomorrow I'll find out where the ambulance took him and you and I'll go there. You'll see. We'll get him back, I swear we will.'

Nolan stretched naked on the hearthside rug, sweeping his hand down the long arch of Vanessa's back. A bit too muscular for his liking – muscle should define a woman's curves, not embolden them – yet her flawless skin, gilt by firelight, felt like satin beneath his touch. Cradled by the fur on which they lay, a pelt of luxurious warmth and texture, the effect was overwhelmingly sensual.

'Your hands are cold,' she murmured, staring away from him into the flames.

'Want me to throw on another log?' Starting at her nape he began trailing kisses across her left shoulder. When he reached its apex he worked his way back, burrowing towards her neck to whisper his next words into her ear. 'Or would you rather just retire to the bedroom?'

Dark hair tumbled across her face as she turned her head towards him. 'No, we'll stay here. I'm sure we can find some other way to warm them.'

He laughed and rolled her onto her back. Christ, he needed this! After the day he'd had such mindless diversion wasn't just welcome, it was therapy.

The cabin at least had been a pleasant surprise. Two bedrooms, fully furnished with a huge open fire and a view of some lake – the name of which had ten syllables he couldn't pronounce, let alone remember. The only lodging for a hundred square miles, it was normally rented by vacationers seeking to truly get away from it all. But with the foliage season nearing its end and the skiing season not yet begun they'd been lucky in finding it unreserved.

Now, after a long hot shower and a meal of venison stew and crusty wheat bread – purchased from the general store – he was ready to put the day behind him. Along with all thoughts of three feral boys and what would happen if they weren't caught.

Vanessa moaned softly, arching against him. As he bent to her breast, he noted dimly that his mobile was ringing.

'You'd better get that.' Her voice was husky.

She couldn't be serious. 'Message bank.'

Taking his head in both her hands she pushed him away, then swung up to sit with her back to him.

Nolan swore. How did women just turn off like that? With a muttered curse he took up the phone from the coffee table.

'I could've sworn my last words to you were to keep me informed.'

Nolan's mouth went instantly dry. 'Tragg.'

'Yet here it is going on ten o'clock and I haven't heard a single word from my buddy. I was starting to worry.' The man's rough whisper made even the most innocent words a threat.

'Tragg, listen, I was just about –'

'Where the fuck are you?'

'Deadwater. Maine. The town where the kids ended up. Vanessa's here, too. We're at a cabin by a lake.'

'Having a little vacation, are you?'

'What? No! We've been searching all day. Got some good leads. Vanessa's sure that by tomorrow –'

'You mean you haven't found them yet.'

Five minutes later when he hung up the phone, Nolan's cold sweat had raised gooseflesh over his body. Suddenly no fire in the world could warm him.

Vanessa nodded at his shrivelled erection. 'I take it Tragg wasn't happy.'

He shot to his feet and began pacing. 'This is all that kid Ballinger's fault! I swear to God when I find that smart-ass little prick –'

'You won't do anything,' Vanessa cautioned in a level voice. 'Be clear on this, Nolan. At this stage our goal is to get them back alive.'

He laughed as he balled his hands into fists. 'I'm sure Tragg won't mind a mark or two.'

Chapter 20

With a white-knuckled grip on the Chevy's steering wheel, Shyler sat staring at the back of Bill's shop. Her palms were already slick with sweat, her breathing rapid. And she hadn't even shut off the engine yet! Twice on her drive in she'd nearly turned around and gone home again. If not for the fact she was out of just about everything in the cabin she wouldn't have come.

Three trips to town in as many days was definitely more than she was ready for. In the last ten months, desperate to limit her exposure to anything that might trigger an attack, she'd made only four trips altogether. Yesterday's had already proved her concerns were well founded, resulting in one of the turns she so feared. And as if that wasn't enough to unsettle her, there was the dream she'd had last night.

She wouldn't have thought anything could be worse than her usual nightmare where she relived what had happened. But dreaming of Jesse alive and whole, holding him, touching him, knowing the joy of his return, only to wake and find it an illusion, had been the cruellest form of torment.

Why? Why would her dream suddenly change? The strain of the second anniversary of his death? Encountering children two days in a row? An unplanned trip to the doctor's office? A combination?

Whatever the cause, she couldn't see the change as a sign her condition was improving. If anything it was getting worse. The dream had felt so incredibly real, a part of her had wanted to remain in that realm. And a sense of what that would mean in reality told her she was possibly nearing a crisis point.

Staring up at the back of Bill's store she again felt the pressure to turn and run. In her current state, who knew what another trigger might do? But she had to eat.

She shut off the engine and looked around. Early morning, no other cars in the parking lot and there hadn't been any out front on the road. The odds that Bill was alone inside were as good as they were going to get. She pulled on her hat, climbed from the car and closed the door.

Before locking it she checked for movement in the woods that bordered the back of the lot. As always her gaze was drawn to the thicket. Broad and leafy, the copse of moosewood was a perfect screen for an ambush. Ample cover for five young men, their leader a brute with a fish hook scar, his second a scarecrow with flaxen hair . . . another with a jaunty beret . . .

She stopped, took a breath and closed her eyes. Slowly she opened them, willing herself to see only what was real, only what was there.

Nothing. No shadows, no movement, no threat of any kind. *They* were long gone. *It's only the ghosts that live in your mind.*

'You said you'd find out where the ambulance went. You said we'd go there and get Corey back.'

'We will, I promise. I just need to get something to eat first, okay?'

Zack looked down into Reece's troubled face, feeling only slightly shamed by his lie. In truth he had no idea how he was going to find out about the ambulance. He couldn't very well walk into the doctor's office and ask. But just at that moment, and as bad as it made him feel about himself, Corey wasn't his top priority.

After vomiting all he'd eaten the night before he just had to get something into his stomach. His hunger was like nothing he'd ever known. It overrode every other sensation – the biting cold, even the growing pain in his leg – and was so demanding he couldn't think about anything else.

'You're hungry, aren't you?' he said to Reece.

The boy bowed his head. 'Starving.'

'Well, all right then. We do this first, then we find Corey.'

Zack turned back to the general store. From their vantage point amid the bushes at the far end of the lot, he could see a woman in a white woollen hat standing a few steps from the back door. For his plan to work he needed at least one other customer inside the shop. Why was she just standing there? Why didn't she go in? What was she doing staring off into the woods like that? What the hell was she waiting for?

'Do you think it's far, where they took Corey?'

'Will you forget about Corey till after we do this? I need you to concentrate. Now you remember what I told you to do, right?'

Reece shoved a knuckle into his mouth.

Zack pulled it out again. 'Well, do you?'

'Yeah, but . . . I'm scared.'

'There's nothing to be scared of. They can't do anything to you if it's an accident. You just have to make sure it looks like one.'

'But I don't know how.'

Zack clenched his jaw. 'I told you how. You just drop something or knock something over. But not a little thing; it has to be something big and noisy.'

113

'What if the man gets mad at me?'

'So let him get mad! You want to eat, don't you? Or would you rather have breakfast from the garbage can again?'

Reece grimaced and shook his head.

Zack sighed at the pathetic sight. 'I don't know what you're worried about. I'm the only one who could get in trouble. I'm the one who'll be stealing stuff.'

'What if they catch you?'

In that one mournful question Zack finally heard the boy's true fear – if he were caught, Reece would be alone. 'Get real. It's not like I've never done this before.'

'It's not?'

'You kidding? I've shoplifted heaps. And that was in department stores with lots of people and security guards. This is nothing, just one little old man.'

Reece finally managed to return his smile.

Zack looked over at the store again. The woman was just walking through the back door. He got to his feet. 'Okay, you ready?'

Reece swallowed and gave him a nod.

'Right, let's go.'

'There!'

Nolan roused from his partial doze at the wheel of the rental car. After Tragg's phone call the night before he hadn't slept well, but the sound of Vanessa's excited voice brought him fully awake in an instant.

They were parked some thirty yards up the road from the general store with a view of both its front and rear doors. Raising the binoculars, he spotted two small figures dashing across the parking lot for the building.

'It's them!' he said. 'Well, two of them anyway.'

'Can you tell which ones?'

'Looks like Ballinger and the middle one.'

'Perfect. The little guy must be hiding somewhere. If we catch these two, he won't hold out long on his own.' Vanessa gave his shoulder a slap. 'Didn't I tell you they'd come back here?'

'Yes. As always you were right.'

Impervious to his sarcasm, she pointed ahead. 'Pull up along the side of the building. Then you go in the front and I'll take the back.'

Chapter 21

'Missed you yesterday,' Bill said, stepping up behind the counter. 'Found the boxes you left out back but you'd gone by the time I opened up.'

'Yes, I'm sorry. I had to go.' Shyler shot another glance around her. The store appeared empty, as she had hoped, but it didn't do much to ease her anxieties.

'No problem. I mighta been a few minutes late.' Bill reached for a slip of paper and slid it across to her. 'You had a few more sales this month. That's yer total – not counting what's on the tab.'

'Thank you.' The figure briefly caught her attention. The amount was more than she'd seen since mid-summer. She'd be able to get everything she needed and pay off a little of what she owed him. 'I'll take it in groceries again, if that's okay?'

'Fine with me.'

She moved quickly about the aisles, putting her purchases into a cart. Where once she might have shopped with care – comparing prices, choosing only the best quality produce – speed was now her top priority.

She was halfway through her list of items when she looked

towards the back of the shop and froze. Two young boys stood close together near the freezer units. Where had they come from? She hadn't heard the shop door open. Had they been here all along and she just hadn't seen them?

In a matter of seconds a panic attack was bearing down on her. *Run. Now. Before they see you. Before they come close!*

She turned away, trying to slow her breathing as she scanned the list in her trembling hand. She couldn't go yet. If she left without getting the things she needed she'd only have to come back again tomorrow.

Just don't look at them. Keep your distance and get out of here as fast as you can.

Grimly she forced herself to walk on, throwing things into the cart as she went.

Zack started up the aisle furthest from the man at the counter. He'd been looking for a potential source of distraction but so far hadn't spotted anything. Reece was sticking like glue to his side, growing more fearful by the second. If he didn't hurry up and decide on something the kid would lose his nerve for sure.

Stopping before a display of garden tools, he tested a cluster of iron rakes. When he jiggled one handle the entire bunch moved, their tines interlocked. This would do.

He leaned down to Reece. 'Okay, all you have to do is pull on this one and they'll all fall over. It'll make a lot of noise but it won't break anything so the man won't get angry.'

Reece didn't answer.

'When the guy comes over, keep him busy as long as you can. As soon as you see me leave the store, you leave too.' When again the boy gave no response, Zack shook his arm. 'You hear me or what?'

Reece raised his head, face streaked with tears.

Zack muttered all the bad words he knew. 'Don't be such a baby. All you gotta do is knock this down and then stand here. That's it.'

Cowed by his tone, Reece nodded meekly.

'Fine then. Let's do it. Just give me a minute to get in position then watch for my signal.'

Reece clutched his arm. 'Where are you going?'

'Over there.'

'Why?'

'Because there's no food in this aisle, dummy. You want to eat compost and cow manure?' Zack pried his arm from the boy's desperate grasp. 'Everything we want is on that side of the store. That's the idea. Just let me get over there and wait for my nod.'

Zack walked off without waiting this time. The little creep's fears were getting contagious – if he didn't act soon he'd lose his own nerve!

Pretending to inspect the goods on the shelves, he wandered to the head of the third aisle over. Twin walls of treasures stretched before him – salted nuts, crackers, potato chips, Fritos. He nearly cried at the sight of them all. He stretched up to peer over the shelf at Reece and gave a nod.

The boy didn't move.

Zack shot a glance back towards the counter. The owner was ringing up a customer's groceries, almost done. Any minute now the woman would leave and their chance would be gone.

He looked back towards Reece. Do it! he mouthed, with a fierce expression.

Reece bowed his head and started towards him.

*

Shyler dumped the last of her groceries on the counter. With only the occasional curious glance, Bill continued to tally her purchases and pack them in boxes. As fast as he filled them she piled them into the cart again.

'That comes to just under your last total sales. What do you want to do with the difference?'

'Put it towards what I owe you, please, Bill.' She swung the last box onto the cart, returned his goodbye and started away from him.

Fear snapped her heels as she raced up the aisle. The palpitations had already started. She had to get out!

The back door was just past the end of the counter. Almost there. But cutting the corner, she caught a display with the front of her cart. The slatted crate teetered then fell with a crash. And twenty-five pounds of McIntosh apples cascaded over the wooden floor.

Zack jumped at a rumbling sound from the far side of the shop. The owner was emerging from behind the counter. He walked a short distance, bent and picked something up off the floor. The customer he had just been serving was doing the same, muttering apologies.

At the end of the aisle, Zack saw a small red object roll by. Then several more. He pulled Reece close and started shoving groceries down the neck of his sweatshirt.

'What are you doing?'

'Change of plans. Hold the bottom so nothing drops out.'

Reece clutched his waistband, glancing nervously towards the counter. 'But I thought you –'

'Some lady just dropped a bunch of apples. The owner's busy – now's our chance.'

With Reece's shirt as full as he could pack it, Zack turned to start on his own. The woman had just gone out the back. They had seconds at most.

He'd just laid his hand on a bag of Fritos when movement at the window drew his eye. He looked up to see a face peering in at them. A masculine, smiling, familiar face.

Zack dropped the corn chips and stumbled back, dragging Reece with him.

'What is it?' the boy said, following his gaze. The groceries he was holding crashed to the floor when Nolan stepped through the door in front of them.

They got only ten steps up the aisle when another familiar face appeared, this one near the rear of the store.

Vanessa flashed them her sweetest smile. 'Hello, boys. Doing some shopping?'

Nolan was coming up the aisle behind them. Zack grabbed a can off a shelf and threw it. Unprepared, the man copped a hit to the shoulder and swore.

The boys raced on, reaching the end before Vanessa could cut them off. But around the corner, Reece, in his panic, veered up the aisle while Zack went straight. And as the boy flew blindly around its end, Nolan was there.

'Zack! Zack!'

Zack stopped dead in the next lane over. He snatched a fishing rod off its stand, stepped up onto the lowest shelf and whipped Nolan about the head. The man dropped Reece and started after him.

'Here now, what are you people doing?' The owner stood gaping in disbelief.

Zack doubled back. Vanessa had moved towards the front of the shop – the back door was clear. But Nolan's footsteps were closing behind him. As he passed the display he'd checked out earlier, he grabbed at a handle. The entire bundle of iron-tined rakes crashed into the aisle. A second later, another crash as Nolan sprawled over them. Zack raced on.

'No! Lemme go! Zack, help!'

The screams drew him up ten feet from his goal. He turned back to see Reece now firmly in Vanessa's grasp, with Nolan getting to his feet. He looked the other way. Ten paces only to the door and freedom.

With a cry of despair he ran for the door.

Chapter 22

The trembling had moved inward towards her core. It wasn't just her hands shaking now, but the larger, more powerful muscles of her arms, legs, and back as well. It gave her the sense that unseen hands had taken hold of her and were trying to rattle her very bones.

Shyler opened the car's back door and dumped the first of her boxes on the seat. The knocking of her heart against her ribs wasn't so much painful as frightening. How could it beat so hard and fast without causing damage? Without exploding?

She shoved the first box across the seat and stacked the second and third on top of it. Why had she taken the car this morning? The pick-up was so much faster to load. Just because it had looked like rain and she didn't have a tarp to cover the bed . . . Who cared about a few wet groceries?

Turning for another box, her gaze shot once again to the woods. Deprived of its earlier sliver of sunlight, the thicket was now steeped in shadow, shifting and crawling with secret menace – the ghosts amassing to mock her in her fight for control.

*

Zack burst through the shop's back door. He flew down the steps, ran three paces and skidded to a halt in the near-empty lot. Nolan was only seconds behind him. He'd never make it to the cover of the woods without the man spotting him. And even if he did he'd never outrun him in open forest.

A car stood nearby, a woman leaning in through its gaping rear door. When she straightened and turned to the cart beside her, he darted past and dove in the back seat. There was nowhere to hide. Half the seat was crammed with boxes and the half that wasn't was too exposed. He looked out just as the woman turned towards him.

Their gazes locked. Her eyes grew wide as she stood unmoving. The box she was holding slipped from her hands and landed, teetering, on the rim of the cart.

Zack swore silently. The crazy lady from yesterday morning. He hadn't recognised her in the hat, and she'd been driving a pick-up yesterday. He had no hope of escaping now. Even if she didn't start screaming, her weird behaviour would draw attention.

From behind her came the sound of the shop's door slamming. The crunch of gravel. Running footsteps.

Nolan felt precious seconds tick by as he stood turning circles in the parking lot. He kicked at some gravel. The kid hadn't had that much of a lead on him. How could he have disappeared so fast?

He stepped towards a woman loading groceries in her car. 'Did you just see a kid run out here?' He scanned the woods, hoping to catch a flash of movement. 'Just in the last couple of seconds. Brown hair, brown eyes, about ten years old?'

At getting no reply, he shot her a look. The bitch was acting like she hadn't heard him.

He grabbed her arm and spun her around. 'What are you, deaf? I said did you see him?'

She gaped at him with a frozen expression. More than startled. Afraid? Confused? Uncomprehending? Maybe the bitch sensed something was wrong. Had she seen where Zack went? Was she trying to protect him?

He was just drawing breath to ask her again when she shifted her gaze to the woods behind him. Nolan smiled. Did she realise she'd just given it away, told him exactly what he wanted to know?

He let go of her arm and raced for the trees.

Stiff with dread, Shyler turned slowly back to the car. The part of the seat she could see from this angle showed nothing unusual, just the worn grey fabric of her aging sedan. She eased a bit closer, grabbed the top of the door for support and bent down to look inside.

Nothing. Just the boxes she'd loaded.

She squeezed her eyes tight. Dear God, what was happening to her? A moment ago she was certain she'd seen . . .

She clenched her hands. No, not certain. Of course not certain. She *thought* she'd seen him. A trick of the light. Her raincoat lying there, dropped down off the back of the front seat where she'd draped it, creating – as it would to any sane mind – the impression of a small figure sitting in her car.

She straightened and moved one last time to the cart. The box she'd dropped lay on its side, its contents spread out over the bottom. She gathered the items, loaded the box, shut the door and climbed in the front.

Behind the wheel she sat taking deep breaths, working to free the residual tightness from her lungs. After a moment she felt a bit better. Her ordeal was over for another two months. She was going home. Where no one would find her, no one could bother her, and the ghosts would never dare intrude.

Chapter 23

The car rocked slightly as someone got in. Nolan or the woman? The driver's door closed, the engine started. Movement – the car pulling out of the lot.

Peering from under the edge of the raincoat, Zack glimpsed an elbow between the front seats. He let out his breath – the woman was driving. She slowed the car over a bump, then turned left. Picking up speed. Not roaring off like she'd done yesterday, but a normal acceleration.

Zack eased the raincoat away from his face. Trees swept past the opposite window. He pushed himself out of the narrow crevice behind the driver's seat and cautiously raised his head to see out.

They were still on the short lane beside the parking lot. Scanning across it, he caught sight of Nolan running along the edge of the woods. The woman hadn't given him away after all.

For a moment, relief engulfed him so fully he rested his forehead against the glass. But on lifting it again his spirits plunged. Coming down the store's front steps were Vanessa and Reece.

Everything inside him seemed to clench. Reece wasn't even putting up a fight. The boy looked totally dejected. Defeated.

Abandoned, whispered a voice in his head. *First Corey, now Reece. You deserted them both.*

Zack jerked at hearing the words. It wasn't true. He would never –

Admit it, you thought they were pains in the butt. Always whining, asking questions. You wanted them gone.

No! There hadn't been a choice in either case. He'd done everything he could to help Reece escape. If he'd stayed, he just would have been caught as well. At least this way, with one of them free, there was a chance he could –

What – rescue them? As if you'll even try. And anyway what do you think you can do? A pathetic, useless loser like you.

Pressing his face against the seat, Zack fought to silence the awful voice. He'd done the right thing. He hadn't deserted them. He hadn't. He hadn't!

Finally he lifted his head and stared out at the passing landscape. They were heading in the opposite direction from the depot and were now in an area he'd not seen before. The towering pine trees had become a backdrop to mixed hardwood forest, the flames and golds of its autumn foliage setting the surrounding hills on fire.

The only problem was there weren't any houses. The further they went along this road, the further he got from food and shelter. He couldn't imagine the crazy lady had much of a house.

Still, better there than back at the store. Now that they'd spotted him, Nolan and Vanessa would no doubt be keeping an eye out for him. They might even put his picture up somewhere, in which case he couldn't let anyone see him.

He eased back down into the tiny space, careful not to nudge the seat in front of him and let the crazy lady know he was there. A few days ago he probably wouldn't have fit in a space this small. But all that time without any food . . .

127

Reminded of his hunger, he noticed the boxes stacked around him. Perched on top of the last one she'd loaded was a plump soft roll, not even wrapped. Now that he'd seen it he could smell it as well. He reached up, grabbed it and crammed it in his mouth.

A half hour later, when the woman turned off the gravel track and into the woods, Zack was starting to wonder where the hell they were going. He'd had visions of her living in a tree some-where and was surprised when he caught a glimpse of a cabin. As she followed the driveway around to its front he ducked down and covered his head with the raincoat.

They rolled to a stop. The engine shut off. The driver's door opened, then closed again.

Zack held his breath. *Please don't reach for the raincoat first.*

The back door opened. The scrape of cardboard as the woman slid the top box from the stack. Receding footsteps.

He peeked out to see her going up the steps to the cabin's front porch. When she vanished inside he raised his head further.

In front of the car stood an open garage with some kind of shed built off the end. Parked to one side was a pick-up truck, the one she'd been driving the day before. Forest pressed in around the small clearing, nothing but trees in every direction.

Zack squeezed out of his tiny chink. On legs wobbly and cramped from confinement, he hobbled off into the deepening shadows.

'What's eating you?' Allen said from behind his newspaper.

Chase shifted his gaze from the computer to the man having breakfast at the table beside him. Now that his father had drawn attention to it he realised he'd been muttering to himself. 'Nothing. I'm just thinking about a case.'

'Complicated, is it?'

'It didn't appear so at the start, but it could turn out that way.' Chase returned his attention to the screen.

'So what's the problem?'

'The problem is I need to follow up on a certain . . . subject . . . but I can't find the relevant information.'

'Wouldn't give you her phone number, would she?'

His head snapped around. 'What?'

'Your mother was the same in the beginning. Had me jumping through all sorts of hoops with her hard-to-get games.' Allen noticed his startled expression. 'Well, that's what we're talking about, isn't it? This woman you met?'

'Am I made of glass or something?'

'Oh, come on, it's pretty obvious. You've been mooning over that carving she gave you like it was the Venus de Milo.'

'I haven't been mooning.'

'A high school football team on a year-long bus tour wouldn't do as much mooning as you have these last two days.' Allen lifted the paper again. 'Don't get me wrong, I think it's great. As long as it's love and not obsession.'

'Obsession? When have I –'

'You know what I mean. That thing you do where you have to take care of everyone.'

'You mean being a doctor?'

'It would be the best thing for you to finally have a serious relationship. I was starting to wonder about you, to be honest.'

'I don't know why I open my mouth.'

'So she wouldn't give you her phone number. Big deal. Just look it up.'

Chase quickly closed down the site he'd been perusing, then decided his father had probably seen in. 'I've tried every search engine on the net and just about every directory in the state.'

'And this is you not obsessing about it.'

'Dad, this is serious. She could be in trouble.'

'I would've thought you'd be more concerned about that boy you found in your waiting room yesterday.'

'I am concerned. But I've done everything I could for him and he's now getting the care he needs. I'm not sure the same can be said for this woman.'

Allen set the paper down in his lap. 'So what kind of trouble do you think she's in?'

'Never mind.'

'No, no, come on. You haven't gotten her pregnant, have you?'

'I've only just met her!'

'Well, then what kind of trouble could she be in?'

'I don't know. If I knew I wouldn't need to find her so badly.'

For once his father had no smart reply.

'It's nothing I can put my finger on at this stage. I just have a feeling something's wrong.'

'A feeling.'

'Yes.'

Allen lifted the paper again. 'Looks like I was right to be worried.'

Chapter 24

'What the hell am I going to tell him?'

Nolan paced the cabin's living area, running a hand through his wind-ravaged hair. He'd spent the entire afternoon scouring the woods behind the general store and found not a trace of the other two boys. 'He's left me six messages. I've got to call him back. But what do I say?'

From her seat on the couch Vanessa said, 'Tell him the good news. Tell him we caught one of the little bastards.'

'One out of three. That's your idea of good news, is it?' Nolan huffed. 'I doubt Tragg'll see it that way.'

'So don't tell him anything. Don't call him back till we catch the others.'

Nolan stopped and turned to glare at her. 'Were you even listening last night when I told you what he said he'd do if –' His swallow made a clicking sound in his throat. 'The man's a psychopath. Pain is his profession and he enjoys his work.'

Vanessa shrugged. 'Can't argue that.'

'Ballinger's the critical one. He's the one we should've gotten back.' Nolan resumed pacing. 'That bitch must have helped him. She sent me into those woods deliberately because Ballinger was hiding in her car. He had to have been. He couldn't have disappeared so fast otherwise.'

'So tomorrow we just start looking for her. When we find her, we follow her and she takes us to him.'

'And what if Ballinger's talked by then? What if he's told her –'

'The kid's a punk; she'd never believe him. And if she has doubts . . .' Vanessa smiled. 'That's where your acting skills come in. We flash our IDs, give her the same song and dance we gave the Learys and the problem's solved.'

Nolan stood with a hand to his brow. Yes, it all sounded perfectly logical. But the thought of telling Tragg of their failure, of confessing that the boy with knowledge of Lazaro's affairs had not only escaped but was now being helped –

On the coffee table his mobile trilled. He picked it up, read caller ID and fumbled it open. 'Tragg! My man, I was just going to call you. Yeah, great news – we caught the bastards.'

Vanessa blinked at him, her mouth dropped open.

'Yup, all three of 'em. They're right here in the cabin with us, safe and sound. And the best part is they never talked to anyone. So everything's cool.'

Nolan listened, feeling Vanessa's gaze bore into him. 'Well, there's just one problem. You see it . . . it's been raining up here, really bucketing down, and the only road into town is washed out. It could be a day or so before we can leave.'

Hearing the words he'd been praying for, Nolan let out his breath in relief. 'Oh sure, we'll take good care of them. Yeah. Great, see you then.' He disconnected.

Vanessa shook her head in disgust. 'You're pathetic.'

'You're the one who said we'd as good as caught them.'

'Have you any idea –'

'If I hadn't lied he'd have driven up here!' Nolan struggled to lower his voice. 'Besides, if you're right, he'll never find out. He wanted us to meet him at the warehouse tomorrow but that story about the road bought us some time. We now have an extra twenty-four hours to find the others.'

Vanessa rose slowly, stepped in front of him and pressed the point of one stiletto fingernail up under his chin. 'You screw this up for me, lover, and I'll have your nuts in a blender.'

Nolan stared into her cold green eyes. 'If *we* screw this up I'm pretty sure Tragg will beat you to it.'

She turned away from him. 'Okay, get that Reece kid out of the closet and let's find out what he knows.'

Tragg pushed out through the hospital doors, oblivious to the cold. Even the rain, slashing across the driveway in sheets, couldn't dampen his present mood. His head was clear, his body pain-free and the matter that had threatened to become a major problem had been taken care of. He was getting the fuck out of this dump.

He turned up his collar and dashed for the rental car Nolan had left for him, parked just across from the main entrance. He unlocked its door, climbed in and sat adjusting the seat and mirrors.

He was heading home, back to Boston. No point slumming it in some New Hampshire motel when Nolan wouldn't get there for another day or two. He had people keeping an eye on the warehouse; the money wasn't going anywhere. He'd only need to get there when Nolan and Vanessa arrived with the kids.

Till then he'd have nothing to do but wait. Something that never improved his mood. Still, the important thing was they'd caught Ballinger before he'd talked. Before they'd been forced to silence the lot of them.

Starting the car, Tragg felt a smile pull at his mouth. In a way he was looking forward to greeting them – the three runaways and the bungling fuckwit who'd let them escape. Looking forward to that very much.

He reversed the car from its parking spot and started towards the exit at the rear of the grounds. As he rounded the building a staunch female figure in a nurse's uniform emerged through a side door. Standing beneath its overhang she swung a coat up over her head and prepared to launch herself out into the weather.

Tragg smiled. Yes, it was her – the sagging matron so fond of giving orders. The ward's head bitch, so puffed up by her dollop of authority she wielded it like a battle-axe over patients and subordinates alike.

Perhaps I'd better hold onto that mobile for you, Mr Tragg, until you're discharged. We don't allow them on the wards.

Tragg looked around. The lot was empty and shrouded from view of the windows above by the swirling rain.

When the doctor says complete bed rest, that's exactly what he means, Mr Tragg.

A laugh escaped him. Clutching the wheel he bent towards the windshield.

I hope you're not leaving, Mr Tragg. The doctor hasn't authorised your discharge yet.

The woman stepped out from under the portico and commenced her jostling run towards her car. Tragg touched the gas, timing his approach, the acceleration. For a moment she was nothing but a blur in the darkness. Then she broke out into the flood of his headlights.

The woman whirled, ghostly white. Her features, wrenched by shock and fear, captured in a camera's flash. She threw herself back.

Tragg heard the satisfying thud of her body bouncing off the nearest parked car.

Chapter 25

Zack sat hunched on a granite outcrop shielded by a massive evergreen. The wind had picked up since that afternoon, subtracting another ten degrees from the chill of approaching night. Dead leaves and twigs swirled around him as he stared across the clearing at the lighted windows of the cabin.

In the hours he'd been here he'd had a look around, inspecting more closely the two-car garage, the carpentry workshop built off its end, the lean-to for firewood and the remains of a vegetable garden out back. He'd walked a wide circle around the premises, keeping the cabin in sight at all times, and discovered his initial impression had been correct – there were no other houses anywhere nearby. He couldn't have asked for a better hideout. Except for the fact that he was freezing to death.

Clamping his hands beneath his armpits, he braced himself against another fierce gust. He was also starting to feel a bit sick. He'd thought that after eating that roll he'd feel a bit better, but instead he felt worse. Sick to his stomach and with a strange sense of fullness in his groin.

Weirdest of all, the cut on his leg was sending out pulses of stabbing heat perfectly timed with the beat of his heart. Yet maybe he'd been feeling that for a day or so. It was hard to tell. Taking care of Corey and Reece had kept him so distracted that he hadn't paid much attention to himself. Now that they were gone and . . . he was alone . . .

Alone. Somehow the word made him feel even colder.

He looked towards the cabin. Smoke was billowing out of the chimney. The crazy lady had lit a fire. He slid from the rock, limped to the edge of the clearing and stood debating.

He'd seen no evidence the place was inhabited by anyone but her. Even the washing that hung on the line suggested she was on her own. What would she do if he went inside, just walked in? Would she scream? Throw him out? Call the police? What possible reason could he give her for being here? Yet, being crazy, maybe she wouldn't even ask for one.

With a burst of resolve he started forward. Cold gnawed his fingers with razor teeth and his body shuddered. He couldn't stay outside a minute longer. If she called the cops he'd just run away before they got here. He tip-toed up the cabin steps and across the porch. Took a deep breath and opened the door.

One big room. A couch and two armchairs squared off an area before a stone fireplace; a kitchen, table and chairs behind it. On his right a ladder rose to a loft, and on the left, two doors – one open, one closed. The crazy lady was nowhere in sight.

He stepped inside, leaving the porch door open behind him in case he needed a fast escape.

His gaze swung instantly back to the fire. Even from across the room he could feel it, its warm arms reaching out to embrace him, urging him nearer. Yet something stopped him moving towards it.

The scents of wood smoke and pine enveloped him. No stench of cigarettes, no reek of beer. The furniture was comfortably worn yet clean, not a fast-food wrapper or bottle in sight.

For some reason tears were burning his eyes.

Light in the darkness. Warmth in the cold. Home as it should be. Safe and snug and bright and –

The crash tore a startled cry from his throat. Heart thudding he swung towards the sound. The crazy lady stood in the doorway off the kitchen, the fragments of the jar she'd been holding strewn at her feet.

Zack cleared his throat, swallowed hard, but her look was so wild, so filled with alarm, he couldn't speak. Clearly, this had been a mistake. He turned and left.

The seven-year-old seated at the table before him was possibly the sorriest sight Nolan had ever seen. The boy's clothes were filthy, his sweatshirt torn. His brown hair was matted and his grimy face was streaked with tears. Nolan couldn't have cared less.

'Well now, Reece, it's time you and I had a little talk. I'm going to ask you some important questions and I want you to tell me everything you know. Because right now you're in a world of trouble, and unless you help us find Zack and Corey things are just going to get worse for all of you. Understand?'

The boy nodded.

'All right, first question – what did Zack tell you?'

'About what?'

'Well, for starters, why did he want you to run away from us?'

'I don't know.' Reece shot a glance aside at Vanessa, who was standing against a nearby counter. 'He just said we had to get away from you.'

'That's it?'

He nodded.

Nolan let doubt creep into his words. 'That's all he told you and you went along with him? We tell you we're taking you to a great new home, he tells you we're not, and you believe him, not us.'

A spark of resentment lit Reece's eyes. 'Zack never lies to us. He takes care of us.'

Nolan laughed. 'He's sure done a bang-up job for you so far.'

The boy stuck out his bottom lip.

Rising from his chair, Nolan crossed to the fridge and opened it. 'So did Zack mention anyone else to you?'

'What do you mean?'

'Did he talk about a man we were taking you to see? Did he say any names?' Nolan pulled a plastic-wrapped bundle from a shelf, closed the door and returned to the table.

Watching his approach, Reece shook his head.

'You sure about that?' With an innocent smile Nolan slowly unwrapped the bundle, lifted its contents and took a big bite.

Reece didn't answer. His gaze had locked on the chicken salad sandwich. He watched as Nolan picked up a morsel that had dropped to the table and popped it in his mouth.

'Oh, hey, I'm sorry. You must be starving. You want some of this?'

Reece looked warily from one to the other then reached out his hand. The sandwich jerked back before he could touch it.

'Tell me the name first.'

'What name?' Tears had sprung to the boy's round eyes.

'The one Zack told you. The name of the man.'

'He didn't . . . There wasn't . . .'

'Who's the woman you two were with, then?'

'We weren't with any –'

Nolan slammed the table. 'I said no lies!'

Reece burst into tears. 'I don't know! I don't know! Zack never said!'

Vanessa was suddenly at Nolan's side. She nudged him off the chair then pulled it closer to Reece and sat down.

Putting her arm around the boy's shoulders she stroked the tangled hair from his brow. 'There, there, sweetheart, don't let him upset you. He's just worried because we haven't found the others. He's afraid something might happen to them out in the forest all alone. And so am I.'

Gradually Reece choked back his sobs.

'So tell us – there was only you and Zack at the store. What happened to the other boy? Where's Corey?'

'He got . . . sick and we had to . . . take him to the doctor.'

With a muttered curse, Nolan turned and started pacing.

'Oh no, poor Corey,' Vanessa said. 'What doctor did you take him to?'

'The one just up the road from the store.' Reece wiped his eyes. 'But Corey isn't there any more. An ambulance came and took him away.'

She clamped her teeth. 'When did this happen?'

'Yesterday. When it got dark.'

'What did you tell the doctor about him?'

'Nothing. We didn't even see the doctor. Zack just carried Corey inside and ran out again before they saw him.'

'Well, that's something, at least.' Nolan stepped closer and bent down to Reece. 'You said Corey was sick. What was wrong with him?'

The boy cringed back. 'I don't know. He said his stomach hurt.'

'You mean like a tummy-ache? He was throwing up?'

'No, it got hurt in the accident. He had a mark. Then he fell asleep and we couldn't wake him up.'

Nolan straightened, pulling Vanessa aside for a conference. 'If the kid was unconscious they'd've shipped him off to the nearest hospital. The question is, where?'

She narrowed her eyes. 'I might just know a way to find out.'

Chapter 26

They were only small, half-grown at most. Yet dragging the two of them down the long corridor took most of his strength. Like all those who'd walked this stretch before them they were fighting to the last.

Why did they do it? With no hope of escape, no prayer of swaying him from his purpose, they still pulled and clawed, jerked and strained. How it must hurt, their collars tightening around their necks. If they just wouldn't fight, it would all be over so much faster.

The garage yawns low and wide before them now. The chamber door stands agape, leaking fumes and the throaty purr of the idling engine.

He bends to lift them, the pale one going limp in his arms, at last surrendering. But once inside last-stand panic revives their struggles. Their faces, unrevealed until now, twist and distort as they call his name. He slams the steel door closed on their screams . . .

Zack shot upwards from the depths of his dream, a drowning swimmer clawing his way through polluted waters. He surfaced with a gasp, tangled in the burlap sack that had been his blanket for the night.

It had been his old nightmare but with a twist. In this version, instead of the victim, he'd been the offender, dragging Reece and Corey to their deaths. He closed his eyes against the memory of their twisted faces, their hands reaching out to him, their shrill voices calling his name. What did it mean? He would never do anything like that in real life!

He shivered, waiting for his heart rate to slow. Morning sun slanted through the open garage but behind the snow-plough blade where he'd slept – on a pile of rags gathered from the work shed – the shadows were deep and chilled with night.

He pushed to his feet, took a step and winced at the pain knifing through his groin. The fullness he'd experienced the day before had overnight become a throbbing fire spreading upwards into his belly.

Hearing the clunk of footsteps outside, he hobbled to the door and peered around it. The crazy lady was coming down the cabin steps.

He watched her walk toward the pick-up truck parked directly in front of the garage. As she came toward him he studied her face. For a nutcase she was kind of pretty. Probably about the same age as Vanessa but soft and light instead of dark and tough-looking.

He ducked back as she climbed in the truck. The cops hadn't shown up last night as he'd feared so either she hadn't called them or there weren't any in this one-horse town. The engine started and the truck drove off.

Zack stepped out and watched it disappear around the side of the cabin. He wasn't all that afraid of the woman seeing him, so long as no one else did. If she caught a glimpse of him now and then and realised he wasn't a danger to her maybe she'd get used to him and let him inside. Until then . . .

He looked towards the cabin. How long would she be gone? They were miles from anywhere so probably a while. Time to sneak in and get something to eat.

The instant Chase hung up the phone and stepped from the treatment room Elaine spoke up. 'So what's the word on our little John Doe?'

'Well, he's stabilised but beyond that they aren't saying much. Until they locate his parents they don't want to give out any information.'

'You mean to say they haven't found them yet? How can that be?'

'Presque Isle police say missing persons has no report of a case child meeting the boy's description. They're sending someone over here later today to talk to us and canvass the area.' He frowned. 'You're absolutely certain you didn't recognise him?'

'Trust me. I know all the families in the area. If he'd been a local I'd have recognised him. Poor little thing.'

'He must've been with people passing through town, then.'

Elaine was incredulous. 'If a family's missing one of their children how long do they wait before raising the alarm?'

'Maybe they couldn't. Something might've happened, some kind of accident.'

'Then how did he get here? He was unconscious – someone would've had to carry him in. Unless he came in by himself and passed out after he lay on the couch.'

'No, you're right, he still would've had to get here from some-where. If the accident was close enough for him to walk, someone would've seen it.'

Elaine sat frowning. 'Maybe somebody dropped him off. Found him injured and left him here without saying anything because they didn't want to get involved.'

'Or the person did the damage himself and ran before he could be charged for it.' Chase didn't realise he'd spoken his thoughts until he saw her studying him.

They were silent a moment as she sipped her coffee.

'I suppose you would've seen a lot of that in Boston,' she said at last. 'That clinic of yours was in a rough neighbourhood.'

'We did see our share of abuse cases, yes. A big reason I wasn't sorry to leave there.'

She regarded him over the rim of her mug. He could almost see her mind ticking over, her antennae rotating towards him. 'It must have been hard, never knowing whom to trust, what story to believe.'

'Yes, it was.'

'And of course, being human, you doctors can't always get it right. There'd be times you'd fail to pick up the signs a child was at risk.'

'Sometimes there isn't any way you can know.'

'And still you'd wonder,' she went on, her voice hushed, '"if I'd only asked a few more questions, if only it hadn't been so busy that day, if I'd just seen that bruise on the mother's arm . . ."'

Chase stared past her. 'Yes,' he whispered. 'Sometimes you wonder.'

Zack dropped the cookies back in the box and closed the drawer. He couldn't believe it. After nearly three days with hardly any food he wasn't hungry. His stomach just hurt too much to eat. He left the kitchen in search of the bathroom.

Ten minutes later he was perched on the rim of a claw-foot tub, pants legs rolled, bare feet submerged in several inches of warm soapy water. Aiming to leave no evidence of his presence he used wet tissues to gently wipe the back of his leg. Layers of grime and crusted blood slowly dissolved to reveal the source of his growing pain.

He swallowed hard. He'd had infected cuts before but nothing like this. The wound was surrounded by a patch of red flesh the size of his palm, and the cut, though swollen shut, was leaking a mix of pus and blood. Strangest of all were the squiggly red lines snaking away from it towards his knee. He dried his legs with another wad of tissues, swung them over the rim to the floor and drained the tub.

In the medicine cabinet he found antiseptic and smeared some over the affected area. His socks were too gross to put back on so he stuffed them into his pockets, grabbed up his sneakers and went to see if the crazy lady had something he could wear.

Like the rest of the house, her bedroom was tidy. A double bed draped with a patchwork quilt stood against the wall with a tallboy and dresser on either side.

In the second drawer he checked he found what he was after. He burrowed in search of a thick pair of socks till his fingers scraped something neither cotton nor woollen. He pulled it out.

Three handsome faces smiled at him from the photo encased in a large wooden frame – the crazy lady, a ruddy-faced man and a boy about six or seven years old. By the way they were clustered, the boy in the centre, they looked like a family.

Zack felt a funny stir of emotion. A boy who'd actually known his father. A mother who hadn't shoved him in foster care just so she could marry some loser.

Where were the boy and his father now? Clearly, they didn't live in the cabin. Were they dead? Had the man and the crazy lady divorced? *Had* she deserted them? Had *they* dumped her because she was crazy? If they were her loved ones, why did she keep their picture in a drawer?

His gaze kept returning to the woman. She looked so beautiful, so happy and normal. How long ago had the picture been taken? What had happened to change her since?

A shiver washed over him. His face was burning but his feet were like ice. He buried the picture where he'd found it, grabbed some socks and closed the drawer.

Back in the main room he sat on the couch and pulled on the socks. His shivers continued, the cold having seeped through the rest of his body.

The remains of a fire burned in the hearth. Even its dying warmth felt wonderful. He drew up his legs, curled in a ball. He'd just stay a minute, soak up what warmth and comfort he could, before going outside again.

Chapter 27

'Marilyn Roswell?'

Vanessa looked up at hearing the false name she'd given the receptionist. The man standing in the waiting room's archway was tall and dark-haired with an earnest expression. Though he wasn't what she'd call break-your-heart gorgeous, he radiated an aura of quiet strength.

'Doctor Hadley?' She got to her feet.

His smile, though reserved, softened his features from overly serious to warm and concerned. She felt a slight kick in the middle of her chest.

He greeted her then motioned to the hallway behind him. 'Would you come this way?'

As she followed him across to the treatment room she found herself revising her plan. She'd originally thought to complain of insomnia – something with no visible symptoms to reveal her lie. But now that she'd seen him she suddenly felt the urge to change her complaint to one that would require him touching her. Why the hell not? There was no reason this had to be totally boring.

He ushered her into a brightly lit treatment room and indicated the chair by his desk. She let her skirt hike up as she sat, but he'd turned his attention to the form before him and didn't notice.

Only after taking down the usual details did he finally look up at her. 'Now, Ms Roswell, how can I help you?'

'I wonder if you'd check my ankle for me, Doctor. I had a fall yesterday and it's been hurting a bit.'

'Certainly. If you'll just come over here.'

Chase led the woman across the room, watching how she carried her weight. Strange that he hadn't noticed her limping on the way over from the waiting room – she certainly was now. He took the hand she extended towards him as she climbed onto the treatment table. Then he rolled over the stool and sat down before her.

'I don't think it's broken,' she said, slipping off a three-inch heel. 'But I wanted to make sure nothing else was wrong.' Toes pointed, she raised her leg and lowered it into his hands.

The sensuous nature of the gesture surprised him but he dismissed it. Surely just his imagination. 'How did you fall?'

'I didn't so much fall as twist it coming down the stairs of my cabin.'

'I see.' Initial perusal of the site showed nothing. Chase began testing the joint with his fingers. 'Your cabin. Would that be one of the rentals out by the lake?'

'Why yes, it is.'

'Nice spot for a vacation.'

'Oh, I'm not on vacation. I'm on my way to a conference in Toronto and thought I'd break up the trip.'

'Well, you picked a nice spot.' Still at a loss to find the problem, he smiled. 'Can you show me exactly where it hurts?'

Like a cat unfurling after a nap, she stretched forward slowly, running her hand down the length of her leg till her fingers skimmed the side of her foot. 'Just in here.'

There was no mistaking her movements this time. Nor could he miss the view now displayed with her blouse hanging open inches from his face.

Keeping his gaze fixed on her foot, Chase began rotating the ankle gently. No swelling, no contusions. Warning bells had started to sound in his head.

'When it happened I felt like such an idiot,' she laughed. 'It got me thinking – what if I'd really hurt myself? I mean, this area is so remote. What do you do if someone gets seriously injured or sick?'

'Presque Isle hospital is only an hour's drive from here. Any pain when I do this?' Chase flexed the joint. Suddenly he didn't feel like making small talk.

'No, that's fine. Well, it must be a comfort to the folks who live here, having a hospital so close by. Do you have to send people there very often?'

'I sent a patient there only yesterday as a matter of fact. Aside from that I can't really say – I haven't been here all that long.' He extended the rotation just a bit further. 'How about this?'

The woman arched back her head and closed her eyes. 'Oh yes, that's the spot.' Her voice was more breathy than edged with pain.

He lowered her foot. 'Your ankle looks fine, Ms Roswell. It's certainly not broken and there's no sign of tendon or ligament damage. At worst I'd say you sprained it. Slightly.' He got up and returned to his desk.

'Oh, thank you, Doctor. That's such a relief.'

Vanessa slipped on her shoe again. Feeling somewhat slighted by his lack of interest she slid off the table, returned to the chair and sat watching him write in her file. 'So you haven't been here all that long.'

'I only took over the practice three weeks ago.'

'You poor thing. I imagine it gets pretty lonely out here.'

Chase gave a tight smile. 'Lucky for me I don't live alone.'

When he left his office a few moments later he found Elaine leaning over her desk watching Ms Roswell walk down the hall. She turned to him worriedly. 'Everything all right?'

'As far as I know. Why, is there a problem out here?'

'Oh no, no, everything's fine. I just wondered . . .'

He arched a brow.

'I thought you might have had trouble with that one.' She jerked her head towards the hallway.

'You mean with Ms Roswell? What sort of trouble did you think I might have?'

'Come now, Doctor. Don't tell me a city boy like you can't spot . . .'

He maintained his expression of bewildered innocence.

Elaine leaned towards him and lowered her voice even though they were totally alone. 'A woman of that sort.'

'Ah.'

'All that make-up. And those shoes!' She shook her head. 'No woman wears shoes like that unless she's . . .'

'That sort,' Chase supplied.

'Well, they aren't built for comfort, I can tell you.'

'The women or the shoes?'

She narrowed her eyes at his burgeoning smile. 'Maybe you haven't heard about female patients seducing doctors and then later suing them for sexual assault.'

'Actually I have. But I thank you for your concern, Elaine. If she comes again I'll be sure to have you in the room while I treat her.'

Elaine humphed and returned to her filing.

*

At the sound of his mobile, Nolan pulled the car to the side of the road. It wasn't out of concern for safety. It was simply that without a current destination he could accomplish just as much standing still.

He eyed the phone on the seat beside him. Then again if it was Tragg on the other end the conversation might well have an adverse effect on his driving. He picked it up and put it to his ear.

'I just left the doctor,' Vanessa said without preliminaries.

Nolan slumped against the seat in relief. 'And?'

'They sent the kid to Presque Isle hospital. I'm heading there now. You stay and keep an eye out for Ballinger. I'll see you at the cabin when I get back.'

'I got a better idea. How about I go to the hospital and you stay and look for Ballinger?'

'That's your baby, Nolan. Just find the woman and you find the kid.'

'And how do you propose I do that exactly?'

'For Christ's sake, it's a fly-speck burg with one main road. Drive around long enough and you'll run into everyone who lives here.'

'Well, if it's so damn easy –'

'Hospital's only an hour's drive. I'll call you when I get there.' The line disconnected.

Nolan threw the mobile onto the seat.

Vanessa drove to the parking lot exit, sat looking up the road towards Presque Isle, then pulled out and headed in the opposite direction. She was making an unscheduled stop before leaving. Back to the cabin. Just for insurance.

When she'd heard Nolan lying to Tragg last night, the writing on the wall had lit up like a neon sign. The man had not just outlived his usefulness, he'd become an outright liability.

Listening to his voice on the phone just now had confirmed those fears. Nolan was done. He was too freaked out to do the job. He wasn't going to find this mystery woman and he wasn't going to get Ballinger back.

Well, she would not go down with his sinking ship! Yes, she'd slipped up. Yes, she'd let Ballinger get information about Lazaro. But she hadn't let the boys escape. That was totally Nolan's doing and she wasn't going to share the rap for it. Or for his lies.

She had to distance herself while she could. Tragg would be wild when he learned the truth. But if she could convince him she'd done her bit – more than her bit – if she could return to him with two of the boys Nolan had lost, he might overlook her part in the rest. Especially if she did it right.

Vanessa drove on with renewed conviction. She'd always known Nolan was totally spineless. Now that he had lost it completely it was time to cut the dead weight loose.

Chapter 28

The plank pulled free with a tortured groan and hung by a single supporting post. Shyler stepped across to the anchored end and drove the crowbar beneath its last nail. A moment later, it lay with the others at her feet. She bent and examined a piece more closely.

The timber was in a perfect state of deterioration – beautifully weathered but with no sign of rot. Like the other old shelters she'd dismantled that summer it would provide the raw materials for a dozen projects. Indeed, with what she'd already scavenged she hardly needed to collect any more.

So why was she here?

She gathered up the planks, carried them to the pick-up and laid them in the back. The track she'd parked on was little more than a driveway's width, trees crowding in on either side. For perhaps the tenth time since she'd arrived there she paused to take a look around.

The morning's mist had left the forest fragrant and sparkling. In places where sunlight pierced the canopy, maple leaves gleamed on the ground like rubies. Morels and puff balls poked shy faces through the mulch and the ghostly swan necks of Indian Pipes arched gracefully beneath the hemlocks. In every direction all she could see was virgin forest, all she could hear was bird song and the wind gently stirring the leaves.

Yet something was wrong. She'd been here a couple of hours now and still felt no better than when she'd arrived. Work of this sort, performed in solitude and surrounded by nature, normally soothed her. But today the diversion just wasn't working. Today she just couldn't get her mind off the dream.

In the newest version she'd had last night Jesse had actually spoken to her. He'd prattled for what had felt like hours, telling her about his friend's new rabbit, the bike he wanted, the hit he'd gotten at Little League training. He'd held her hand and asked her to sing him his favourite song, then laughed when she couldn't remember the words.

Smiling, she recalled the excited gleam in his almond-shaped eyes as he spoke of the pretty new girl in his class. Her little boy was getting so big, so grown up. And still, his face had been smudged with dirt, his tousled hair in need of a trim, his . . .

She leaned against the truck and closed her eyes. No, her Jesse wasn't getting big, he wasn't growing up. He would never grow up. Fish Hook and the others had seen to that.

She groped for the driver's door, yanked it open, and threw herself in. Gripping the wheel she sat, head bowed, fighting to make sense of her whirling thoughts.

It seemed to be getting harder and harder to pull her mind from what she so desperately wanted to believe. And it wasn't just in sleep any more. She'd seen Jesse in the cabin last night. She'd stepped from the pantry and there he'd been, standing in the doorway, plain as day. He'd looked older. Not as she had seen him last on the bridge but as he would if he had lived.

She'd dropped the jar of peaches she was holding, she'd been that shaken. Yet when she'd looked up from the mess at her feet, her boy had gone. Only to reappear this morning in her rear-view mirror as she'd driven off to collect her wood.

With trembling hands she started the engine and guided the truck back through the forest. At the road she waited for a car to pass. The driver slowed and for a moment she thought he was going to stop – a lost vacationer? – but in the end he drove on. She pulled out and turned in the opposite direction.

Even as she sped up the track towards home, she knew she couldn't outrun her fears.

Nolan drove at a reasonable speed till the pick-up vanished from his rear-view mirror. The minute it was out of sight he swung a U-turn and started back after it.

Clearing a bend he spotted the vehicle up ahead and slowed again. It was her, he was sure of it! He'd seen her face clearly, if for but an instant, when he'd passed her at the edge of the road. Just as well she'd been stopped there or he might have missed her. All this time he'd been looking for the sedan she'd had at the general store yesterday.

With a growing sense of anticipation, he forced himself to hang back far enough to avoid drawing the woman's attention. He'd follow her till she led him home then, one way or the other, he'd solve the problem of Zackary Ballinger.

He couldn't wait to get his hands on the kid. All the trouble the little shit had caused him – threats from Tragg, abuse from Vanessa, traipsing around this godforsaken wilderness . . .

He didn't have long to wait. Ten minutes after commencing his pursuit the pick-up turned down a lonely dirt track. He briefly lost sight of it around a bend then saw it pulling up to a garage adjacent to a small log cabin.

He stopped at once and reversed well away. Through the binoculars Vanessa had brought he watched the woman get out of the truck and begin unloading some timber planks from the back.

Now was his chance. If Zack was inside the cabin he could sneak in the back, grab him while he was alone and not have to deal with the woman at all. Even if Zack had told her something, she wouldn't have any idea where he'd gone so she couldn't tell the cops.

Nolan reversed his car beyond the blind bend and turned it around for a speedy getaway. He checked his watch. One forty-five. He might just make his meeting with Tragg in time after all.

Leaving the keys in the ignition, he got out and started towards the cabin.

The light above the couch was weird. A wide band of metal, like the rim of a wagon wheel, with animals and trees cut around its upper edge. When sunlight came through the window just right, shadows of bears, bobcats and moose stalked across the cabin walls. Zack lay disoriented, staring up at them, as slowly his situation returned to him. With effort he pushed himself onto one elbow. The cabin interior spun around him and he clenched his jaw against a rush of nausea. Sounds had awakened him. Something outside. But he couldn't quite think . . .

A car pulling up. Yes, that was it. God, he must've fallen asleep. If the woman was back he had to get out of here.

He managed to push himself halfway up, then something hit his chest and slammed him down again. A hand clamped tightly on his mouth. All remnants of sleep dissolved in an instant as he stared at the man's face hovering over him.

'You so much as squeak and I'll break your neck.' Nolan hauled him to his feet by his shirt. Maintaining a grip on his mouth the whole time, he dragged him through the kitchen and out the back door.

Zack stumbled along unresisting, too stunned to put up a fight at first. If he'd cried out at all it would have been in pain, not fear. The sleeping horror had awakened in his leg the instant he'd put his foot to the floor.

But once outside his courage returned. If Nolan was so desperate to keep him quiet it had to mean someone else was nearby to hear. He bit down on the smothering hand. Nolan squawked and released his grip.

The instant the hand pulled away from his mouth, Zack drew breath and screamed his loudest.

Shyler dropped the armload of planks and spun back to face the open door. For an instant she stood, muscles locked, intent on the sound she thought she could hear, a sound that seemed to be coming from the woods on the far side of the cabin. She lurched forward, hesitated, then launched herself out into the sunlit clearing.

The sound stopped the instant she stepped from the garage. *If* it had ever been there at all. In the silence, there was only the thump of her heart, the rasp of air scraping her throat.

With a hand to her mouth she bowed her head. The sound had gone through her like rusty barbed wire, ripping and tearing. All at once she'd been back on the bridge, watching him fall, watching that beautiful head of brown hair vanish beneath the swirling waters.

Jesse.

Sinking her teeth into one of her knuckles, she used the pain to pull herself together. Wind. A bird. The echo of something farther away. That's all it had been.

She was just turning to go back to her task when the sound came again. She closed her eyes, threw up her hands to cover her ears. *Please, no more.*

The sound wouldn't stop. It seemed so real. She ran for the cabin.

The blow knocked him flat. Stars exploded before Zack's gaze, a roar filled his head. He crawled a few inches, struggled to rise, but couldn't get his feet beneath him.

Hands pulled him up. His legs felt rubbery but with Nolan keeping a grip on his arm they carried him forward. He walked in silence, resistance gone. No one had heard him. No one would help.

A parked car appeared through a break in the trees. Nolan marched him steadily towards it.

But with every step Zack's fear was reborn. Suddenly it wasn't the forest he walked but the long dark corridor of his nightmare. And now before him, not a car door opening but the gate to the chamber of the idling truck.

He turned and kicked out.

Nolan managed to block the worst of it. The kick just grazed its intended target, enough to enrage but not incapacitate. He swore and threw Zack to the ground.

As the man stood hunched, Zack scrambled backwards away from him. 'Help me! Somebody! Please! Help!'

'I told you to shut up.' Nolan straightened and started towards him.

'He's killing me! Please! Don't let him hur –' His voice choked off as the man's hands closed around his throat.

He tried to buck but couldn't move. He flailed his arms but the pathetic blows had no effect.

'You just don't get it, do you, kid?' Nolan bent over him. 'She doesn't care. Nobody cares. No one in this whole world gives a rat's ass about a worthless piece of shit like –'

A sickening thud. A guttural grunt. The man pitched forward.

Zack lay gasping. The pressure on his throat had eased but Nolan's full weight now lay crushing him. With the last of his strength he heaved the man sideways.

The crazy lady stood above them holding a rifle, its butt end angled forward and down. Was that the horrible sound he'd heard? She'd bashed in Nolan's head with the rifle? No blood or brains were leaking out, but the man wasn't moving. He didn't even seem to be breathing.

Slowly he turned his gaze back to her, fighting to focus. She seemed to be fading. He opened his mouth but nothing came out.

It didn't matter.

The world had gone.

Chapter 29

Vanessa stood near the group of visitors, hoping she'd be mistaken for one of them. So far no one on the children's ward had given her a second glance and she'd been able to eavesdrop on a conversation between a female police officer and one of the doctors.

It appeared that when Corey Ingles had arrived last night he'd been suffering hypothermia and damage to his spleen. Since commencing treatment he'd improved steadily and was expected to make a full recovery. Best of all, though the kid was awake, he was refusing to speak so the authorities still didn't know who he was.

But the news wasn't all good.

Vanessa watched the cop disappear up the hall then glanced back at the doctor, who was now on the phone. From what she'd overheard they were trying to track down the hospital shrink to see if he could get Corey to talk. Which meant she hadn't much time to intervene.

With no cops or nurses anywhere in sight, she edged up the hall and into his room.

Holding her breath, she moved towards the bed. The fact

he'd bonded with her back at the 'safe house' hopefully meant he'd believe her lies now. She stepped into view. The boy's eyes widened.

'Oh, sweetheart!' she whispered, rushing forward and taking his hand. 'Thank God you're all right! I was so worried!'

She bent and covered his cheek in kisses. 'I'm so sorry I sent you away with those men. I had no idea what they were like. Can you forgive me?'

Corey's initial fear turned to joy. 'Vanessa!'

'Shhh, don't talk.' She pried her hand from his desperate grip, then reached into her bag for the clothes she'd brought. 'Here, put these on. Nolan and Tragg are on the way. We have to leave before they get here.'

She helped him dress then led him over to stand near the door as she groped in her bag for the lighter. She tore a page from the chart on his bed, set it alight and waved it beneath the smoke detector. Five seconds later the ward erupted in a wailing alarm. She swung back and lifted Corey in her arms.

Out in the hall the scene was chaos – visitors milling, patients yelling, nurses running. Clutching her prize, Vanessa walked calmly towards the exit.

Shyler staggered across the cabin and laid her burden on the couch. She slid the rifle from her shoulder and set it on the coffee table within easy reach. Not that she expected to have to use it right away. The man was dead – *God help me, what have I done? You had to, there was no other choice!* – and from what she could see from the tracks near his car, he'd been alone. The others would surely show up eventually but for now, Jesse was safe.

She dropped to her knees and smoothed the hair away from his face, then gently examined his upper body. He didn't look injured. A scratch on his cheek, bruises forming around his throat, but no major blood loss or broken bones.

He was, however, burning up.

She quickly removed his shoes and socks and lifted his legs up onto the cushions. A moan escaped him.

'Jesse? Sweetheart, are you hurt?'

When she couldn't rouse him, she bent and checked his legs more closely, and let out a gasp.

Twenty minutes later she was pacing the cabin. The fire was going, Jesse lay swaddled in a quilt on the couch, his wound washed, disinfected and bandaged. It wasn't enough. The infection was serious. He needed antibiotics fast.

At the window she scanned the clearing, the woods beyond. No way would she risk taking him to the doctor. If they knew he was injured that's just where they'd be waiting to grab him. No, the cabin was safe. It always had been. She must keep him here.

She swung round and paced to the opposite wall. She could go and see Doctor Hadley herself but what could she tell him? To say the medicine was for her son would put Jesse in every bit as much danger. Not from Hadley himself necessarily but if he ever mentioned it to anyone else –

With a hand to her head, she turned again. No, that would never work. A doctor wouldn't give out medicine for a patient he hadn't seen. And she wasn't sick or injured herself so she couldn't pretend the drugs were for her.

Jesse moaned. She rushed to the couch. Before, he'd been shivering; now he was sweating. She drew back the quilt, dipped the washcloth in the bowl of water and draped it gently over his forehead.

She slid her hand down the side of his face and cupped his cheek. 'Don't worry, baby. I'll work it out.'

The bandage encasing her thumb drew her gaze.

Slowly she raised her hand before her and studied the sterile layers of gauze, visualising the wound beneath. The sutures in her thumb were healing nicely, not the slightest hint of infection. But hadn't Doctor Hadley said, if the cut had been deeper, and not as clean . . .

She swallowed hard. Looked from her hand to the boy lying flushed and feverish before her. Then she pushed to her feet and walked to the kitchen.

Chapter 30

Chase looked up from his computer to the treatment room door. Elaine had left a half hour ago, not long after his last appointment, but he could've sworn he'd just heard someone moving around in the outer office.

'Elaine?' Had she forgotten something and returned? He pushed his chair back from the desk.

Beyond the door a shadow slid along the far wall. A silhouette too slim to be his receptionist appeared in the doorway, then stepped forward into the treatment room light.

'Ms O'Neil!' Stunned, he got to his feet. 'What – I wasn't expecting you till next week. We're actually closed at – Not that it matters, I mean –'

He let out a huff and shook his head. He'd been searching for this woman, thinking about her, casually inquiring of everyone he'd met if they happened to know her, since she'd left his office three days ago. Now here she was standing in front of him and he couldn't string two sentences together!

'Please, come in. I'm glad to see you. I hope you haven't had any problems with –' His smile faded when he saw her hand. The dressing he'd applied was still intact but above it a filthy blood-soaked rag encased her arm from elbow to wrist. 'Apparently it's something else that's brought you.'

She stood silent, her gaze darting around the room, taking in the corners, flitting to the window, searching the area beyond the treatment table.

'Ms O'Neil?'

Her attention shot back to him. 'I've had another accident.' Without hesitation she crossed to the table. In the time it took him to step to her side she'd ripped off the bandage and thrust out her arm.

Chase took the soiled rag from her hand, frowning at the injury revealed. 'Two lacerations requiring stitches in less than a week. You certainly are having a run of bad luck.'

He tossed the bandage into the bin and noted the feel of dirt on his fingers. Hard to imagine she couldn't have found something cleaner to use. He started for the sink, then turned back when something caught his eye.

Swinging the lamp down over her arm, he bent to examine the wound more closely. The edges of the six-inch laceration had three distinct notches, suggesting that whatever object had caused it had paused in its track across her flesh.

He felt a sickening chill wash over him. 'Shyler, how did this happen?'

'I was cutting some wood and slipped with the saw.'

'A saw?'

He looked up when she didn't respond. He'd lapsed and called her by her first name but she hadn't noticed. Nor had she noted his doubting tone. Her gaze had strayed to the window again. Her pulse was racing, her breathing rapid. She was even more anxious than at her first visit, only this time it seemed about something outside.

With her attention distracted he turned her hand to examine the wrist. Nothing. The skin was free of scars. Partly relieved, he reached for the other hand.

She jerked it away. 'I'm sorry, Doctor, but I'm in a hurry.' Her face was only inches from his, her green eyes wide, their pupils dilated despite the glare of the overheads.

'Shyler, what's wrong?'

'Nothing. My arm, that's all.'

He lowered his voice. 'You know I only want to help you, don't you?'

'Of course.' She swallowed. 'That's why I'm here.'

He held her gaze a moment longer, then, sensing she wouldn't respond well to pressure, he got to work.

Throughout the procedure she remained distracted, seeming more intent on sounds from outside – a gust of wind, a car going past, the scrabble of dry leaves across the roof – than to any discomfort she might have experienced. He held off on the small talk this time, in part because the procedure demanded his full attention but also because he doubted she'd hear it.

Ten stitches and a tetanus shot later he rose from the stool. 'Shyler, this cut was obviously more extensive than the one to your thumb, and you didn't manage to keep it as clean. I'd like to give you a course of antibiotics, just to be on the safe side.'

'Yes, all right.'

He went to the cupboard and dispensed the tablets. When he turned back she was standing by the door.

'Before you go, there's one other thing.' He took up a pen and pad from his desk. 'It seems you forgot to leave your details with Elaine last time. If you'll just write them down for me I'd be grateful.'

She glanced towards the door. 'Doctor, I –'

'It'll only take a second. Address and phone number is all I need.'

For a moment he thought she was going to run. Then she took the pen, scrawled some words across the pad and handed them back. After assuring himself he could read her writing he held out the bottle – but didn't let go when she reached to take it.

Startled, she looked up, their hands overlapped.

'It's getting cold out. Would you like a hot drink before you go?'

The offer surprised him as much as her. The urge to detain her had hit him suddenly. If he kept her here he could keep an eye on her, make sure she took the pills he'd given her, see she didn't have any more accidents, keep her safe from whatever dangers were lurking outside.

But she was already pulling the bottle from his hand, stepping away. 'I . . . I'm sorry, I forgot to bring something to barter this time. I –' She stopped, her gaze fixed on something behind him.

Turning around, he saw it was the row of carved wooden figures that lined the shelf behind his desk.

He shrugged and smiled. 'I'm a fan of your work.'

Chapter 31

It was dusk when she reached her driveway again but beneath the trees it seemed much later. Rounding a bend, her headlights glinted off the stranger's car standing where it had been when she'd driven out.

She slowed as she neared it. Something was wrong. Something had changed. From her current perspective she ought to have been able to see . . .

But, no, she couldn't. Not even when she pulled up twenty feet away and shone her beams directly on the spot where he'd fallen.

The body was gone.

Twisting in her seat, she strained to see out into the surrounding gloom. She'd hit him so hard, she was sure she'd killed him. Where could he be? Was someone else here? Had they dragged him away?

A sudden thought snapped her gaze towards the cabin. Was that person right now inside her home, intent on finishing what his partner had started?

She unclipped her belt and reached for the rifle on the seat beside her. Even as her fingers closed on its barrel her door flew open. Hands thrust in, grabbed for her throat.

He pushed her back. She tore at his arms, struck at his face, but his grip was relentless. Forced sideways, she groped the seat again. The rifle was gone, knocked to the floor.

She stamped with her foot, hit the accelerator. The car shot forward, churning wheels throwing up rocks and debris.

Incredibly the man held on. But the force he exerted as he hung from her neck, legs dragging, threatened to wrench her from the seat. She yanked the wheel, turning the car to side-swipe a bush. With a final shout, the man fell away.

Shyler sped on. She drove around to the front of the cabin, threw wide her door, found the rifle and jumped from the car. By the time she'd cleared the side of the porch all she could see of her attacker was his car's tail lights disappearing down her driveway.

The rifle trembled in her hands as she stood gasping. Her heart was a time bomb inside her chest. Had he really left? Had he called for help while she'd been gone? Was someone else here?

'Well, well, look who it is.'

She spun at the sound of the voice from behind her. No one was there. They'd sounded so close. How could the person have vanished so –

'Some mother you are.'

A different voice. Yet somehow familiar, as the other had been. She swivelled again, but again there was no one.

She raised the rifle and stepped towards the woods. 'Where are you? Show yourselves.'

'Here.'

She swung back.

All at once they were standing around her. Scarecrow with his flaxen hair, Beret, Snake, Puppet with his twitching hands . . .

'Where's Jesse? What have you done to him?'

Fish Hook jerked his head towards the cabin, ignoring the rifle she aimed at his chest. 'Didn't look after him very well, did you?'

'What do you mean *didn't*?'

'What kinda mom leaves her sick kid alone?' Scarecrow leered.

'I went to get medicine.'

'Ain't gonna do him much good now,' Puppet whispered across her shoulder.

She whirled to face him. 'No. You're lying.'

'Getting it off with the doctor, were you?' Fish Hook bent closer. 'You liked those big strong hands of his, didn't you? The way he touched you, pretended to care.'

She bowed her head, squeezed shut her eyes. *No. No.*

'Been a while, hasn't it? Yeah, we know. And I'm sure the kid would've understood. If only you'd got back in time to explain it to him.'

'No! You're lying!'

Pushing past them, she ran for the cabin. She charged up the steps, burst through the door, then fell against it, slamming it shut.

A small still figure lay on the couch. She flew to his side, dropped to her knees and placed her hand on his smooth, dry, over-heated brow.

A sob clawed its way up her throat. Hot, not cold. Jesse was alive.

She jumped up again and raced to the window. Not the slightest movement or deeper shadow disturbed the near-total darkness outside. Fish Hook and his gang were gone.

If they'd ever been there at all.

*

Nolan stumbled through his cabin's back door, head screaming, vision blurred. It was a miracle he hadn't killed himself driving back. Several times he'd veered off the road, twice to the shoulder, once into the oncoming lane. Thank God this hick town had so few people there hadn't been anyone coming the other way.

He groped to the kitchen and hunched over the sink. Judging by how dark it had been when he'd woken, he'd lain unconscious on the forest floor for several hours. Only moments after he'd pushed to his feet, he'd spotted headlights coming through the trees, giving him the seconds he needed to hide. But when the woman had pulled up right in front of him, he'd lunged at her car with one thought in mind – to snap the fucking bitch's neck.

But even that had been too much for him. After she'd scraped him off her car it had been all he could do to get back into his own and drive away. He knew what Tragg would say of his efforts but there was just no way he could deal with the bitch in his present condition. Especially seeing as she had a rifle and he was unarmed.

He turned and stumbled into the bathroom. Light hurt his eyes but he needed to survey the damage. Bracing himself, he flicked the switch.

A rivulet of blood streaked his face from scalp to chin. Gingerly he probed for the source, wincing when his fingers touched an egg-sized lump in the centre of his crown. He wet a washcloth, swiped at his face, then staggered out again.

Somehow he ended up in the living area. He eased himself down onto the couch, lay back and closed his eyes. He had to rest. Just for a while. Just until the room stopped spinning. Then he'd work out what to do next.

Chapter 32

The sudden jolt of her head lolling forward snapped Shyler from her doze. Instantly alert, she looked around. The cabin was quiet, the room lit only by the gentle glow of the hurricane lamp beside the couch. An occasional crack and sputter from the fire was all that disturbed the pre-dawn stillness.

She checked the clock above the hearth. Four twenty-five. She hadn't been dozing for more than a few minutes but she couldn't risk nodding off again. She got up, threw another log on the fire and walked to one of the windows that faced the front porch.

The full moon's light revealed not a single unfamiliar shape in the clearing outside – no figures, no movement. Were they hiding further back in the trees where the light couldn't reach? Somehow she sensed the answer was no. They weren't here yet, but they were coming. Soon. Probably when it got a bit lighter.

She looked at the rifle in her hands and felt sick. A single weapon. Against all of them. It would never be enough. They'd encircle the cabin, create a diversion, attack from one side to draw her attention. And while she was busy defending that front, one of them would sneak in and –

She turned to Jesse asleep on the couch. Maybe she should

take him away after all. Someplace where they'd never be found. But was he well enough? His fever hadn't broken yet. Could she risk taking him out in the cold?

She let the curtain fall back and went to him. Even from several paces away she could hear the difference in his breathing – deeper and steadier than it had been all night. She bent and lay her hand on his brow. It might only be her imagination but his skin seemed cooler.

She stood gazing down at him, her heart constricting. Her beautiful boy – how big he was growing. Those almond-shaped eyes with their long dark lashes. Those glorious dark curls – wildly untidy at the moment, of course, but then he was sick. As soon as he was well again she'd brush out the tangles. As soon as they were safe . . .

The thought went crashing around her head. She clutched the rifle to her chest. One weapon. Against all of them. Never enough. But there were other alternatives to guns. Ways to level the odds a bit. Eliminate as many of them as possible, before they even reached the cabin. Yes, there were ways.

With a final look at the sleeping boy she went to the door. She watched through its window, assuring herself as much as possible no one was there. Then she slipped out and closed it silently behind her.

Chase rubbed his eyes and took a sip of his extra-strong coffee. The clinic was having a quiet morning – two early appointments, the third one cancelled, his next not until that afternoon. It was just as well. He wasn't yet firing on all cylinders.

Shyler's visit the previous day had preyed on his mind through much of the night. Her agitation. Her hyper-vigilance. Jumping at every sound she heard. Two injuries in as many days, one that possibly wasn't an accident . . . She had assured him there wasn't a problem but could he believe that? Would she have told him even if there was?

He tapped his shirt pocket, felt the slip of paper she'd written on. The only thing easing his fears at the moment was knowing he now had her contact details. He could go and see her whenever he wanted.

But the very fact she'd given them to him had alleviated one reason he should. Contrary to what Elaine suspected, Shyler hadn't been withholding her details. And surely that alone suggested he had less cause for concern.

Still, it was a comfort to know where she was. He could go and see her today if he wanted. Drop by to check how she was doing – pretend he was making an old-fashioned house call.

Yet, why pretend? Why not just call her? Ask her out? A picnic on the lake. A drive to Presque Isle for dinner and a movie. If she got to know him, maybe she'd open up to him more. Then he could stop all this second guessing.

Yes, why not?

With his worries for the moment allayed he stepped from the treatment room into the office. 'Elaine, did you find that paper I left on your desk?'

'The one with Ms O'Neil's contact details? Yes, I found it. I meant to ask you, who gave them to you?'

'She did. She came in yesterday after you'd left. I made sure I got them from her this time.'

Elaine stopped typing and shook her head. 'Which is why you're the doctor and I'm the receptionist.'

'What are you talking about?'

'That address she gave you doesn't exist.'

'What?'

'There's no Pine Tree Drive in the Deadwater area. Here, see

174

for yourself.' She smiled faintly as he studied the map she'd pulled from a drawer. 'You sure your mind wasn't on other things when you wrote that down?'

'I didn't write it, she did. That's just a copy I made for you. Hers is right here.'

He pulled the paper from his pocket. Elaine fished her copy out of the trash. They set the two side by side on the desk.

They were the same.

Chase straightened slowly. He took up the phone, punched in the number inscribed on the page, then gently set the receiver back at hearing the out-of-service recording.

'Elaine, I have to go out for a while.'

Chapter 33

C hase turned onto the doctor's road and saw a moving van dead ahead. Pulling his Land Rover up behind it, he spotted Dan Muir standing in the yard talking with one of the moving men.

The doctor broke off his conversation and came towards Chase as he climbed from his car. 'Lucky you caught me. I was just saying goodbye to the place. Heading to Caribou to be near my daughter.'

'That's great, Dan. I'm sure you'll love it there.'

'Probably gain twenty pounds the first month. That woman is just too good a cook. So, what can I do for you?' The man gave him a knowing smile. 'This still about Shyler?'

'I won't step around it, I'm worried about her. She came to see me again yesterday. Another laceration, ten sutures this time. That's two in three days, Dan.'

'I don't see what's so strange about that. She works with tools. You ever seen a carpenter's hands?'

'The larger cut had three distinct notches.'

Muir went still, his face growing dark. 'Hesitation marks?'

'That's what they looked like.'

'Aw, no.' The man slumped and closed his eyes.

'You said when you saw her back in November she seemed depressed.'

'*Possibly* depressed. How do you diagnose something like that from a ten-minute talk? She never said anything.'

'I know.'

'She was quiet, sure, but I never figured her to be self-harming. Never saw the slightest evidence of it. If I had –'

'Dan, I'm not judging. Even when I asked her, she denied there was a problem. And when I finally pinned her down about her contact details she flat out lied.'

'She did?'

'Address and phone number totally bogus.'

Muir took a deep breath. 'Guess you were right about there being a problem. How can I help?'

'I need to find her. You said she lived in a cabin somewhere.'

'Yes, but I wouldn't have a clue where it is.'

'You don't know anyone else who would?'

Muir thought for a moment. 'Sorry, no.'

'You said she vacationed here with her parents. Can you remember their names?'

'That was twenty years ago!'

'Try, Dan, please.'

The man was already shaking his head when his frown suddenly lifted. 'I treated her.'

'Who? Shyler?'

'No, the mother. Just once. It would be in the files. You'll have to go through them.'

Chase took the details and turned for his car. 'Thanks, Dan. That's a big help.'

*

Tragg pulled his arm from beneath the pile of platinum hair on the pillow beside him. The body attached to the outrageous mane was plump and luscious. A real little tigress who'd served him outstandingly for most of the night. But already he was tiring of her. For some reason, no matter how well they performed, he never liked the look of them in the morning.

Pushing himself off the king-sized bed he scuffed to the bathroom. Outside the window of his North End apartment, Boston Harbor glittered like a lake of diamonds in the mid-morning sun.

Back in the bedroom after his shower he flicked on the TV. The blonde groaned noisily at the disturbance but simply rolled over and went on sleeping. As he dressed, Tragg listened absently to a news report on the storms that had swept New England. The weather had never interested him much and wouldn't have this time if it hadn't been for one particular line the reporter said.

'Residents of Maine, forecasted to receive the brunt of the storm, narrowly escaped the violent weather when the front swung easterly sooner than expected.'

Tragg turned, still buttoning his shirt. A weather map filled the screen showing satellite imagery of the storm's course over the last forty-eight hours. A thick band of cloud was clearly visible passing over Connecticut, New Hampshire and Vermont. But nowhere else. He waited, hoping for more information, but the report switched to another topic.

With an uneasy feeling, he walked to the desk and opened his laptop. After a brief search he found a site giving weather information for the state of Maine. The uneasy feeling took a stronger hold. No rain had been recorded north of Orono in the last seventy-two hours.

So how could the Deadwater roads be flooded?

Tragg sat staring at the map. Maybe the rain had been localised over a very small area. So small it didn't show up on satellite imaging. Deadwater was remote – few people lived there. Would they even bother recording rainfall? He turned from the screen and picked up his phone. Nolan's number didn't answer. Cut off in such a backwater where could he be? The uneasy feeling became full-blown disquiet.

Tragg rubbed his jaw. It would take him eight hours to drive up there. A wasted trip if there was a logical explanation for all this. Yet if something was wrong the situation could deteriorate further, perhaps irretrievably, in that amount of time. If there was just some way to check things out faster.

He snatched up the phone again and speed-dialled a number. 'How's the fishing?' he said when he heard his old friend's greeting. No matter the reason it was always good to talk to Jake Farrell.

'Tragg, my man! The sweet voice of reason in a troubled world. The fishing sucks – haven't caught squat. Wish you were here, though.'

'Yeah, me too.' They shot the breeze for a couple of minutes then Tragg got serious. 'Listen, you had any rain up there lately?'

'Rain? No. Been dry as a nun's nasty all week.'

Tragg swore softly. Moosehead Lake, where Farrell was staying, was maybe ninety miles south of Deadwater. It was starting to appear ever more certain that Nolan had lied to him. What the hell was going on up there?

'Anything I can help you with, man?'

'Well, now that you ask . . . No, forget it, you're on vacation.'

'What, are you kidding? You'd be doing me a favour. All this peace and fresh air is giving me a fucking headache.'

Tragg smiled, instantly relieved. If anyone could get him what he needed it was Farrell.

Chapter 34

Zack opened his eyes. Flames danced in a granite fireplace, a long low table on the rug before him. White log walls, sunlight slanting through lace-curtained windows. Where the hell was he?

He rolled on his back and frowned at the ceiling – a light with animals carved in the rim. The last thing he remembered was lying in the forest. Nolan on top of him. Pushing the man aside and seeing –

'So, you're awake.'

He caught his breath. The crazy lady had stepped out from behind the couch. In a flash the details came flooding back. The awful sound of her rifle connecting with Nolan's skull, her standing over him, the look of horror on her face.

She lowered herself to the table beside him. 'How are you feeling?'

For a second he couldn't answer. She'd killed a man. Even though she'd done it to save his life, it still made her a little bit scary.

'Okay,' he croaked.

He tried not to flinch when she reached towards his face. Her palm rested briefly against his brow, then slid to his cheek. So cool, so gentle.

'Well, you certainly seem better.' She withdrew her hand. 'I don't mind telling you, you gave me quite a scare, young man.'

'Sorry.'

Her smile was like the sun coming out. 'You don't have to be sorry, sweetheart.'

Sweetheart? 'What's going on?'

'What's going on is you're sick. You have a fever.' She drew up the blanket and tucked it closer around his neck. 'Don't worry, I got you some medicine and it seems to be working. As long as you keep taking it you'll be fine.' She pushed to her feet. 'Feel up to eating? I made you some of your favourite soup.'

He blinked at her. When had he ever told her –

'Chicken noodle. Don't tell me you don't like it any more.'

'I like it okay.'

'Then you just lay there and I'll go get some.'

She was back in a moment with a bowl in her hand. A hand with a bandage wrapped around it. Another peeking out from the end of her sleeve.

'What happened?' he said.

'This? Oh, nothing. I had a little accident.' She raised the spoon. 'Now come on, open up.'

The first taste brought his hunger awake like a raging beast. Suddenly he realised he couldn't remember the last time he'd eaten.

'How is it? Too hot?'

He shook his head and was rewarded with another of her beautiful smiles.

When the bowl was empty he lay back wondering what he'd been so worried about. So the woman was a little weird. It didn't mean she was psycho-dangerous. She treated him nice. She made great soup.

'Now I want you to try and sleep some more. You need lots of rest if you're going to get better.'

Yes, he already felt a bit sleepy. 'How come . . .'

'How come what, sweetheart?'

He shook his head. Did he really care why she was doing this? Why she'd suddenly gone from flipping out at the very sight of him to being this loving almost-Mom. She'd saved him from Nolan. That's all that mattered.

She leaned down and started stroking his head. 'Everything's going to be all right. I'll take care of you, don't you worry.'

Suddenly it hurt to swallow. Had anyone ever said that to him before?

'I won't let them hurt you, Jesse, I promise. You're totally safe. My precious boy.'

Through the fog deepening inside his head, he fought to reply. 'My name's not Jesse.'

She stroked his cheek. 'Just get some rest.'

Seated at the desk in his treatment room, Chase opened the file before him.

After leaving Dan Muir he'd returned to his office and pulled out all the records for the years Shyler's family had visited the area. Perusing only those for the summer months, it had still taken him over an hour to find the right one. At least he hoped it was.

Patricia O'Neil had come to see Muir in July of 1995. Her file gave a Presque Isle address and phone number. But even if this was Shyler's mother, after nearly twenty years, what were the odds she was still living there?

He took a deep breath, picked up the phone, and entered the number.

A woman's voice answered on the second ring. 'Hello?'

'May I speak to Patricia O'Neil, please?'

'Speaking.'

Chase felt his heart rate kick up a notch. 'Forgive me, I'm not sure I have the right person. Do you have a daughter by the name of Shyler?' Silence so long he thought they'd been cut off. 'Hello?'

'Who is this?'

'My name is Chase Hadley. Doctor Hadley. I have a practice in Deadwater Maine.' He waited but the woman didn't respond. 'I take it you do have a daughter named Shyler.'

'What do you want?'

'I recently treated Shyler at my office. Nothing too serious. I sutured a couple of cuts she had. I was wondering if you could tell me how I can get in touch with her as we don't seem to have her contact details.'

'I can't help you.'

Chase hesitated. 'I'm sorry, does that mean you don't know where she lives, or that you don't want to tell me?'

'It means I can't help you. Shyler is no longer a part of my life.'

'I'm sorry to hear that, Mrs O'Neil, but really all I need –'

The line disconnected.

He blinked at the phone in disbelief, nearly entered the number again, then decided it would do no good. From the woman's tone it was obvious she wouldn't answer.

Chase sat debating, staring at the address scrawled in the file. If the telephone number was still in use . . .

He grabbed the receiver and dialled again.

His father picked up on the seventh ring.

'Dad, did you still need to go to Presque Isle?'

Chapter 35

Nolan spluttered awake against the deluge washing over him. Sitting up abruptly made his head whirl and he dry-retched over the side of the couch. When the vertigo eased he slowly looked up, wincing at the light streaming through the cabin windows.

'Who the hell are you?'

The man standing over him – tall and rangy with shoulder-length black hair tied in a ponytail – tossed the bucket he was holding aside. 'Farrell. Tragg sent me.'

At the mention of the name, Nolan's situation hit him so hard he nearly retched again. That was daylight coming through the windows. Daylight, as in *another day*.

'I can explain.'

'Well, now, that's why I'm here.' The man dragged over a kitchen chair, swung it around and straddled it, facing him. 'Tragg wants to know what's going on. He told me to use whatever form of persuasion I needed to get the facts but . . . Well, you seem like a reasonable guy.'

'I am, I am. I'll tell you everything. Just give me a second.'

'Sure.' He smiled. 'Whenever you're ready.'

Nolan exhaled. 'All right, here it is.'

By the time he'd finished half the story Farrell was staring in disbelief. 'You lied to Tragg?'

'No! Not exactly. I mean . . . I really thought we'd catch the last two and make it back in the time I told him.'

'So what went wrong?'

'Vanessa drove to Presque Isle yesterday to grab the youngest one out of the hospital. She hasn't rung me so I assume she's got him and is on her way back here.'

'Meanwhile you decided to tie one on.'

'I'm not hung-over!' Nolan held his head. It hurt to talk. It hurt to think. 'A local woman was helping Ballinger so I tracked her down and followed her home. I grabbed the kid, but before I could get him into my car she bashed me with a rifle.'

'The woman did?'

'Nearly split my fucking head open.'

'Christ, no wonder Tragg's in a state. So of three missing kids you managed to get back only one of them. Where's he?'

'The middle one. Dennings.' Nolan pointed. 'Locked in the closet.'

Farrell went to the door and opened it. 'This another make-believe story?'

'What are you talking about?' Nolan rose and staggered over. His eyes widened as he stared down into the empty space. 'What . . . No. He was here, I swear it!'

'Looks like he wandered off. Again.'

'He couldn't! The door was locked from outside. There's no way –' Nolan's jaw dropped, this time in sudden comprehension. 'That bitch!'

'Who are we talking about now?'

'Vanessa. She took him. That's why she's not back from Presque Isle – she went back without me!'

'So you're pissed off because she did what Tragg wanted.'

'Don't you get it? We were supposed to go together. She must've figured I wouldn't catch Ballinger and decided to ditch me. She's bringing Tragg the other two just to kiss ass.'

'Rats deserting a sinking ship, eh, Nolan?' Farrell laughed.

As Nolan raved, Farrell stepped aside, opened his phone and punched in a number.

Tragg lowered the phone from his ear and stood clenching it in his fist. As he'd suspected, Nolan had lied. The Deadwater roads weren't flooded, and he'd only captured one of the boys. At least Vanessa – bless her black self-serving heart – was on her way back with the younger two.

The bad news was, Ballinger, the biggest threat to Lazaro, was not only still on the run but also now being helped by some local woman. Which meant there was a very good chance he had talked.

Tragg fought down a surge of rage. Nolan's payback would have to wait. At the moment the most pressing issue was what to do about the kid and the woman.

He narrowed his eyes as he weighed the facts. Ballinger had told him back at the 'safe house' that all three boys had seen where Giles hid the case. Was he smart enough to lie about something like that? Maybe. He'd been smart about a hell of a lot of other things.

Still, even if he'd lied, at this stage the decision was about priorities. Since Ballinger was their greatest risk and Vanessa now had the other two . . .

Tragg put the phone back to his ear. 'Farrell?'

'Right here. What's the verdict?'

'Kill the woman and get the kid back alive if you can. If you can't, do 'em both.'

Zack lay watching the crazy lady from across the room. He'd woken intermittently throughout the day and, except for the one time she'd brought him some lunch, she'd been in the exact same spot every time.

For a while the sight of her seated at the window, rifle in hand, had reassured him — she was watching out for him, taking care of him, just as she'd promised. But as the afternoon wore on, her obsessive vigilance was slowly starting to creep him out. If Nolan was dead, who was she watching for? How did she even know there were more people after him?

The other thing was, she kept calling him Jesse. That was more than a little bit weird. He'd tried to tell her his name was Zack but she'd laughed like he was making a joke. So was she actually truly crazy? The thought he was being guarded by a nutcase wasn't all that reassuring. Still, better than no one, he supposed. And, crazy or not, she had killed Nolan.

So who the hell was she looking for out there? Ghosts? Monsters? Hideous mutants only she could see? Maybe she was just making sure, playing it safe. Probably a little creeped out herself. Anyone would be after killing a man.

Then again, maybe she hadn't killed Nolan. What if she'd just knocked him out and he'd woken up later and run away? Back to Vanessa. To get reinforcements. Maybe the two of them were out there right now, sneaking up on the cabin with guns. And maybe this time they weren't alone.

He pushed himself up. 'You see anyone?'

The crazy lady's head snapped towards him. For an instant

the rifle pointed his way. Then her face cleared and she rose from the chair.

'Hey now, you get back under those covers. You're not ready to be up and around yet.' She set the rifle on the table and gently eased him down to the pillows.

'Is there?' he said.

'Is there what?'

'Anyone out there.'

'No, sweetheart, nobody's there. And anyway, I told you, you don't have to worry. I'll look after you.'

Zack stared up at her. Did she really think she could protect him? If Tragg found them, she had no idea what she'd be up against.

Shyler stroked the side of his face. She could see her words hadn't assured him; the glint of fear was still in his eyes. Her poor little boy, he'd been through so much. She needed to distract him.

'Would you like me to make you another sandwich?'

He shook his head.

'Milk and cookies?'

'No thanks.'

She smoothed a lock of hair from his brow. 'Maybe you should try to get some more sleep.'

'I'm sick of sleeping.'

She smiled. 'That's a good sign. It means you're getting better.' She settled onto the floor beside him. 'How about I tell you a story then?'

He nearly laughed. Was she kidding? What kind of baby did she think he was? Still, her voice and touch were so soothing. And he just couldn't seem to get enough of her smile.

He sighed and lay back. 'Yeah, okay.'

*

They left Farrell's car hidden among trees and approached the rear of the cabin on foot.

'Here's where I struggled with Ballinger,' Nolan said, indicating the furrows in the mulch. 'I nearly had him in the car when that bitch snuck up and clobbered me.' Spotting a patch of dried blood on a leaf – *his* blood – he felt a rush of anger. God, when he got his hands on these two . . .!

Farrell had walked on, ignoring his excuses. Nolan caught up to him behind a boulder just as he was closing his mobile.

'You called Tragg?'

'The man likes to be kept informed. Just letting him know we found the place and that there looks to be somebody inside.'

'How do you know?'

Farrell held up a pair of binoculars. 'Smoke's still coming out of the chimney and I can see some kind of lantern burning.' He tucked the glasses back in his pack, pulled something else out and shoved it at Nolan.

Nolan stared down at the cold alien object in his hands. 'Strange as it may seem in this day and age, I've never fired a gun before.'

'You don't have to hit anything,' Farrell said, loading a clip into his automatic. 'Just stay back here and, when I give you the signal, fire in the air every few seconds till I tell you to stop.'

'What if I run out of bullets?'

'Your magazine holds thirty rounds – that should be plenty. But just in case . . .' He slapped another into Nolan's hand, then got to his feet.

'Where are you going?'

'Around the front. Only take me a couple of minutes to get in position so be ready.'

Nolan took his arm before he could leave. 'I know what you're doing. You're using me to draw her fire.'

189

Farrell's gun rose to an inch from his face. 'Maybe you'd rather draw mine instead.'

When Nolan let go, Farrell grabbed the front of his shirt. 'You're here to stop them running out this way. You're here to fix the enormous fuck-up you allowed to get out of hand. So whatever I tell you to do, you do.' He shoved Nolan back and walked away.

'Stop! I don't want to hear anymore.' Zack pressed his face into the pillow to hide an unexpected rush of emotion. He was starting to feel like maybe he was a baby after all.

'Why, what is it? Are you in pain?' The crazy lady sat bending over him.

'No. It's a stupid story, that's all. I don't want to hear it.'

'But Hansel and Gretel was always your favourite. You always loved –'

'Well, I don't any more!' He turned with the words, in time to catch her startled reaction. The outburst surprised him as much as her. He didn't even know if he was angry or sad.

'Jesse, what's wrong?'

Christ on a broomstick! Jesse again. Hadn't he told her . . . And how did she know what his favourite story was? 'Nothing.'

'Of course there is. Come on, tell me.'

'Are you deaf? I said it's a stupid story!'

'All right, what's so stupid about it?'

He closed his eyes. He was being a jerk, an absolute shit. And she wasn't even shouting or anything.

Suddenly all his anger dissolved. 'Why did the father send his kids away if he loved them?'

She thought a moment. 'His new wife didn't like them, I suppose.'

'Why didn't she like them? What was wrong with them?'

'Nothing was wrong with them. I think she was jealous. Maybe she could see how much the father loved them and she was afraid he'd never love her that much.'

He shook his head. 'That's not why.'

'No? Well, what do you think the reason was?'

'They were lousy kids. The father never really loved them. He was just too weak to dump them until the new wife forced him to.'

Her mouth fell open. 'Why on earth would you think that?'

'Because I know.' His anger was returning. 'And it works both ways. Mothers ditch their kids when they find a new guy. A guy who doesn't want their bastards.'

She reached out and took his face in her hands. 'Jesse, I don't know where this is coming from, but I want you to know you are the most loved and cherished little boy on the face of this earth.'

He choked back a sob. Were he only able to accept her words his world would change. But it wasn't him she was saying them to. All that love, all that caring, was for someone else!

'You crazy cow! I'm not Jesse!'

She drew back and gaped. Slowly astonishment changed to confusion, fear, denial. Had it finally sunk in? Was she really seeing him? What now, if she was? After all she'd given him, what had he done?

'I'm sorry,' he said and reached out a hand.

It was then the lamp beside them exploded.

Chapter 36

Suddenly Zack was on the floor, the woman's weight bearing down on him. The cabin's front windows blew inward, spraying a blizzard of glass through the room. Dishes shattered on the kitchen counter. Pots came to life and flew off their hooks. Stuffing filled the air like confetti as bullets stitched across the couch.

The woman rolled off him. 'Come on! This way!' She flipped the coffee table on its side for cover and on hands and knees they circled the couch.

Around the back he fell against its sheltering bulk and hunched in terror. Though the woman was frantically waving him on, he could go no further; his muscles had locked.

Her arm swept around him. With the rifle in her other hand she propelled them towards the kitchen table. They'd just slid beneath it when the chair she'd pushed aside jigged convulsively, leapt into the air and hit the wall in a mass of splinters.

A hail of bullets glanced off the table top. He cowered and screamed. The woman seemed suddenly undecided. She'd been heading for the back door. She must have planned to get out that way. Why had she stopped? Had she lost her nerve? Was she just going to sit here and let them get slaughtered?

Shyler sat frozen as reality sank in. Her efforts to secure the cabin had failed. Through a brief lull in the gunfire from the front of the house she'd distinctly heard single shots coming from the back. Though this was the very scenario she'd feared, though she'd done all she could to keep it from happening, somehow they'd found a way through her defences.

Bullets strafed the table and Jesse cried out. She clutched him to her. How could she have let this happen?

But was the cabin completely surrounded? She strained to listen and could make out only two distinct weapons, presumably being fired by only two men – one at the front, one at the back. Which meant the side windows might be clear.

She grabbed Jesse's shoulders and turned him to face the nearest wall. 'The ladder to the loft,' she yelled above the din. 'Run to it and climb up as fast as you can.'

Zack judged the distance as less than six feet. It might just as well have been six miles. 'No way! I can't.'

'I'll be right behind you. Do it. Now!'

Committed to action by her shove, Zack scrambled out from under cover. He half-ran, half-crawled, reaching the ladder just as more shots slammed the table.

Panic seared through him. Had the woman been hit? But even as he took his first step up he felt her body against his back.

'Jesse, go!'

He struggled to climb. It seemed like a lead weight was tied to his ankle. 'I can't. My leg!'

Shyler knocked a picture frame off the wall and hung her rifle from its hook. Shielding his body with her own she pushed him up. Each step seemed to take an eternity. Each seemed certain to be their last. When a volley of pellets hit her back she nearly fell, but it was just shards from a shattering vase.

They were nearly to the top. She'd just curled her fingers around the last rung when the firing from the front of the house cut off. In the echoing silence an image filled her head: that of the gunmen charging the cabin.

Nolan held the gun above his head and fired. The first few shots had stung his hand but now he was used to the pistol's recoil. In a way, he liked it. There was a tremendous feeling of power in that kick. And the more he thought about what the woman had done to him, what the boy had caused him, the more he wanted to aim that deadly power at them.

He got to his feet behind the boulder. Screw this firing into the air bullshit. He wanted to get closer, wanted to see if he could actually hit one of them. The bitch hadn't fired a single shot yet. Clearly, she was overwhelmed by their assault.

He peered out from behind the rock and sighted a large tree nearer the cabin. From there he'd be able to see in the back window. The bitch would be so distracted by Farrell she wouldn't notice him until too late.

Nolan broke cover. As he ran for the tree he heard Farrell's fire abruptly cut off. It didn't matter. The man had told him to keep shooting until he said stop and that's exactly what he planned to do. The only difference was, now, he'd be shooting at someone.

With a final heave, Shyler pushed Jesse into the loft. She followed him up then reached down to grab her rifle off the hook. Her fingertips had just brushed its strap when the front door burst open and a figure in black fired an arc of bullets around the room.

She pulled back, praying the man hadn't spotted her. With luck he might check the other rooms first and she'd still have a chance to retrieve her weapon. But as she held her breath in the silence that followed she heard not the creak of the gunman's footsteps but her rifle scraping against the wall as it swung on the hook.

No doubt the gunman had seen it as well and now knew exactly where they were.

Outside, Nolan charged.

Leaping over a fallen log he felt like Bruce Willis in *Die Hard 2*. Maybe he could get a job with Farrell. Guns were his thing, he was fast discovering. Nothing he'd done in his life before compared to this.

With a final burst of speed he ran for the cabin. His target tree was just up ahead. Twenty paces with nothing to stop him. He dodged a branch, jumped one last rock. And collapsed, screaming, to the ground.

Zack watched the woman scrambling around the loft on her hands and knees. She'd lost it for sure this time – fear had taken out the last of her marbles. As scared as he was, he couldn't help hating her. Wasn't there a grown-up in this world he could count on?

She pawed through the bedding on the double mattress then moved to the little chest beside it. In the second drawer down she found what she'd apparently been searching for. Though what possible good a nail file could be against men with machine guns he had no idea!

Clutching the tool, she returned to the ladder. As she lay face down – doing God knew what – Zack stole a look over the edge of the loft.

The man was closer. He'd reached the couch and was inching around it. Suddenly his eyes flicked upwards. Zack's heart stopped as their gazes met.

He nearly shrieked when the woman grabbed his arm and pulled him away. 'Stay back,' she hissed, then immediately returned her attention to the floor.

He watched her hands. She was doing something to the top of the ladder, to the screws that anchored it to the loft. Nothing that could possibly save them. And even if it was, she'd never get it done in time.

He stole another glimpse over the edge again. This time his query was met by a burst of machine-gun fire. Bullets hit the ceiling directly above them. Which meant they had come from directly below.

'He's on the ladder! He's coming up!' Zack grabbed her arm and tried to pull her.

She fumbled the file and snatched it up again. 'Get behind me!' She shoved him towards the back of the loft.

Where did she expect him to go? Out the window? Leave without her? He was just reaching out to grab her again when the gunman's face appeared over the edge.

Incredibly the woman ignored him. With dogged focus she kept to her task.

Another rung and the man's shoulders came into view. 'Like fish in a barrel.' He started to swing his weapon around.

Shyler dropped the file and threw herself back. Bracing her foot to the top of the ladder she kicked out with all her strength. The gunman's smile turned to surprise as his support teetered. He made a grab for the edge of the loft but she kicked his hand away.

The silence was shattered by a startled shout. Followed by a crash of splintering wood.

As Zack sat clutching the woman's arm another sound emerged through his shock. Someone screaming. But it wasn't the man who'd just done a back flip off the ladder. This noise was coming from outside the cabin.

When the woman pulled away from him he followed her forward. Side by side they crept to the edge of the loft and looked down.

The gunman lay sprawled on what remained of the kitchen table, now collapsed to kindling beneath him. His head was twisted at a weird angle and a sliver of the table leg stuck through his neck.

Shyler reached down and grabbed her rifle off the picture hook. She sat back and took Jesse's face in her hands. 'Are you all right?'

He nodded, eyes wide.

'Right, let's go. We have to get out of here.'

'But the ladder –'

'This way.' She crawled to the window, pulled it up and knocked out the screen.

She eased her head through the opening and listened. No more shooting. No one in sight. Had it really just been the two of them? Screams were still coming from the rear of the house so at least she knew where that one was.

She turned back to Jesse. 'Get up on the sill and give me your hands. I'll lower you onto the lean-to roof.'

Shyler jumped down and motioned for Jesse to slide towards her. When he neared the roof's edge, she shouldered her rifle then reached up and lowered him to the ground.

They ran for the garage diagonally opposite. At the door she stopped to survey the interior, rifle poised. Except for the pick-up, the shed stood empty. To the sound of the man still yelling out back she helped Jesse into the passenger seat then circled and got in behind the wheel.

The spare key was beneath the mat where she always left it, but when she turned the ignition nothing happened. With a silent prayer, she tried again. Nothing. What had they done to it?

'Wait here,' she said and climbed out again, then froze at the silence. The man had stopped his yelling. Did that mean he was on the move? Had he found his dead friend? Was he coming for them?

In the clearing just ahead she spotted the Chevy. Their last chance gone. The tyres were slashed.

Gunshots resounded from the rear of the house. She leapt inside and pressed back against the garage wall.

Breathless, quaking, she felt the paralysis taking hold, stripping her reason, shutting her down. All at once she knew it was over. The monsters were here. Fish Hook. Puppet. Beret. Scarecrow. She could see their faces, their sneers, their scars –

Small arms clamped around her waist. With a gasp she looked down. Jesse stared up at her, his wide frightened eyes drawing her into a place of stillness and sudden clarity. With every second she stared at his face her courage returned. She pressed a trembling hand to his cheek. No, the monsters hadn't won yet!

Hugging him close, she turned for the door, glanced at the sky – twilight streaking the clouds with gold – then into the woods. They hadn't a chance against five armed men and they weren't going anywhere in either vehicle. But in another hour it would be fully dark.

And no one knew these forests better than she.

Chapter 37

Chase pulled his Land Rover to the side of the quiet suburban street and shut off the engine. He sat staring out at the green shingled, two-storey Queen Anne with its manicured shrubs and cottage garden. A blue sedan was parked in the driveway. He climbed from the car and started up the path.

On the open front porch he rang the bell. After a moment a shadow appeared behind the glass panel that flanked the door.

'Mrs O'Neil? It's Doctor Hadley. I called this morning regarding Shyler. I still haven't been able to locate her. I wonder if I could ask you a few more questions.'

The shadow lingered but the door didn't open.

'I'm concerned about her, Mrs O'Neil. It's important I find her.'

The door cracked an inch. 'I thought you said there was nothing seriously wrong with her.'

'There's nothing seriously wrong with her physically, but I'm worried . . . Look, do you think I could come inside and talk to you? It's not the sort of thing –'

The door opened wider and a woman's face appeared, thin and hard-featured. Chase could barely see the resemblance.

'I told you I can't help you. I haven't spoken to my daughter in years.'

'That's okay. At this stage all I want to do is find her. I know she's living in the Deadwater area, I just don't know where.'

The woman stared back as though debating. 'The cabin.'

'Yes, someone said something about a cabin, but they didn't –'

'It's on the north side of town, off one of the old logging tracks. We used to vacation there when Shyler was young. She and her father built the place and when he died he left it to her.'

'Mrs O'Neil, I'm new to Deadwater. It would be a tremendous help to me if you could draw me a rough map to find the place.'

More debating. 'All right, come in.'

A flight of stairs leading to the second floor lined one side of a wide hallway. As she moved to the desk beside the door, Chase saw the picture frames covering the walls.

'I really appreciate this,' he said, stepping closer to scan the photos. Most were of the same young girl at various ages. For someone who claimed not to care about her daughter, Patricia O'Neil kept a lot of mementos.

'These pictures are all of Shyler growing up?' He pretended not to notice the completed map she was holding out to him.

'Yes.'

'She's an only child?'

'That's right.'

He leaned to take in a particular shot, more to buy time than anything else. How could he get this woman to open up?

She lowered her hand. 'Go ahead and ask your questions, Doctor. It's clear I won't get rid of you until you do.'

Where to begin? How did he ask about an experience that might have destroyed a young woman's life? Perhaps by approaching the subject indirectly.

'I see Shyler used to play the piano.'

'Yes. She was very talented.'

'Is that so?'

'By age six she was playing the Bach Inventions. Mozart, Chopin and Brahms by high school. She could have gone to any music school in the country. I would know, I was her teacher.'

The pride in her voice was unmistakable. 'Could have? So it didn't turn out that way?'

'Shyler was talented at a good many things. She could have done anything she wanted with her life. Gone to any college, pursued any number of challenging careers. Instead she fell pregnant and married the father.'

His head snapped towards her. 'Shyler's married?'

'They've since divorced.'

He waited but she didn't elaborate. She seemed to be struggling to meet his gaze. 'Was that when you stopped having anything to do with her? When she got married?'

She looked away. It was answer enough.

'How did your husband feel about it?'

'He agreed with me. We refused to see them, even after the baby was born. It wasn't until —'

'Until?'

'When the boy turned five, Robert, my husband, came to me and confessed he had contacted Shyler. It was the one and only time he ever disregarded my feelings on the issue. On any issue, for that matter.'

'What changed his mind?'

'He said he'd been having . . .' She swallowed with effort. 'That he had some health problems and wanted to get to know his grandson before . . .'

Chase could fill in the blanks from there. 'Your husband was dying.'

'I didn't know it at the time but, yes.'

She drew herself up and fixed her attention on one of the photos. 'Shyler had always been close to her father. The two of them were much alike – similar natures, similar interests. When Robert told me he wanted Shyler back in our lives . . .' She closed her eyes. 'We fought about it. A terrible argument. And we never fought normally. If I'd only known . . . If he'd only told me . . .' She covered her mouth.

'Mrs O'Neil?'

'Robert collapsed. A heart attack. That was the health problem he'd been keeping from me.'

'So your husband died while the two of you were fighting. Which you wouldn't have been doing if not for Shyler.' Chase took a quick mental stock of the facts. Had he stumbled onto part of the problem? If Shyler felt responsible for her father's death, a parent she adored, a man she'd unwittingly forced to choose between her and her mother . . .

'I . . . I'm sorry, Doctor, you'll have to excuse me. I'm very busy.' She tried to urge him towards the door.

Chase stood his ground. 'Mrs O'Neil, are you aware Shyler is exhibiting symptoms of a possible psychological disorder?'

'I . . .'

'Did you tell her how you felt all these years? That you blamed her for her father's death?'

'Blamed her! I never blamed Shyler, I blamed myself. If I hadn't been so – I'm sorry, Doctor, I'm really not well. You'll have to leave.'

He stepped reluctantly out on the porch. 'Your estrangement wouldn't be the only cause. I'm sure if you saw her . . .'

'I tried. If you only knew how . . . But Shyler refused and I couldn't blame her.'

'Things may have changed. She could feel differently now.'

She shook her head, noticed the map still clutched in her hand. Snatching a pencil from the desk she scrawled a few lines and handed it to him. 'This is her ex-husband's name and phone number. He can help you better than I.'

She swung the door towards him, then pulled it back.

'Please, Doctor Hadley, help my girl.'

Chapter 38

Zack fell gasping to the ground. For a while the woman had helped him along, held his arm, half supporting him. But ten minutes back she'd pulled out in front and had been getting farther and farther ahead of him. With darkness rapidly closing in, soon he wouldn't be able to see her at all.

'Hey, wait up!'

Her footsteps halted in the gloom ahead, then resumed, coming back to him.

'Jesse, what is it? What are you doing?'

'I need to rest.' He'd given up trying to tell her his name.

'We can't. It's not safe. We have to keep going.' She crouched beside him. In the ghostly half-light her eyes were wide.

'But we got away. There isn't anyone after us. See.' He indicated the trail behind them. 'If they were coming they'd have caught up to us by now, don't you think? We haven't been going all that fast.'

She took a deep breath and swung down to sit on the ground beside him. 'I suppose we can rest a little while.'

He slumped in relief. She hadn't been trying to leave him behind. Despite his doubts about her sanity he'd much rather be with her than alone.

'You were pretty cool back there,' he said once his breathing had slowed. 'I thought we were history but man, you beat them, you really did. The way you pushed that guy off the ladder. That was awesome!'

'Jesse.' Her tone was gently admonishing, as though she didn't like him talking that way.

'What, you think I'd be freaked out by something like that? No way. That dude had it coming.'

They sat in silence, straining to hear any sounds of movement or approaching footsteps above the burble of the nearby stream. Until she noticed he was shivering. 'Here, put this on.' She took off her jacket and draped it around him. Her warmth and scent gently enfolded him. She felt his brow, then his cheek, but kept her judgments to herself.

'So, that other guy. The one who was screaming.' Zack swallowed. 'What happened to him?'

She peered around at the deepening shadows. 'We should keep moving.'

'You did something to him, didn't you? Planted some kind of booby trap or something.'

She got to her feet. 'Come on. If you can't walk I'll carry you a ways.'

He sighed in defeat. 'I can walk. Just not so fast, all right?'

She helped him up then immediately turned and started off.

'Hey!' he called.

She stopped and looked back.

'It's getting kinda weird not knowing your name. What do I call you?'

'Silly. You call me Mom, of course.'

Shyler went back, wrapped her arm around his shoulder and held him close as she ushered him along. It had to be the fever coming back that was making him ask such peculiar questions.

He hadn't felt hot when she'd checked him just now but he would be soon. The shock of what had happened, the exertion and cold would all take their toll. And as if that wasn't bad enough . . .

How could she have forgotten the antibiotics? He wasn't nearly recovered enough to go without them. As soon as his last dose wore off his infection would flare and resume its spread. Even in her panic she should have remembered!

It was too late now. They couldn't go back. She'd just have to get him some more. But how? The doctor's office was a good ten miles. He'd be struggling to make it another ten yards!

She held him closer as an idea spawned. A mile west of the doctor's office was Heron Pond – the body of water into which her trout stream eventually fed. It was still ten miles. But if they used her canoe, followed the stream . . .

She changed direction.

'Can we stop again?' Jesse said weakly.

'Not yet, honey. Just a little further. Then you can have a good long rest.'

Chapter 39

'Tragg? It's Vanessa.'

'Where the hell are you?'

'On my way back. I just crossed the border into New Hampshire. I've got two of the boys with me.'

Tragg felt a curious mix of feeling. Relief that the intel he'd got through Farrell had proved correct, anger that he'd had to go to such lengths to get it, and a touch of admiration for this woman's shrewdness in escaping a no-win situation. 'Any problems?'

Looking away from the sporadic traffic, Vanessa shot a glance at the sleeping figures on the car's back seat. 'Nothing major. One's still recovering from that accident you had, and I had to sedate them both for the drive. They'll need a day or so to recover.'

'And which two boys are we talking about?'

'The youngest ones – Ingles and Dennings.'

'What about Ballinger?'

'Nolan's bringing him.' A second's pause. 'Isn't he back yet?'

Tragg couldn't help a begrudging smile at the polished innocence of her surprise. Nor had he missed her subtle reference to the accident *he* had had. Just how deep would she dig herself in? 'Should he be?'

'I would've thought so. It's what we arranged.'

'What time did the two of you leave Deadwater?'

'Well, we didn't actually leave together.'

'No? Why not?'

'I didn't see a need. I had my kids ready so I left and figured Nolan would follow.'

Tragg's smile broadened. So far she'd carefully skirted the issue. Time to raise and see if she'd fold. 'How were the roads?'

Son of a bitch! Vanessa straightened after jerking the wheel, sweat instantly beading her lip. All this time Tragg had been baiting her. Somehow he'd learned she'd walked out on Nolan. She had maybe three seconds to make a decision.

She made it in two. 'The roads were fine. Nolan lied. He told you they were flooded to buy himself time.'

'Time for what?'

'To catch Ballinger. He lied about that, too. He didn't have all of them when you talked to him last.'

'But he did when you left him.'

She worked to speak but no words would form. The laughter issuing from the other end made her skin crawl.

'Not a real team player, are you, Nessa?'

She cringed at his use of her uncle's pet name for her. 'I brought back two of them. Was it too much to expect him to bring the third?'

'You left before the job was done.'

'I did my part. Nolan was supposed –'

'He's your playmate. You were responsible!' Tragg let her writhe in silence a moment. When he spoke again his voice was controlled. 'Luckily the situation is being resolved even as we speak. I sent someone up to give Nolan a hand. Someone reliable.'

'That's a relief.'

Another laugh. 'I'm sure it is.'

'So what do you want me to do with these two?'

Tragg gave her the name of the motel where his men were staying. 'Keep 'em out of sight and first thing tomorrow get down to the warehouse and find that stash.'

'You mean you want *me* . . .?'

'That's right, I want you to do it. You did such a fine job of playing mommy. You bonded with those brats. They trust you now.'

She felt a shiver climb her spine. Did Tragg know the rest? Her moment of weakness, her brief insanity. Had Nolan told him?

No, he couldn't have. Nolan didn't know himself.

It had happened coming out of the hospital, carrying the little one in her arms, his soft curls warm against her throat. With the alarm still wailing she'd had the sense she was rescuing him, his noble protector.

But once in the car she'd started thinking about where they were going, what was in store for them – him and the other one – the true role she had played in it all. Whether they knew where the money was or not, it would end the same way.

She'd got as far as buying them clothes, little backpacks in bright colours, planning their escape route into Canada. Reality struck as she'd stood at the checkout, a large stuffed alligator under her arm, and watched a kid in the next line throw a tantrum on the floor. She'd walked outside, ditched what she'd bought in the nearest dumpster, turned the car around and headed for New Hampshire. She wasn't cut out for that sort of life. And yet . . .

'You hesitate, Nessa?' Tragg's voice hissed in her ear. 'I'm giving you the chance you've always wanted. Prove to your uncle you've got what it takes.'

She clamped her jaw to staunch a response. There was no way he could know what she'd almost done and yet he seemed to be mocking her for it. The absurdity of her compassion. The notion she could have such feelings at all.

'What if they don't know where Giles hid the case?' she said through her teeth.

Tragg paused to consider her words. Yes, there was that possibility and he wouldn't much relish informing Lazaro if it came to it. In the days his people had been searching the warehouse they'd turned the place upside down and not found a thing.

Then again, there was still the chance Farrell would bring Ballinger back alive, though getting him to cooperate might be a different story. The kid wasn't just smart, he was gutsy. Not only had he arranged the accident that had allowed him and the others to escape but also he'd managed to evade recapture, making Nolan and Vanessa look like fools.

With a grim smile Tragg saw again the look of challenge in the boy's eyes back in the 'safe house'. *Must be hard to get laid with a face like that.* The kid had been shitting himself at the time yet he'd still found the balls to spit in his eye. In fact, looking back, the only weakness he'd ever shown . . .

'Keep 'em alive,' he said into the phone.

'But if they don't know anything –'

'They could still be useful.' His smile broadened when she didn't respond. 'Don't worry, Nessa, when the time comes, the job is yours.'

Chase pulled the Land Rover into his driveway, shut off the engine and rested his head against the seat.

Ten thirty-five. He'd planned to be home well before this. Even at nine, when he and his father had left Presque Isle, he'd hoped he might still look for Shyler's cabin tonight. But he had to accept it was too late now. He couldn't just happen to show up at her place at this late hour. He pulled the key from the ignition and rubbed his eyes.

'Anything wrong?' Allen said from the seat beside him.

'Just tired.' He took out his mobile and checked missed calls. Shyler's ex-husband hadn't called back yet, despite the several messages he'd left.

He was starting to wonder if he'd ever get his answers. He'd gone to Presque Isle thinking Shyler's mother wanted nothing to do with her. But after talking to her he realised he had gotten that wrong. Whatever estrangement existed between them, Patricia O'Neil cared about her daughter. So what was keeping her from coming to see Shyler? If she knew her daughter was having trouble –

'You break all land speed records getting back here and now you just plan to go to bed?'

Chase sighed and slipped the phone in his pocket. There was no point in arguing. 'I was hoping to see someone tonight, that's all.'

'First I hear of it.'

'I know. Don't worry, it's no big deal.'

'I bet *she* thinks it is.'

Despite his frustrations he managed a smile. 'It's too late now. I'll see her in the morning.' He climbed from the car, hefted his father's chair out of the back, wheeled it round to him and opened the door.

'You should've told me,' Allen said as Chase helped him out. 'I wouldn't have suggested we stop for dinner.'

'It's okay, Dad. It was good to get a decent meal for a change.'

'Oh, is that so?' Allen grunted. 'Wait till you see what I cook you tomorrow night.'

Chapter 40

Flashes of light danced on the water. The nearly full moon skimmed the tree tops, bringing objects on shore into colourless relief – boulders, bushes, a toppled pine. And a single large silhouette standing in the shallows as they rounded a bend.

Shyler stopped paddling. The current continued to carry them along; there was no way she could halt their advance. She could head for the farthest side of the stream but doubted it would make any difference now.

They'd already been spotted.

Slowly she lowered the paddle to the floor and picked up the rifle.

'You're not going to shoot him, are you?'

She jumped at the words but kept her voice low. 'Jesse, you scared me. I thought you were asleep.'

Yeah, right. Curled up on the bottom of a boat with his hands and feet numb and something digging into his back. 'You're not, are you?'

'Not unless I have to. Just keep very still.' She braced the gun stock against her shoulder.

'But why would you have to? It's just a moose. It's not like a grizzly bear or a wolf.'

'It's coming up to mating season,' she whispered. 'The bulls can get quite . . .' *Aggressive. Deadly.* 'Unpredictable.'

She shuddered at the memory. Autumn of the year she'd started high school, the poor lone fisherman caught off guard, she and her father trying to save him . . . trying to stop the bleeding . . .

Across the water the animal raised its head. No antlers. She lowered the rifle. 'But this one's a female so we don't need to worry as much.'

As they drifted past it, Shyler laid the gun back at her feet and took up the oar again. She checked the sky. They were getting close. Judging from the stars it was well past midnight; they had to be three-quarters of the way at least.

Her main concern now was that she wouldn't recognise the spot when they reached it. Landmarks were hard to make out in the dark. The pond was small, little more than a widening in the stream. If she overshot the mark and had to go back, paddling upstream might be more than she could manage with her injured arm.

'Is it much further?' His voice quavered slightly.

'Why? Are you cold?'

'A little.'

She slid off the seat and onto her knees. As she bent towards his face she could hear his teeth chattering, even above the murmur of the water. 'My God, you're frozen. Why didn't you say so?'

She pushed back onto the seat and began paddling for shore. However close or far they might be hardly mattered if Jesse caught pneumonia getting there. She'd light a fire, keep him as warm as she could for the night and go the rest of the way in the morning.

*

Zack sat against a moss-covered tree trunk watching the woman feed another branch into the fire she'd just kindled. Opening her backpack, she pulled out a water bottle and handed it over.

He accepted it but took only a tentative sip. His stomach felt hot and tight as a fist – a symptom nothing to do with his infection. A thought had occurred to him in the hours they'd drifted along the stream and, like a worm in an apple, it was burrowing slowly around his guts.

The scene at the cabin kept playing over and over in his mind. He couldn't stop seeing the man with the gun. The way he'd smiled when their gazes met. The look on his face when the ladder tipped. The table leg sticking out of his neck.

He hadn't recognised the man but knew without a doubt who had sent him. And that's what had caused the worm in the apple. The realisation. Nolan and Vanessa had been trying to *catch* him, but the dude at the cabin . . .

He tried to block his next thought from forming but couldn't stop it. Clearly the situation had changed or he'd been wrong about their intentions in the first place. Either way it meant that Reece . . .

He stifled a groan. At least Corey had gotten away. He was safe in a hospital somewhere. Being looked after by kind doctors and smiling nurses, getting all sorts of food and attention.

Assuming he had survived his injuries.

Injuries sustained from . . .

Wincing at the gut punch the thought delivered, he struggled to force his attention elsewhere. Beside him, the woman took back the water bottle and shoved it and the matches into her pack.

'How did you know to bring all this stuff?'

'I always stow a pack of emergency gear in the bottom of the canoe. First aid kit, insect repellent, matches, water bottle and a blanket. Actually, there might even be . . .' She rummaged around. 'A-ha! Here you go, have a granola bar.'

He felt his stomach rebel at the thought. 'No thanks. You have it.'

'Tummy-ache?' Her voice sounded worried. 'You haven't eaten since lunch at the cabin.'

He bowed his head and gave it a shake.

'Still cold?' She moved closer, pulled the blanket up over the back of his neck and left her arm around his shoulders. 'How's that?'

Somehow the gesture only worsened his pain. He bit his lip.

'Jesse, what is it?'

He swiped at his tears. Now that they'd managed to squeeze from his eyes there was just no stopping them. 'I did a bad thing.'

'Oh, sweethcart, I'm sure it's not as bad as all this.'

'Yes, it is. It's terrible, the worst thing ever.'

She hugged him tighter. 'All right, tell me. What did you do?'

'I was supposed to look after somebody. They were little and I was meant to take care of them, but I didn't.'

'Who were you meant to take care of?'

'My . . . friends.' His stomach clenched as though someone had stepped on it.

Zack, where are you? The voice from his dream. Reece and Corey screaming as he pushed them into the chamber of the idling truck.

'I ran away and left them.' He turned his face into her neck. 'And now they're probably dead.'

The woman said nothing. She didn't try to stop him or refute what he'd said. She didn't tell him everything would be all right, maybe because she knew it wouldn't. After what he'd done, how could it ever? Rocking gently, she just let him cry.

Eventually the touch of her hand quelled his sobs. His breathing slowed. The tears prickled his cheeks as they dried. To the feel of her gently stroking his hair, in the knowledge she would still be there when he woke, he let himself drift towards the edge of sleep.

The tumbler exploded against the wall, the last of its twelve-year-old Chivas Regal spraying a starburst across the panelling. Tragg grabbed his phone and keyed in a number. Though it violated established procedure and could possibly put the receiver at risk, he couldn't wait a minute longer.

After Farrell's initial call informing him of Nolan's deception, Tragg had received only one other update – when the two men had returned to the woman's cabin where Ballinger was supposedly hiding. Since then he'd waited interminable hours to hear the matter had been resolved, but the follow-up call had not yet come. Now, at going on 1 am, he had to concede it wasn't going to.

The phone rang out and switched to a private message bank. He hung up without recording a message. Something was wrong. Farrell would never have left him hanging like this.

He keyed in a second number. There was no other choice. He had to go to Deadwater himself and see to things personally. Something he clearly should have done when he'd left the damn hospital!

The call was answered and Vanessa's sleepy voice said, 'Yeah?'

'Where are you?'

'Tragg? At the motel. Why? I caught up with Quinlan and Stokes like you said. I'll –'

'Still no word from Farrell or Nolan. We're going back.'

'What? *We*? Why do –'

'You know the area.'

A rustle of covers as she sat up in bed. 'What about these kids?'

'Leave 'em with the others. Pick you up in a couple of hours. Be ready.'

Chapter 41

The screaming came from far away. It threatened to weave itself into his dreams, twisting them towards the realm of nightmare. But the unfamiliar was too distracting. A woman's voice. In the end it dragged him from the pit of sleep and spewed him into confused consciousness.

Zack looked around. She was standing in the half-light at the forest's edge, shrieking her protests across the water. 'No! Let him go! Leave him alone!' Her terror suffused him and for a moment he thought they were under attack. But peering closer he saw she was alone. He pushed himself up.

The new perspective only confirmed it – there was no one else there. The last he'd been aware she was lying beside him, spooned against his back for warmth. Now she appeared to be sleepwalking, trapped in some horrible alternate reality.

'Please! I'll give you whatever you want! Just let him go!'

Sickened by the pain he heard in her voice, he struggled to his feet. Only to find he had no idea what to do. Weren't you never supposed to wake a sleepwalker?

'Stop! He can't swim! No! Don't!'

He watched, dumbstruck. Was this the same woman who'd

beaten two men with kick-ass weapons, climbed out a window, guided him through a pitch-black forest, and then down a stream past dangerous animals? She'd held it together through all of that and now here she was freaking out over something that wasn't even there?

'Hey!' he called out to her. 'Over here!'

She spun around, a silhouette against the shimmering water. Arms outflung. Body braced. Did she even see him?

'Jesse!'

Suddenly she was flying towards him, stumbling over obstacles in the dark. She dropped to her knees, threw her arms around his waist and sobbed her words against his chest. 'Jesse, oh God!'

Zack stiffened at the sound of the name. Who the hell was this kid? Was it the boy in the picture he'd found in her drawer? If so, what happened to him? Did the man in the picture take him away? She'd been shouting, 'Let him go, leave him alone.' Had someone hurt him? Did he die?

'Jesse, my God, you're really all right?'

Zack clenched his jaw. If the kid was dead why did she keep thinking he was Jesse? The boy in the picture had dark hair and eyes like he did. But they weren't the same. Couldn't she see that? What was wrong with her?

Another thought slapped him and he reeled from the blow. All those things she'd said and done, they hadn't been for him at all. It hadn't been Zack she'd held and rocked, it hadn't been his face she'd stroked so tenderly. What was so great about Jesse anyway? Why hadn't anyone ever loved him this much?

All at once he was fighting to pull from her embrace. But at the sound of something rustling in the undergrowth he froze again. It was probably just a possum or an owl but it doused his anger with a frigid splash of realisation – men were after him trying to kill him, he was still really weak, he had no idea where the hell he was and the only reason this woman was helping was because she thought he was someone else.

The last of his anger ebbed away. How could he have been such a dummy? The question he should be asking himself was, how long did he have? Because the minute she snapped out of her fantasy trip she'd ditch him just like everyone else. She'd never go on risking her life for a reject like him. So rather than insist she see him as Zack, the smart thing to do would be to play along. At least till he was strong enough to make it on his own again.

'Jesse, you're all right? They didn't hurt you?'

'I'm fine. Honest.' Why did the words burn his throat so badly?

'They . . . they had you. They were going to . . . they would've –'

'Yeah, but they didn't.' He blinked the acid sting from his eyes. 'Because you got me away from them. You saved me. See.'

She lifted her gaze. Crying and laughing she swept her hands over his face as though to confirm her eyes weren't deceiving her. 'My precious boy. You're really here.'

Zack gazed into her upturned face. Even if it had been a product of insanity, her courage had made her a hero in his eyes. If she needed so desperately for him to be Jesse, then how could he not?

He cleared his throat. 'Yeah, Mom. I'm here.'

Chapter 42

Mist rose from the dawn-lit track and seeped through the trees on either side. Tragg eased the Jaguar slowly forward, tearing the gossamer membrane to shreds.

'This guy you sent to help Nolan,' Vanessa said, rubbing her eyes – she'd barely slept on the night-long drive – 'he's not one of Lazaro's people.'

'No, he's freelance.'

'And you trust him?'

'Like that drop-kick faggot boyfriend of yours?' A soft chuckle from the man at the wheel. 'Farrell and I go way back, grew up in Roxbury together. Closer to me than my own brother.'

Vanessa peered through the swirling tendrils. 'How do you know they came this way?'

'Farrell's last update. Man always gives his location, he's thorough like that.' An admiring smile appeared on Tragg's face. 'If there's one person in this whole frigging world I'd give my life for it'd be Jake.'

A four-wheel drive appeared through the mist, standing amid a grove of saplings. Tragg pulled his car up behind it and shut off the engine.

Taking her cue from his silent exit, Vanessa got out and, with weapon poised, began circling the Cherokee with him. It appeared undamaged, at least on the outside. Clearly, the two men had arrived here safely. They'd just never left.

From opposite sides they stepped to the windows. A brown pig skin jacket lay on the front passenger's seat. Vanessa recognised it at once as Nolan's. Seeing it filled her with a sense of foreboding.

She shot a look across at Tragg, noting the tight forward thrust of his jaw. Without a word he turned away and started through the woods. She hurried after him.

They followed the track – a driveway she realised now – as it swung a wide arc. A few moments later they were crouched in the undergrowth before a cabin. Most of the glass had been blown from its windows and the bullet-riddled front door stood wide open.

At a nod from Tragg they started towards it, across the clearing and up the steps. They paused at the door, then burst inside with weapons raised.

All was silent. What remained of the furnishings lay in splinters, shards and billows of stuffing. They eased through the room, around the couch and stopped at the sight of what lay beyond.

Vanessa heard a strange sound escape Tragg's throat – half-moan, half-growl. He approached the body cradled in its bed of shattered wood that had once been a kitchen table. The remains of only one leg stood upright, held in place by the torn flesh and bone of Farrell's neck.

Under the guise of searching the rest of the house, Vanessa quickly walked away. Though she'd taken no part in what had happened here she felt suddenly and keenly at risk, threatened by the sheer force of dark energy radiating off Tragg in squalls.

In passing she noticed a small bottle sitting on the end table beside the couch. She picked it up, read the label, saw who the prescribing doctor was. At once she turned. But, seeing the storm still masking Tragg's features, thought better of speaking and slipped the bottle in her pocket instead.

She went through each of the rooms in turn. After giving him what time she thought he'd need, she returned to Tragg to report her findings. 'No sign of Ballinger or the woman anywhere in the house.'

Tragg stood quaking. In a voice more animal than human he said, 'Find Nolan.'

Vanessa shuddered as she backed away. 'I'll check outside.'

Chapter 43

Light flickered across his eyelids, teasing them open. Zack took a deep breath of pine-scented air, scraped the dead leaves off the side of his face and rolled onto his back.

The sun winked down at him through shifting pin holes in the forest canopy. It was well past dawn, probably later than the crazy lady had wanted them to sleep, but who cared? Where did they have to be anyway? As long as no one had followed them here they were perfectly safe.

At the thought, he pushed himself up. Apart from the canoe at the water's edge there was no sign of human presence as far as he could see. He cocked his head to the woods behind them. Not a sound other than the chatter of birds and the soft sighing of wind through the branches.

He gazed down at the woman beside him. She seemed so peaceful, her head cradled on one of her arms, the fingers of her other hand curled beneath her chin. Pine needles and leaf litter clung to her hair but somehow it only made her look prettier, like some kind of fairy. Did he need to wake her? After the night she'd had she probably needed to sleep a bit more.

He peeled off the blanket, covered her with it, pushed himself up and limped towards the water.

The stream was wider and slower here, more like a pond. Huge slabs of granite stood along the shore, ranging in size from a chest-high boulder off to the left, to the jumble of smaller ones on the right. The canoe lay between them, marking the only clear path to the shallows.

As he walked towards it, a fish broke the surface, leapt a foot into the air and fell back with a splash. Ripples spread outward till they reached the reeds and cat tails beyond the rocks.

Why did fish do that? he wondered idly, bending down to wash the sleep from his eyes. Probably for the same reason human beings jumped into water. Because it was fun.

A strange sound suddenly broke through his musings, a faint pulsing, like distant music. He rose, spun around but couldn't see the source. Until he looked up. In the clear patch of sky above the pond a V-formation of Canada geese winged their way south announcing their passage with boisterous honking.

Zack smiled as he watched them fly over. When they'd passed he stood marvelling at the pink horse-tail clouds that curled across the lightening sky. It wasn't so bad out here really. He almost wished they could stay in the woods. As long as the weather was nice like this. As long as they were together and could find enough to eat and no one bothered them.

He turned and looked back at the sleeping form beside the fire. But they wouldn't be together for very much longer. Sooner or later – probably sooner – the woman would see him for what he was. A useless throw-away who wasn't as smart or cute or brave or any of the other things Jesse surely was.

As if she'd heard him, the woman stirred. She threw off the blanket and sat up quickly. On her feet in an instant, she stood looking around in confusion. After a moment she turned towards the water.

She seemed to see him and started running, but ten feet away she slowed to a stop. Probably wondering what to say to him. After his breakdown the night before he could understand. In fact, what was he going to say to her? Should he mention her nightmares? Could he ask her about them? Would she even remember?

Zack took a step and opened his mouth.

She stopped him dead with her whispered command. 'Jesse, don't move. Stay right where you are and don't make a sound.'

Chapter 44

'Careful, there are probably more of them around.'
Nolan heard the words through a red haze of pain. A familiar voice, seemingly distant, but one he had to reach at all costs. He struggled towards it, pushed through the fog, opened his eyes.

The form standing over him slowly took shape. Dark hair, female build . . .

Tears stung his eyes. 'Vanessa, thank God.' He licked his lips, tasting salt and dirt. 'My leg . . . it's broken. Been here all night. Couldn't . . . get the damn thing off.'

Nolan fell back. He was cold. So cold. Just the simple act of raising his head had brought him close to blacking out again.

The pain of the steel jaws clamping his leg, grinding his splintered bones together, was beyond enormous. Each time he moved, a firestorm seared up his leg, along his spine, until it consumed his entire body.

Over the hours he'd lain there he'd tried repeatedly to open the trap. But he just couldn't force himself into a position where he could exert the required leverage. Sometime in the darkest hours of night, when the pain had dulled and numbness set in, he'd grown convinced he was going to die. In this stinking, rotten hell-hole of a place. Phillip Nolan was going to buy it.

He'd thought about praying, asking forgiveness. Perhaps he had, he couldn't remember. But now, blessedly, it didn't matter. Vanessa was here. She hadn't gone off without him after all. How she'd found him he couldn't imagine and cared even less. All that mattered was that she had.

He opened his eyes again searching for that image of hope and reassurance. But something was wrong. She hadn't moved. She was just standing there looking down at him. Her face devoid of all compassion.

'For Christ's sake, help me.'

Without a word she stepped aside and another figure took her place. Nolan felt all hope seep away into the ground beneath him.

'Hey there, buddy.' The man's smile was a work of pure evil.

'Tragg. Oh God, please, you gotta help me.'

'Well, sure I will. That's why I'm here.'

The false assurance stole the last of his courage. Nolan sobbed. 'I know I screwed up, I know I lied but . . . Oh, man, please. I can't feel my foot.'

'No? How about now?'

Nolan screamed.

Darkness returned.

Thirty minutes later Vanessa walked cautiously up the cabin's front steps. Throughout her comprehensive search of the area she'd been dogged by the alternate screams and silences of Tragg's interrogation of Nolan. But ten minutes ago she'd heard a single echoing gunshot and knew Nolan was finally out of his misery.

She hadn't wanted to return to the cabin before that moment for fear Tragg, in the blackness of his current mood, might turn his rage on her as well. Now that he'd vented the worst of his anger, she felt it relatively safe to enter. She crossed the porch and peered inside.

Tragg was there, standing once again over Farrell's body. He didn't stir as she stepped through the door, didn't look around as she crossed the room. Assuming he hadn't noticed her, she stood uncertainly beside the couch.

'What did you find?'

Despite having half-expected to hear it, his voice made her jump. She cleared her throat. 'They headed into the woods on foot. I picked up their trail leading down to a stream but there weren't any tracks on the other side. Could be the woman had a boat or canoe.'

Tragg stood another moment in silence. Then he stooped to examine the wooden ladder that lay full-length over Farrell's body. Gently he pried the dead man's fingers from the top-most rung. He inspected the brackets fixed to its shafts then looked up at the loft to which they'd been bolted.

'Tear this place apart. I want an address book, letters, computer files, emails – anything with the name and address of someone this bitch might go to for help.'

He prodded one of the holes in the bracket and a loose screw fell out into his hand. He clenched it in his fist. 'And while you're at it, find me a map. I want to know where that stream ends up.'

Chapter 45

Shyler stood frozen. The rifle. Where was it? Dear God, she'd left it back by the fire!

If she ran for it now the moose might charge. At the moment it was simply watching them, but that would change the instant it felt threatened. And to make matters worse – what the animal perhaps hadn't noticed yet – was that Jesse, poised amid a break in the rocks, was blocking its only access to land.

Shyler motioned him to hold where he was, then leaned to one side to see around him. The bull stood in shallows not ten yards beyond, head high, nostrils flaring – a creature she would, at any other time, have considered magnificent. Now all she could see were the massive antlers, the body nearly seven feet high at the shoulders.

Her stomach dropped. Even if Jesse were one hundred per cent healthy he couldn't outrun a charging moose over open ground. He wouldn't make it to the nearest tree, let alone the fire.

Legs trembling, she hissed her instructions. 'When I tell you, run for that boulder. If you can't get up on it, circle around it. Keep it between you and him. Understand?'

Jesse's nod was barely perceptible. Despite her warning to remain motionless, he'd shot a quick glance over his shoulder and now knew the monster lurking behind him. His eyes were huge in his ashen face. He was hardly breathing.

But his fear would work in his favour at this point. If he just stood frozen a few moments longer . . .

The bull snorted and lowered its head. Swinging its hind-quarters around, it charged.

Spray flew before it as it lunged for shore.

'Run!' she yelled and started forward.

Jesse veered, taking uneven strides towards the boulder. Even at its present lumbering gait, the giant was gaining. Once it cleared the resistance of the water . . .

Shyler roared and waved her arms. Never in her dreams would she have imagined herself playing chicken with a charging moose. But a brute this size surely wouldn't get challenged often. If she could startle it, even just confuse it, she might buy Jesse the seconds he needed.

The bull hadn't slowed. Heading straight for her, it broke from the water. She turned and ran. Her best hope now was to lead it away.

Ten paces on, she dared a look back. Jesse had reached the massive rock, but with no footholds he couldn't climb up. As she'd instructed, he started around it. But the bull had fixed on this new moving target and swerved to follow him.

Shyler cut left, paralleling the animal's course. Jesse vanished behind the boulder; the bull slowed, sniffing the air. Though hardly enough protection to suit her, the rock was proving an effective barrier. As long as Jesse stayed out of sight –

She froze in horror. A small running figure had appeared further left, heading across the rocky spit that banked the stream's inlet to the pond. *Jesse, no!* She sprinted after him.

Even as she angled down to meet him, the bull emerged through the rocks and saw him. By the time she reached him, the animal had resumed its charge.

Jesse stumbled; she helped him up. The spit was littered with river stones and cluttered with jumbles and slabs of granite. The moose hadn't gained any distance yet. But the same loose footing that was slowing its progress was slowing theirs.

She glanced around. The forest was now even further away. Would they make it before the bull was on them? Even if they did it was no guarantee. Yet surely better than out in the open.

She grabbed Jesse's arm and pulled him aside.

'No! This way!' He broke free and started in the other direction.

She darted after him. 'Jesse! Wait!'

Ahead, a cluster of car-sized rocks stood tightly spaced amid the rubble. A fallen pine tree leaned across them, creating a small but protected crevice. All at once, she understood.

They reached the shelter with seconds to spare but one of the branches blocked the entrance. Together they pulled it until it snapped. Her bandage caught. She wrenched her arm free, feeling something tear at her flesh. Then, to the clatter of approaching hooves, they pushed through into the tiny space.

Wrapped in the woman's solid embrace, Zack stared down at the monster's muzzle snorting just inches from his foot. They'd huddled together for several minutes as the bull tried various ways to reach them.

With each failed attempt he grew more relieved. Now that the danger was largely past, he felt embarrassed being held in her arms. He pushed himself forward and swung around to sit facing her.

Shyler did her best to sound stern. 'You, mister, are in big trouble.'

'Why? What'd I do?'

'I thought I told you to stay by that boulder.'

'I couldn't! There was this massive rock on the other side blocking the way. If I'd stayed there that thing would've had me trapped.'

A long quivery sigh escaped her. 'Okay, you're off the hook. But what made you head in this direction?'

'I saw all these rocks and figured there had to be a place to hide.'

'Oh, did you? Well, you were right.' She reached out and brushed some dirt from his face. 'Clever boy. You were very brave.'

'I was?'

'Are you kidding? You saved us. I was headed back into the woods. And I'm not all that sure we would've made it.'

The smile lingered, her face glowing with pride and affection. He loved it when she looked at him like that. God, why couldn't things stay this way? Why couldn't they each just pretend to be what the other one wanted?

Turning away, he checked the entrance. No muzzle, no sound of movement. 'You think he's gone?'

'Probably. But we'll sit tight for a few more minutes just to be sure.'

Zack laid his head back, swallowing against a wave of nausea. The throbbing had started in his leg again and the longer he sat, the worse it got. 'It's hot in here.'

Again she reached out and touched his face. When she drew back this time her smile had vanished.

Chapter 46

Chase drove slowly down the wooded track. From the map Patricia O'Neil had drawn him he'd found the old logging trail without any problem. Locating Shyler's cabin from here would simply be a matter of taking the next turn-off he came to.

A narrow track appeared on his right and he made the turn, slowing at the sight of a sunlit clearing just beyond. Shafts of golden rod, purple loosestrife and Queen Ann's lace swayed in the Indian summer breeze. Sumac lined the meadow's verge like a ring of fire.

Chase drove on, moving at his previous turtle's pace. Truth be told, he wasn't lingering to enjoy the scenery. He hadn't yet decided how best to approach Shyler with his concerns. Given how remote her cabin was and the extremes she'd gone to to keep him from finding it, he couldn't very well drive up and say, 'Hey there, I just happened to be in the neighbourhood and thought I'd drop in.'

What's more, she might consider it an invasion of privacy that he'd gone to see her mother. Was she in hiding as much from her family as everyone else? Was it her choice, and not Patricia's, that the two had so little contact with each other?

The problem was he was flying blind. He had no idea how profound Shyler's condition actually was. Or even if she had one, for that matter. There was still the chance he was wrong about her and all her 'symptoms' had a perfectly logical explanation, though at this stage he very much doubted it.

What little Patricia had told him could explain some aspects of Shyler's behaviour but certainly not all. Guilt over her father's death might contribute to her being reclusive, even self-harming, but he couldn't see it causing her hyper-vigilance and heightened anxiety. Those were more symptoms of PTSD.

Yes, post-traumatic stress disorder did seem a better fit in some ways. But the problem with that was, her father dying of a heart attack, however hard that might have been for her, just didn't seem traumatic enough to have been the cause. Which meant there were still some pieces missing from the puzzle. A lot of pieces.

Spotting a cabin through the trees, Chase took a deep breath. He'd just have to wing it. Do the best he could to gain Shyler's trust and let her know help was available if she wanted it. He couldn't force it on her if she didn't. At the very least he could check her injuries and make sure she hadn't done any more damage to herself.

He pulled around the front of the cabin, came to a stop and shut off his engine. Any doubts he was in the right place were allayed by the sight of Shyler's old Chevy standing at the foot of the cabin's steps. But something was odd. The car had not one but two flat tyres. She must have been driving over some pretty rough terrain to have caused that much damage.

With a frown he climbed from the Land Rover and stood, taking in his surroundings. There was a strangely desolate feel to the place. The cabin's front door stood open but the area within looked dark and lifeless. There wasn't a sound above the wind and the birds. Steeling himself, he started forward.

Disquiet exploded into all-out fear as he climbed the steps. The windows were smashed. Glass lay strewn across the porch. The spots on the logs he'd thought to be knots were actually bullet holes. He ran inside.

The interior confirmed his darkest fears. Rushing through the bullet-torn living area he stumbled to a halt at the sight of the man lying dead on the floor.

Chase stood gaping. He had treated victims of all sorts of injuries, attacks with weapons of every kind, but never had he been first on a murder scene. Somehow it was different. Seeing the violence laid out before him, frozen like a snapshot, chilled him through. At the thought there might be more bodies here, other victims . . .

'Shyler!'

And at once he was running to search the cabin.

Chapter 47

Gravel spewed from the Land Rover's tyres as Chase took a corner at high speed. His office was just a half mile further – the nearest place he knew of with a phone, since Shyler's cabin hadn't had one. He had to report his gruesome discovery to the police.

Driving one-handed, he tried again to get through on his mobile. Still no signal. Either the cloud cover was too thick or it was all the trees. He threw the phone on the seat beside him but it bounced to the floor.

Looking up he saw the car was drifting, nearly off the road, and yanked it over. He fought again to rein himself back. It wouldn't help anyone if he ploughed into a tree before making his call. Certainly nothing could help the victims. But the memory of what he'd seen at the cabin, and what more it could mean, kept spurring him faster.

He'd found the second man lying outside. The sight of the massive trap clamped to his leg had made him feel sick. With the thought there were more of the things around he'd suddenly felt he was standing in a mine field. Before moving closer he'd picked up a branch and used it to test every patch of ground he intended to step on.

When he'd finally got a good look at the victim, he'd made a bewildering discovery. While the man in the cabin had died hours ago – twelve at least, judging from the rigor – the one in the trap appeared to have been shot much more recently. From yesterday afternoon to this morning. Had the siege gone on for that long? Or had someone come back and finished the second man hours later? If so, why?

But by far the most disturbing fact he'd uncovered was that there was no sign of Shyler anywhere. Both her car and truck had been disabled so either she'd fled into the forest on foot or there'd been more men there and they'd taken her away. And the heart-stopping prospect of this last possibility was what had driven him here at such speed.

He slowed to pull into his office parking lot then sped 'round the back. That monstrous trap! Who in their right mind would set a bear trap just yards from their back door? It had to have been deliberately placed there as a booby trap. Which meant Shyler had to have expected trouble. Did she know all this time that someone was after her? Was that why she lived such a reclusive existence? Perhaps there was a logical reason for her behaviour after all.

Skidding to a stop, he leapt from the car and ran for the building. He'd unlocked the back door and was halfway down the hall to the front when the sound of breaking glass stopped him dead.

He stood in mute shock. Yes, it had come from *inside* the building. More muffled noises now. Bottles clinking. Drawers opening. It sounded like someone was in the treatment room. What the hell was going on? Was the entire area under siege?

The store room was two steps back on his left. He ducked inside it, scanned the shelves, and grabbed the snow shovel off its hook.

Recalling the two dead men at the cabin – one with a bullet

hole in his forehead, the other still clutching a high-powered rifle – he hesitated before going on. But despite the timing, these couldn't be the same men who were after Shyler. Most likely they were kids. At worst an addict. Didn't they know he didn't keep narcotics on the premises?

At the end of the hall he paused to survey the reception area. Elaine's work station looked undisturbed. Nothing seemed amiss in the waiting room opposite. The sounds were definitely coming from the treatment room. He inched around the corner and, brandishing the shovel, stepped through its door.

A slight figure, possibly a woman, stood with her back to him, hunched before the medicine locker.

'What the hell do you think you're doing?'

She rose and spun around.

'Shyler! You're all right! I – What on earth . . .'

Glass was everywhere. Some from the window she'd smashed to get in, the rest from the shattered cabinet doors. What was she after? If someone was chasing her why come here? Why tear up his treatment room? Lifting his gaze to search her face, he noticed for the first time what she was holding.

Slowly he raised one hand in the air. 'Easy now. Everything's going to be all right. I didn't realise it was you. I'll just set this down over here.' He stepped aside and placed the snow shovel on his desk.

Her rifle never wavered from its aim at his chest.

'Shyler, it's me. You don't need that.'

She stood unmoving, eyes wide. She really was spooked. Understandable after what he'd found at her cabin. Had she killed those men? Had it been self-defence? He wanted to think so.

'Are you all right?' He scanned her quickly, spotted the blood. 'Your arm –' But the instant he moved towards her, the rifle came up again.

'It's okay, I just want to help. It looks like you might have torn out some stitches. We can fix that. But I need to know, are you hurt anywhere else?'

She just kept staring. Not the look of someone in shock but of one trying to reach an important decision.

'Please, answer me, are you hurt?' He was fighting to smother a fresh wave of panic. If she'd been shot . . . Was *that* why she'd come? 'Shyler, for God's sake –'

'I need more medicine.'

He blinked at her. 'Medicine?'

'The tablets you gave me the other night. The antibiotics.'

'What . . .?' He did his best to go with the flow. Surely this would all become clear in a minute. 'What happened to the ones I gave you? You didn't take them all at once, did you?'

'I didn't take any of them. They weren't for me.'

When her gaze flicked aside he turned to follow it. Behind the door sat a dark-haired boy about ten years old, face flushed, brown eyes glassy, leaning to one side as though in pain. It took him a moment to register who the boy had to be. 'Your son?'

'Yes.'

'He has a fever?'

'The last few days. He has an infected cut on his leg.'

'Will you let me examine him?'

That look again. Uncertain, debating, filled with distrust. Then she nodded and lowered the rifle.

Chapter 48

Zack stiffened, trying not to shrink away. The man's taut body angled above him like a leaning tower.

As though sensing the effect his size was having, the doctor pulled over a little stool, sat down on it and put out his hand. 'Hi, I'm Chase. What's your name?'

The 'z' sound was nearly out of his mouth before he stopped it. 'Jesse,' he answered. With Tragg still after him it seemed the smart thing to go on being somebody else.

'Nice to meet you, Jesse.'

The man smiled more with his eyes than his mouth, eyes blue as marbles with rooftop brows. Now that he was sitting, he wasn't so scary. But his voice helped too. Even when the crazy lady – Shyler, it was good to finally know her name! – even when Shyler pointed her gun at him he spoke really calm. Like old lady Harriet trying to coax her cat from a tree.

Zack shook the hand extended towards him. So this was the man who'd treated Corey and sent him to the hospital. He hoped he'd spoken as softly then as he was now – Corey would have been so scared. The impulse to ask about his foster-brother nearly overcame him, but he couldn't give himself away.

'Your mom says you've got an infected leg. Mind if I have a look?'

Zack hesitated, then stuck out his foot.

The doctor gently pushed up his jeans, removed the bandage and examined his cut. It was hard to see any change in his face but Zack thought he saw those rooftop eyebrows scrunch up a bit.

'Is it sore?'

'Better than it was. But . . . I think it's getting worse again.'

'Your mom gave you medicine. Can you remember how many of the pills you took?'

'Two, I think.'

'Three,' Shyler corrected from the window. 'He had his first the night you gave them to me, one yesterday morning and the third at lunch.'

The doctor tossed the old bandage in the bin and began replacing it with a fresh one. 'Why'd you stop taking them? What happened to the rest of the medicine?'

'We left it at the cabin.' Zack shifted, knowing what the next question was likely to be. 'We had to leave in kind of a hurry.'

'Why can't you just go back there and get it?'

Zack glanced at Shyler but she'd turned away to peer out the window.

Chase sat back and addressed them both. 'Okay, I know what happened out at your cabin. The fact is, I just came from there.'

Shyler spun around. 'You *what*?'

'The place is shot up and two dead men are lying in the wreckage. Maybe you can tell me what's going on.'

'But how . . .?' Her confusion changed to resolve. 'You're not calling the police.'

Chase eyed the rifle that had swung his way. 'You aren't serious.'

242

'How did you know where my cabin was?'

'I talked to your mother. I got her name from one of Doctor Muir's old files.'

'Why?' She stepped closer. 'Why did you want to know where I lived?'

'Because you lied to me. The address you gave me the other night doesn't exist.' He got to his feet, gently took hold of her injured arm and drew her aside. 'Because I was worried about you,' he whispered. 'I knew this cut was self-inflicted.'

She looked at the bandage, now in tatters, then back at him. No denial.

'Shyler, please, what's going on?'

She slid her arm from his grasp, her expression giving nothing away. Was she wondering why he would be so concerned about just another patient? Did she sense his feelings ran deeper than that? Or did she think he was one of the men who were after her?

'Just take care of Jesse.'

He watched her walk off. Fighting the urge to press her for answers, he opened a drawer, grabbed the thermometer and returned to his patient.

'Jesse, tell me, do you hurt in here?' He pointed discreetly to his own groin.

The boy nodded.

'Anywhere else?'

'It's kind of like I fell off my bike. I hurt a little bit everywhere.'

'That's a good description. I know just what you mean.' He shook the thermometer then held it out. 'Just hold this under your tongue for a minute.'

As he checked the boy's pulse he glanced aside. Shyler had resumed her vigil. With a white-knuckled grip on her twenty-two, she sat staring anxiously at the road.

He had no problem reading her thoughts. Were they out there? Had they followed them here? The same questions had occurred to him. And her single rifle wasn't much comfort. That and his snow shovel would hardly stand up to the type of destruction he'd seen at the cabin. He could understand it might take her some time to trust him. The question was, how much did they have?

He withdrew the thermometer and read the bad news. 'I saw they slashed the tyres on your cars back at the cabin. How did you get here?'

'Canoe,' Jesse said. 'We ran through the woods till we got to this stream, then Sh – I mean Mom – told me to get in the boat and we floated away.'

Chase nodded and managed a smile. The boy seemed willing enough to talk. Perhaps he could get more answers from him. 'When was this that you went down the stream?'

'Last night. After . . . what happened at the cabin.'

Chase met his gaze. 'You want to talk about it?'

He shook his head.

'All right, so you floated down the stream. Then what?'

'We camped by a pond overnight. Then this morning we walked here.'

'You're talking about the pond behind this building? That's a fair hike; you must be exhausted.' Chase reached up and gently palpated beneath the boy's jaw. 'From the time you left the cabin to the time you got here did you see anyone?'

'Nope. No way. Unless you count mooses.'

'So you're fairly certain you weren't followed?'

'I'm positive we weren't.'

'Well, that's good news, eh?' He started to lower his hands and stopped. Slowly he reached out and drew Jesse's T-shirt collar aside. Contusions encircled the boy's throat.

'Jesse, you've got some bruising here. How did this happen?'

For a moment Zack couldn't think what he meant. Then he remembered – Nolan's attack. No way could he tell the doc about that. 'I . . . I fell.'

'These marks go right across the front of your neck. Did you fall on something?' Chase leaned closer. A chill washed over him at the unmistakable sight of a thumb print. 'Jesse, did someone –'

The sound of a car engine cut off his words.

Shyler gasped and jumped to her feet. 'Oh, God, it's them!'

Chapter 49

On the sun-drenched lane in front of the office a second car had pulled up behind the first. Men were getting out – two from the first car, two from the second; she could see more silhouettes still inside. If they all had guns . . .

Shyler took aim at the man running up the path towards the office.

'No!' Chase shoved the barrel to the sill.

'It's them!'

'No, it's not. They're loggers. There must have been an accident on one of the lines.' His voice, now calm, seemed a lifeline she could cling to.

A pounding on the front door made her jump. She tried to turn but he still held the barrel.

'That's Harvey Lediston. Trust me, I know him, he's one of the foremen.'

'Doctor Hadley, you in there?' came a muffled voice.

A third car sped into the parking lot. Shyler turned in time to see it disappear around the side of the building. She looked up into Chase's calm gaze. If he was lying it meant they were now surrounded.

'Shyler, I have to go and see what they –'

'No!'

He held both her arms. 'Listen to me. Someone's been hurt. Maybe several people. I have to help them.'

She hesitated, suddenly uncertain what frightened her more – that he might be lying or that she had no choice but to trust him.

He pointed towards a second door off the treatment room. 'Just through there is a room with a bed. Take Jesse in there and have him lie down. You'll be perfectly safe. No one will see you.'

'You'll tell them we're here.' Her protests were weakening. Whatever he said she had to believe him.

'I won't. I promise.'

Men's urgent voices were coming down the hall from the back of the building. He didn't seem to hear them. His gaze held hers as though nothing could hurry him from her side.

'You'll call the police,' she said, pleading to be denied.

He nodded towards the sick room. 'There's a phone on the desk in there. You'll know if anyone makes a call out because the light will come on. If you're worried, pick up and listen in.'

'Doctor Hadley!' The voices were closer.

With a final desperate scan of his face, she lowered the rifle. 'Jesse, come on.'

As Chase stepped away, Jesse hobbled towards her. Shyler wrapped an arm around his shoulder and guided him through the sick room door. Before she closed it she looked back at Chase.

He too had turned, concern and reassurance in his eyes. 'I'll come and check on you as soon as I can.'

The car pitched and bounced as Tragg negotiated a rocky stretch in the forest track. Opening the map she'd taken from the cabin,

Vanessa again found the squiggly line that marked their present course.

'The stream flows into a pond just a mile and a half from the town's main road. If they did have a boat they'd most likely have left it at that point. Why don't we just go straight there?'

'We follow the creek,' Tragg said flatly, never taking his eyes from the trail.

She stifled a sigh. They'd been doing just that for nearly an hour and hadn't covered a quarter of its winding length. 'There's nothing but wilderness between here and there. There's no other place they could've gone.'

'We follow the creek.' This time Tragg did look over at her, his expression chilling. 'We follow every inch of it all the way to wherever it leads. And every time we lose sight of it *you* get to get out and take a hike.'

Vanessa folded her hands over the map. She'd already taken two such hikes. Each time the water disappeared from view he'd made her get out and follow it on foot till stream and trail met up again. Once she'd lost her footing on a stretch of steep, bramble-covered bank. Her boots were now soaking, her socks full of prickles and her face was covered in black-fly bites.

But trying to dissuade the man from his plan was clearly a mistake. She'd been fool enough to think his lingering silence had meant he was over the worst of his fury.

'So what do you say? That sound like a fucking plan to you?'

She stared straight ahead. 'Yeah, sounds fine.'

Chapter 50

Four steps – turn – four steps – back. Four of her strides. That was the entire length of the sick room. After two hours shut up inside it, and on top of all her other fears, Shyler was beginning to feel claustrophobic.

During that time she'd divided her attention between Jesse – now dozing on the bed – the phone, and watching out the window. It appeared Chase had at least told the truth about the men being loggers. So far none of them had burst through the door and tried to kill them. But there was still the matter of the police.

The phone light had come on several times – once when Chase had rung the hospital to summon an ambulance, the rest when the men had called their families to tell of the accident. With her heart in her throat she'd listened in on every call. None of them had been to the police. But that didn't mean they weren't coming. Someone in this building would surely have a mobile.

Yet as bad as that possibility was, there was still a worse one: that the men from the cabin had tracked them here. That they were, even at that moment, gathering outside. She'd certainly given them every chance. By staying in one place she'd allowed them the time to follow their trail and make preparations for a fresh assault. She never should have agreed to stay here this long. They should have left the instant she'd gotten the medicine!

She reached the wall again, turned and surveyed the narrow room. Like many old New England buildings the ceiling was low. So low she could reach up and touch it. Or was that simply her imagination? Just as it might be her imagination that it was now getting lower by the second.

Twisting the rifle stock in her hands she tried to slow her breathing. Ten counts in, ten counts out.

Please, not now.

Beads of sweat broke out on her face. She felt the sudden drenching beneath her armpits, the familiar flutter inside her chest. When the door opened she almost screamed.

Chase slipped silently into the room. 'I'm sorry I couldn't get away sooner but I had to stabilise one of the men.' He went straight to the bed, pulled up the chair and placed a hand on Jesse's forehead.

Shyler stood taking in slow steady breaths. The attack seemed to be easing off. Even the ceiling was slowly receding. Perhaps the brief instant the door had been open . . .

'How has he been?' Chase said.

'Sleeping, mostly.'

At hearing the residual tremor in her voice Chase turned around. 'What about you?'

She nodded, then shrugged.

'You'll have to let me look at that arm later. I'm afraid it's going to need re-suturing.' He pushed to his feet and ran a hand through his dishevelled hair. 'Shyler, I . . .'

She went rigid. 'What?'

'There's an ambulance coming to pick up one of the injured men. It'll be here any minute. When it leaves, I think Jesse should be on it.'

Her eyes widened. 'To a hospital? No.'

'Shyler, listen to me. I didn't get a chance to say this before but I'm afraid Jesse is very sick.'

'Well, of course, he's got a fever but –'

'It's more than a fever. He may be developing septicaemia.'

Fear raked her heart as she turned to stare down at the boy.

'If the infection reaches that stage he'll need to be hospitalised. I don't have the facilities here to care for him properly.'

'But he was getting better. Back at the cabin, his temperature went down when he started the antibiotics.'

'It's certainly an encouraging sign, yes. Unfortunately he missed two doses and his fever's up again. I can't guarantee it'll work a second time.'

Shyler stood weighing all the factors – the chance of infection, the risk of people asking more questions, the possibility they might be followed.

'We'll stay,' she said.

'Shyler, please –'

'You'll treat him here. If he doesn't get better we can take him then.'

'But why take a chance when –'

'You don't know what could happen to him there!'

Chase paused, lowered his voice. 'No, I don't. Can't you tell me?'

When she didn't respond he took a step closer. 'Shyler, I know you have no one. Your father's dead, you're estranged from your mother, your husband's gone. Wouldn't you feel better facing whatever this is with someone helping you?'

His words brought the sting of tears to her eyes. That he should know such things about her – let alone that they were true – seemed an absurd humiliation.

She looked up and met his gaze defiantly. 'I'm not alone. I have Jesse.'

Chapter 51

The bed of dead leaves crunched beneath Vanessa's boots as she kicked it apart. Judging from the still warm remains of the fire, Zack and the woman had been here only a few hours ago. If Tragg had listened to her and come straight here they would have been in time. They could have caught them! But she'd put out her eye with a rusty screwdriver before mentioning that fact to him just at the moment.

She slid a cautious glance at the man as he stood, shoulders stiff, expression grim, inspecting the camp. He hadn't said a word since leaving the car. She almost pitied the two runaways when he finally caught up to them. She turned away.

At the edge of the pond directly below them lay a red canoe. It had to belong to the woman from the cabin because there were no other buildings or people in sight. No fisherman would abandon their only means of transport. Plus there were the tracks. Two sets of footprints – one adult, one child – leading up from the water's edge.

Consulting the map, she faced the direction the pair would have headed after leaving the area. 'This is the closest they could get to town. Just over that hill is the general store, a few houses, the offices of the logging company and the local GP.'

Her thoughts trailed away, diverted by a sudden connection. She reached in her pocket, pulled out the bottle she'd found at the cabin and stared at its label. 'Maybe we should pay the doctor a visit.'

'You feeling sick?'

'No, but I think one of them might be.' She tossed him the bottle. 'I found that at the cabin. They're antibiotics. Bottle holds thirty and there's twenty-seven left. I counted them.'

'So, one of them's got a cold.'

'You don't take that stuff for a cold. It's powerful. I had it for an impacted wisdom tooth once.'

He sent her a glare – get to the point.

'I saw bloody bandages in the trash at the cabin. And there was gauze and a tube of antiseptic cream lying near the couch.'

Tragg returned his gaze to the bottle. 'You think the kid's hurt.'

'Whichever one it is, they'll be feeling sick again fairly soon. Three doses wouldn't have been enough to cure anything.'

He thought a moment. 'It's Sunday. Doc's office won't be open.'

'There might be a contact number on the door, maybe an address. If they're desperate enough they might try to see the doctor at home.'

Tragg clenched the bottle in his fist. 'Let's go.'

Chapter 52

The light in the room was more golden than before. He must have been asleep for quite a while. Shyler still sat at the sick room window, peering out between the partly drawn curtains.

'What's happening?' he said.

She looked around at him, then pulled her chair up beside the bed. 'We're just waiting for the last of the loggers to leave. How are you feeling?'

'Okay,' he lied. 'Still kinda hot.'

'That's the fever. Don't worry, the doctor's taking good care of you.'

Zack shook his head. 'He gives me medicine. *You* take care of me.'

She leaned down and stroked his face. 'You bet.'

For a moment he let himself drift on the feeling. She had more than a couple of marbles missing, yet he trusted her totally. The knot that had tied up his guts for so long almost unravelled. But as always a shadow passed over the sun. 'What's going to happen to us?'

Her smile dimmed. She didn't answer.

'We don't have any money. We don't have a car. We don't even have any other clothes.'

She laced her fingers through his hair and tugged gently. 'Now you listen to me. I don't want you to worry about those sorts of things. That's my job. You just concentrate on getting better. Okay?'

He didn't know what made him do it but suddenly his arms were around her neck. It wouldn't last, he knew it wouldn't; it never did. Maybe that was why he was trying to hold on.

Chase pressed the last strip of tape in place, securing the cardboard over the window. The hole was now sealed against the weather. Tomorrow he would get the glass replaced.

He'd already swept up all the shards and plucked the slivers from the cabinet door. If he was going to abide by Shyler's wishes – something he had vast misgivings about – he had to convince Elaine he had been responsible for the office breakages. Otherwise the first thing she'd do when she came in tomorrow would be call the police. With the matter now sorted he stepped to the sick room door and opened it.

Shyler sat bending over the bed holding Jesse in a tight embrace. Though her gaze flicked across to see who had entered she made no move to pull away.

Chase waited. After a moment she laid the boy back and he took a step closer. 'Everyone's gone.'

The pair stared up at him, Shyler with her arm still draped protectively over her son's chest while holding the rifle in her other hand. By the red-rimmed look of Jesse's eyes Chase sensed he'd interrupted something.

'I'm sorry it took me so long. After the second ambulance left I still had the minor injuries to deal with. Then I had to wait for the last man's wife to come and pick him up.'

Again no answer. With the rigid wariness of prey for the hunter they simply watched him.

He stood a moment tugging his earlobe then threw up a hand. 'Well, I don't know about you two but I'm famished.'

Their wariness dropped a notch to uncertainty.

'We've got a kitchen here, but there's not much in it besides tea and coffee, and the general store's closed. So you have your choice – you can either let me run home and bring you back something –'

'You're not going anywhere,' Shyler whispered.

'Or,' he continued, ignoring her words, 'you can come there with me.'

She blinked at him as though he'd gone mad. He couldn't blame her. An hour ago, when he'd first had the thought, he'd felt the same way. But further contemplation had changed his mind.

After seeing how agitated she'd become just from having the loggers here, and knowing that tomorrow the office would be open . . . Well, he couldn't imagine she'd cope any better with patients coming and going all day. Armed with a rifle and in an agitated state she might injure someone, if only accidentally.

But at home, in a quieter, safer environment, she might relax. Perhaps even enough to let him call the police. And since there was little chance the pair had been followed he wouldn't be placing his father at risk.

'Jesse needs to eat if he's going to recover,' he reasoned softly. The last thing he wanted was to make her feel pressured.

Shyler turned to the bleary-eyed boy.

'I am kinda hungry,' Zack confessed.

'That's a good sign.' Chase looked at Shyler. 'What do you say? You can even stay there. I've got two spare rooms, both with beds, and I can bring everything with me I need to treat him.'

'Do you live with anyone?'

'Just my father. But he's in a wheelchair and never comes upstairs, which is where you'll be. He'll never even see you.'

She reached out again and cupped the boy's face. As though gaining courage and strength from the contact, she finally nodded.

Chapter 53

A cold front had moved in since they'd left the pond. Rain glazed the windshield, reducing their view of the doctor's office to a house-sized blur. In the waning light the place looked deserted, but the sign near the gate gave the doctor's name, address and phone number.

Vanessa knew his name already, of course, but saw no reason to mention that to Tragg. In fact she saw one very good reason not to tell him that Corey had been treated here or that she'd come here herself in order to learn where they'd sent the boy. The man's mood was black enough at the moment.

She located the address on the map and felt her heart sink. 'Well, so much for my idea.'

Tight-lipped and glaring, Tragg waited for the explanation.

'The doctor's house is a good six miles from here. If one of them's as sick as I think they are, it's doubtful they could've walked that far.'

She slapped the map down as though disappointed. In truth she wished only to hide her unease. Tragg's silences were every bit as frightening as his outbursts.

'There's always the chance they called someone,' she reasoned, nervousness making her blurt her thoughts. 'But the bitch didn't even have a phone at her house. What are the odds she's carrying a mobile?'

She turned to stare out at the deserted building. Anything to avoid Tragg's unrelenting gaze. She felt it boring into the back of her head and gave a shudder.

'I think they're nearby, though,' she offered hopefully. 'They must be. They'll keep out of sight and wait for the office to open in the morning.'

Tragg reached down with a black-gloved hand and shifted the car into drive. 'Which leaves us with nothing better to do than stake out the doctor's house till then.'

'Stop right here!'

Startled by Shyler's anxious words, Chase hit the brakes, stopping the Land Rover twenty yards short of the foot of his driveway.

'I thought you said you only lived with your father,' she accused.

'I do.'

'Then who are all these other people?' She pointed at the six cars parked in front of and across from his house.

'I'm sorry, I forgot. It's my father's book club. They meet every Sunday afternoon.'

'And what else have you forgotten to tell me?'

He angled the rear-view mirror to better see her face. 'There's nothing to worry about. They'll all be in the living room. We'll go in the back and I'll take you up the kitchen stairs. No one will see you.'

'You can't be sure of that.'

'All right, I can't. But even if they do –'

'No. No way. Take us back to your office.'

Chase turned around. 'And what then? Are you going to let me leave again?'

'No, Jesse needs you.'

'Well, then you don't eat. And what's more, what do you think my father will do when I don't come home tonight?'

Shyler hesitated. The man seemed sincere, but had he planned all this? 'You'll just have to call him and give him some excuse.'

'I could. But wouldn't it be easier to just stay here?'

The simple statement silenced her for a moment. She looked down at Jesse, cradled against her, then closed her eyes. She almost wished the enemy would come. There could be no end to this short of that ultimate confrontation. And as stressful as all this was on her, it had to be ten times worse for a child.

'Think about it,' Chase said. 'If someone's after you, wouldn't it be better to have people around?'

'*If* someone's after us? You think I'm imagining there are men trying to kill us?'

His expression grew earnest. 'Shyler, I was at your cabin, remember? I have no doubts at all that the threat against you is absolutely real. I also think you shouldn't have to face it alone.'

Chapter 54

Wrapped in the blanket from the sick room bed, Zack found himself bundled from the car towards the doctor's house, up a ramp and through the back door. Without pause he was ushered through a cluttered kitchen – dishes in the sink, counters strewn with utensils and plates – and up a narrow staircase off the eating area.

He held his breath as long as he could but by the time they reached the second floor he just had to inhale. And there it was. Nothing bad. Nothing even anyone else would notice. Just the smell of strangeness. Another strange smell from another strange house.

As they walked along the hallway the scents of coffee and food from downstairs mixed with the woodsy smell of the floor, the faint drift of soap and men's deodorant. Why did these things always hit him so hard? He knew without doubt that if he ever went blindfolded into one of his old foster homes he'd be able to tell which one it was just from the smell.

Of all of them, Shyler's cabin had been the best. That remote but soul-warming little cottage had smelled of homemade soup, pine, wood smoke and . . . her. And though he'd spent the least amount of time there of anywhere he'd lived in the last three years, somehow that was the smell he missed now.

At the end of the passage the doctor opened a door on the left. 'This is one of the spare rooms. The other is just across the hall. Make yourselves comfortable. I'll be right back.'

Zack stood with Shyler's arms wrapped around him in the middle of the room. There wasn't much in it besides a bed, a night stand, some drawers and a chair. Before they'd even moved from the spot, the doctor returned, setting some clothes and towels on the bed.

'The bathroom's next door if you want a shower. I'm sorry, I know these clothes won't fit either of you but they're all I have. If you give me yours I can wash and dry them in an hour or so.'

They stood staring back at him.

'Well, I'll leave you to it, then.'

'Where are you going?' Shyler said, not quite masking the fear in her voice.

'Downstairs to get some food. I'll just be a minute.' His words didn't alter her worried expression. 'Did I lie to you about the men at my office? Did I tell anyone you were hiding there? Did I call the police?'

She looked away.

'I didn't then and I won't now. Even though I think the best thing would be to call the police, I won't because you don't want me to. Obviously you have your reasons. I trust that they're good ones.'

His voice was a whisper, his tone earnest. Arms around her waist, Zack felt Shyler's body relax.

'Go ahead,' she answered.

The door closed gently and they were alone.

Zack stood unmoving. He didn't want to do anything else, just stand there with his cheek against her chest. In the sudden silence he could hear her heart beating. He closed his eyes to block out everything else.

'Well, how about we get you freshened up?' she said after a moment.

He didn't answer.

She cupped his cheek. 'You okay?'

'Yeah.' Zack stepped back, knowing in that instant the spell was broken.'Come on, then. You'll feel better once you're clean. And a cool bath might help bring your temperature down.'

She led him next door and settled him onto the edge of the tub. In silence he watched her put in the plug, turn on the water and adjust the temperature. It was strange having someone look after him again. He hadn't really thought about it up to that moment – probably because he'd been too sick and scared.

Suddenly he wasn't that sure he liked it. It had been all right when he was little but he was almost eleven now. And for much of the last three months at the Learys' he'd been left in charge of Reece and Corey. Why would he need anyone to take care of him?

Shyler left the room and returned with the items the doctor had given them. He watched her go through them and set aside things for him to wear. Remembering how he'd thrown his arms around her neck back in the sick room suddenly made him cringe. What a baby! He never should have done that. And he wouldn't have if he hadn't been sick!

He pushed to his feet. 'I can do that.'

'I know you can, sweetie. It's all right, you rest.'

'I don't want to rest.' He snatched the sweatshirt out of her hand. 'I said I can do it.'

Shyler blinked at him. 'Jesse, what is it? Are you –'

'Yes, I'm all right! I just want to do it myself, okay?'

'Sure, honey, if that's what you want.' She managed a smile

and backed from the room. 'I'll be next door in case you need me.'

Uncertain what Shyler and Jesse might like, Chase prepared a variety of sandwiches – two ham and cheese, one egg salad, a tuna and lettuce and a peanut butter and jelly. What they didn't eat he surely would. He was just slicing them all into wedges when his father glided into the kitchen.

'Hey there, I was wondering where you'd got to. Haven't seen you since breakfast. Did you find your friend?'

Chase pulled a platter from under the counter and set it on a tray. 'I did but that's not what took me so long. I stopped at the office on my way home and got hung up – there was an accident at one of the logging sites.'

'Anybody seriously hurt?'

'Had to send a couple cases to PI. They were pretty banged up but they'll recover. It could've been worse.'

'That's good anyway.' Allen sat eyeing the massive platter his son was arranging. 'That all for you or are you hiding someone up in your bedroom?'

Chase let out a laugh. 'Guess I'm pretty hungry. I missed lunch.' He opened the fridge and pulled out a container of apple juice.

'Well, the group's just having coffee and nibbles.' Allen nodded towards the living room. 'Why don't you come in and join us?'

'Thanks, but I've already made this.'

'Bring it in and eat it with us. Then have dessert. Between six women they made enough to feed an army.'

'I'll be fine with this. Thanks anyway.'

Allen wheeled closer and lowered his voice. 'Actually you'd be doing me a favour. It's getting a bit tense in there.'

Chase set three glasses on the tray and began pouring juice. 'What could be tense about a book club? I thought you said it was just six women.'

'Just? Are you kidding? They're all trying to out-do each other with the food. They're hovering around me like . . . like they expect me to sample it all and then pick the winner. I feel like first prize at a bake-off competition.'

'That's what you get for being the only eligible male over fifty in a small town.'

'So what do you say? You going to help your old man out, or what?'

'Sorry, Dad, I've got a few things to do upstairs.'

Allen slumped back with a hearty sigh, his gaze falling on the three glasses of juice. Arching a brow he regarded his son. 'Thirsty as well as hungry, eh?'

Chase pursed his lips around another smile, picked up the tray and stepped around him. 'Good luck with your lady guests.' He headed for the stairs.

Chapter 55

Shyler sat in the upstairs window seat, rifle resting across her lap. She would have preferred a view of the road, but at least she could see the back yard from here – lawn bathed in moonlight surrounded by trees, garage, porch, a bit of the driveway. She'd spot it if anyone slipped from the woods and tried to break in through the kitchen. She only hoped the activity downstairs – the club meeting that, according to Chase, was going on far longer than usual – would be enough to deter someone coming in the front.

She eyed Jesse asleep in the bed. The most recent addition to her list of concerns was her son's increasingly belligerent behaviour. After finishing his bath, he'd returned to the room and climbed into bed, refusing any help from her. And when Chase had brought up the tray of sandwiches he wouldn't let the doctor take his temperature or even look at him.

His use of bad language didn't bother her. The fact that it was so out of character did. Was his behaviour simply a delayed reaction to all they'd been through? Or was it the fever? It had started so suddenly. Did it mean his infection was getting worse?

Out in the hall the floorboards creaked. Her body tensed, then relaxed again when a familiar figure appeared in the doorway – Chase, in a red flannel shirt and jeans, his hair still wet from a recent shower.

She sat a moment just taking him in. She'd only ever seen him in white before – the medical coat he wore at his office, the sweater he'd had on all that day. Somehow the red shirt made his eyes bluer, the plaid adding sharpness and breadth to his shoulders. Combined with the jeans' stone-washed denim, the effect was more rugged outdoorsman than doctor.

'May I come in?'

She shrugged. 'Your house.'

'True, but you're the one holding the rifle.'

Another time she might have smiled. She wanted to smile, wanted to get to know this man. This man she could almost come to trust. But with the risks so great she couldn't let herself. 'Therefore a wise person wouldn't provoke me.'

He gave a soft chuckle. 'I promise to be on my best behaviour.'

Silently he crossed to the bed and sat on the desk chair he'd brought in earlier. So gently he didn't disturb Jesse's sleep, he inserted a thermometer into his ear.

Shyler waited. Jesse had had more medicine with dinner, his second dose since leaving the cabin. His temperature then – two hours ago – had been a hundred and two. One degree higher than when they'd first reached Chase's office. Was it too soon to hope there had been a change? Had she been wrong? Should she have let him be taken to the hospital?

Chase removed the thermometer and read it. Though she scrutinised his face, she couldn't read his thoughts. She forced herself to stay where she was till he picked up the chair and brought it over to sit before her.

'No change,' he whispered.

She bit her lip.

'It's too soon to expect one, really, so don't lose hope. As long as his temp doesn't go any higher there's still a chance the medicine's working. We should have a better idea in the morning.'

She nodded. If they survived till then.

At the thought, a wave of dread crashed over her. She slumped under the weight, exhausted to the point of feeling physically ill. Even if they made it through the night, what then? Where would they go? When would it end?

'Why don't you get some sleep?' Chase said. 'The bed's all made up across the hall. I'll stay with Jesse.'

She drew herself up. 'I'm fine right here.'

'How did I know you were going to say that?' He opened the black case he held on his lap. 'Well, as long as you're staying, how about you put the rifle down and let me take a look at that arm?'

'Don't worry about it.' She turned away, stared out the window.

'At least let me change the dressing. You won't be much good to Jesse if you end up with an infection as well.'

Shyler focused on the lawn below, keeping her injured limb tucked to her side. When she felt Chase's hand settle over hers she glanced back around.

For a moment she found herself held by his gaze, his eyes both kind and gently coaxing. She must have communicated something in return without even realising it, for with no further comment he drew her arm towards him and began unwrapping it.

She gave up the fight. He was right – she couldn't allow herself to get sick. Not while Jesse was still in danger.

He swabbed the area and inspected the wound. 'Well, the good news is you didn't tear out any stitches. What you've got is a fresh laceration. A simple bandage is all it needs.' He got out the tape and a pair of scissors then opened a packet of sterile dressing.

He squeezed antiseptic cream on his finger and began spreading it over the cut. 'You know, it would've been a lot less painful if you'd just brought Jesse in to see me.' His gaze lifted briefly, confirming he'd figured out why she had cut herself.

There seemed little point in denying it now. 'I couldn't.'

'Why not?'

'You went to my cabin and you have to ask that?'

'So you thought I was one of the men trying to kill you?'

'Well no, I . . . I . . .'

He held up a hand. 'It's all right, I understand. Trust must be hard to come by in your situation. Whatever it is.'

Frowning, she leaned back; vaguely disturbed, yet not sure why.

'So you know who they are.'

She blinked at him. 'What?'

'The men who came after you. Out at your cabin.'

A chill shivered along her neck as she recalled the man peering up at her from the ladder of the loft. No, she hadn't recognised *him* but . . . Suddenly there were other faces. Scarred and battered. Savage and leering. Fish Hook. Puppet. Scarecrow. Beret.

'How long have they been after you, Shyler?'

She tried to remember. Forever, it seemed. 'I . . .'

'Is that why you lied to me about where you lived? Why you gave me a false address?'

Her frown deepened. That at least seemed something she should know. And yet – 'I'm . . . not sure . . .'

'But you know what they want. You know what they're after.'

She darted an anxious look towards the bed.

'Jesse? Is that it? Why, Shyler? Why do they want him?'

She closed her eyes. When she tried to think of the answers to his questions she felt almost dizzy. As though the reasons were spinning around her so fast she couldn't latch on to them. They were images out of focus, garbled words that didn't make sense.

'Does Jesse have something they want?' he persisted.

She swallowed against a wave of nausea. The spinning was getting worse by the second.

'There must be a reason. He must have seen or heard something that –'

'Does it matter?' The words came out louder than she'd intended, but they had the desired effect. The questions stopped. The spinning slowed enough that she could open her eyes again.

Only then did she notice how tightly she was clutching his hand. How close he had moved. How his arm had come up behind her back, spreading warmth across her shoulders.

She let her gaze lift to his chest. What would it hurt to collapse against him? To feel his strength and protection envelope her? To trust once again in another human being?

He dipped his head. Their breath mingled. 'Shyler.' The word a caress on her cheek. *What would it hurt . . .*

She let go of his hand and pulled away, taking up the cold hard steel of the rifle. She knew all too well who it could hurt.

Beside her she felt him draw away, pack up his things and rise from the chair.

From the bed behind them, lost in shadow, Zack tracked the man as he left the room.

Vanessa slid her hands beneath her armpits. The car was freezing. Mainly because Tragg insisted on keeping his window open so the windshield wouldn't mist up. From the top of the rise at a bend in the road they had a clear view of the doctor's house and had been watching it for the last four hours.

The prolonged surveillance had left her not only shivering with cold but also absolutely ravenous. 'We should go to the place Nolan and I stayed at. The cabin we rented.'

From the box in his hand, Tragg shook a Junior Mint into his mouth. 'Why?'

'Because if Nolan didn't check out when he left with Farrell we can still use it. We can get some sleep, start fresh in the morning.' She lowered her voice. 'Maybe even grab a cup of coffee.'

'Not a priority.'

She stifled a sigh. Of course it wasn't a priority for him, he'd just put away a mixed cold meat sub, a bag of chips and a can of Coke – extra provisions she hadn't thought to buy from the last gas station they'd stopped at on the drive up here. Tragg hadn't offered to share his meal and she hadn't asked. She knew how much he'd have gotten off on seeing her beg and then refusing her.

She tried a different tack. 'There's a chance Nolan might have left me a message there. Maybe something to do with the kids. The poor sap was probably still expecting me to come back for him.'

Tragg kept staring out at the house. 'I'm pretty sure he told me everything he knew.'

Vanessa winced, recalling Nolan's screams. 'I haven't eaten since this morning,' she blurted.

Tragg turned slowly. Meeting her gaze with dark flat eyes, he held out the box. 'Have a mint.'

She swallowed hard and shook her head.

As she turned away she realised she was no longer hungry. Even after fifteen hours without food, one look from Tragg could destroy any appetite.

Chapter 56

Even when the thermometer slid into his ear, Zack didn't move. He'd heard the doctor enter the room and murmur a soft 'good morning' to Shyler. He'd heard the floorboards creak near his bed, sensed their shadows sliding over him and then a hand brushing his hair aside.

All the while he'd kept very still, eyes closed, breathing steady. He wanted the doctor to think he was asleep, wanted to hear what he said to Shyler when he thought her little boy wasn't listening.

The thermometer gently slid from his ear. The doc probably thought he was being real smart, sneaking around, taking his temperature when he wasn't aware. But Zack knew all right. And he'd go on pretending to be asleep because *he* was doing some sneaking of his own.

'Still no change – a hundred and two.' The doctor's voice was a whisper above him.

He opened his eyes a crack. The two of them were standing over him, Chase in a navy blue terry-cloth robe. Light from the bedside lamp frosted Shyler's hair but did little for the shadows beneath her eyes or the worry lines that creased her brow. He would have liked to comfort her, to tell her not to worry about him. But of course the doctor was doing it for him.

'It doesn't mean he's not getting better. We'll just have to wait a little while longer before it shows.'

Zack watched them closely. He knew the doctor had a thing for Shyler. He could tell just from the way he looked at her. What he hadn't worked out yet was whether Shyler knew it or not. And, if she did, how she felt about it.

Back at the office when she'd held the gun on him it had seemed pretty certain she didn't like him. But things had changed a bit since then. Now she seemed to be listening to him, trusting him more. And last night when he'd actually touched her . . .

Beneath the blanket he clenched his fists. At the time he hadn't been able to figure out why he'd become so angry at seeing them like that. But after the doctor had left and his anger slowly died away he'd found another feeling hiding beneath it. A secret feeling that had made it hard for him to breathe.

Fear.

Not the kind he felt for Tragg. No, this was different. More like the feeling he got from his nightmare. Only ten times worse.

He squinted at the woman standing over him. In the beginning he'd thought, 'Well, she isn't much, but she's all I've got.' Now that too had changed. He didn't even care any more whether or not she protected him from Tragg. In three years of being passed from one foster home to another he'd never found anyone as brave and smart and wonderful as her. And he wasn't going to let some stupid doctor come along and take her away from him!

'When he wakes up, make sure you get plenty of fluids into him,' the man was telling her. 'I'll bring up some juice and breakfast before I go.'

Her head snapped towards him. 'Go? Go where?'

He consulted the clock on the bedside table. 'I've got to be at work in a couple of hours.'

'You aren't serious.'

'Don't worry, I'll come back at lunch and check on him then.'

'That's not what I meant.' Her voice had risen above a whisper.

'You're not still worried I'll call the police, are you? I could've done that any time last night.'

'Call your office and tell them you're sick.'

'And if there's an emergency they'll come here to find me. Is that what you want?'

Zack opened his eyes a bit further. They weren't paying any attention to him now.

'Then tell them you have to leave town for a while.'

He blew out a breath. 'Shyler, think about it from my perspective. The minute I walk out the door it means my father's here alone with you. I'm not going to do anything to endanger him.'

'Endanger.' She took a step back. 'You think I would hurt him?'

'What I'm saying is, if I called the police and they showed up here –'

'I might use your father as a hostage, is that it? I would never –'

'It doesn't matter if you would or not, that's how the police would see it. And that, apart from the promise I've already given you, is why you can be sure I'm not going to call them. Because I do not want to create that situation.'

Shyler stood, considering his words. Slowly the tension eased from her stance, her breathing slowed. 'All right, go. Just so long as you're back by lunch.'

'I give you my word.'

The man kept staring as though he wanted to say more. Or, worse, do more. Zack smiled at his disappointment when Shyler turned away, crossed to the window and resumed her post staring down at the lawn.

His smile broadened when the doctor sighed and walked from the room.

Chapter 57

Two hours later, showered and dressed for work, Chase carried a breakfast tray up to the guest room and stopped in the doorway.

Shyler sat slumped in the window seat, rifle resting across her lap. Dozing at last. She certainly needed it. From what he'd seen she hadn't closed her eyes all night. Jesse, on the other hand, was now wide awake. Chase crossed the room and set the tray on the bedside table.

'Morning,' he whispered, pulling up the chair. 'How are you feeling?'

Jesse glared up at him, his expression more hate-filled than distrusting. The intensity of it set him back. What had he done to alienate the boy?

'You're looking better, not as flushed. I wouldn't be surprised if your temperature's down.' He held up the thermometer. 'Should we check and see?'

Jesse yanked the blankets over his head and rolled away to face the wall.

'I don't seem to be very popular this morning.' He set the thermometer back on the table. 'Well, your breakfast is here when you get hungry. Toast, fruit, cereal, juice, some donuts for later and coffee for your mom. You won't forget to take your pill, will you?'

He waited for an answer but the boy didn't stir.

'Well, I'll head off then. I'll be back to check on you both around lunch time.'

'She doesn't like you.'

Halfway out of his chair, Chase stopped. 'Who? Your mom?' He sat down again. So that's what this was all about. 'How can you tell?'

'Same way I can tell you like her.'

He nodded to himself. Fear of abandonment. Hardly unknown among children of divorced parents. 'It scares you that I like her, does it?'

Jesse rolled over. 'Why should it? If she doesn't like you I got nothing to worry about.'

'And if she did?'

The boy's eyes narrowed.

'You'd still have nothing to worry about. Liking one person doesn't mean you can't like another. Anyway I'm not out to take your mother away from you.' He gave a huff. 'I pity any man who ever tried.'

If anything the boy appeared even more troubled.

'Was that what happened at your cabin? Did those men try to take you away from your mom?'

He chewed his lip.

'Jesse, I have to be honest with you. I'll do everything I can to help you and your mom – I'll hide you, feed you, treat your injuries, I'll drive you anywhere you need to go. But I think you can see there's not much I can do against men with guns. If someone's still after you, and you know who they are, wouldn't it be best to . . .'

Once again he found himself staring at the back of Jesse's head. On impulse he reached out and laid his hand on the boy's shoulder. 'We'll talk more about it later if you want. In the meantime try not to worry.' He got up, slid the chair aside and started for the door.

Seeing Shyler slumped in the draughty window seat he paused long enough to grab the throw off the end of the bed and drape it over her.

Further up the hall he ducked into his study to pick up the magazines he'd bought for the waiting room. He'd just reached his desk when the phone rang. Fearing the sound would waken Shyler, he snatched it up before the first ring had died.

'Chase Hadley here,' he said in a low voice.

'Doctor Hadley, this is Greg Linnell. You left a message on my service to call you.'

Chase blinked a moment then remembered the name. With all that had happened he'd forgotten the call he'd placed to Shyler's ex after speaking with her mother.

'Mr Linnell, yes. Thank you so much for calling back.' Chase sat down. More than ever he needed to speak to this man.

Shyler jolted awake in the window seat. She didn't know what had awakened her but was grateful something had. She couldn't keep dozing off like this. She had to stay alert.

Throwing off the blanket that was draped around her – had Chase put it there? – she slid from the seat and looked towards the bed.

Jesse appeared to still be asleep. On the night stand beside him sat a tray of untouched food, steam still rising from a mug of coffee. Chase must have been here only moments ago. Was he still nearby? Had he left for work yet?

Her gaze shifted back to the steaming mug. Coffee. Just what she needed. On legs trembling from stress and fatigue she started towards it only to stop after two steps, her attention drawn by the murmur of voices. One voice anyway, coming from somewhere just up the hall. It sounded like Chase.

A chill spread through her as that thought soaked in. His father was in a wheelchair and couldn't come upstairs. So who was he talking to? Was someone else here?

Taking up the rifle she went to find out.

'Your message said it was a matter of some importance.'

'Yes, that's right. I hope I didn't alarm you. You see . . .' Chase hesitated. In the seconds since hearing Greg Linnell's voice a thought had occurred to him. If he divulged what had happened at Shyler's cabin, her ex might call the police himself. What's more, there was even the remote possibility *he* was the man Shyler and Jesse were fleeing from.

'Doctor Hadley?'

'Yes, still here.'

'So what is this about?'

Chase cleared his throat. He supposed it wouldn't hurt to simply ask what he'd wanted to know when he'd first called this man. 'Mr Linnell, I contacted you because I was hoping you could give me some information about your ex-wife. I'm Shyler's doctor.'

A second's pause. 'Shyler. Good God.'

Hearing what sounded like stunned concern, Chase spoke quickly to reassure him. 'Oh no, don't worry, nobody's hurt. She and Jesse are perfectly fine.'

The silence this time was deep and incredulous. 'Is this some kind of joke?'

'A joke? Why would –'

'You sick son of a bitch. Who put you up to this?'

The ferocity of the words brought Chase up short. 'I . . . I'm sorry, I don't understand.'

'You don't, eh? Well, let me explain it to you. Jesse's dead. My son is dead. He died two years ago when Shyler threw him off a bridge.'

Chapter 58

Chase felt the floor drop away beneath him. He moved his lips but nothing came out.

Movement encroached on the edge of his vision – a shadow creeping across the desktop. Someone behind him. He spun to see.

Shyler. Coming at him. The stock of the rifle aimed at his face.

He dived from the chair. The stock swooped down – once, twice – smashing the phone into dozens of pieces.

The barrel swung towards him. 'You called the police.'

'What? No!'

'Don't lie to me. I heard you talking to them!'

Hands raised, he pushed to his feet. 'Shyler, you're wrong. I was –'

'Be quiet!'

The rifle thrust closer, trembling in her hands. He held his breath. If what her ex had just told him was true, she was far more unstable than he'd ever imagined.

'We're leaving,' she announced with sudden conviction.

'What?'

'You heard me.' With the rifle she motioned him towards the door. 'Let's go. Back in the other room.'

He wavered, searching for a way to dissuade her. Why would her ex-husband lie about Jesse? Why would she? And if Jesse was dead, who was the boy she was protecting?

Whatever the reason, if she truly believed he was her son . . . 'Shyler, you can't leave. Jesse's too sick. He needs constant medical care.'

She pointed the rifle at the centre of his chest. 'I know. That's why you're coming with us.'

'Over there. Sit down.' Shyler gestured to the chair by the bed. Holding the rifle on Chase the whole time she picked up her knapsack and threw it across to him. 'Put the food in that.'

Chase took the fruit and donuts off the breakfast tray and dropped them in.

On the bed beside him the blankets stirred and a small head appeared. Seeing them both Zack sat up. 'What's going on?'

'It's all right, honey, nothing to worry about. We're just getting out of here. As soon as we put a few things together.'

'Why? What happened?'

Shyler checked the clock on the bedside table. Nine forty-five. She knew of no sheriff in the Deadwater area. Which meant the police would be coming from Presque Isle. That gave them maybe an hour and a half, two hours at most to get far enough away that they couldn't be followed.

'What happened?' Zack repeated.

'Our helpful doctor called the police.'

'Shyler, I didn't –'

'I told you to be quiet.' She waved the barrel at the bottle of pills. 'The medicine too. Put it in the bag.'

Slowly he lowered his hands and stood up. 'No.'

Clutching the rifle she took a step closer. But the battle within her only made the gun shake uncontrollably. Why was this so hard? After what he had done it should be easy!

'Shyler, listen to me. Don't do this. Whatever –'

'Your father's downstairs.' The words came out before she even knew why she'd spoken them.

Chase on the other hand seemed to know at once. He grew very still, clenching his jaw in lieu of a response.

'You know that situation you didn't want to create? The one where I take your father hostage?' *Back down, Chase. Please back down.*

'All right, I'll do whatever you want. Just leave my dad out of this.'

'Put the medicine in the bag and slide it across to me.'

He did as instructed.

'Now wrap Jesse in the blanket and pick him up. You're going to carry him out to your car.'

Chapter 59

Chase laid the boy on the Land Rover's back seat and tucked the blanket in around him.

The boy. He couldn't think of him as Jesse any more despite the kid's willingness to accept the identity. Which in itself raised another good question – why was he posing as Shyler's son?

Chase closed the car door and straightened beside it. 'Where are we going?'

'West,' Shyler said, throwing her knapsack in the back.

'Into Canada?'

'I suppose you want to go east, the direction they're coming from.'

'Shyler, nobody's coming. I keep trying to tell you –'

'Get in the car.'

He climbed behind the wheel. When she'd gotten in beside him he turned to face her. 'We're not going to make it whichever way we go. Not on a quarter of a tank of gas.'

'That's all you have?'

'Plus, I should warn you the car's been playing up lately. It might not start.' He turned the ignition and it fired instantly.

'Nice try, Hadley. Pull out and turn left – we'll fill up at the store.'

As he drove the distance, Chase tried to think. He had only minutes in which to decide. What could he do to stop their leaving that wouldn't endanger himself or the boy? How could he convince this woman to trust him?

Through the rear-view mirror he noted the boy watching fearfully out his window. If he wasn't Shyler's son then who the hell was he? Who were his real parents? Where were they now? He certainly didn't seem afraid of Shyler and showed no signs of wanting to escape.

'Pull up at the pump,' Shyler said as they neared the store.

When he'd shut off the engine she nodded at the rifle she held concealed beneath the dashboard. 'I'll be watching through the window so don't try anything. You'll only be putting others at risk.'

Chase looked out at the two cars parked along the side lane. 'They're pretty busy. This could take a minute. You know old Bill's alone in there.'

'Just stay where I can see you and don't talk to anyone.'

Chase got out and moved to the pump. There was no point in arguing. She was right – the faster he did this, the safer for everyone.

As the tank slowly filled he stared through the car window at her profile. Could it be true? Could she really have killed her own son? Had it been negligence? An accident? If she'd murdered the boy surely she'd have been imprisoned by now, unless –

An unseen hand latched onto his throat. Was that why she lived in such isolation, refusing to give her name or address? Bartering for her needs, anxious and watchful, suspicious and wary . . .

You're not calling the police – her very words to him as she'd held him at gunpoint in his treatment room yesterday.

He groaned with the pain that lanced through his chest. Could it be the dead men back at her cabin weren't killers but police having finally tracked her down?

He bowed his head and covered his eyes. 'Oh, Shyler.'

Chapter 60

'Pull around back. I've got an idea.' Vanessa pointed down the lane that led to the rear of the general store.

Tragg made the turn and swung into the parking lot. 'Let's hear it.'

Talking quickly she filled him in.

After a night spent huddled in a freezing car she'd greeted the new day with little hope of resolving their dilemma. But less than fifteen minutes ago, she'd been roused from her bleary-eyed despair by the sight of their target leaving the doctor's house. And when she'd spotted the woman – the first time she'd actually laid eyes on the bitch – forcing Hadley to his car at gunpoint the solution to their problem had suddenly come to her.

Slight and fair-haired, their wild-card heroine hardly seemed capable of having bettered Farrell in a fire fight. The bitch must have qualities far beyond those she made plain to the world. And it was clear she'd taken it upon herself to be Zack's protector, to the point of risking her life to save him. But that very devotion would be her undoing. Her reasons for helping him didn't matter. That they made her seem desperate and irrational did.

Tragg listened closely as she spelled out her plan, then leaned back and flashed a tight-lipped smile. 'I'll wait here.'

She reached for her door and he grabbed her arm. 'Just so we're clear. This isn't about catching this kid any more. This is about Farrell. We finish these two here and now.'

Vanessa nodded and climbed from the car.

Standing second in line at the counter, Chase felt someone ease up behind him.

'Doctor Hadley? Remember me?'

His stomach dropped when he saw who it was. The woman who'd consulted him with a bogus sprained ankle. The last thing he wanted was to get hung up talking to her right now. 'Ms Roswell. How's the ankle?'

'Please face forward, Doctor, and listen carefully.'

Chase turned around, stunned once again. Was there no end to the shocks he'd be hit with this day?

'I'm sorry I had to deceive you the first time we met but it was necessary. I'm a child social worker. I've been in the area for the last ten days trying to locate a runaway boy.'

Chase felt something slip beneath his arm and looked down to see her photo ID.

'Our department now has reason to believe the child we're after was kidnapped by the woman sitting in your car.'

'Kidnapped?'

'Please, Doctor, don't turn around. She's watching and I don't want her to know we're talking.'

Chase shot a glance out the store's front window. Sure enough Shyler was looking their way. He angled his head so she couldn't see his face and whispered over his shoulder. 'Are you sure she kidnapped him? I've been with them since yesterday and the boy appears to want to be with her.'

'As a runaway he very well might. After all, she's been helping him hide from us. Unfortunately he's a little too young to understand she could be a danger to him.'

'A danger? It didn't seem to me she's a danger to him. If anything –'

'Doctor, we don't have time to discuss this. Obviously we don't have all the facts, but we know enough to be certain it's imperative we get the boy away from her.'

Chase exhaled. If this woman had come to him an hour sooner he never would have believed her. But on top of what Shyler's ex had told him, and who the dead men at her cabin might be . . .

'What do you want me to do?' he said.

'When you finish here, go back to your car and drive in whatever direction she tells you. When you come to a deserted stretch of road, pretend to have car trouble and pull off to the side. I'll stop and offer to lend you a hand.'

'She has a rifle.'

'We're prepared to handle the situation.'

'We?'

'There's a police officer in my car.'

His heart sank. 'You'll make sure neither of them gets hurt?'

'It's our top priority. And you can assure it by playing your part.'

God help him. 'I'll do my best.'

Chapter 61

Zack peered out each car window in turn – at the store, the road both ahead and behind, the woods across the street – wondering who would find them first, Tragg and Vanessa or the police.

They were sitting here, just sitting here, in plain view of everyone. He felt like Howard, his bug-eyed goldfish, the one the Masons had flushed down the toilet.

In the front seat, Shyler sat with her gaze fixed on the store's front window. She seemed more worried now than she had at the house, shoulders tense, hands gripping the twenty-two.

Zack's stomach tightened. He'd told her so many stupid things – that he didn't need her help, that he wanted to be alone, that he could manage just fine on his own. He only hoped she hadn't believed him.

He didn't know why he'd said those things. Maybe because he was afraid she was going to do them anyway. Better to be the one who walked away than the one who got left. That's what he'd figured anyway.

'Did Chase really call the cops?' he asked.

'Yes, Jesse, he did.' Her words sounded muffled against the glass.

'How do you know?'

'I went in his study and caught him doing it.'

'He was talking to them?'

'Yes.'

'What was he saying?'

'Jesse, please, I have to keep watch. I didn't hear his exact words anyway.'

There was an edge to her voice he'd not heard before, a suggestion that her control was slipping. He knew he shouldn't, but he just couldn't stop himself – he had to keep talking. 'Then how do you know?'

'How do I know what?'

'That it was the cops.'

'I heard him say both our names. Who else could he have been speaking to?'

Zack couldn't think of anyone else either. 'So what are we going to do?'

'We get as far away from here and as fast as we can.'

'Well, why are we waiting then? Why don't we just steal his car?'

'Because he has the keys.'

Zack slumped back. Beneath the blanket his limbs were shaking, and this time it wasn't because of any fever. Maybe she just didn't want to leave the doctor no matter what he did. Maybe she liked the guy better than him.

'You must be pretty mad at him, huh?'

She seemed to think about that for a moment. 'I suppose it depends on why he did it.'

'What do you mean?'

'He might have thought he was helping us.'

'But you didn't want him to call them.'

'No.'

He studied her profile, suddenly realising how odd that was. He knew why *he* didn't want the police to get involved but why didn't she? Most grown-ups in their situation wouldn't have hesitated to call for help.

'What do you think they'll do if they catch us?'

'The police?' She laughed. 'Arrest me.'

'You? What for?'

'They'll go to the cabin, find the dead men and figure I killed them. And they'd be right.'

'But *they* came after *us*!'

'Oh, we'll tell them that, but it won't make any difference. They'll ask a lot of questions, write down all sorts of information, then walk away and leave us to fend for ourselves.'

Zack didn't speak. She sounded both frightened and angry now, and what she'd said seemed a bit mixed up.

'We'll describe what happened over and over till we can't bear it any more. We'll tell them what they looked like – their scars, their eyes, the clothes they were wearing – and still they'll do nothing. They'll say they can't find them. And even if they did they couldn't arrest them. Not enough evidence. No other witnesses.'

Zack sat gaping. What was she talking about? 'Can't find who?'

She turned so sharply it made him jump. 'Them, Jesse. Don't you remember? Fish Hook. Puppet. Those monsters. Those –'

He shrank into the blanket. The way she was staring at him – scared and angry yet really confused . . . For the first time he was actually a little afraid of her.

Slowly she reached her hand towards his face, as though touching him would help her understand something. He let her fingertips trail down his cheek, but her look of bewilderment didn't fade.

The driver's door opened and Chase got in.

Chapter 62

'You still want to do this?' Chase said, pulling his seatbelt across him.

Her face turned away from him, Shyler nodded.

'You all right?'

'Drive.' She waved her hand.

Chase pulled out in the direction she'd indicated. He tried to drive as though nothing was wrong. As though bile wasn't oozing up the back of his throat, his chest not tight.

He was grateful that whatever had happened in his absence was keeping Shyler staring out her window. So far she and Jesse had been so preoccupied, neither had noticed the car that had emerged from the lane behind them and was now following at a cautious distance.

Despite this good fortune he still fought doubts. Could he go through with this? What would happen if he just kept driving? Would the others stay with them? Would they force a confrontation in some later setting where the outcome might not prove as safe?

He took a deep breath and blew it out again. For better or worse he was committed. He cleared the next bend, eased the right tyres into a rut and began to slow down.

Shyler straightened. 'Why are we slowing?'

'Flat tyre.'

'I didn't hear anything.'

'Can't you feel it?' The rut was doing a passable job of creating vibration but she wasn't convinced.

He pulled to a stop. 'It'll just take a minute. I'll put on the sparc and we'll be on our way.'

She reached out and stopped him turning off the engine. 'I don't believe you. There's nothing wrong.'

'Shyler, come on. If I drive on it this way it'll ruin the wheel.'

'Someone's coming!'

At the boy's frightened words, Shyler looked back.

As Chase had planned, the bend had obscured the Jaguar's approach so it swung into view only thirty yards behind them. It started slowing down at once.

'Get us out of here.'

'Shyler, relax. They probably just want to give us a hand.'

She pressed the barrel of the gun to his knee. 'I said get going.'

'Hey now, careful. I can't drive with a shattered kneecap.'

Composure fading, Chase reached down and grabbed the rifle. If he could keep holding on to it he just might prevent anyone getting hurt.

'It's them! It's them!' The boy began pounding the back of his seat, voice shrill with panic. Had he spotted the social worker in the other car? His fear seemed a bit excessive for that.

'Jesse, get down!' Shyler shouted, trying to wrench the rifle free.

Chase held on to it. 'Shyler, no!'

As they struggled, he looked in the rear-view mirror. The Jaguar hadn't veered over yet. He'd expected them to pull up behind him; instead, they seemed headed to come alongside. That and the speed at which they were approaching suddenly seemed odd. But disquiet turned to panic when, three car lengths back, he saw what protruded from the passenger window.

'On the floor!' He let go of the rifle and pushed Shyler down, then threw the Land Rover into reverse.

'Hang on!' he yelled but his words were drowned by the rear side window exploding inward. Glass and bullets showered the cab, taking out the window on the other side. He stomped on the gas.

Shyler, who'd raised her rifle to fire, fell against the dash when the Rover shot backwards. Chase caught a split-second glimpse of a man staring in at him as the Jag swept past in the other direction.

Reversing full speed, he weaved side to side, hoping to avoid the fire flying from the man's automatic. A few of the bullets still found their mark, sparking off his hood and cracking the windshield. When the Jag finally slowed and started a U-turn Chase slammed the brakes and did the same.

The instant they were racing forward again Shyler dropped the rifle and scrabbled around to look over the seat.

Chase gripped the wheel, knowing it wasn't the Jag she was checking on. 'Is he all right?'

She didn't answer.

Chapter 63

'Is he all right?' Chase repeated.

'Yes, he's okay! No thanks to you!' Shyler turned and hunched down in her seat. 'Why didn't you listen to me? Why did you just sit there when –'

She cut off abruptly, her expression one of dawning realisation.

'Your car's driving fine. There's no flat tyre.' Her mouth dropped open. 'You stopped deliberately to let them catch us!'

Chase checked in the rear-view mirror. The Jag had halved the distance between them. He rammed the Land Rover into third and stamped on the accelerator. 'One of them approached me in the store, said she was a social worker, the other a cop. What could I do?'

'So you just went along with them? What, did they offer you a reward or something?'

A volley of bullets strafed the car, the last one taking out Chase's side mirror. 'Can we discuss this later? Right now I'd like to get us out of this.'

Shyler looked out at the woods speeding by. 'We're headed back to town.'

'If you have a better idea I'm listening.'

'Oh, *now* you're listening!'

The Jag was looming like a semi in his mirror. 'One thing's for sure, we can't outrun them. Not in this heap.'

At the sight of the track coming up on their right her eyes grew wide. 'No, but maybe we can go where they can't. Turn in here!'

Chase fought the wheel as the Rover threatened to reject the sharp turn. Three heartbeats later they were bumping through pines over a rough, barely discernible track.

'Shyler, this is a logger's trail.'

'How does this thing handle water?'

He turned to her. 'What are you talking about?'

'Your Rover! How does it cope with streams?'

Chase felt a flutter in the pit of his stomach. 'How deep are we talking?'

'No idea.'

The flutter became a full-blown migration.

Zack slammed against the Land Rover's door as they took a hard turn. His ears were ringing, heart pounding like a blue-light disco. Tragg had found them. They were dead for sure.

Spitting out crumbs of broken glass, he straightened on the seat. He couldn't believe it. The doctor had actually ratted them out. After all his talk about wanting to help he'd gone and made a deal to hand them over. Zack glared daggers at the back of the man's head. The only good thing was that he would now cop the same thing they did.

The car dropped into what felt like a crater, nearly throwing him off the seat. Where the hell were they? He stuck his head up and took a peek.

The road they'd been on had disappeared, replaced by a narrow trail winding through trees. Skidding around another turn, a huge fallen branch came into view, angled, half-propped, across their path.

Chase never slowed. He swerved left, aiming for the gap with the greatest clearance.

Zack clutched the seat. Still too low – they'd never make it!

Metal screeched as the branch scraped the roof. The Rover caught briefly, tyres churning, then lurched free.

Shyler spun round. 'They've dropped back a bit. At least they've stopped shooting.'

'They're still coming, though.' Chase fought the wheel through another tight turn. 'All this has done is buy us some time.'

'Trust me. Just a little bit further.'

They burst from the trees into blinding sunlight. On either side the hills were bare, scalped to a stubble of foot-high stumps. Zack shielded his eyes from the glare. It looked like a buzz cut on a giant's head. And they were the fleas.

The track ahead wound down and left, disappearing behind a slight rise. The stretch in between was fully exposed. If Tragg cleared the forest while they were still on it . . .

Bullets glanced off the Land Rover's roof.

Chase hit the gas. They flew down the slope, took the turn and were briefly airborne when the track bottomed out.

Zack's eyes widened at what stretched before them.

'Chase, slow down!' was the last thing he heard before the Rover plunged over the bank of the stream.

Chapter 64

The wave from their impact sluiced away and Shyler peered out through the clearing windshield. Luckily Chase had braked in time to avoid hitting the boulder at the stream's edge. Steering around it, he started slowly forward again.

She looked both ways, trying to judge the best path across. Along their shore grey-green water churned between shelves and islands of granite, some large enough for shrubs and saplings to have taken root. But it was the calmer stretches in the middle that worried her. Pockets that gave no indication of what lay beneath.

Chase eyed the water with the same misgivings. 'How deep is it out there?'

'I told you, I don't know.'

'But you knew it was here. Haven't –'

'I've canoed along it, never driven across.'

Gunfire from behind them.

'Guess we'll find out.'

The instant they cleared the top of the rise, Tragg swore savagely. The trail they'd just driven had been bad enough – rocks and pot holes to knock out his fillings. But a creek? No way could he drive the Jag across that.

Hanging from the window he fired a desperation sweep at the Land Rover. It was already halfway across and nearing the deepest part. Water splashed up over its fenders. It seemed set to reach the far side in seconds. Then suddenly its front end dipped sharply.

Tragg caught his breath. A pot hole. Or better yet, they'd bottomed out. With water now skimming the lip of the windows, another few feet could see them go under. If they started to sink they'd have only two options – stay in and drown, or bail out and swim.

Raising his gun, he took aim at the doors. He'd be ready and waiting the second they opened.

Zack couldn't tear his gaze from the window. When the first splash of water had hit his face he'd tried to pretend he was just in a car-wash and forgotten to roll the windows up. But with the sharp nosedive the car had just taken that calming image had deserted him.

'What's happening? Are we sinking?'

Ignoring him, Shyler leaned towards the dash, trying to see the bottom through the swirling current. 'Aim for those rocks.' She pointed ahead.

Chase eased them forward another foot and the Rover's back end dropped down level with the front.

Water surged against their side, spilling over the top of Zack's door. He shrieked and scooted across the seat. 'Water's coming in!'

'Jesse, stay calm.'

Calm? Was she kidding? They were going to drown!

Chase kept going. The Land Rover yawed over unseen

obstacles, lifting their right side clear of the torrent, the next minute plunging it back again. Icy talons ripped at Zack's feet.

'It's coming in faster! We have to get out!'

Chase spun towards him. 'Don't touch that door!'

Zack jerked his hand away. The doc had never raised his voice before. Weird that it would actually make him feel calmer.

For a second anyway.

Till the Rover took another sharp lurch to one side.

Chapter 65

'That's it, we're clear!' Shyler yelled. 'Go, go, go!'

Chase hit the gas. Rocks and gravel churned beneath their wheels. With a shudder the tyres caught and they shot upwards onto the opposite bank.

In fighting the current they had drifted slightly, but the trail was there. Just a few yards over, rising through the forest that resumed on this side – a hill thickly timbered in maple, oak, hemlock and pine. Bullets ripped the foliage as they entered its cover and climbed into shade as dense as twilight.

Shyler fell against her seat, took a few breaths, then turned around again.

'Are they coming?' Chase said.

'I don't think so.'

He slowed and she peered through the criss-crossing branches. 'They're turning around. They're going back.'

When the Rover sped on she gazed down at Jesse. Her heart tightened. He was trying so hard to be brave but his eyes were wide, his face so pale. She reached out her hand. 'How are you going?'

Jesse took hold of her but for a moment he seemed unable to speak. Then he swallowed and managed a feeble smile. 'Just a little wet is all.' He nodded at the water sloshing against his seat.

'What about the windows, the broken glass? You weren't cut?'

He shook his head.

'We'll stop in a minute and see if we can clean things up for you back there.' She squeezed his hand and let it go.

'You want to stop?' Chase whispered disbelievingly the moment she was facing front again. 'It's safety glass. It's not going to cut him.'

'He's wet. With all that cold air blowing in on him –'

'All right. When we get to the top of this hill. But just for a second.'

Ten minutes later, standing on a bend where the trail levelled out, Shyler wished she had chosen not to stop. 'Why won't it start?'

Chase straightened from under the hood and swept the damp hair off his face. 'Take your pick. Either we were hit or something got wet that shouldn't have.'

'Can't you fix it?'

'Fix it? I don't even know what's wrong.'

'He's lying,' Zack said from where he sat drying his shoes in the sun. 'He wants us to sit here, he wants us to get caught.'

Chase sighed. 'I can understand why you would think that but it isn't true.'

Cradling the rifle, Shyler scanned the sky. There were maybe six hours of daylight left. To their right the trail wound back to the road. On their left a rocky ridge cut a break through the trees leading down and away towards the next stand of pine.

'We better get moving.' She started around the back of the car.

Chase walked after her as far as the driver's door. 'You mean on foot?'

'That's just what I mean.'

'Moving where?'

'That way.' She pointed along the ridge.

Frowning, he surveyed the rugged terrain then turned in the direction they'd been driving. 'Wouldn't it be better to keep following the trail?'

'Right now our friends are checking a map to see where that leads. They'll go out the way they came, swing around and try to cut us off. In the Rover we might've beaten them out. On foot we'd simply be walking straight into them.'

Shyler reached through the broken rear window, grabbed the knapsack and started back. When she reached him she stopped, staring in silence into the face of the man who had nearly killed them.

She could almost have forgiven him for calling the police. *If* she'd been certain he'd done it out of concern for their safety. But this second betrayal, to the monsters who wanted Jesse dead . . . He claimed they'd lied about who they were. Could she believe that?

Chase held her gaze. 'So who were those people?'

She didn't answer. If she started to explain she just might forget how much she still needed him. How much she still . . . For an instant tears stung her eyes. God help her, she'd wanted so much to believe –

'You know it isn't only your lives at risk any more,' he said. 'They're after me now, too. Doesn't that give me the right to know what's going on?'

She slung the knapsack onto her back. 'I'll take this. You carry Jesse.'

At hearing her words, Zack jumped up. 'No way! I'm not letting *him* carry me!'

Shyler stepped towards him and touched his face. 'You're not strong enough to be walking yet and we have a long way to go.' When he still seemed reluctant she tousled his hair. 'Just pretend you're riding a horse.'

Zack's mouth twitched as he looked up at Chase. 'Not a horse, a donkey. A big, dumb ass.'

Chapter 66

The ridge top afforded a spectacular view of the stream they'd just crossed, the forests beyond and a range of pine-covered hills rolling into the distance to their left. Most impressive were the rocky escarpments jutting from the mountain directly ahead. With clear autumn sunlight warming their faces, they headed for the woods on the clearing's far side.

Chase plodded on, unmoved by the scene. He was too aware of the hostility radiating from the child on his back. Finally, unable to bear it any longer, he spoke over his shoulder, 'I know you won't believe this but I'm truly sorry I helped those people.'

The boy didn't answer. It was no doubt going to take some coaxing to regain even the shaky ground they'd been on before.

'I guess I just never imagined a woman could be involved in such a nasty business. That's sexist, I know. I should've suspected. If I'd had more time I probably would have.'

Nothing. Not so much as a snide remark.

He tried one last time. 'Then again if you and Shyler had told me the truth I might not have listened to them.'

'You want *us* to tell the truth but it's okay for you to lie?'

Bingo.

Shyler was no more than four yards in front of them. Chase slowed his pace, falling back further out of her earshot. 'You know you're right, I haven't been totally honest with you.'

'No shit!'

'Okay, how's this?' He gulped in some air – the terrain plus the extra weight he was carrying were getting his breathing and heart rate up. 'You know that call I got back at my place? It wasn't the police, it was Shyler's ex-husband. He was returning my call from two days ago. I wanted to ask him some things about Shyler.'

'What kind of things?' The small voice had lost a bit of its venom.

'About her life, things that might have happened to her. I was worried about her. But my concerns had nothing to do with the people who are after you because this was before what happened at the cabin.'

'So why were you worried?'

'Shyler had been to see me a couple of times and on both occasions I thought she acted . . . Well, to be honest, a little strangely.'

'You thought she was crazy.' The belligerence was back in his tone.

'I thought she might have some problems, yes.' He was quiet a moment.

'What did you think could be wrong with her?'

'I didn't know. I had a few theories but I needed more information to be sure.'

'So what'd the guy say?'

'The guy? Her ex?' Chase nearly smiled at the unconscious slip. 'Don't you mean your father?'

The boy's grip tightened on his shoulders. When he failed to respond, Chase went on. 'Well, one thing he told me was that Jesse was dead. Naturally that made me wonder who *you* were and why you were pretending to be Shyler's son.'

Again no response.

'In fact he didn't just say that Jesse was dead, he said Shyler killed him.'

'What? That's nuts! *I'm* Jesse and I'm alive!'

'Then why would your father say you were dead?'

'He's the one who's crazy! He's making it up!'

'Actually that was my thought as well, that it all had to be some kind of mistake. I've seen how Shyler is with you – loving, gentle, willing to risk her life for you. She wouldn't be like that with a stranger, now would she?'

The boy's hands were claws digging into his shoulders.

'Unfortunately my instincts aren't always right. And as the two of you wouldn't answer my questions I started to have doubts. So when that woman approached me in the general store and told me Shyler had kidnapped you –'

'Kidnapped!'

'And that she might hurt you –'

'What? No way!'

'That was why I agreed to her plan and stopped on the road so she could catch up.'

'Well, she was lying. Shyler's not crazy. She'd never hurt me!'

Chase let the words fade into silence. 'Shyler?' he murmured. 'Don't you mean Mom?'

Chapter 67

'You're sure this is the trail they were on?' Tragg steered the Jag around a rocky outcrop and up the rise on the other side.

'Absolutely. It's right here on the map. There are no other turn-offs they could've taken.'

'You said we'd cut them off before they reached the road.'

'Well, yes, we have to. According to the map –'

'Then where the fuck are they?'

Fingers fumbling, Vanessa smoothed a crease from the paper. What had she missed? She didn't see anything. They were exactly where they were supposed to be.

After doubling back from the stream, with Tragg once more behind the wheel, they'd reached the main road and headed north to where the logging trail eventually came out again.

There was no way the Land Rover could have reached that turn-off ahead of them. It was three miles coming from that direction. Three miles of rugged twisting track that even in a four-wheel drive would have taken twenty minutes, whereas the Jag had had to travel less than half that distance over gravel road. They couldn't have gotten out ahead of them. They couldn't!

Yet with each passing second she felt less certain. If they were coming this way surely they should have run into them by now. Were there other smaller tracks that weren't on the map? If so, Tragg could hardly blame her –

'There!' she said as they rounded a bend and the Rover came in sight up ahead.

Tragg put on a burst of speed that snapped her head back. They skidded to a stop beside the four-wheel drive, grabbed their weapons and jumped out.

Wind stirred the treetops. From somewhere below, the sound of water murmuring over rocks. Otherwise silence.

The Rover was empty.

'Why'd they leave it?' Tragg said, scanning their immediate surroundings.

Vanessa stepped closer and surveyed the ground behind the vehicle. 'They were losing oil. Must've cracked the sump.'

She peered in through the broken back window. 'They've taken with them whatever they were carrying. They can't be more than a half hour ahead of us. We can still catch them.'

'If we knew which way they went.'

Vanessa began checking the ground again. She moved out in ever-widening circles, finding what she sought where the forest opened on a narrow clearing – a residual swathe, an all but imperceptible parting in the meadow's weeds. 'They went out along this ridge.'

Tragg came over. 'You can track them?'

'Three summers of army survival camp. Lazaro has no use for daughters.' She winced inwardly. Under this man's scrutiny she always blurted out more than she wanted.

'Good. Then from here on there'll be no excuses.'

Chapter 68

The murmur of running water echoed from the shallow steep-sided ravine they'd been following for the last half hour. Afternoon sunlight speared through the narrow breach in forest cover, making Shyler blink. Shifting the pack straps on her aching shoulders, she picked up the pace.

They could not slow down even for an instant. The others couldn't be far behind. Fish Hook, Puppet. They were coming, she knew it. Scarecrow. Beret. Like an approaching storm, she could feel it in her bones, sense it in her struggle to take a full breath.

She didn't understand why they'd chosen Jesse. She would never understand! All she knew was that they wanted him dead. And she was the only one who could stop them.

Oh, she'd tried to tell people, but who had listened? She'd begged for help, but who had believed? Now she was through with looking to others. It was up to her and no one else. And this time . . . this time . . .

The words echoed around her head.

This time.

How odd. Almost suggesting . . .

She faltered a step, for some reason suddenly a bit off balance. *This* time. Did that mean there had been another? Did that mean all this –

She staggered to a halt. The movement in her head had started again. Like near objects glimpsed from a speeding train, thoughts and images swept through her mind. So fast. So disorienting. Her stomach churned.

A hand took her arm. 'You all right?'

She looked up, gasping. Chase was beside her, Jesse peering over his shoulder, concern etched on both their faces.

'Yeah, fine.'

'We can stop for a minute if –'

'No. We keep going.' She shrugged him off and continued on.

In ten quick strides she'd pulled out ahead again. *Push their pace. Keep them moving.*

They had stopped only once since leaving the Rover and that just long enough to get food from the knapsack so Jesse could eat and take his medicine. The one bright note in their day of terror was that Chase now felt Jesse's fever had broken. A joyous turning point they couldn't take a single second to celebrate. Even such a short break had no doubt let the others catch up a bit.

At the thought, she quickened her pace yet again, pulling out further in front. They had to move faster, make up the distance. She dipped beneath a low-hanging branch, straightened and stopped at the sight that greeted her.

A large white pine, its top sheered off by a lightning strike, had lost its tenuous hold on the bank and lay toppled across the ravine. A natural phenomenon, she told herself. Hardly an unusual sight in these forests. Yet all at once she was breathing faster than even her hurried pace could account for.

Confused at the power of her reaction, she stumbled back. By the sudden dread that gripped her chest it was as though a precipice yawned before her. Turning aside she hurried on.

Ten feet further, the terrain dipped sharply down a rocky slope offering a view of a wooded valley. Beside her the water began a long cascade over tumbled boulders and ledges of granite. Scanning the vista to confirm her bearings, she prepared to start down the steep descent.

'Hang on a minute,' she heard Chase call.

She stopped and turned but didn't walk back to him.

The log was as thick as a telephone pole and firmly supported at both ends. Judging from the sound of rushing water, it spanned the ravine at the crest of a waterfall – a clear indication, in Chase's mind anyway, that the way to go was across, not down.

He pointed over at the other side. 'Isn't that the way to town? Wouldn't it be faster to cross here?'

'No,' she said simply and turned away.

'No what? Town isn't that way or that way isn't faster?'

'Both.'

He frowned. 'What are you talking about?'

Joining her where the ground sloped away, he pointed to the distance. 'Town's over there. If we cross here we'll cut off all that.' He waved a hand at the area in question.

Shyler stood silent.

Incredulous, he stared down the slope. 'I'm flattered you think my energy reserves are inexhaustible but this way's not just longer, it's steeper and a lot more rugged.' He dropped his voice. 'What if I slip?'

Shyler glanced anxiously up at Jesse then towards the makeshift bridge. Chase couldn't fathom it. Was she worried the log wasn't strong enough to hold them or was it a simple fear of heights?

'It's perfectly safe.' He turned and started walking back. 'I'll help Jesse across first and then –'

'Get away from there!' Her words echoed along the ravine.

Chase spun around. From her tone he'd thought she'd spotted something – a bear, a snake or, worse, the others bursting from the trees to gun them down. But she was simply standing frozen in horror at their proximity to the fallen tree.

Stepping away from it, Chase lowered Jesse to the ground and nudged him towards a rock. 'Sit here while I go talk to her.'

Not since their brief initial exchange had the two of them spoken. Yet as Chase started forward the boy reached up and grabbed his hand. 'What's the matter with her?'

'I don't know. But if you give me a minute I'll try to find out.' *If we have that long.*

The boy eyed the fallen tree. 'You really think we should go that way?'

'Yes. But I don't know these woods like she does.'

Chapter 69

Zack watched the doctor walk away. He still didn't trust him but the man was right – they should cross the stream here. The path on the other side looked heaps easier than the way Shyler wanted them to go.

What was she scared of? The log was plenty wide enough. Even if they fell they wouldn't get hurt. Well, not as bad as if they tumbled down that rocky hill. And if she was worried about him she could relax. He could run across that thing with his eyes closed!

Zack watched Chase talking to her, trying to convince her. He could see the doctor moving his hands, pointing one way then the other. Mr Honesty. Mr Calm and Reasonable. Mr I-only-want-to-help.

Shyler didn't seem any happier. She was still standing with her chin stuck out, holding the gun like she was ready to point it at him again. It probably didn't help that Chase was so much bigger than her. She'd feel scared no matter how calm he was.

Zack stood up. This was taking way too long; they had to get out of here. He didn't like taking the doc's side against Shyler but his way wasn't just easier, it was faster. Maybe he could do something to help convince her. Maybe if he showed her the log was safe . . .

Vanessa scanned the ground in desperation. She'd been bluffing her way for the last half hour hoping to pick up the trail again. So far no dice.

The bitch she was tracking had kept her group to rocky ground as much as possible and over the last such stretch their trail had simply disappeared. It didn't matter how much training you had, no one could track a person over solid rock. But she knew Tragg wouldn't see it that way.

So, in the interests of self-preservation, she had been keeping it her little secret. She'd simply continued in the direction the others had been going before she'd lost them. She walked with assurance, gaze on the ground as though there was actually something there to see, and so far Tragg hadn't caught on.

'You sure this is the way?' he spoke up suddenly as though reading her thoughts.

'Absolutely. Trail's crystal clear.'

'I don't see anything.'

'Trust me, it's there.'

Another ten yards and she caught the sound of running water. A short distance further they pushed through some bushes to find a rocky fault line cutting across their path, disappearing into forest in either direction. At the bottom of the ten-foot-wide ravine, a stream followed the gentle slope away to their left.

Vanessa pretended to check for traces, stalling for time while she made up her mind. Would the bitch have headed uphill or down? She chose the latter.

'This way,' she said, as though her decision had been based on physical evidence.

'You wouldn't be bullshitting me, would you?' Tragg said after another twenty yards. 'Back at the car you were sure they weren't more than half an hour ahead of us. So why haven't we caught up to them yet?'

'They must be moving faster than I thought.'

'With one of them sick? How the hell –'

The pair stopped dead at the sound that echoed up the ravine. The exact words were indiscernible, but it was clearly a woman shouting.

Chapter 70

Chase fought against his sense of urgency. They didn't have time for this. Shyler was clearly distressed about something but they had to get moving. 'Please, just tell me, what's the problem with crossing here?'

'We can't. It's too –' She clamped off the words.

'The log? It's too what? Too thin? Too high? Too weak? What?'

She didn't answer.

'If you're worried about Jesse, I told you I'll help him.'

'No! He mustn't go anywhere near it!' Body hunched, gaze darting, she clutched the rifle.

Chase watched her in disbelief. This was the woman he'd seen in his office – anxious, hyper-vigilant and uncommunicative. A reaction to something beyond their current situation. Behaviour that worsened every time he mentioned crossing the ravine. Or, more specifically, whenever he mentioned Jesse crossing it.

A thought exploded. Could that be it? The tree was a bridge? Hadn't her ex said Shyler had thrown their son off a –

'Hey, look at me!'

At the sound from behind them they turned in unison. Jesse

was standing in the middle of the log, legs braced, waving his arms. 'See, Mom? It's okay!'

Shyler staggered a single step, emitting a sound like a strangled sob.

'Come on! It's easy,' the boy called out. 'Just follow me!'

He turned to continue his passage across when the peace was shattered by a gale of gunfire.

Resting the barrel of her Weatherby Mark V against a boulder, Vanessa paused to calculate drop to target.

On rounding a bend in their downhill course and glimpsing the boy standing on the log below, she and Tragg had had nothing to lose and everything to gain by opening fire. And though the view from their vantage point was partially obstructed by over-hanging trees, Tragg currently had their target pinned by a steady stream of automatic fire.

Placing her eye to the telescopic sight she caressed the trigger. 'Hold it right there, you little shit.'

Chapter 71

At the first burst of gunfire Jesse flinched, nearly losing his balance on the log. Arms outstretched, he started for the opposite bank. A volley cut across his path and with his next backward step his foot slid off the side.

Suddenly he was hanging from the log, not standing on it.

Chase sprinted towards him. Running beside him, Shyler fired blindly up the ravine. An effort he prayed would give them all a few seconds' cover.

They reached the log and started across. Jesse was clinging to the shattered remains of one of its branches, splinters flying about his head. Shyler fired her second round and as Chase reached down to pull the boy up there was a moment of silence.

Almost at once the din resumed. Heedless of the drop to the rocks below they raced for shelter. On the far side Chase pushed the others behind a boulder, then turned and ran back.

The doc was nuts. They were safe, they'd made it! All they had to do was run into the forest. What the hell was he going back for?

Catching his breath, Zack stood gaping. Beside him Shyler was reloading her rifle. When she finished she jumped up and ran back as well.

Zack stretched up to see the two of them. Chase had grabbed the end of the log and was trying to lift it. He was clearly struggling but Shyler wasn't helping. Instead she stood at the bushes next to him, aiming her rifle into the foliage. 'Come out of there! Now!'

From above them the automatic fire resumed. An arc of bullets struck the log and began swinging in Chase's direction. 'What are you doing?' he yelled to Shyler. He'd managed to lift the log an inch. 'Either help me or get back.'

Shyler thrust her gun towards the bush again. 'I know it's you! I swear I'll shoot if you don't come out!'

Straining with his burden, Chase began walking it to one side. Zack finally got what he was trying to do. But the gunshots were almost to his hands!

'Shyler, for God's sake, there's nobody there!'

The man's desperate words gave Zack an idea. Breaking cover he rushed to Shyler, grabbed her arm and spun her around. 'They went back behind us!' he yelled, pointing up the ravine.

Shyler swung the rifle around and fired. In the resulting brief silence she pushed Zack away then looked down and saw what Chase was doing. Firing her last round up the stream, she shouldered her weapon and dashed to help him.

Chapter 72

'I lost them!' Tragg called from behind the tree he'd been using as cover. 'Have you got a fix?'

'Too many branches. Let's move down.' Before Vanessa had finished her sentence the man was running.

Together they raced along the ravine, pausing only where terrain or foliage provided cover for a possible ambush. When they reached the spot where Zack had stood on the fallen log, they found both him and his accomplices gone.

Stepping to the edge, Vanessa peered into the ravine. There it was – their fastest, easiest way across, smashed to splinters on the rocks below.

She stiffened at the feel of Tragg moving up to stand beside her. Then flinched when, in unchecked frustration, he fired a volley blindly into the forest on the other side.

'There's got to be another way across,' she said when the shots died away. 'All this has done is buy them some time.'

Vanessa paused to catch her breath. It had taken them a good half hour to work their way down the rocky slope, and another before the ravine had narrowed enough that they could jump across. Now, as they stood on the opposite side overlooking the flat stretch ahead, she suddenly had an uneasy feeling.

'I think we should go back to where they crossed and follow them from there.'

Tragg looked up the slope they'd descended then back at her. 'They're heading for town; that's over that way.' He pointed to their left. 'We keep going straight we'll cut 'em off.'

She frowned. 'That's what's bothering me.'

'What the hell are you talking about?'

'I'm not sure the bitch would keep going that way. She'd know we'd expect her to and change direction.'

'So which way do you think she's going?'

'I don't know. That's why I'm saying –'

Tragg swore.

'If we go this way we'll be walking blind,' Vanessa reasoned. 'If we climb back up I can find their trail again.'

'Which'll put us at least two hours behind them.'

'Better than losing them completely. Besides, if they aren't heading for town we've got all the time in the world to catch them.' She held out the map for his inspection. 'There's nothing but wilderness in every other direction.'

Chapter 73

Shyler stepped out on the narrow escarpment and looked to the distance. The last rays of sunlight warmed her face and formed a golden pool along the horizon. Undulating mountains, streaked in the sepia tones of dusk, sprawled like a giant bedded down for the night.

Shifting her gaze to the valley floor, she wondered for perhaps the twentieth time if her ploy had worked. Their pursuers would no doubt have expected them to head for town after crossing the ravine so she'd done just the opposite and kept to high ground. If they hadn't picked up on what she'd done they were down there right now, floundering in the dark, unable to find any trace of their quarry. Which meant for the moment Jesse was safe and they could allow themselves a much-needed rest.

But although she was tired enough to drop in her tracks, she doubted she would get any sleep. Her behaviour at the ravine still haunted her. With every step she had taken since, she'd grown more convinced only a small part of what she'd experienced had actually been real.

The prospect was terrifying. It was as though a black hole existed in her mind, a well of secret unspeakable horrors. She sensed that understanding those images was vital to the decisions she was making now. Yet the thought of shining a light on that space and actually seeing what was there . . .

She shuddered as the forest's chill washed over her. The sun was gone now, leaving her to face her dawning realisations with fading hope. If it was true, if she had lost touch, then she couldn't be trusted to take care of Jesse. More than that, it meant her lapses – face it, her madness – might actually place him in greater danger.

She heard a muffled grunt as Chase, having caught up to her at last, tripped over something in the deepening gloom. His footsteps halted at the forest's edge. 'You must have eyes like an owl. What do you say we stop for the night?'

She stayed as she was, unable to answer.

'Yeah, I'm hungry,' came a supporting vote.

At the sound of Jesse's voice, tears were suddenly burning her eyes. And with them a phantom freed from its grave – a voice in her mind, repeating the same words over and over. *What have I done? What have I done?*

Chase walked a stone's toss back into the woods. He wanted to camp near enough to the cliff to profit from any moonlight available but not so close that one of them might wander off the edge in the night.

Crouching down, he let his passenger slide from his back. 'Looks like we'll be camping here.'

'It's cold.' The boy peered around at the deepening shadows.

'I know. We can't light a fire, unfortunately, but if we sleep close together we'll be all right.' Chase pulled the blanket around the boy and gave his shoulders a vigorous rub. Perhaps cold wasn't the only thing bothering him. 'Get yourself settled and I'll bring you some food.'

By the last of the fading light Chase walked over to stand beside Shyler. She seemed unaware of him, deep in thought. He lowered his voice so the boy wouldn't hear. 'Shyler, where have we been headed these last three hours?'

She didn't answer.

'Even I know we weren't this far from town. Where have we been going?'

'Away from where we were.'

'Could you perhaps be a bit more specific?'

'I don't know.'

Her voice had been even softer this time – he couldn't possibly have heard her correctly. 'What was that?'

'That's right, I have no idea.' At last she turned to him. 'All I know is what we're running *from*.'

'You mean we're lost.'

'I didn't say that. I know exactly where we are. I just don't know where we can go that's safe.'

At the strain in her voice his chest grew tight. He gave her a moment then reached up and gently took her shoulders. 'Shyler, we can't wander around these woods forever.'

Her body sagged and for a moment he thought she might actually lean against him. Instead she straightened.

'I know.' She swallowed. 'Which is why at first light tomorrow you're going to take Jesse and head for town.'

'I am?'

'When the sun comes up I'll show you the way.'

'And what will you be doing in the meantime?'

'Waiting here.'

'For them, you mean.' When she gave no answer he understood. 'No, I'm sorry, that's not an option.'

'Look, I know what's happening, I know that I'm –'

Her words cut off, somehow leaving him with the impression

327

it had been her own state of mind she'd thought to discuss. Or maybe that was only what he wanted to believe.

Her behaviour back at the ravine had disturbed him. For a few crucial moments she'd appeared to disengage from reality. And she'd been distant and preoccupied ever since, even to the boy. Now he grew hopeful. Awareness that a problem existed was the first step in treatment. 'What, Shyler? What do you know?'

But the moment had passed. She shook her head. 'As far as I can see it's the only option. I stop them here or it never ends.'

'And if you don't stop them?'

She lifted her gaze. 'Then it'll be up to you. All that matters is to keep Jesse safe.'

Reluctant to upset her yet unwilling to commit to such a plan, Chase tried to stall. 'What do you say we discuss it in the morning?'

She hefted the rifle and turned for the forest. 'There's nothing to discuss.'

Chapter 74

Zack sat huddled with the blanket around him. He could hear Chase and Shyler talking a short way off but couldn't make out what they were saying.

In the past few hours he'd been thinking lots about the doctor. Maybe the man had been telling the truth when he said he'd thought Tragg and Vanessa were cops. If he really wanted the others to kill them he never would have driven away or helped them across the ravine.

Zack hugged himself, remembering the feel of his foot sliding off the side of the log, that horrible sensation of dropping into open space. The rocks had looked a long way down as he'd clung to that branch. He'd thought he was going to fall for sure.

Then suddenly a big hand had closed around his wrist and he was flying upwards. Set on his feet, a large presence protecting his back, he'd been guided across by those same sure hands, then pushed to safety behind a rock.

He shook his head. He still didn't get it. Even with the others shooting at them Chase had helped him. Why? To score points with Shyler? Because he felt guilty? If all he'd wanted was to save himself, wouldn't he just have run off and left them?

At the sound of footsteps Zack looked up. Chase was walking towards him carrying the backpack. 'Shyler's taking first watch,' he said. 'I'll relieve her in a couple of hours.'

Chase sat down, opened the pack and began rummaging through it. 'Well now, Jesse, what would you like for your first course this evening? Apple or pear?'

Zack hesitated. There were things he desperately wanted to know and this man was the only one who could tell him. No way did he trust him a hundred per cent, but maybe the little he did was enough. 'A pear,' he answered. 'And it's Zack, not Jesse.'

Beside him the doctor went still for a moment. Then he held out what was in his hand. 'Good to finally meet you, Zack.'

Zack accepted the piece of fruit and took a big bite as the doctor did the same with his apple.

'So tell me, Zack, why have you and Shyler been pretending you're her son?'

'I'm the only one pretending. She really thinks I am her son.'

'Why would she think that, do you suppose?'

Zack blew out a ragged breath. It was the question he'd been asking himself for the last four days. 'I saw this picture back at her cabin. It was of her and some guy and a little kid. Could be her family.' He shrugged. 'Guess I look like the kid a bit.'

Chase dug the ground with the heel of his boot and dropped the apple core into the hole. 'So why were you pretending to be Jesse?'

'I told her I wasn't but she just kept calling me that. At first it kinda made me mad. But then when Nolan came and tried to kill me Shyler stopped him. I figured she wouldn't keep doing that if she knew who I really was.' Zack straightened sharply. 'You can't say anything. You can't tell her I told you this.'

'I won't tell her anything you don't want me to.' Chase reached into the pack again. 'So is Nolan one of the men who're after you?'

'He was, but . . . Not any more I don't think.'

'I gather he's one of the casualties back at Shyler's cabin, then.'

Zack didn't answer.

'Well, since you've started down this road maybe you can finally tell me why these people are after you.'

Zack straightened and hardened his voice. 'First you gotta tell me something.'

'All right. If I can.'

'Last week, in your office . . . You treated a kid . . .'

'I treated several children last week, Zack. What was his name?'

'Corey. But . . . you wouldn't know that.'

'I wouldn't? Well, how –' A heartbeat of silence. 'The John Doe child. You know him? He was with you? *You* brought him in?'

Zack braced himself to relate the details. 'There were three of us at the start – me, Reece and Corey. Corey was the youngest and when he got hurt . . . Well, me and Reece . . .'

Chase heard the pained uncertainty in his tone. 'You did the right thing. Corey definitely needed medical attention.'

'So what was wrong with him? We saw the ambulance come. Where did they take him? Was he all right?'

'They took him to Presque Isle hospital, about an hour's drive from here. As for his condition, I don't have the equipment to run all the tests but I suspect he may have injured his spleen.'

'Is that bad?'

'It depends on how severely he damaged it. Do you have any idea how it happened?'

Zack bit his cheek, feeling the food turn sour in his stomach. 'There was an accident.'

'In a car, you mean?'

'It was how we got away. The car drove off the road into a ditch.'

For the next few minutes, Zack gave the details of their ordeal – from their life with the Learys to learning the truth about their rescue to their ultimate escape and arrival in Deadwater. In answer to the man's gentle probing he even blabbed stuff about his real mother – why she'd left him, that she'd died, where he'd been since.

'So what happened to the third boy, Reece?' Chase asked.

'Nolan and Vanessa followed us here and found us in the general store. They caught Reece but I got away. Nolan never saw me 'cause I jumped in the back of Shyler's car.'

They sat in silence.

'You've certainly been through a lot,' Chase said finally. 'But why didn't you feel you could tell me any of this?'

'Yeah, right, like you'd really believe me.'

'Why wouldn't I?'

Zack held the words in as long as he could but at last they burst out. 'Because I make promises and then don't keep them! I'm a liar and no one should ever believe me!'

The man thought a moment. 'You promised to take care of Reece and Corey, didn't you?'

Fighting his tears, Zack looked down.

'Sounds to me like you did your best. Were you going very fast when the car hit the ditch?'

'Not too fast.' Zack wiped his eyes.

'Then I'd say Corey's injuries probably wouldn't have been too severe.'

'Probably? You mean you don't know? Didn't you call the hospital to see how he was?'

'I did. Several times. They wouldn't tell me.' Chase explained why.

'Then for all you know Corey could be . . .' Zack bowed his head again. This time he had no hope of winning the battle.

After a moment he felt the man's arm slip around his shoulder. The same strength that had helped him across the log was there for him now. He didn't really want it. He certainly didn't need it. But if the doc thought it was helping he could knock himself out.

Chapter 75

Chase kept his arm around Zack's shoulders until they stopped quaking and his body relaxed. When he thought the boy was finally asleep he eased him to the ground and tucked the blanket close around him.

The truth was worse than he had feared. At hearing this innocent speak the name Lazaro a knot had tightened inside his chest. The man was a well-known Northside thug – to possess knowledge that could put him in prison would be frightening to anyone, let alone a ten-year-old.

We don't even know where that guy hid the case! And even if we did, they'd kill us anyway!

Chase gazed down at the sleeping form with a sense of awe. Zack's ingenuity in arranging his and his brothers' escape and getting them safely as far as they'd come was truly amazing.

As for pretending to be Shyler's son, it didn't take a genius to see his motives went beyond simply trying to evade his enemies. Having to leave his brothers behind had clearly caused him tremendous guilt. What better way to escape feeling hateful than to assume the identity of a child adored? And for a kid who'd been abandoned by his mother and spent the last three years shunted

334

from one foster home to another, Shyler's devotion would have seemed a dream come true.

And that could be the most serious problem – a danger even worse and more immediate than the thugs who were after them. Shyler herself.

'You really think she killed her kid?'

Chase looked down at the drowsy boy who'd just asked the very question he'd been contemplating. What could he say that wouldn't destroy the child's fragile hopes? What should he answer – what he'd been told or believed in his heart?

'Zack, you know . . . sometimes things happen to grown-ups. Things that make them . . . well –'

'Never mind.' The boy rolled over, pulled up the blanket and settled again. 'Even crazy, Shyler's the best mom there ever was.'

Chase sat unmoving. He waited nearly half an hour this time, torn between urgency to complete his next task and wanting to be sure the boy was asleep.

At last he got quietly to his feet and slipped his hand into his pocket. The mobile was there, right where he'd put it after snatching it up off the floor of the Rover before they'd abandoned it.

Had Shyler killed her son? He wanted desperately to believe she hadn't, but wanting wasn't enough. With all that was at stake he had to be sure.

He turned towards the cliff. He could just make out her silhouette outlined by moonlight where she sat leaning against a large rock. Keeping her in sight, he walked a short way through the trees, just enough to ensure neither she nor Zack could overhear him. The forest had been a problem before but here on the cliff top he should get a signal.

Taking cover behind a tree he opened the phone and hit a stored number. After three rings his call was picked up. 'Mr Linnell?'

The man recognised his voice at once. 'You again.'

'I'm sorry, we were disconnected last time.'

'We weren't disconnected, I hung up on you. Just like I'm going to do now.'

'No, wait! Please, this is important. I need to ask you about Shyler and Jesse.' Chase held his breath. No answer but no disconnection either. 'Mr Linnell, please. I understand it's difficult for you, but I need to know how Jesse died. You said Shyler killed him.'

Again no reply.

'Does that mean you were there? You saw what happened?'

'I wasn't there but I know what happened.'

Chase thrust a hand through his hair. He didn't have time to decipher riddles. 'Please, Mr Linnell, I need to know.'

'Well, what version do you want to hear, Doc? Shyler's or the cops'?'

'I take it they differ.'

'You could say that.'

'Start with hers, then.'

'Right, the Gospel according to Shyler.' A second's pause as the man prepared himself. 'She picked Jesse up after Little League training, just around dusk. They were walking home when some drugged-out punks trapped them on a bridge and demanded money. Shyler didn't have much and when she handed it over they thought she was holding out on them. To force her to pay, they grabbed Jesse and held him over the side of the bridge, at which point either they dropped him or he slipped. By the time Shyler got down to the water he'd been swept away. According to her.'

Chase frowned. 'But you don't think it happened that way.'

'The cops didn't believe her. Why should I? They never found a trace of the five men she talked about, despite her detailed and colourful descriptions. You know, she actually gave them all names based on some aspect of how she'd imagined them. Fish Hook was the leader. Puppet was the one who grabbed Jesse. And then there was Snake and Scarecrow, and some other one I don't remember.'

Chase tried to keep the man on track. 'So what did the police –'

'They think it was a simple case of negligence. Shyler wasn't paying attention and Jesse climbed up on the railing. When he fell and died, she made up her story to cover her guilt.'

'Was Shyler normally careless with Jesse?'

'No, not usually.' His tone was grudging.

'Then why would they think –'

'Because they never found anything to support her claims. Not one shred of proof. Not a footprint, not a witness, not a fingerprint. Nothing.'

'That still doesn't mean . . .' He couldn't believe it. 'Shyler was your wife. Didn't *you* think she was telling the truth?'

'I tried, believe me. All through the investigation, the months afterwards. In the end, I just had to accept their version of things.'

Chase gripped the phone. *Of course you did.*

'I stuck around as long as I could after that. But it was no good. Shyler sensed how I felt by then.'

'So you just walked out on her.'

'Hey, don't you judge me, you arrogant bastard! You know what it's like to sleep beside the woman who murdered your child? You have any idea what that's like?'

Chase took a breath. 'Did you ever bother to check how she was going?'

'I heard from a friend she was having problems – panic attacks, nightmares, weird spells where she'd relive the whole thing while she was awake.'

'Intrusive flashbacks.' Chase squeezed the bridge of his nose. 'Sir, the things you've described are symptoms of post-traumatic stress disorder. They suggest Shyler really did have some kind of horrific experience. Did she ever receive treatment?'

'She had a bit of counselling after it happened but she stopped it herself. Said she didn't need it any more.'

'This condition would've made it difficult, if not impossible, for Shyler to function. She'd have struggled to hold down a job, go out in public, even carry out everyday errands.'

'I guess that's what guilt does to a person.' The line disconnected.

Chase stood a moment fighting his anger. He looked towards the cliff, to the woman keeping watch over a child who wasn't hers. A woman so desperate to erase the memory of an event totally beyond her control that she would create an alternate reality in its place.

Slowly his outrage changed to conviction. In every conflict he'd ever known he'd always managed to see both sides. Not this time. This time for better or worse he had chosen. He'd known it before he'd even placed the call. For once in his life he was truly, wholly, unswayably committed.

'You should've believed in her, Mr Linnell.'

Chapter 76

Chase closed the phone and bowed his head. Never had he felt such a sense of relief, nor vindication that his intuitive faith in a person had been justified. Now, with the information he'd gained, he might finally unlock some of the mysteries surrounding Shyler.

First and foremost, she hadn't killed her son. Yet, like her ex-husband, she could very well blame herself for what happened, a common reaction in people who'd experienced such trauma as she had.

Unlike others, however, Shyler had had no support in coping. Her husband had left, her father was dead, she was estranged from her mother. And, if she followed the pattern of most PTSD sufferers, she'd withdrawn from friends.

Slowly her behaviour began to make sense. Her overriding goal in everything she did would have been to avoid any situation that triggered memories of her ordeal. And if she were forced into such a scenario – like crossing the ravine – she could well be expected to experience symptoms. Like seeing the men who'd killed her son hiding in the bushes on the other side.

Surely, for Shyler, the greatest threat of triggering bad memories would arise from contact with children. Zack's presence around her cabin would have placed her under enormous stress. She might have dealt with it for a time by denying his presence, blocking him out. Which she'd managed to do, according to Zack, by simply ignoring him. But when Nolan showed up and tried to kill him that would have tipped her over the edge.

At that point everything would have changed for her. Forced to take action in a situation far too similar to her original trauma, her denial would have shifted – from not seeing Zack at all to seeing him as Jesse. The son she would give her life to protect.

Chase looked down at the phone in his hand. He still had a signal. Just one more call to make. There was no reason not to any more. Shyler's fear of the police clearly stemmed from their treatment of her in regard to Jesse's death. If she were thinking clearly now he had no doubt she'd agree to letting him contact them.

Entering nine-one-one, he waited. He didn't know their exact location but the police would hopefully be able to triangulate –

A scream from the darkness stopped his heart.

Dropping the phone he ran for the cliff edge.

The others had found them! That was all Chase could think as he raced towards the sound. At the wood's edge he stopped. The cliff beyond was littered with rocks. He snatched one up, drew back to throw it, then froze with his hand above his head.

Only one silhouette stood in the moonlight. Shyler. Still screaming, rifle forgotten. In the throes of a nightmare? She'd fallen asleep? Stumbling perilously close to the edge!

Rushing forward, he pulled her against him and slid his free hand over her mouth. If the others were near enough to hear her screams –

Shyler grew frantic. She kicked and flailed.

He pressed his lips to the side of her face. 'It's okay, it's me. There's no one else here. You're all right, you're safe.'

Still she swung at him, straining to reach around and claw his face.

Chase took a chance. From what he now knew of her ordeal he could guess what her nightmare had been about.

'Listen to me. They're all gone. Fish Hook? Puppet? They've all run off. You drove them away.'

Her struggles stopped but her body was rigid within his arms.

'You hear me, Shyler? They're gone, every one. Snake. Scarecrow. All of them. Gone.'

When she still didn't move, he slowly slid his hand from her mouth.

'Jesse?' she hissed, between ragged breaths.

'He's fine. See.' He turned her slightly and pointed through the trees. 'He's asleep, just there. Safe and sound.'

Her tension eased down another notch. 'Fish Hook. The others. They're really gone?'

'Yes, they're really gone.' *And one day they'll be gone for good, I promise.* Closing his eyes, Chase breathed the leafy scent of her hair. He brushed his lips across her brow, pressed a light kiss to her temple.

Without warning she turned in his arms. 'Chase?'

'Shyler.' He brushed a stray lock out of her face.

'I . . . I'm not . . . I don't think . . .'

She was trembling now. He wrapped his arms around her again. 'Easy, it's all right.'

'You have to promise. If something happens to me, you'll take care of Jesse.'

He held her closer. 'Nothing's going to happen to you.' *I won't let it.*

'I don't just mean if I should get hurt. I mean . . . If you see that I'm unable . . . If I'm not doing what's best for him . . .'

'When have you ever –'

'Promise me anyway!'

He took her face in both his hands. 'All right, I promise.'

Vanessa blundered as far as she dared through the murky shadows. The woman's screams had given her a bearing. Frustratingly brief, but enough to guide her through the forest a good quarter mile closer to their quarry.

She stopped and listened. Nothing but the wind. If they heard no more screams they'd have to wait till the sun came up to move again. But that was fine. At least she knew now she'd made the right call. They were close. Very close.

She settled down against a tree. The crunch of dry leaves a short way off told her Tragg was doing the same. She smiled to herself. He would never admit she'd been right in climbing back up the slope, yet the fact he wasn't questioning her decision to stop again said it all.

Leaning her head back she laid the Weatherby across her thighs. She would rest for now, but remain alert to the slightest sound. If the screams came again she'd be ready to run.

She smiled as she closed her eyes. The bitch had been smart, changing direction, but not smart enough. Clearly, she'd under-estimated her opponent. And tomorrow, at first light, Vanessa would show her just how wrong she'd been.

Chapter 77

Zack stretched his legs, feeling a familiar presence beside him. When a hand touched his cheek he opened his eyes to see Shyler's sweet face gazing down at him.

'Morning, Sunshine. How are you feeling?'

He nodded, then reached from beneath the blanket to take her hand. She'd been with him all night, allaying his fears and transforming a simple pile of leaves to a warm, secure bed. And now, though he knew they had to leave, he didn't want the feeling to end. He let out a sigh and watched the silvery plume of his breath dissipate in the pre-dawn light.

Shyler smiled. 'We should get going.'

'Ready when you are,' came an answering voice.

Zack looked around to see Chase sitting propped against the nearest tree, holding the rifle. Had he been there all night, watching over them? Shyler must have decided he could be trusted if she'd given him the gun.

Zack eyed the man with a curious feeling. It was weird, the three of them together like this. If it wasn't for the constant sense of fear, they could almost be on a camping trip. A vacation or something. As though they were . . .

He swallowed a sudden tightening in his throat. A family. That's what it was like, a family. He shoved the thought away and got up.

Shyler rose as well and started away from them. 'I just want to take a quick look from the cliff before we leave.'

'Here, take this.' Chase handed over the rifle as she passed then pushed to his feet.

He walked a few paces in the opposite direction, then started searching around on the ground. 'How's the leg this morning?'

'Yeah, okay.' Watching the man's movements, Zack pulled the blanket tighter around him. 'What are you doing?'

'Looking for my phone.'

Zack stood blinking. Had he heard the man right? 'You've got a mobile?'

'Couldn't get a signal before last night. Then afterwards I dropped it and couldn't find it again in the dark.'

'Afterwards? You mean you used it! Who'd you call?'

'Shyler's ex.'

Zack felt his stomach relax a bit. 'What did he say? Did she or didn't she?' The doc would surely know what he meant.

'No. I'm convinced Shyler didn't kill her son.'

'Told ya!' Smiling, Zack began scanning the ground with him. 'So if you already talked to him why do you need to find your phone?'

'To call the police.'

He froze. 'You can't.'

'Zack, our only way out of this is to get some help.'

'You don't understand. They'll send me back!'

Chase stepped towards him. 'Zack, whatever happens I give you my word you'll never end up in a place like the Learys' ever again.'

'How do you know?'

344

'Because I'll make sure of it.'

Zack stared up at him. Make sure how? Was he saying he would foster him himself? It wouldn't be bad living with the doctor as long as Shyler was there too, but – No, that was crazy. What was he thinking? They'd never do that.

'Bastard! You're just like every other grown-up! You think it's okay to lie to kids to get what you want!'

'Zack, I swear to you –'

'Everybody says that! Everyone promises! And no one's ever kept them but *her*!'

Chase took his shoulders. 'Listen to me –'

'No, lemme go! I'm staying with Shyler!' Zack twisted free and stumbled away. His heart was already clubbing his ribs but the next sound made it leap in his chest – a gunshot echoing along the cliff.

From the very direction Shyler had gone.

Blinding terror seared through his veins. 'Mom!' he screamed. Before Chase could grab him he was running for the cliff.

Chapter 78

Shyler dragged herself behind a boulder. The shot had come from the woods beyond. Her arm was screaming where she'd been hit. Worst of all, she'd dropped the rifle and couldn't see it anywhere. How was she going to protect Jesse!

Bracing her good hand against the rock, she tried to push up. Pain swamped her senses. Darkness encroached at the sides of her vision and she slumped back down. *Don't pass out. Damn it, don't faint!*

She opened her eyes. The rising sun was spreading long shadows across the cliff top. By the burgeoning light she opened her jacket and had a look. The bullet appeared to have passed right through but a good chunk of flesh had been ripped from her arm. Even if she didn't faint from blood loss, shock and pain would take their toll.

She choked back a sob. She had to try again. Now, while she could, while she still had the strength. She had to get up, had to reach him, had to –

Oh, God. Jesse, no!

Panic overrode her pain. He was running towards her out of the woods. Breaking cover.

'No! Get down!'

Another shot echoed along the cliff top. He dived for cover behind a rock not much bigger than his own little body. Twenty feet away from her.

He might just as well have been at the ends of the earth.

Vanessa stalked slowly towards the cliff. She had little to fear. Her first shot hadn't just hit the bitch; it had sent her rifle flying over the edge. With their only weapon now beyond reach, the remaining two targets were completely defenceless.

Still, she had to be careful. The boy was unharmed and could still make a run for it. If he reached the woods he might get away. Tragg would have heard her shots and be running to join her, but she couldn't count on him stopping the kid.

Besides, she wanted to finish this herself.

Slipping from the trees, she started out across the ledge. Rocks to her left gave limited cover. She raised the Weatherby, stepped around and smiled at the terrified boy crouched behind them. With the drop-off less than six feet away he had nowhere to run but over the edge.

So here it was, her moment of truth. When Tragg had told her – whether as punishment or because he'd sensed her weakness, her conflict – that the job of killing the boys would be hers, at first she'd despaired. But the closer she'd got in tracking their prey the more she'd seen what he was offering. This was her test, her initiation. The act that would ultimately earn her a place among Lazaro's favoured.

Zack's eyes widened as she levelled the barrel. In a useless gesture he threw up his hands. But the last thing she saw before squeezing the trigger was a dark shape darting across from the side.

Vanessa jumped back.

The body that sprawled across the granite wasn't the boy's. With an unexpected stab of regret she stared down at the doctor's face. Blood was spreading from beneath his head, already forming a little pool in a hollow of rock.

'You killed him!' Zack shrieked.

She clutched the rifle as again her weakness fought to the surface. Pity? Remorse? Tragg would never have suffered such doubts. Damn this kid for making her feel them!

'No, Zack, *you* did, just like the others. That bitch who was helping you. Reece and Corey. They're all dead now and it's all your fault.'

Zack felt the blow in the middle of his gut.

'You just couldn't keep your mouth shut, could you? Had to drag strangers into it. Had to tell your little brothers everything. Boy, you really took care of them, didn't you?'

'No! You're lying! They aren't dead!'

Vanessa smiled and raised the rifle. 'Don't worry, you're not going to miss them for long.'

Even as her finger curled round the trigger, a second, much smaller figure sprang from the rocks. Never slowing, Shyler slammed into her, driving her the last few steps towards the edge.

And vanished with her over the side.

Chapter 79

Zack stood rigid, too horrified to move or even cry out. When the scream from the drop-off finally faded, his paralysis broke and he ran towards the edge.

Shyler was there, four feet below, sprawled on a small ledge jutting from the cliff face. She sat up weakly and reached for a handhold. He grabbed her sleeve and helped her climb up.

The instant they fell back onto the summit a volley of gunfire exploded from the woods. They rolled behind rocks. With Shyler's good arm around his shoulder, he pushed them both up. They took off shambling along the cliff top.

The initial shock from her wound was wearing off. She was moving faster now, nearly running. Leafy fingers snatched at their hair, vines writhed up to ensnare their feet. Clutching Jesse's hand, Shyler stumbled through the forest.

Gone was all sense of plan or direction other than keeping to the cover of the trees. She'd lost her bearings the moment they'd veered away from the cliff edge. Through the next wall of foliage could be a road, more forest or another drop-off. She only ran faster.

Even in her panic she sensed it wasn't fear of death alone that was driving her. It was something else, something far worse. A flickering awareness that, once fully realised, would rip through her mind the way no bullet could tear her flesh. Something was stirring in the depths of the pit, slithering upwards, determined to show itself.

Turning her focus to the woods behind them, she listened for footsteps. They'd heard nothing since leaving the cliff. No more shots since . . .

Her heart clenched. A pain sharper and more soul-destroying than the one in her arm. Chase. She tore her mind from the image of him lying still and bloodied. Not now. Jesse! Rounding a tree, she urged him faster.

Despite the silence, she wasn't fooled. Whoever had shot at them wasn't far behind. She'd had neither the time nor presence of mind to conceal their trail. Only the trees were now protecting them.

Plunging through a tangle of undergrowth she stopped, gasping at the sudden loss of cover. A clearing. A single-storey shed sprawled in its centre. One of Downeaster's small local sawmills. It was early but some workers might already be inside.

She hurried towards it, pulling Jesse with her through a yard littered with machinery, equipment and piles of logs. They reached the building and fell against its door. Jesse helped her push it open.

Whatever hopes she'd had for assistance vanished the moment they stepped inside. The place was deserted. In fact – Oh God, hadn't she heard the company had closed one of its mills last spring?

She looked around, fears deepening. Except for one walled-off corner, the building was nothing but a huge open room. Benches and racks filled much of the space but nothing big enough to hide inside or protect them from gunfire.

'Come on.' Jesse yanked her towards the corner room.

A pitted sign hung askew on the door: LOADING BAY: NO OPEN FLAME. Inside, a garage, dark and empty. They ran for the roller door at its far end, but even together they couldn't lift it.

Cursing her useless arm, she straightened. She spotted a lever mounted to the wall, grabbed it and heaved.

With a shriek of protest it yielded an inch. A flurry of sawdust showered over them. The lever didn't work the roller door at all. It was connected to a pair of drop-away panels in the ceiling. The sawdust had fallen through a crack between them. Some kind of storage compartment for shavings.

Her hopes flickered – could they hide up there? She glanced around and felt them deflate. Not without a ladder. She wiped the stinging grit from her eyes and pulled Jesse back to the door they'd entered by.

Eyes streaming, they stepped through and froze. A silhouette was sliding past the opposite window. Their pursuer was here.

Chapter 80

Shyler pulled Jesse behind her and side-stepped along the wall. As the door across from them creaked open they rounded the corner of the garage and slipped back into the mill's deeper shadows.

'Hey, Zacky, you in there?' came a man's voice.

Shyler's heart kicked. That name again. The woman at the cliff had used it as well. Why were they calling her son Zack? Had they mistaken him for someone else?

'Trick or treat.' The door flew back. The man burst in and opened fire, sweeping the room in a hail of bullets. She shoved Jesse down behind a bench and threw herself over him.

When the ear-splitting din finally stopped, the voice called again. 'Guess this is it, Zacky-boy. Not many places to hide in here.'

Shyler clamped Jesse in her one good arm. Jesse. He was Jesse! She could feel him trembling and held him tighter. *It's all right, baby. I'll never let go.*

But the voice in her head just wouldn't stop. There was more to her terror than this man with the gun. She couldn't stop hearing the name he'd spoken. Couldn't stop feeling –

And at once she knew. This was the monster scrabbling from the pit. This was what had driven her from the cliff in such desperation. Not fear of death, but fear of truth.

The man spoke again, closer this time. 'Don't expect any promises, will ya? Your chances for quick-and-easy are gone. It's payback time, Zacky-boy.'

With death perhaps only moments away, she had to know. She pried the small arms from around her and eased the boy back. Cupping his cheek in her trembling hand, she lifted his face.

Zack thought his fear couldn't get any worse until he looked into Shyler's eyes. Something was wrong. She seemed in pain. Had she been shot again?

'You're not Jesse,' she barely whispered, trailing light fingers down his face. 'You're not my boy.'

His stomach dropped a thousand storeys. She knew. Reality had finally come to her. The dream was over.

Something crashed and he flinched at the noise. Still he couldn't tear his eyes from her face. Her filthy, tear-streaked, beautiful face. Tragg had won. They were going to die. Yet all he wanted was to scream at her that it was okay, he could still be Jesse, they could go on pretending. He just couldn't get the words to come out.

'Come on, kid, you know it's no use. Just show yourself and let's get this done.'

Tragg's voice was even closer than before. The man was moving down the side of the room across from the garage.

Zack grabbed Shyler's arm and shook it. 'What do we do?' But she'd bowed her head and was quaking silently. It was over. The truth had destroyed her.

'I'll make you a deal,' Tragg called out. 'Whoever that bitch is that's been helping you, she can go free. You step out now and I'll let her go. I never wanted her in the first place.'

It was a lie, of course, but it didn't matter. Tragg sounded no more than ten feet away now. If they stayed where they were, he'd see them the minute he stepped round the bench.

Zack sat up. Their only hope was to make a run for it. But could he get Shyler moving again? Her eyes were streaming and so full of hurt it seemed she would break apart if he pulled her.

Yet even as he watched, something changed. Her gaze focused, her body straightened. Shifting to get her feet beneath her, she pushed off his hand.

What are you doing?

She leaned forward, kissed his brow. And then she was gone.

Chapter 81

He choked back his scream as she rushed away from him. Hunched below the bench top, she moved to its end and vanished around it.

Zack sat frozen in horror and panic. She'd actually gone. The minute she'd realised he wasn't Jesse she'd left, just like that. Just like he'd feared. Just like he always knew she would!

Yet sitting there lost he suddenly realised a part of him had thought it might end differently. Talk about crazy. In his secret dream he'd imagined her saying it didn't matter, he was just as good. That she wanted him as much –

A shuffling sound from the rear of the building. An explosion of gunshots from a hell of a lot closer.

He shrank into a ball and covered his ears. Tragg had to be in the very next aisle, practically on top of him.

The shooting stopped. Heavy steps thudded away to his left. Zack turned to see a large figure dart past the end of the bench. He rolled and scurried in the opposite direction.

At the aisle he turned towards the front of the building. Tragg hadn't seen him. Maybe he could get out the way they came in.

He crawled a few yards further and stopped. Were those

footsteps? Someone breathing? The shed had a strange way of echoing sound. He couldn't tell if it was in front or behind him.

On impulse he turned left away from his goal, took two rights, then swung back on course. He stopped, breathing hard, trembling violently and strained to listen. Nothing.

He forced himself on.

Another bench over, the garage came in view on the opposite wall. The shed's front door was now just twenty feet or so to his left. But the area between was a lot more open. If he made a run for it and Tragg was nearby, he'd see him for sure.

Holding his breath, Zack chanced a look over the top of the bench. Not a shadow stirred. He ducked back down, turned and launched himself. He rounded the bench and had halved the distance when he stopped in his tracks.

Something was there in front of the door, some kind of cabinet, a metal locker. The crash he'd heard earlier. Tragg had dumped it there to block their escape.

Zack turned to see the man step from the shadows. He dived for cover past the corner of the garage as Tragg opened fire. Flattened to the wall, he screamed when a hand reached out and grabbed him.

Stumbling back, he fell through the door into Shyler's good arm. Before he could speak she was dragging him towards the end of the room. What was she doing? They were trapped in here!

When they reached the roller door, she let him go and slipped something around his shoulders. 'Keep this over you no matter what.'

Zack clamped his arms around her waist as she lifted her jacket hem up over his head. The last thing he saw before darkness descended was Tragg stepping through the loading bay door.

Chapter 82

With the boy's arms wrapped tightly around her, Shyler fell back against the wall. Her strength all but gone, she clung to the lever for support.

A figure slunk forward out of the shadows. Ugly sneer, eyes like a shark. Icy fingers touched her heart. Fish Hook, Scarecrow, Puppet, Snake . . . they were innocent children compared to the horror in this man's gaze.

He moved to the middle of the chamber and stopped. 'So you're the fucking whore who's been helping him.' He smiled. Trapped and helpless was clearly how he preferred his victims.

He raised his weapon. 'Just so you know, that guy you killed at your cabin was my friend.'

Shyler tightened her grip on the lever. 'Just so you know, the boy you're trying to kill is my son.' She heaved down with all her weight.

The panels dropped.

At the sound overhead, the man looked up, taking the first wave of sawdust in the face. He ducked and swerved but there was no escape. Debris billowed out, filling the air whichever way he turned. He dropped the rifle and threw up his arms.

Eyes shut tight, face pressed to the top of Zack's head, Shyler groped along the bay wall. She fumbled to the back, found the door through which they'd entered and pushed him through it.

The instant she released him he threw off her jacket. A cloud of dust puffed out around their legs. They closed the door and fell against it.

She pressed her ear to its cold steel. The man's roars of anger had choked off into hacking coughs. But even these were now growing weaker. A few seconds more and they'd died altogether.

'Is he dead?' Zack whispered. 'He dropped the rifle, I heard it fall.'

Shyler stood quaking, reluctant to move. She had no idea how much sawdust had actually fallen out of the bin. Enough to temporarily blind the man, yes, but enough to kill him?

At a screech from behind them she spun around. Someone was forcing the mill door open, pushing back the locker the man had put before it, in order to enter. Dear God, not another one! For some reason she'd thought there were only two of them. She grabbed Zack's arm. But where could they run, where could they –

'Shyler! Zack!'

She froze at the sound. A voice she'd thought never to hear again. A hand appeared through the gap, then a shoulder.

With a final heave Chase squeezed through, hunched and bloodied but very much alive. He limped three steps and sprawled across the nearest saw bench. When he started to fall Shyler ran towards him.

They were all right. Shyler hadn't left him. Chase was alive.

Zack couldn't hold back his tears any longer. His thoughts were a jumble but one thing stood out. These people had come for him. They'd risked their lives. Even when they'd had the chance to run they hadn't left him.

Slumped against the loading bay door, he watched them embrace. It didn't bother him like before. In fact it actually made him feel good. And when they turned and reached out their arms to him he had to fight not to blubber like a baby.

He started forward and suddenly he was on the floor, thrown aside by the loading bay door flying open. The expressions on Chase and Shyler's faces told him everything. Tragg wasn't dead. He'd dropped his rifle but he still had that little gun he kept in his shirt.

Sprawled on his back, Zack drew his legs up – no way was this dude gonna wreck things now! – and kicked at the door with all his strength.

It slammed shut with a hollow clang.

A single gunshot resounded from the chamber.

The building rocked as though hit by a tank.

Chapter 83

A roaring sound. Choking black smoke. Whatever had exploded had started a fire in the loading bay. He could feel the heat of it even through the door. Zack rolled onto his hands and knees and started crawling.

He bumped into something big and wooden and ran a hand over it – one of the benches, knocked on its side. A little further he came to another one. He looked above it and, through the smoke, saw the now-shattered window beside the main door.

Panic seized him. Shyler and Chase had been standing right there before the blast. Where were they now? He couldn't see them!

He scurried faster, groped round the bench and gasped when he felt something soft and silky beneath his fingers. Hair. Oh God!

'Shyler!' Smoke filled his throat and he broke off into a fit of coughing. He felt her face, her shoulder, her arm. She wasn't moving. 'Shyler! Get up!'

Eyes streaming, he grabbed her shirt, tried to pull. The fabric tore. He forced his hands beneath her arms and tried to drag her. She seemed to weigh a thousand pounds. 'Mom! *Please!*'

A figure emerged through the haze across from him. 'Help me.'

Chase pulled Shyler to a sitting position and looped her arm around his shoulder. When he struggled to rise, Zack did the same with her other arm and together they got her to her feet. The door was only a few steps further. They squeezed through the opening Chase had created coming in.

Outside the day seemed stunningly bright, the air sharp and clean. They weaved across the clearing and dropped to the ground at its furthest end.

Chase propped Shyler against a tree, bent down and put his ear to her chest.

'Is she dead?' Zack couldn't keep the terror from his voice.

Even as the man straightened, Shyler groaned. Her eyes opened. She looked from one of them to the other and started to push up.

'Relax,' Chase said, settling her back with a hand to her shoulder. 'It's over.'

She blinked at him. 'There was an explosion.'

'The gunman's shot ignited the sawdust.'

'Then he's . . .'

He nodded.

She turned to Zack. 'You're all right?'

Zack couldn't answer. He couldn't move.

'He'll be fine,' Chase said, slumping beside her.

'And you?' She clutched his hand and squeezed, nodding at the gore that streaked his face. 'Dear God, I thought . . .'

His smile was crooked. 'Scalp wound – always masses of blood. Sprained ankle. I'll survive.'

Zack sat watching them both and crying.

Shyler tipped her head, her own eyes growing bright with relief. She touched his cheek. 'Hey, you didn't think I ran out on you, did you?'

Zack gulped a breath. The tears were coming faster now – he could barely see her.

'I was trying to lead the gunman away from you. It was the only way I could think of to . . .' Her frown deepened. 'You didn't really think . . .'

He let out a sob.

'Oh, sweetheart, come here.'

He collapsed against her, burying his face in the crook of her neck. With her arm tight around him he vented the worst of his shock and fear.

After a moment Chase pulled something out of his pocket. 'The police are on the way.' He tapped a number into his mobile and handed it to Shyler. 'Maybe you can tell them where we are.'

When she'd finished the call, Chase closed the phone and set it beside him. Zack lay between them, clutching their hands, fearing that after all they'd been through, these people who now meant everything to him might somehow disappear.

They were both still there, cradling him, when the police arrived an hour later.

Chapter 84

Zack scuffed aimlessly along the corridor from the nurses' station to the vending machine at the opposite end. It was the first time he'd been out of his room since he, Chase and Shyler had arrived at the hospital two days ago. Physically he was fine, if still a little weak. It was just the not-knowing, the growing, twisting lump in his stomach, that was making him feel so restless and sick.

At Chase's request the two of them had been allowed to share a room, with Shyler close by, just up the hall. Zack had slept pretty much the whole first day and all that night. An easy, totally dreamless sleep of exhaustion and relief. But the very next morning the nightmare had returned – when he'd had to tell the police his story.

Shyler and Chase had insisted on being with him as they questioned him and, while he knew why they'd done it, their presence had only made things worse. When he'd come to the part about Reece and Corey – how he'd left them behind, how they'd died because of it – it wasn't the policeman's face he'd been watching, it'd been Shyler's. And when she'd bowed her head and started crying, his own hot tears had forced out as well.

The doctor had given them both something then to make them sleep again. But even as he'd drifted off in Shyler's arms he'd known it would probably be the last time she ever held him.

It seemed he'd been right. For this morning the nightmare had only deepened; so much so, he just couldn't lie still any longer. He'd learned they were going to be released in a few days. Yet so far neither Shyler nor Chase had said anything to him about where he'd be going.

Having reached the vending machine yet again, he turned and started back in the other direction. His stomach hurt, but pacing at least helped take his mind off it.

If they wanted him with them, surely they'd have said something about it by now. Yet as the time for their release drew nearer it seemed less and less likely it was going to happen. And who could blame them? Who'd want a kid who ditched his own brothers to save himself? Especially when they ended up –

He trudged on towards the nurses' station, stopping as he neared Shyler's room. Through its open door he could see her in the chair at the foot of her bed, Chase beside her in a wheelchair, talking to the stranger who'd been in there for ages. The guy wore street clothes so it wasn't a doctor. And it wasn't the cop who'd asked him questions. What did that leave?

The thing in his stomach started twisting again.

When the stranger suddenly got up to go, Zack darted behind a linen cart that stood against the wall. He listened to footsteps fade up the hall, then peeked out – in time to see the man get on the elevator.

A social worker. It had to be.

Zack stepped out and stood staring after him. Maybe he should just run away. Better than having to hear them say it – that they didn't want him, that he'd be going to yet another new foster home. Or, even worse, back to the Learys.

But, no, it was no good. He had to know. Head down, he went through the door.

Chase sat helping Shyler thread her injured arm through the sleeve of a sweater. A bandage encased his sprained left ankle. A second on his head concealed Vanessa's handiwork – the bullet wound that had split his scalp, requiring a dozen stitches to close. Once Shyler's arm was through the sleeve, he gently slipped the sling back around it, then bent and kissed her on the lips.

Zack stood watching, feeling the tightness build in his throat. He gritted his teeth – he wasn't going to cry, no matter what. 'Who was that guy?'

They both looked around at him.

'What guy?' Shyler said.

'The one who just left.'

She glanced at Chase before replying, 'Just another doctor.'

Zack clenched his fists. Why was she lying? To his horror he felt the Bad Boy stirring. 'No, he wasn't. He didn't have a white coat or one of those things around his neck.'

Chase smiled. 'Not all doctors wear white coats.'

'Zack, one of the nurses has a son your size and brought you some clothes.' Shyler pointed to the stack on the tray top. 'Would you like to –'

'No! I don't want to try on stupid clothes, I want to know who that guy was.'

A knock from behind him. Zack turned to see a cop poke his head in – the same one who'd asked them all the questions.

'Got a second?'

Chase wheeled himself from the room. 'Be right back.'

Zack walked after him, stood in the door and watched the two men go up the hall. They stopped in front of the nurses' station, the cop sitting on a bench facing Chase.

'Zack?'

Ignoring Shyler's summons, he kept staring. The cop was doing most of the talking. Chase sat nodding, hand to his chin. Zack felt the lump in his stomach do a flip.

He turned around.

Shyler patted the covers beside her. 'Come here, I need to talk to you.'

Despite his growing urge to run, his feet dragged him forward. He reached her bed and slumped against it.

She stroked a loose bit of hair off his face. 'You've been through a terrible ordeal, something no child should ever have to face. But you are also the strongest, bravest little boy I have ever known. That's why I think you can understand that sometimes things can't work out exactly how we'd like them to.'

So, there it was. That familiar opening line. The heaviness changed into something else – he couldn't feel his body at all now.

'Over these days that you and I have been together you might have noticed me behaving a little strangely at times. I'm not even sure myself everything I might have done. But I need you to know that I never ever meant to hurt you.'

He nodded dully. *Never meant to hurt you*. Yeah, he'd heard that one, too. Despite what he'd vowed, his eyes were burning.

'Those things I did were because of something that happened to me before I met you. You don't need to worry about any of that. What you do need to understand is that when a person has these sorts of problems they're not in the best position to take care of someone else.'

Right, so that's the excuse they were using. Zack pushed up. He'd heard enough.

'Sweetheart, wait. It's not that I don't –'

'Yeah, whatever.'

She grabbed his arm with surprising strength and turned him

back. 'Don't you imagine, even for a second, my heart isn't big enough for two sons.'

Her tears were too much. He pulled free and hurried away, determined she wouldn't see his reaction. Whatever she'd meant by that last statement, the reality was the same – they weren't going to be together.

Blinded by his tears, he ran out the door – straight into Chase who was just returning.

'Whoa, there, partner.' The man caught his arm. 'Where are you going? Don't you want to hear what that policeman told me?'

Zack swiped his eyes. 'What?'

'Reece and Corey are still alive.'

The words zapped through him like a jolt from an outlet. 'But . . . but Vanessa said they –'

'For whatever twisted reason, she lied. Either that or she just didn't know.'

Zack moved his fingers, touched his legs. Every part of him seemed to be buzzing. 'You mean it? They're really –'

'With the information you gave the police, they tracked down Lazaro's men at the warehouse and have already made some initial arrests. They found Reece and Corey recovering in a motel room, safe and unharmed.' Chase's hand settled on his shoulder. 'You saved them, kiddo. Just like you promised.'

Zack bowed his head. The hand rocked him gently as he cleared his throat. 'When can I see them?'

'Well, now that's the only bad part. Not for a while, I'm afraid. You see, Child Welfare has already lined up a new home for the two of them.'

The two of them. So this was why he'd been reluctant to believe – deep down he'd known there was something else coming.

He raised his chin. 'Then what about –?'

Just up the hall the elevator opened and a woman stepped out, pushing a man in a wheelchair. To Zack they looked like somebody's grandparents but Chase raised his hand to catch their eye and they started towards him.

'Thanks so much for driving him in,' Chase told the woman when they stopped before him.

Zack waited as the adults talked, then Chase turned their attention to him.

'Zack, I'd like you to meet my father, Allen, and Shyler's mother, Mrs O'Neil.'

The pair greeted him, said a few more words, then the woman looked around uncomfortably. Chase nodded towards Shyler's room and she gave a brave smile and walked through the door.

Sensing the interest of the two men in wheelchairs, Zack watched with them as the woman crossed the room and stopped just short of the patient in her chair. Shyler slowly pushed to her feet, her expression first stunned, then growing distressed. Zack took an unwitting step towards the door.

Chase put his hand out. 'Give them a minute. They haven't seen each other in a long time.'

'How come?'

'To be honest, I don't know the whole story, but . . . Well, sometimes people have disagreements and it takes them a while to get over things.'

Zack found himself pinned to the spot. Shyler's *mother*. No other word had this effect on him. He felt his whole body leaning forward, eager, hopeful. Waiting to see what would happen between them.

They were talking now. At least the mother was. Shyler just stood with her hand to her mouth.

'Mrs O'Neil lives here in Presque Isle,' Chase whispered, as though he was feeling their tension as well. 'Since Shyler's going to be staying a while to get treatment for another condition I was hoping maybe . . .'

Mother and daughter stepped towards each other and enfolded one another in a tearful embrace.

'You thought Shyler could live with her mom until she gets better?' Zack finished for him.

'Looks like maybe it could work out. We'll just have to wait and see.'

They turned from the door to find Allen eyeing Chase's wheelchair. 'Guess I won't be the only one doing exercises now. Hope that ramp of yours holds up.'

'It's just a sprain, Dad. I won't need the chair at home.'

Allen gave Zack a nudge in the side. 'What do you say – think I can take him in a drag down the hall?'

Zack cocked his head. 'Are you really his dad?'

'Hard to believe, isn't it? Me being so much better looking. So,' said the man, returning his scrutiny, 'are you the young fella that's going to be living with us?'

'What?'

Chase laughed. 'Actually, Dad, I haven't discussed it with him yet but . . . Yes, if that's all right with him.'

Allen grunted. 'Thought you never got anyone pregnant.'

Zack stood speechless. He'd been waiting ages to learn his fate, and now everything seemed to be happening too fast.

He opened his mouth, but found his gaze drawn back to Shyler. *Never imagine, even for an instant, my heart's not big enough . . .*

'We'll drive here and visit her every weekend until she comes home to us,' Chase whispered.

Zack swallowed and accepted his hand.

Chapter 85

'So what's our defence? Same as last time?' Chase stood hunched in the middle of his back lawn, hands on his knees, breathing hard.

Zack narrowed his eyes in thought. 'No, let's swap. They'll never expect it.'

'Good idea.'

They broke their huddle and turned to face the opposition – Reece, Corey and Wayne Seavers, the boys' new foster father.

'Stop the clock!' Wayne quickly knelt to tie Corey's shoelace. His shaggy blond hair was nearly as pale and wind-blown as the boy's.

Chase heard a tapping sound behind him and turned to see Shyler at the dining-room window. She held up two fingers, then flashed him a smile that warmed the chilly November afternoon.

'Just got the two-minute warning, guys,' Chase announced as the teams squared off again. 'Dinner's almost ready. This'll be our last play.'

Wayne called out a series of numbers ending with 'Hut!' then tried to hand off the ball to Reece, who promptly dropped it.

When the man bent to grab it, Zack charged and shoved his hip, and he fell to the ground with a satisfying grunt.

Before he could rise, Reece and Corey jumped on top of him.

'What are you doing? You're not supposed to tackle *me* – I'm on your side!' He started tickling them.

As they tumbled about in a giggling heap, Chase felt the knot inside him ease. No matter how many assurances he'd given Zack that his brothers had gone to a caring home, Chase knew he'd harboured secret concerns these last two months. Seeing now how happy they were was hopefully putting his mind at rest.

He reached out and placed a hand on his shoulder. 'Feel better?'

Zack looked up, smiled and nodded.

Shyler set a dish of stuffing on the table, lit the candles and crossed the dining room. At the window she raised her hand to the glass, then stopped and lowered it.

Behind her, the final-stage bustle from the kitchen – Allen carving the turkey, her mother making gravy, Janis Scavers mashing the potatoes – created a soundtrack for the scene being played out on the lawn beyond. The talk and laughter of family and friends, mixed with the sights of their love for each other.

Feelings welled and swirled within her. Nostalgia, hope, a measure of sadness but, above all, gratitude. Though she still had a long way to go in her recovery, though there were surely still downs and setbacks ahead, one thing was certain – she had far more good days than dark ones now. And it was all because of the support of these people.

At the sight of Wayne struggling across the lawn dragging two small boys from his legs, a sound escaped her at once so fragile and unfamiliar it startled her to silence. Laughter. Dear God, how long had it been? She gave it another tentative try, discovered it carried no after-effects, and let out another unrestrained burst.

She watched as Wayne fell to the ground and Reece and Corey piled on top of him. Janis had confided over setting the table that they'd commenced proceedings to adopt the boys.

With the same joy she'd felt at hearing that news, Shyler turned her gaze to Chase and Zack. One day she too would be ready. When she was well. And perhaps the only hurdle remaining was a lack of closure. The thought the men who had taken Jesse might never be caught . . . But with help she'd deal with that as well.

She reached out and tapped her knuckles on the glass.

'Dinner's ready,' Chase announced, at seeing Shyler's wave from the window. 'Come on, let's eat!'

They trooped across the lawn to the patio, Reece riding high on Wayne's shoulders, Zack with Corey astride his back.

As the others filed through the back door, Chase paused to pick up his phone from a bench. Even as he touched it, it started to ring. 'Hello?'

'Is that Doctor Hadley?'

'Speaking.' He stifled a sigh. It wouldn't be Thanksgiving if he didn't get a call just as he was sitting down to dinner.

'Doctor, I don't know if you'll remember me. It's Greg Linnell.'

Chase shot a quick glance through the window. The others were finding their seats at the table. He turned away and said into the phone, 'Shyler's ex-husband. Yes, I remember. What can I do for you?'

'I'm sorry to disturb your holiday, Doctor, but I was wondering if you were still in touch with Shyler. If you know where she is.'

'I am and I do. As a matter of fact she's here right now. Would you like to speak with her?'

'Shyler's there?' A beat of silence. 'Oh. I see. No, actually I'd rather not. If you could just pass on a message for me.'

Coward. 'What is it?'

'I thought she should know . . . Well, she'll have to, if this goes ahead. I mean, if it's what I think it is.'

'Know what, Mr Linnell?'

An intake of breath. 'There's been an arrest. Three men were caught mugging a woman in Eastwich, New Hampshire. Apparently they ambushed her . . . on a bridge.'

Chase felt a tingle crawl up his spine. Shyler had long since told him her story. The possible significance of what he'd just heard –

'The police who handled Jesse's death were notified because . . .' Linnell cleared his throat, 'one of the muggers had a snake tattoo and another had a scar at the side of his mouth.'

Make that indisputable significance. 'Well, I certainly agree. Shyler will be very interested to hear this.' Chase fought down the urge to say more.

'That's all they've told me at this stage. I'll be in touch as soon as they get back to me. Of course, if these *are* the same men, Shyler will have to identify them, there'll be a trial . . .'

'I'll make sure she knows.' *In fact, better that it comes from me than you.*

Silence stretched.

'Was there something else?'

'So, Thanksgiving and Shyler's there. Am I to take it you two are together?'

'We are, very much.'

'Well you must be relieved, then.'

'Relieved?' Chase frowned. 'Why is that?'

'After what I told you back in September, about the way the police said it happened . . . I just thought you might have had some concerns.'

Chase laughed outright. 'No, Mr Linnell, I wasn't concerned. I never had the slightest doubt things happened just as Shyler said they did.'

Shyler placed the last bowl on the table and looked up as Chase came through the back door. She'd seen him take a call on his mobile and hoped it didn't mean he was leaving.

'Everything all right?' she said as he joined her near the head of the table. 'Don't tell me you have to –'

'No, it wasn't a medical call. Just someone . . .'

She tipped her head at his curious expression. 'What?'

He took her face in both his hands, his kiss deep with promise and longing. 'I'll tell you later.'

Acknowledgements

My number one thanks go to my editor, Beverley Cousins, for giving me this chance to realise my dream, and to the fabulous team at Random House Australia for their work in putting this book together.

Special thanks to my critiquing partners, Alison Manthorpe, Kathy Blacker and Mary Gudzenovs, who helped me through every stage of this project, from the first glimmer of an idea to the final edit, and without whose feedback, friendship and encouragement it might never have been finished.

Sincere thanks also to the writers, readers and fellow retreaters who gave me their generous support along the way: Rowena Holloway, Helen van Rooijen, Carol Lefevre, Esther Campion, Aileen Pluker, Sandy O'Grady, Monica McInerny, Dr Christine Lucas, Liz Jones, and the members of Eyre Writers.

And to my wonderful family, both in Australia and the US, for believing in me and always giving me their total support. Thank you for letting me live my dream.

About the Author

Diane Hester is a former violinist with the Adelaide Symphony and the Rochester Philharmonic, US. Born in New York, she now lives in Port Lincoln, South Australia with husband Michael. *Run to Me* is her debut novel and she's currently hard at work on her second – another fast-paced Hitchcockian thriller.

Loved the book?

Join thousands of other
readers online at